H. E. Stewart

The Birds of our Country

H. E. Stewart

The Birds of our Country

ISBN/EAN: 9783337227210

Printed in Europe, USA, Canada, Australia, Japan

Cover: Foto ©Andreas Hilbeck / pixelio.de

More available books at **www.hansebooks.com**

THE

BIRDS OF OUR COUNTRY

BY

H. E. STEWART, B.A.

WITH ILLUSTRATIONS BY A. THORBURN, J. GIACOMELLI
G. E. LODGE, K. KEYL, AND R. KRETSCHMER

London

DIGBY, LONG, & CO, PUBLISHERS

18 BOUVERIE STREET, FLEET STREET, E.C.

1897

PREFACE

THE object of this work is to give to the young collector a book which will not be beyond his means and which at the same time will contain an account of all the birds which he is likely to meet with in the British Isles.

Some years ago scholastic work took me to a school on the borders of the New Forest in Hampshire. Natural history pursuits always occupied a prominent place among the recreations of the boys, and many an enjoyable day was spent rambling through the Forest in search of something which might be deemed worthy of a place in our collections, and possibly of a paragraph in a natural history paper to be read at one of our social evenings afterwards. At another time our excursion would be directed through Harewood to Andover, or over the Downs to Salisbury, or we would even run down to Southampton and, crossing the Solent, spend an enjoyable day roaming over part of the beautiful Isle of Wight in pursuit of our favourite hobby. Perhaps no county in England affords such scope to ornithologists as sunny Hampshire.

On all these occasions our "takes" were carefully recorded, and anything of special interest made a note of, much of the present work being the outcome of these enjoyable summer excursions.

In compiling the book, reference has been made to the writings of Seebohm, Hewitson, Bewick, Morris, Gilbert White, Atkinson, and others, to whose works I am indebted for assistance where my own information has been scanty.

Throughout the work the classification of Seebohm has been followed, the common birds of each family being taken first ; while the rare birds which have only visited our shores a few times have been mentioned at the end of each group, in order to make the book as complete as possible. The family PASSERIDÆ has been placed first, since it contains the greatest number of our better known birds.

Wherever a bird is described, the description, unless otherwise stated, is that of the male.

WYLLIES, CUCKFIELD, SUSSEX.

MISSEL THRUSH.

TURDUS VISCIVORUS.

Family PASSERIDÆ. Sub-family TURDINÆ. Genus TURDUS.

Misseltoe Thrush—Storm Cock—Holm Thrush—Shrite—
Missel Bird—Shrike Cock.

THIS handsome bird—the Storm Cock, as it is sometimes called, because it may be seen perched upon the
top of some high bough pouring out its wild, half-heard
song through the driving storm in the early spring—is
through the greater part of the year one of the shiest
and wariest of birds. In the breeding season, however,
it seems to lay aside all fear, and frequently chooses
for its nesting site a spot in a garden close to some
dwelling. The orchard is a favourite place, in the fork
of some apple tree, or on an outlying bough of a fruit
tree away from the trunk, but never placed in the
more slender twigs. I have seen the nest built and a
brood reared in one of the compartments of an old
disused pigeon-cot. No effort seems to be made at
concealment, the nest often being overlooked from its
very conspicuousness. The bird becomes very angry
and abusive when its nest is approached, and has

I

been known'to successfully drive off hawks and other
intruders. Missel Thrushes feed on grain and insects,
but they are also very fond of berries and fruit, such
as cherries, gooseberries, and raspberries. Meyer relates a curious tale with regard to this. In a garden
were two whitethorn bushes close together full of
berries. For several weeks a Missel Thrush took
possession of one of these, driving off in turn any
Blackbird or Thrush that attempted to steal a berry,
though he raised no objection to them feeding off the
other bush, which gradually became bare. After
some time, however, a pair of Missel Thrushes appeared upon the scene and put to death the single
inhabitant of the tree, and in their turn took possession.

He is popularly supposed to feed on the berries of
the mistletoe, and Pliny tells us that the seeds of
this plant will not grow unless they have previously
passed through the intestines of some bird, generally
the Missel Thrush ; but this, of course, is not borne
out by fact. In the autumn these birds congregate
in small flocks, but as the winter advances they dis-
perse, and either live alone, or in small parties.

The Missel Thrush can always be easily distinguished from any other British Thrush on account
of his much larger size.

The nest is a large one, very similar to the Blackbird's in its construction. The outside is composed
of grass, sometimes interwoven with wool, lichen,
rushes, and a few small twigs to strengthen it ; on
this is placed a coating of mud and clay ; and the
whole is lined with a thick carpet of grass.

The eggs, seldom more than four, but more frequently only three or two in number, are bluish-white

in ground colour, sometimes tinged with reddish brown, spotted and blotched with rich purple brown markings, which however vary considerably, in some cases the blotches being very bold, while in others the markings are confined to a few spots.

The Missel Thrush is easily tamed if reared from the nest, and given plenty of room will lead a perfectly happy life.

SONG THRUSH.

TURDUS MUSICUS.

Family PASSERIDÆ. Sub-family TURDINÆ. Genus TURDUS.

Throstle—Mavis—Common Thrush.

There seems to be no doubt whatever now that the Song Thrush is a regular migratory bird, coming over to us as early as February, but leaving us in the winter for warmer climes; so that where they may be said to swarm in the summer very few will be found in the winter; the Redwing being, no doubt, often mistaken for him. Seebohm tells us how, on their migration, the inhabitants of Heligoland watch for favourable nights, and it is no unusual thing for several hundreds to be captured in one night in nets set for the purpose.

The Thrush is a very early riser; he is one of the first to greet the returning day, and one of the last to cease his evening song. A singularly beautiful song too. Two or three notes whistled and repeated, sometimes again and again, as though he were proud of their effect, before he goes on to a fresh strain.

He is a skulking bird, and like the Blackbird prefers to keep to the thick shrubberies and hedgerows rather than the open. He is very fond of snails. Which of us has not seen a small heap of broken snails' shells on the road, and near at hand a good-sized stone, which has been used by the bird to crack the shells on? He takes the snail in his beak, and raising his head, brings the shell down upon this stone; constantly he returns to the same spot with a fresh victim to be offered on the altar; hence the collection of shells. Sometimes having selected a stone, he mounts into the air with the snail to a considerable height, and then with unerring judgment drops the snail on to it. Although the gardener looks upon him as an enemy and a robber of the cherry orchard, yet the Thrush is a very useful bird in the kitchen garden amongst the cabbages and turnips. He is also very fond of worms and grubs, and his food is always more animal than vegetable.

The Song Thrush commences to build his nest very early. There is an instance on record of a nest with four eggs being taken on the 6th January, 1853, at Bicester, in Oxfordshire; but you will be fortunate if

you find eggs before the middle of March. The nest is
known to all of us, with its lining of clay and decayed
wood. The outside is composed of grass, straws,
small twigs, moss, leaves and roots. A favourite spot
for it is in some yew or holly bush five or six feet from
the ground in the garden shrubberies or against the
trunk of a tree, supported by some little branches.
We are all familiar too with the beautiful blue eggs,
generally four or five in number, with their deep brown,
almost black, spots on the larger end. Sometimes
eggs are found spotted at the smaller end. Sometimes, but seldom, the eggs are taken with no spots at
all. A Thrush's nest was taken near Ipswich on 2nd
May, 1880, with the unusual number of eight eggs
in it.

The Song Thrush, like the Missel Thrush, can be
reared from the nest with a little care, and is one of
our favourite cage birds.

BLACKBIRD.

MERULA MERULA.

Family PASSERIDÆ. Sub-family TURDINÆ. Genus MERULA.

Black Ouzel—Amzel—Ouzel Cock—Merle.

This beautiful songster is familiar to us all. Shy he
is ; more so even than the Missel Thrush, or the Song
Thrush, and like the latter he prefers skulking under
the laurel bushes and shrubberies to flying in the open,
so that when we get a view of him it is only as a rule
in the act of a hurried flight to some sheltering bush
or hedgerow. We all of us recognise too the harsh
scream which he utters when startled and driven from
his retreat. It is only the male bird that boasts the
beautiful shining black plumage which we know so

well ; the hen bird presents a dusky brown appearance, very much less showy than her consort's.

From February to June the Blackbird's rich notes may be constantly heard, and he is rightly looked upon as one of our finest songsters. When caged however he will sing through the greater part of the year.

BLACKBIRD.

In the autumn and winter the Blackbird feeds chiefly on berries ; he is very fond also of the larvæ of insects ; it is curious too to watch him after a shower, searching for worms on the lawn ; he hops about, tapping the ground with his beak, and you will pre-sently see him struggling with a large earth-worm, which in all probability has been induced by the tapping to come up and see what is the matter. In the summer, however, he is a shocking thief with the fruit, and so he is frequently shot down by the gardener. The late poet laureate, Tennyson, was apparently very fond of the Blackbird, and seems to have allowed him to thieve undisturbed :—

> Oh, blackbird ! sing me something well :
>   While all the neighbours shoot thee round,
>   I keep smooth plots of fruitful ground,
> Where thou may'st warble, eat, and dwell.

The Blackbird is one of the first birds to begin building its nest. It is generally easily seen. Placed about four feet from the ground in some hedge or copse, or thick bush, it very much resembles the Missel Thrush's in appearance. The outside is perhaps more untidy, made of grass, straws, stalks, fern and a little moss ; this is lined with mud and clay, which again is covered inside with grass. The eggs are four or five in number, pale greenish blue, speckled and blotched with reddish-brown. We all know the look of the Blackbird's egg, and are sure we could distinguish it from any other sort. You may therefore be surprised to learn that sometimes they very much resemble a Thrush's. At one of our School Exhibitions a few years ago a number of Thrush's and Blackbird's eggs were shown arranged in a line, and it certainly would have required an experienced naturalist to say where the Blackbird's ended and the Thrush's commenced ; at each end of the line, where the ordinary normal egg was shown, of course there was no mistaking them ; but since Blackbirds and Thrushes both occasionally lay plain bluish eggs without any markings upon them, it can be easily understood that the division between the two was not very clear.

RING OUZEL.

MERULA TORQUATA.

Family PASSERIDÆ. Sub-family TURDINÆ. Genus MERULA.

Ring Thrush—Rock Ouzel—Mountain Blackbird—Moor
Blackbird.

This bird is by no means so common as those we
have previously mentioned. It is in fact a local bird,
being much more common in the North than in the
South of England. The mountain districts are its
favourite home, and the heather its breeding place.
It has, however, been known to breed in several
southern counties, amongst others in Leicester, Kent,
Cornwall, and Hampshire, where in 1874 a nest was
taken in our kitchen garden at Queenwood, placed in
a pear tree on the wall. This is a case in which, if
a collector in the South should come upon a nest
which he imagines to be a Ring Ouzel's, great care is

necessary, as the nest and eggs are so similar in most cases to those of the Blackbird, that without a sight of the parent birds it would be next to impossible to classify them with any degree of certainty. Its favourite nesting spot is under the shelter of a projecting rock, or beneath the edge of an embankment, protected by the high heather growing around. Generally the nest is placed on the ground, sometimes in a bush, but never at any height. The nest, like the Blackbird's, has its lining of mud and clay, which again is covered thickly with grass and bents. The outside is very loosely put together. The eggs, four or five in number, are pale greenish-blue, spotted, most thickly at the larger end, with reddish-brown.

The Ring Ouzel is a handsome bird, very much resembling the Blackbird, but with a white ring on its neck. It usually feeds on insects, slugs and worms, and like its relation the Blackbird, is very fond of fruit.

COMMON DIPPER.

CINCLUS AQUATICUS.

Family PASSERIDÆ. Sub-family TURDINÆ. Genus CINCLUS.

Water Ouzel—Water Crow—Brook Ouzel—Bessy Ducker.

This merry little bird, that

Flits from ledge to ledge, and through the day
Sings to the Highland waterfall,

is well known to those of us who love to spend our summer holiday with a rod by the side of some of our wild northern streams and mountain burns. There he may be seen perched upon a rock in mid-stream,

singing his song amidst the rush of the water, or ready
to drop in for some tit-bit or dainty morsel. He is a
shy and wary bird, and if you want to watch him you
must approach very cautiously, keeping well out of
sight. Then you will see him wade into the stream,
or perhaps drop from the stone on which he is perched,
and after a moment disappear beneath the surface ; for
the Dipper is a splendid diver, and will move about
between the stones at the bottom, turning them over

COMMON DIPPER.

and searching for his food in the shape of water insects
and beetles. Then up he will come again and float to
the bank, hopping about on the look-out for more
insects.

In Scotland, the North of England, and Wales, the
Dipper's nest may be found ; near the running stream,
generally amongst the rocks, or amongst the tree roots

by the water side you will find it hidden away, and a
lot of finding it sometimes takes, though it is a large
nest, built of moss and lined thickly with leaves, with
a domed roof very much like a large Wren's.   Atkinson tells of a pair of birds that built their nest beneath
a spout which carried off the waste water from a mill,
where they reared their brood beneath this artificial
waterfall.   They seem to like to return to their old
spot every year, and one instance is on record of a
pair and their descendants using the same spot for
thirty-one years, rearing three broods a year all the
time.*

The feathers of this bird are blue-black in colour,
except the head, which is brown, and the neck and
breast, which are white.   He is often persecuted, for he
is frequently seen to dive down into the breeding beds
of the salmon and trout, and so he is accused of eating
the fish spawn.   Seebohm, however, declares that he
is a good friend to the fisher, for in reality he goes
down to catch the insects and other water creatures
that are themselves most harmful to the ova.

The eggs of the Dipper are four or five in number,
generally four, pure white, and in size slightly smaller
than the Thrush's.

The bird occasionally is seen in the South, and instances are on record of it breeding there, but they
are very few indeed.

* Morris's *Nests and Eggs of British Birds*, vol. ii., p. 26.

ROBIN.

ERITHACUS RUBECULA.

Family PASSERIDÆ. Sub-family TURDINÆ. Genus ERITHACUS.

Redbreast—Robin Redbreast—Robinet—Ruddock.

We all love the Robin: he is so confiding and fearless. Watch the gardener turning over the soil or
hoeing up the weeds, and near him you are sure to
see our little friend perched, waiting to hop down and
carry off the first worm or insect that shows its head.
And how trustingly he will come to the window-sill on
a wintry morning and carry off the bread-crumbs
placed for him, leaving his little footprints in the snow
behind. And yet he is one of the most pugnacious
little birds we have got, and will fight any of his own
species that offer battle until "all is blue". He does
not seem so quarrelsome with other birds, however,
for Meyer tells us of one kept in a cage with other
pets, that was always the first to make friends with
any new-comer. At Bramshaw, in the New Forest,
a few years ago a Robin took up its abode in an old
woman's cottage, and refused to leave it; it seemed

very unhappy when she caged it, so she gave it its freedom. In the spring it left her, and she feared it was dead ; but a few weeks later it returned with a family of young ones, and having introduced its children left her and never returned.

The Robin is one of the first birds to commence his song in the morning, and sings right on into the night. Throughout the winter he continues to warble ; indeed throughout the year, except just when he is moulting.

It rears two and sometimes three broods in the year, always building a fresh nest. Very early it begins to make its preparations, and eggs can generally be found the first week in April. Instances are on record, however, of eggs being taken in January, February and even November. I have before me now a note which states that at Merton Hall, Norfolk, a nest of young Robins was hatched on 8th December, 1882. Its nest varies a great deal in the materials of which it is composed, but most commonly it is made of green moss and lined with horsehair. Perhaps there are more instances on record of curious places in which this knowing little bird places its nest than of any other we have. In the cornice of the dining-room where the birds flew backwards and forwards through the open window ; in a flower-pot or water-can ; in the ivy on the wall or the hole of a tree, or securely hidden beneath its roots. I myself took one last year placed quite loosely in a heap of dead leaves that had been piled together and left. Perhaps as curious a nesting-place as any was one which was chosen at Worthing Station in 1884. The spot selected was between the rails over which the goods trains are shunted. The nest was in a battered beer-can, in an old hamper which was lying between the rails; it had four eggs, on which the bird was sitting. Trucks were constantly passing over the spot, and it seems wonderful that the nest was not disturbed. After it was discovered an empty truck was kept over it to prevent any harm coming to it.

The eggs are from four to eight in number; of a beautiful pink tint, which, however, disappears on blowing them, for it is due to the transparency of the shell, and leaves them pure white, spotted with reddish-brown; the markings vary considerably, and specimens have been taken pure white and perfectly free from any spots or blotches whatever.

NIGHTINGALE.

ERITHACUS LUSCINIA.

Family PASSERIDÆ. Sub-family TURDINÆ. Genus ERITHACUS.

This bird, and rightly too, is universally acknowledged to be the Prince of our English songsters. But it is not by any means the only bird that sings at night; the Sedge Warbler, the Grasshopper Warbler and many others frequently do so. Neither is it only at night time, as its name implies, that we must listen for its beautiful rich strains. On a spring afternoon in a five-mile walk I have counted over a dozen of these birds warbling from the coverts by the lane-side. In my part of Hampshire we consider it one of our common birds, and one may lie in bed with open window and listen to their soft notes wafted from every direction till one is lulled to sleep. It is by no means so common all England over, however, for in the North and West it is very rare indeed, whilst Scotland and Ireland are quite out of its range. It has been said that it is only to be found where the cowslip grows, and this may be so, as the same soil which suits the cowslip may produce nourishment for the caterpillars and insects on which the Nightingale feeds. The Nightingale is not always easily observed, for it is fond of keeping to the thick copses and under-

NIGHTINGALE.

growth. Its habits are very similar in some respects to those of the Robin.

Soon after its arrival in the beginning of April its song may be heard; and while the female is sitting, the male bird perched near at hand sings to let her know he is near; after the young are hatched he is too busy with the cares of his family and his notes are heard no more. " Lord, what music hast Thou provided for the saints in heaven, when Thou affordest bad men such music on earth?" said Isaac Walton, speaking of it.

Nightingale's eggs are not found as a rule before May. Nearly all the nests I have seen have been about a foot off the ground, though they are sometimes placed on the ground itself. The nest is made of dry leaves and roots, very loosely put together, so that it is very difficult indeed to remove it without pulling it to pieces; it is generally lined with hair. From four to six eggs are laid in it, of a dull olive brown, or else an olive-green colour. Without great care they will be found to fade badly after a short time, and pains should be taken to keep them from exposure to the light.

The Nightingale has been kept in confinement, but it is not a success as a caged bird. Bechstein mentions an instance in which one was kept in a cage twenty-five years. Goldsmith too publishes a story told by Gerner, and communicated to him by a friend, of three Nightingales which were shut up in three separate cages, and kept dark, and he says that, in the evening or night, they used to repeat the conversations they had heard during the day. This we must take for what it is worth.

Worms, insects and caterpillars are the favourite food of the Nightingale, and it is also very fond of fruit. Its plumage is very plain, being chiefly brown, with the chin and breast a greyish white.

REDSTART.

RUTICILLA PHŒNICURUS.

Family PASSERIDÆ. Sub-family TURDINÆ. Genus RUTICILLA.

Fire Tail—Red Tail—Bran Tail.

This bird is more common in the East than in the West of England, though it cannot be said to be very common anywhere. In Scotland it is rare, and in Ireland almost unknown. It comes over to us early in April, just after the Nightingale arrives, and stays with us till September. The male bird, before the moulting season, is one of the most handsome of our smaller birds: let me describe it, so that you may recognise it when you see it. The forehead and throat are black, upper part of the body dark grey, the breast, sides, and tail bright rust-red, while the wings are brown. The song of the Redstart is not particularly attractive; it sometimes sings on the wing. It feeds almost entirely on insects. Here is an interesting statement of Dean Stanley's with regard to the feeding of their families: " Redstarts feed their young with little green grubs from gooseberry trees twenty-three times per hour, usually with more than one grub at a time ".

May is the time to hunt for the Redstart's eggs. The nest is made of moss, grass and leaves, very loosely put together, and lined with feathers and hair. It is always placed in some dark nook or corner; generally in a hole of a tree or wall, or more rarely in a fork formed by the branches of a tree; but, like the Robin, the places where this little bird builds are very numerous and very curious too. It has been known to place it inside an inverted flower-pot which stood on the garden path, the bird carrying all the materials through the hole in the top, or rather the bottom. A favourite spot for it is beneath the eaves of a house on the rafters inside, or in the moss and ivy-covered walls of old ruins. In a water-can, in a hole in the ground, or fixed between the hinge and the post on which a garden door was hung; no place seems too quaint for this interesting little bird.

The eggs are of a light greenish-blue colour, from four to eight in number, very much like the eggs of the Hedge Sparrow, but smaller and more delicate. To be quite certain of them one should see the bird or nest from which they are obtained. A second brood is generally hatched in June, for which a new nest is built.

These birds will live in captivity.

WHEATEAR.

SAXICOLA ÆNANTHE.

Family PASSERIDÆ. Sub-family TURDINÆ. Genus SAXICOLA.

Fallow Chat—White Tail—Stone Chacker—Chackbird —Clod
Hopper.

This active little bird is commonest throughout Scotland. Throughout England and Ireland it is also pretty
generally distributed, though it is rarer in the southern
counties of England. The open country and wild
tracts are its favourite haunts. They come over to us
at the end of March and leave again in September.

A striking little chap is the Wheatear, as he sits
perched upon a wall or rock eyeing you and jerking his
tail as though to keep his balance, very much as the
Wagtail does. He is not easily mistaken for any other

bird. The plumage on the upper part of the body is a light ashen grey, mottled with reddish brown; the chin and throat are yellowish white; breast yellowish brown; and the wings almost black. Insects and grubs form his favourite food, and he is not averse to fruit when he can get it.

The nest is made in May, built of grass and roots, lined with moss, hair and feathers. It is not always easily found, for the birds like to hide it well away out of sight. Far away under a projecting piece of rock, in a hole in a tree, or in a crevice in an old stone wall; these are the places to look for it. It also not infrequently places it in a deserted rabbit burrow, and Seebohm tells us that another favourite spot is on the moors between the blocks of peat which have been cut and are stacked up in heaps ready to be taken away.

The eggs, four to seven in number, are a long oval in shape, and of a delicate pale blue colour; it is said that their flavour is delicious, and that they are often recommended for invalids; folk must be very far gone if they require nothing more substantial than a Wheatear's egg. The flesh of the bird also is considered delicate food, and on their arrival in this country, they are sometimes caught in large numbers and sold for the table.

WHINCHAT.

PRATINCOLA RUBETRA.

Family PASSERIDÆ. Sub-family TURDINÆ. Genus PRATINCOLA.

Grass Chat—Furze Chat.

This bird is found all over England, and in some parts is common. In Ireland it is rare, and in Scotland it

is still more uncommon. As its name implies, the
gorse and furze plantations are its favourite ground,
as also are the hay fields and meadows. In our
country, Hampshire, it is a fairly common bird. Insects form its staple food, which it is very fond of
catching while on the wing. Small worms too it con-
siders dainty. It is a late bird to arrive in our country,

WHINCHAT.

and we do not see it before the middle of April ; it
leaves us again towards the end of December. It
delights to perch upon some tall grass bent or
delicate little spray at the top of a bush, which one
would think could not possibly support the little bird's
weight ; but he is a light little fellow, and it is pretty
to see him settled there as he clings firmly on, bending

the tiny stalk with his weight. The Whinchat and
the Stonechat are both about the same size.

The upper parts of its body are pale brown, the
throat and the breast are fawn colour, and the wings
brown and white.

The nest is placed in the gorse bushes a few inches
off the ground, or more often on the ground itself,
sheltered by the bush. It is sometimes built too in
the meadows among the thick tufts of grass. It is
made of grass, mosses and roots, and lined with hair.
The eggs, five or six, are of a greenish-blue colour,
rather pointed at the ends, finely marked with minute
brownish-red spots.

STONECHAT.

PRATINCOLA RUBICOLA.

Family PASSERIDÆ.   Sub-family TURDINÆ.   Genus PRATIN-
COLA.

Stone Chatter—Stone Clink—Moor Titling—Stonechack—
Blackcap.

The Stonechat is perhaps the handsomest of those
birds which remain with us throughout the year.* In
its habits and the places it frequents, it is very much
like the Whinchat. It has the same love for flitting
from bush to bush, perching every now and then for
a minute on the highest spray or stalk it can find, its
little tail constantly moving up and down, as it
" chacks " away to its mate somewhere close at hand.
It is however nowhere as common as the Whinchat,

---

* One would expect from its name that it loved to settle on
some rock or old stone wall and warble out its song, but it
does nothing of the kind.

though it may be found in most of the suitable places
in Great Britain. These places are the moors and
large open tracts of uninhabited country, the heaths
and the commons ; especially where the furze bushes,
brambles, and low brushwood abound. In its appearance
too it slightly resembles the Whinchat. Its head, back,
and neck are nearly black, the neck having a white
stripe on each side ; the wings are blackish brown,

STONECHAT.

and its breast chestnut. The food also consists chiefly
of small winged insects, beetles and worms.

The nest of the Stonechat is perhaps as difficult to
find as any we have : partly because it is often placed
right in the middle of a furze plantation, where it is
very awkward to get at, and partly because from the
behaviour of the parent birds it is very hard to guess
in which direction their nest has been built. Then
again the bird will sit so closely sometimes, that she

has been known to keep to the nest even when the bush has been shaken hard. The nest is generally placed on the ground, but sometimes just off it, either at the base of some furze bush, or in the heather, or sometimes in the hedge. It is large and rather shallow, made of grasses and roots, and lined with moss, hair, and feathers. The eggs, from five to seven, are a pale greenish blue colour, freckled with brown, with often a zone of the same colour round the larger end. They can be easily distinguished from those of the Whinchat, as they are much less blue, and the markings are closer throughout.

SPOTTED FLYCATCHER.

MUSCICAPA GRISOLA.

Family PASSERIDÆ.   Sub-family TURDINÆ.   Genus MUSCI-
CAPA.

Bee Bird—Wall Bird—Cherry Chopper—Post Bird—
Rafter Bird.

The Spotted Flycatcher is a common bird all over England while it is with us, but it only visits us to breed. It is one of the last birds to arrive, its visit extending from May to September. In Scotland and Ireland it is not so common. As its name implies it feeds on insects, which it catches on the wing. It watches for them, sitting on some branch or post, and with a sudden spring takes them as it flies, and immediately returns to its station to watch for more. Its song is very seldom heard; and when it does sing it is so low, that it can only be heard a few yards off.

This little bird is remarkable for the various sites it chooses in building its nest. One of the favourite positions is on a horizontal bough of some wall fruit tree, near the trunk, or in a hollow in the wall where a brick has been removed, but anywhere and everywhere one cannot be surprised to find it.   In 1882 a nest was taken with four eggs in a pail full of clothes-pegs, which had been hung up on a fruit tree. It is generally placed four or five feet from the ground, and may be looked for in the last week of May and throughout the

SPOTTED FLYCATCHER.

early part of June. Sometimes this bird displays great fearlessness while nesting. For instance it has been twice known to build in lamp-posts in crowded streets. In 1889 a nest was built here within easy reach in the boughs of a wystaria: by the side of this tree is a flight of steps, up and down which the boys were con-tinually passing on their way from the school to the dining-room ; yet the little bird never seemed disturbed or nervous, being looked upon as sacred by the whole school, and successfully brought off her brood, even allowing a camera to be placed within three feet of the nest and her photograph to be taken without displaying the slightest trepidation. The nest varies a good deal in its construction. Sometimes it bears a very unfinished appearance, at others it is more compact. Small twigs, roots and moss are generally used, and it is lined with wool and a few feathers. The eggs are four or five in number, very beautiful in appearance, of a bluish-white colour, spotted and blotched with reddish brown.

The Flycatcher commences to sit after the first egg has been laid. None of these birds that feed on insects are easily reared, as it is very difficult indeed to supply them. with the proper food. We once tried to rear some, but the last only survived three weeks. Meyer relates a very interesting tale of a nest of young ones which he took and placed in a large cage. The parent bird soon discovered their whereabouts, and used to fly in at the open window, bringing them food ; but these little birds, being unable to leave their perch, could not reach the tit-bits which were held out to them through the bars by the mother. Now in this cage was a robin, and when he discovered the state of affairs he kindly volunteered his services, and from that time he could be seen at any time of the day taking the flies or bees from the mother through the bars and popping them into the little ones' mouths. This continued for six weeks, when, one of the young ones dying, the two others were allowed to fly. This is one of the most interesting tales of bird life on undoubted authority which we have got.

PIED FLYCATCHER.

MUSCICAPA ATRICAPILLA.

Family PASSERIDÆ. Sub-family TURDINÆ. Genus MUSCICAPA.

Goldfinch.

The Pied Flycatcher may be considered everywhere in our island a scarce visitor. It is more likely to be met with in Yorkshire and the Lake District than anywhere else. In its habits it very much resembles the Spotted Flycatcher, though its appearance is quite different. It is rather smaller than its namesake; the head is black, and has a patch of white on the forehead, the back is also black; the chin, throat and breast are white; wings and tail brownish black edged with white. Its food consists chiefly of flies, gnats, and other insects.

The nest is generally placed in a hole in a tree— the oak or birch for preference, it is said—and is made of moss, grass, leaves, straw, and bark, and lined with hair and feathers. Sometimes the hole of a Wood- pecker or Tit will be used, and it is said that like the Nuthatch these birds will fill up the hole, if it is too big, with clay until it is small enough to just admit their bodies.   The eggs, five, six, or even eight in number, are oval in shape, and of a pale greenish-blue colour, sometimes nearly white.

A curious story is told of a pair of these birds which built their nest close to the portico over the hall door of a house in Denbighshire, in 1843.   After the young were hatched a swarm of bees prevented the old birds from entering the hole, and finished up by stinging all the young ones to death.   On the return of the Flycatchers the following year, they were again attacked by the bees, whereupon they left the spot for ever and built elsewhere.*

GRASSHOPPER WARBLER.

LOCUSTELLA LOCUSTELLA.

Family PASSERIDÆ.   Sub-family SYLVIINÆ.   Genus LOCUS-
TELLA.

Cricket Bird.

A summer visitor, scarce all over the British Isles, but pretty evenly distributed.   It is most difficult to

* *Annals and Magazine of Natural History*, March, 1845.

observe on account of its very retired and skulking habits, threading its way through the grass as it hurries away, very much as the corncrake does—in fact, Yarell tells us, it creeps along more like a mouse than a bird. Its note, for it can scarcely be called a song, very closely resembles the note of the Grass-hopper, a long trill continued on the same note, and lasting sometimes two or three minutes. It feeds chiefly on insects and small snails.

You will be lucky indeed if you are fortunate to find the nest of this scarce bird, for it is so cunningly con-cealed that it has sometimes given infinite trouble to discover its whereabouts ; then again, if the bird is disturbed from her nest, she seldom flies up, but drops quietly off and hurries away mouse-like, thread-ing her way through the tufts of long grass, leaving you to find her eggs if you can. I was fortunate to get possession of a clutch of five in May, 1894, the only ones that I have heard of in our county lately. They were brought to me by a keeper. He did not know what they were, and together we went and visited the nest from which he had taken them. We found it in a thicket, placed on the ground and hidden securely away beneath a tuft of tangled grass over which brambles grew, thickly twined and matted together. It was large for the size of the eggs, rather loosely put together, and made chiefly of grass, into which a little moss was woven on the outside. The eggs were pinkish white in ground colour, thickly spotted over with small carna-tion brown spots, rather more profuse towards the larger end of the egg. Two of the eggs had some small thin dark-brown hair lines on them, similar to those one often sees on the eggs of the Sedge Warbler.

SEDGE WARBLER.

ACROCEPHALUS PHRAGMITIS.

Family PASSERIDÆ. Sub-family SYLVIINÆ. Genus ACRO-
CEPHALUS.

Sedge Bird—Sedge Wren.

We may expect to find the Sedge Bird with us about
the last week in April, and we may look for its eggs
early in May.   In all parts of our country it is pretty
common.   It is a retiring little bird, preferring to keep
out of sight in the middle of the bushes which line the
water's edge, for the sedge, as its name implies, is not
its only favourite haunt, and it is equally fond of the
bushes and brambles down by pools and marshes.   It
is a noisy little songster, and has an astonishingly
strong voice for such a small bird.   In the summer
evènings it will frequently sing on into the night, and
its voice is often heard at midnight.   It is also said to
have the power of imitating other birds.   Throw a
stone into the middle of the bush where our little
friend is hidden, and you will always draw a song out
of him, quite defiantly uttered at you as he hops a few
yards off, with an eye to his safety.

The nest of the Sedge Warbler is made of coarse
grass, and lined with finer grass and hair; but the

materials vary : one found in a bush was made of moss and straw. It is generally placed two or three feet from the ground in the bushes or long grass near the water-side, but nests have also been found on the ground itself. Meyer in his *British Birds* says, " We have invariably found the nest of this species suspended " ; Seebohm in his work of the same title says, " Its nest is never suspended, but is supported by the branches ". Who shall decide when doctors disagree ? My own experience is that out of six nests found by me one day last May, four of them, all built in the coarse grass by the side of a ditch in a water meadow, were suspended, three or four stalks being used as supports, and the nest woven round them ; on cutting one of them down I was able to easily slip the stalks through without pulling the nest about at all. All these four nests contained eggs ; two of them had clutches of six. The other two nests I found were placed in thick bramble bushes and also contained eggs ; but these nests were not suspended ; they were supported on the branches. All six nests were within a stone's throw of one another. The eggs are four to six in number. The ground colour is bluish white, but they are usually so thickly mottled and freckled over with yellowish brown, that it is impossible to distinguish it. Very many of them bear small hair streaks of a deep blackish brown.

The Sedge Warbler is of a russet-brown colour, its underparts being a sort of dirty white. Its throat is white, while the feathers on its head are very dark, almost black, forming a sort of cap. It leaves us at the end of September, though it has sometimes stayed until the middle of October. It is considered a good cage bird.

REED WARBLER.

ACROCEPHALUS ARUNDINACEUS.

Family PASSERIDÆ. Sub-family SYLVIINÆ. Genus ACRO-
CEPHALUS.

Night Warbler—Reed Wren.

The last of all our summer visitors to arrive, the
Reed Warbler, can hardly be termed a common bird. It
is undoubtedly common in many of the southern counties and breeds locally as far north as Yorkshire. Above
that, though, it may be regarded as a very rare bird
indeed. It has not infrequently been mistaken for the
Sedge Warbler, which it resembles in size and habits,
and also in the localities it frequents. It can readily
be distinguished, however, as the feathers on its back
are plain brown, instead of being spotted like the
Sedge Warbler's. Its song is softer than this bird's,

and like it, it often sings at night-time. Indeed there is no doubt that people have sometimes mistaken it for the Nightingale, so similar are some of its notes. In marshy districts, down by the river banks, in amongst the rushes that fill the meadow dykes, these are the places where we must expect to meet the Reed Warbler. Its nest is one of the most beautiful we have. Laced in around three or four reeds, some two or three feet off the water, " like a stocking in the process of knitting hanging among its many pins," * it sways gracefully to and fro with the green blades, as every puff bends down their tops. It is a very deep nest for its size, and this is one of the provisions of Nature for the protection of the eggs and young, which would assuredly roll out but for this, since the nest is sometimes bent down by the wind nearly to the level of the water. But this is not the only site which the Reed Warbler chooses for its nest. Sometimes it is placed in a bush near the water, and sometimes it is twined round the young shoots of a willow. Three nests were taken by us in 1894 on the banks of the Test in Hampshire all in this position, one of which contained an egg of the Cuckoo ; and another, found a few days later, close to the same spot, contained a young bird of the same species, which suggests the probability of both eggs having been laid by the same Cuckoo. The nests are built of grass, and lined with a little hair and wool. The eggs, four or five, are greenish white, spotted and freckled with ash green and light brown. One clutch in my possession bears a great resemblance to the eggs of the Whitethroat.

The Reed Warbler is a cageable bird, but is more delicate to rear than the Sedge Warbler.

* Meyer, vol. ii., p. 92.

BLACKCAP.

SYLVIA ATRICAPILLA.

Family PASSERIDÆ. Sub-family SYLVIINÆ. Genus SYLVIA.

Blackcap Warbler—Mock Nightingale—Gǔernsey Nightingale.

Another of our summer migrants, common in most parts of England, particularly the south. In Scotland and Ireland, however, it is a much rarer bird.

The Blackcap, so called of course from its black head, ranks second to the Nightingale in beauty of song, and hence is sometimes called the Mock Nightingale. It may be found in almost any plantation, or in gardens and orchards, which it frequents to pick the insects and caterpillars off the opening leaves and buds of the fruit trees; but later on, I am sorry to say, its visits there are for the purpose of thieving—

ripe cherries being a particularly sweet mouthful for this bird. As a rule, it is a restless, retiring little bird, and if you wish to observe it and listen to its song, it must be approached with great caution. The male can then be easily recognised by its black crown ; the feathers on the head of the female are reddish brown. The breast is yellowish grey in colour, and the back an ash-coloured brown.

The nest is usually commenced in the beginning of May. It is very thinly but compactly put together. It is generally placed in the fork of a bush or a bramble, about two or three feet from the ground, and is made of grass and roots, mixed with a little wool or moss, and lined with roots or hair. The birds resent any interference with their property, and very little meddling will cause it to be forsaken.

The eggs, four or five, rarely six, vary very much in colour and size. The commonest variety perhaps is a pale greenish white, faintly mottled with brown and grey, and spotted and streaked with blackish brown. Some eggs are salmon colour, and others white, blotched with reddish brown. The most uncommon variety is almost brick red, marked with brownish blotches. Care must be taken not to confuse the eggs of the Blackcap with those of the Garden Warbler, which they very much resemble.

GARDEN WARBLER.

SYLVIA HORTENSIS.

Family PASSERIDÆ. Sub-family SYLVIINÆ. Genus SYLVIA.

Pettychaps—Greater Pettychaps.

This beautiful songster arrives very late on our shores, about the end of April or the beginning of May.

It is commonest in the south of England.   In Scotland
it is scarce and in Ireland very rare.   Its notes undoubtedly surpass those of all other birds except the
Nightingale and Blackcap.   They are not so loud nor
so rich in tone as those of the latter, yet they are
very sweet and beautiful.

GARDEN WARBLER.

In size and form the Garden Warbler very much
resembles the Blackcap; the main colour is brown,
with throat and breast brownish white.   In some of
its habits too it is very similar.   It is shy and retiring,
and likes to keep to the middle of the dense growth
and from the heart of a bush utter its song, securely
hidden from view.   For this reason it is often over-

looked, and in consequence considered much scarcer than it really is. Like the Blackcap it is very fond of fruit. As its name implies, the gardens and orchards are a favourite resort, but it can hardly be called a good gardener, for although it is useful in ridding the fruit of insects it is so partial to strawberries, raspberries, currants and other fruit, that most gardeners would willingly part with it.

The nest is built in May. It is loosely put together, reminding one very much of the nest of the Whitethroat. It is placed near to the ground, generally among the tall grass, in a hedge, or in a bed of nettles. I have also found it hidden beneath the leaves of a bramble. Occasionally it is placed in a gooseberry bush or fixed to the twigs of the raspberry canes. It is made of grass or straw, with wool or moss, and lined with roots and hair. The eggs, four or five, are of a dull yellowish grey, or pale purple-brown colour, spotted and streaked, chiefly at the larger end, with light grey and olive brown. So similar are some of the eggs to those of the Blackcap, that the birds should be carefully observed, if possible, to make quite sure of the identity of them. As a general rule, perhaps, we may take it that the eggs of the Blackcap are brighter and more uniformly marked than those of the Garden Warbler and also slightly larger.

WHITETHROAT.

SYLVIA CINEREA.

Family PASSERIDÆ.   Sub-family SYLVIINÆ.   Genus SYLVIA.

Common Whitethroat—Nettle Creeper.

The Whitethroat may perhaps be regarded as the most common of our summer migrants. It may be found

all over Great Britain and Ireland, though it is scarcer
in the north of Scotland. It reaches us at the end of
April, the males arriving a few days before the females.
It is a bird of the lanes, and likes to keep out of sight,
among the hedgerows and thick foliage. The song of
the Whitethroat has been much maligned on account
of its harshness, but it nevertheless has some very
sweet notes, which have gained it many friends. It
feeds upon flies and insects—the " daddy long legs " is
a great favourite with it, but after its young are hatched
it betakes itself to the gardens and orchards, where it
does its best to thin down the fruit.

WHITETHROAT.

The upper parts of the Whitethroat are greyish
brown ; the throat is pure white, shading off to greyish
white on the breast. Though retiring birds, they are not
shy ; according to Morris they delight to mob cats,
and if one makes its appearance, they will keep up
their note of alarm until it has retreated.

Like many other birds the Whitethroat will sometimes feign lameness or illness in order to draw an
intruder away from its nest. Meyer relates a tale of

one which he observed when passing a high bank in a lane. It commenced rolling down the sandy side, moving as if wounded: struggling and shuffling along, it kept just beyond his reach, and finally flew away. A few yards distant he found the nest. Doubtless the old bird's manœuvres were designed to draw him off the scent.

The nest of the Whitethroat is built in May. It is very similar in construction to those of the same genus, made of fine dry grass and lined with rootlets and horse-hair. It is extremely thin; in some you can see the light through; but at the same time it is very strong and compact. It is placed generally low down in a hedge or short bush, occasionally on the ground amongst the tangled grass and nettles, sometimes amongst the brambles and wild clematis by the road-side. The eggs, four to six, vary considerably in their markings. They are greenish white or buffish white in ground colour, blotched and speckled with olive green. On others the markings are a rich yellowish brown with underlying marks of violet grey. The birds leave us again at the end of September.

LESSER WHITETHROAT.

SYLVIA CURRUCA.

Family PASSERIDÆ.   Sub-family SYLVIINÆ.   Genus SYLVIA.

Brake Nightingale.

The Lesser Whitethroat is by no means so common as the previous bird. It is much more locally dis-tributed. It is common in our county, Hampshire, as also in most of the southern and eastern counties of England, but in the northern and western counties and in Scotland it is scarce; in Wales it is very rare and in Ireland it is practically unknown. It reaches our shores about the same time as the Common Whitethroat. Like it, the Lesser Whitethroat is a retiring bird, preferring to keep away out of sight in the hedgerows and thick shrubberies. It is very fond of gardens too, more so indeed than its name-

LESSER WHITETHROAT.

sake; and is even more partial to the cherries and raspberries if that were possible, but at the same time it is very assiduous in destroying the insects and small caterpillars. Whereas the Common Whitethroat is seldom seen at any height from the ground, the Lesser Whitethroat may be frequently observed perched upon the top of a tree, chirping its song, which usually begins with a few soft notes, ending in a harsher shrill shake. It is very like the Whitethroat in appearance, but is more silvery about the breast.

The nest, too, is composed of the same materials as the Common Whitethroat's—dry grass, and a little moss or wool, lined as a rule with rootlets and a little horsehair. It is not, however, nearly so deep. It is usually placed in low bushes and brambles, or in the bottom of a hedge, three or four feet from the ground, and generally more trouble is taken to hide it from view than in the case of the Common Whitethroat. The birds will very quickly desert their nest if it is meddled with before the eggs are laid.

The eggs cannot be very well confused with those of the Common Whitethroat. They are smaller though more elongated, four or five in number, cream-white in ground colour, blotched and speckled mostly at the large end with a rich greenish brown, with under-lying markings of yellowish brown. In all the specimens in my possession, the markings are more blotchy than those of the Common Whitethroat and the finer spots are not nearly so numerous. Some of the eggs are streaked with a very deep brown.

This bird can be kept in confinement.

DARTFORD WARBLER.

SYLVIA PROVINCIALIS.

Family PASSERIDÆ. Sub-family SYLVIINÆ. Genus SYLVIA.

Furze Wren.

This bird, without doubt, seems to be a resident in our island, but it can nowhere be reckoned common. It is most likely to be met with in the counties bordering the English Channel. In our county it is

found in the New Forest, and also in the Isle of Wight,
but it is decreasing. The reason for this seems to be
that it is not a hardy bird, and a keen winter tells
upon it.   In Dorset, where it was once frequently
found, it seems to have been almost exterminated.
Mr. Lister, writing to the *Zoologist* in March, 1891,
says: " The Dartford Warbler usually survives the
cold of our winters, but the extreme severity and

DARTFORD WARBLER.

long-continued snow of 1880 and 1881 killed off every
Dartford Warbler from this district (Lyme Regis).
Year by year I have searched localities where this bird
was abundant before those two disastrous winters, but
have not met with a single individual.   I am told that
they have appeared in some parts of the county since
that date, but they have not extended to these parts."
    The Dartford Warbler is usually met with on the
large heaths and commons where furze bushes abound,

but it is a very shy bird and is in consequence difficult to observe. The upper parts are slate-grey in colour, the head greyish black, while the breast is chestnut brown shading into white on the belly. It is about the same size as the Chiff-chaff, but thinner, and has a much longer tail. It feeds almost entirely on insects, though doubtless it will tackle fruit when it can obtain it. The nest must be looked for in furze bushes. It is very slenderly made, so much so that it is sometimes possible to see the form of the eggs in it when looking up through the bottom. In materials and form it very much resembles the Whitethroat's, made of grass, furze and wool, with a lining of grass. The eggs also are very similar to some varieties of the Whitethroat ; greenish white, speckled with olive brown and grey, forming a zone toward the larger end. You should make quite sure, therefore, of the bird and surroundings, before cataloguing eggs in your possession as those of this rather rare species.

WOOD WREN.

PHYLLOSCOPUS SIBILATRIX.

Family PASSERIDÆ. Sub-family SYLVIINÆ. Genus PHYLLOS-
COPUS.

Wood Warbler—Yellow Wren—Yellow Willow Wren—Green
Wren.

This little bird reaches us late in April, sometimes not till the beginning of May, the males (as in the case of most of the Warblers) arriving a few days before the females. It is not uncommon in England and Wales, but in Scotland and Ireland it is not of fre-quent occurrence. On its arrival, it betakes itself to the woods and covers, preferring to settle in the oaks and beeches, not usually going far from its favourite clump of trees. On the highest twigs of these he delights to perch and give forth his song, which is very sweet. There he will remain, "Singing at intervals from his twig, though ever and anon he leaves it for a short flight after a too tempting insect, which he catches on the wing, and takes to the nearest twig to repeat his song. In such a hurry is he to sing,

WOOD WREN.

that often, when flying from one tree to another, he begins his song on the wing to finish it on his perch."

The back and upper parts of this bird are yellowish green, the chin and breast bright yellow, softening into pure white on the lower part of the breast and belly; the wings and tail are brown.

The nest is of an oval shape, and domed, the entrance being at the side; it is placed among the herbage on the ground, usually in some spot where the sun can penetrate, such as a moss-covered bank, or the slope of a hill, or in the twisted roots of a tree.* It is extremely difficult to find, and as a rule is only discovered by starting the bird or watching it drop down to it. It is made of dry grass, moss and leaves, and lined with grass and hair, but *never* (like ·the Willow Wren and Chiff-chaff) with *feathers.*

The eggs, five to seven, have a ground colour pure white, and are spotted and speckled all over with rich claret-coloured markings and with violet-grey shell markings. They are not likely to be confused with those of any other warbler, especially if the nest and its construction are examined.

WILLOW WREN.

PHYLLOSCOPUS TROCHILUS.

Family PASSERIDÆ. Sub-family SYLVIINÆ. Genus PHYLLOS-
COPUS.

Willow Warbler—Yellow Warbler—Haybird—Huck Muck—
Ground Wren.

This is one of the commonest of our little Warblers, and is found in all parts of Great Britain and Ireland. Early in April they come to us in thousands. The Willow Wren does not frequent lofty trees like the Wood Wren, but keeps to the hedgerows and planta-

* Meyer states that he has taken a perfectly open nest of this bird among the dead branches of an old bramble on St. Anne's Hill in Surrey. It resembled very much the nest of the Whitethroat. This, however, must be regarded as a very unusual occurrence.

tions, especially near streams, where the alder, willow and osier are plentiful, from which it gets its name.

Its song is very sweet and melodious, though powerful for the size of the bird, and is probably familiar to most of us. It is a restless and lively little fellow, but

WILLOW WREN.

very sociable, and will approach quite close to one without showing fear. It seems to be very easily tamed: Meyer speaks of one which he took off the nest and put in a cage, when it immediately began to pick up the insect food which was offered it, not appearing in the slightest degree disturbed at its captivity. Hewitson also mentions one which he caught and put for the night in a large box, and such was its tameness, that when he " took it out the following morning, and would have set it at liberty, it seemed to have no wish to leave his hand, and would hop about the table at which he was sitting, picking up the flies which he caught for it ". Its food is entirely insectivorous; neither this bird nor the Wood Wren nor Chiff-chaff caring for the fruit of the kitchen garden. The upper parts of the Willow Wren are olive brown in colour, the throat and breast are white tinged with yellow. The tail is long for the size of the bird. It is very similar to the Wood Wren in appearance, but rather smaller and of a darker and more dingy colour.

The nest is very large for the size of the bird, and is built upon the ground among the brushwood or under the shelter of a tuft of grass. It is similar to the Wood Wren's in construction, being made of dead grass, moss and leaves, and lined with fine roots, horsehair and a profusion of feathers, which latter, it will be recollected, the Wood Wren's does not contain. It is said that it is the only partially domed nest which is placed on the ground.

The eggs are very difficult to distinguish from those of some of the Tits, but the situation and shape of the nest will always be sufficient to enable one to identify them. They are four to seven in number, of a light pinkish white, but they vary greatly in markings. Some are not much spotted and some are pure white. The spots are pale brownish red.

CHIFF-CHAFF.

PHYLLOSCOPUS RUFUS.

Family PASSERIDÆ. Sub-family SYLVIINÆ. Genus PHYLLOS-
COPUS. .

Lesser Pettychaps—Least Willow Wren.

At the end of March we may expect to meet with
this little bird, for it is one of the earliest of our summer visitors, and at the same time one of the last to
leave us.   Indeed there are many instances on record
of the Chiff-chaff trying to stay with us throughout
the winter. It is not so common as the Willow Wren,
but still it is a common bird in most parts of England
and Wales, though in Scotland and Ireland it is a good
deal scarcer.   When here it is to be found in the

coppices, woods and hedgerows, and often in the osier beds near a river. It is also fond of tall trees, and from them we may hear its somewhat monotonous song poured out above us, " Chiff-chaff, chiff-chaff," though perhaps it more often gives us three notes than two.

It very much resembles the two preceding birds in appearance, but it is slightly the smallest of the three, and has shorter wings and browner plumage. Like them too it feeds on insects and flies, with an occasional caterpillar.

The nest is partially domed, and is very like the Willow Wren's, but it is not so well made. It is formed of grasses, leaves and roots, with sometimes a little bark and wool, and lined with roots, horsehair and a quantity of feathers. I once discovered a nest only just begun with the groundwork loosely woven together, and visited it frequently every day, watching the grassy ball grow thicker and thicker until the thick carpet of feathers was finally deposited and the first egg laid. How wonderful it was! It was placed among the leaves of a bramble, about a foot from the ground ; and at about this height I have invariably found it, though it is frequently placed on the ground itself.

The eggs, very round at the larger end, five to seven in number, are white, and spotted with blackish red or purple brown. In some eggs the spots are paler. This bird may also be kept in confinement and becomes very tame. It is perhaps the most hardy of all the Warblers and the most easily reared.

GOLDCREST.

REGULUS CRISTATUS.

Family PASSERIDÆ. Sub-family PARINÆ. Genus REGULUS.

Golden-crested Wren—Golden-crested Kinglet.

The Goldcrest is our smallest British bird, and is much more common throughout the British Isles than is generally suspected. Its small size may possibly account for this. Some years ago at Queenwood, one of our number had the curiosity to weigh a specimen which he had picked up drowned, and was surprised to find that it just weighed down a three-penny bit, but that a "fourpenny" was considerably heavier. Is it not marvellous that a full-grown bird, with all its flesh, bones and feathers should only just outweigh our smallest silver coin ? It is a very early bird to reach our shores, arriving at the end of March, and leaving again at the beginning of October. Many of them, however, stay with us through the winter, when they may be seen congregating in flocks, but in .

a hard season several of them perish with the cold. In addition to those which stay with us, there is a second migration to our country before winter of birds which come down from the colder northern regions and from the north of Europe. It is wonderful to think of such a small pair of wings carrying the little bird over such a journey.

The Goldcrest frequents the larch and fir plantations. He is very lively and restless, and is nearly always seen hopping about from twig to twig, or clinging to the end of some small sprig of fir, peeping underneath for the insects which he loves to feed on. Sometimes he will fly into the air and catch a passing fly or gnat, just as a Flycatcher might. He is not a bit shy, and any one approaching close to him will not prevent him from continuing his search, as he flits merrily about, peeping everywhere for his prey.

His song is very sweet, but naturally not very loud. It can be caged, and will almost immediately make itself at home, taking its food from one's hand ; but it is a very delicate little bird, and is not likely to survive the slightest injury. At the best one cannot expect to keep it for more than a year or two.

The nest is a most beautiful and pretty little piece of work. It is generally suspended from under the branch of a yew or fir tree by means of grass stalks firmly fastened round. On these the nest is woven, made of moss and wool or grass and lined with feathers. It is somewhat like the nest of the Chaffinch in appearance, but more spherical in shape with its opening at the top. It is usually placed close to the end of the bough, where it sways backwards and forwards with the wind ; indeed it is not an uncommon thing for the bough to be blown so far down that the eggs roll out and are smashed. It is not always easily found, for its similarity in colour to the bough from which it is suspended, added to the fact that it is often nearly hidden beneath the sprays above it, makes it very likely to be passed by.

The eggs, four to eleven, are smaller than those of any other British bird, and very little larger than peas ; they are rather round in shape, of a brownish or reddish white, darker at the larger end.

The plumage of the Goldcrest is olive green on the upper parts ; the under parts are a greyish white, tinged on the breast with yellow. On the top of the head the feathers are a brilliant orange yellow. The wings with a bar of white across them are purplish brown, tipped with yellow.

GREAT TIT.

PARUS MAJOR.

Family PASSERIDÆ. Sub-family PARINÆ. Genus PARUS.

Oxeye—Great Titmouse—Blackcap—Tomtit—Great Black-headed Tomtit.

The Great Tit is the largest among our Titmice, being about five and three-quarter inches in length. It is common throughout the wooded districts of Great Britain and Ireland, and remains with us throughout the year. It is a lively bird and is hardly ever seen still. In searching after its food it seems to assume nearly every attitude conceivable, clinging one moment to a bough head downwards, the next swinging suspended at the end of a twig peering for insects beneath the leaves, now upright, now upside down, ever on the move as it flits from tree to tree ; this is the Great

Tit. Like its namesake, the Blue Tit, it is much persecuted by gardeners, who consider it damages the fruit buds, when it is in reality freeing them from insects. It is also very fond of fat, and may easily be tempted by a piece of fat bacon or even a tallow candle.

Its notes remind one very much of the noise made

GREAT TIT.

in sharpening a saw, for which reason it is sometimes known as the " Saw-sharpener ". Its plumage is very pretty; the top of the head, breast and throat are black, a patch of white on either cheek, and a bar of white across the wings; the cheeks and sides are a dull yellow.

It is an early breeder, making its nest as a rule in the hole of a tree or wall; and not infrequently the forsaken nest of a Crow or Magpie is covered in and lessened. It is an untidy piece of work made of moss and lined with hair and feathers. Many curious sites are recorded where this bird places its nest. It has several times been found inside an unused, or even a used, pump, making its entrance where the handle works up and down. It has also been found in a hole in the ground, in a flower-pot, and even in a cupboard.

The eggs,* from six to nine in number, are white, spotted and speckled with pale red. It is absolutely impossible to distinguish them from those of the other Tits, except by their size ; and even then small varieties cannot be told from large varieties of the others and those of the Creeper. Then the nest and its site must be taken into consideration if the bird cannot be seen.

These birds can be caged, but will become very quarrelsome if placed with other birds, sometimes killing them, and, it is said, eating their brains.

BLUE TIT.

PARUS CÆRULEUS.

Family PASSERIDÆ. Sub-family PARINÆ. Genus PARUS.

Blue Cap—Tomtit—Blue Bonnet—Billy Biter—Blue Mope— Nun.

The Blue Tit must be familiar to most of us. All the year round he remains with us, and may be found all over the British Isles, in most parts being very

* The eggs of the Great Tit are very similar to the small eggs of the Nuthatch, and cannot be distinguished with any certainty unless the bird itself is seen.

common.   A knowing, restless little fellow is the
Tomtit, and very useful, for he destroys an immense
number of grubs, but, sad to relate, he destroys a great
many of the spring buds too in opening them to search
for his favourite food.   Just watch him as he flits
around, clinging to some twig and peeping into the bud
for a grub ; having secured it, he hops off as quickly as

BLUE TIT.

possible to another, and is constantly on the go—never
still, destroying hundreds of grubs and caterpillars in a
single day.   But these are not his only food ; indeed,
he will eat anything, and amongst other things is very
fond of flesh, and will pick a bone quite clean.
    The Blue Tit may be recognised at once by the blue
colour on the top of his head, which is surrounded by
a white band ; the cheeks are white bordered with a

dark blue line, the upper parts are greenish, and the under parts sulphur yellow; the wings and tail are blue. In size he is about an inch shorter than the Great Tit.

He is a very quarrelsome bird, and has no song but a plain "zit, zit," so that, although he can be caged, and becomes very tame, he hardly makes an interesting pet. The nest is not often found before the beginning of May. It is usually made, like that of the Great Tit, in a hole of a wall or tree, and pretty much of the same material—grass and moss, lined with hair, wool, and feathers. The same situation is often used year after year. He often chooses very droll places for nesting. For several seasons past a pair has reared a brood in one of the bell-posts of the school bell at Queenwood— a curious spot to choose, but the little birds seemed quite satisfied with it, and quite undisturbed by the vibration or noise of the great bell.* The spout of a pump is a very favourite place. I have read of an instance where a pair of these birds built their nest in a bottle fifteen inches deep, entering by the neck, which was only an inch in diameter; and more strange still, in the mouth of a skeleton of a murderer that hung on the gibbet. Many other strange places are recorded—in the pocket of an old coat which had been hung up in an outhouse; in an old gun in the grounds of Belvoir Castle; in a letter-box; but perhaps the most curious place of all is one recorded in the Suffolk *Chronicle* of 31st March, 1884. This nest was placed in one of the buffer plungers of a carriage running on the Clacton-on-Sea line. The only entrance to the nest was through a round hole in the centre of the buffer-facing. This hole was of course covered by

* For two years this hole was usurped by Nuthatches, but it is now used again by Blue Tits.

the corresponding buffer of the opposite carriage whenever the train was travelling, so that the bird was a prisoner on each of her trips. On arrival at Clacton-on-Sea one morning the buffer was watched, but although the carriages stood there for about two hours, the bird, which was distinctly seen on arrival, was not observed to leave her nest. No doubt she was afraid of being left behind ; her mate being at the other end of the journey. Unfortunately this nest was destroyed before the eggs were hatched.

The eggs, from six to eighteen in number, are much smaller than those of the Great Tit, and are of a delicate pink white, more or less spotted with clear rufous brown, mostly at the larger end.

COAL TIT.

PARUS BRITANNICUS.

Family PASSERIDÆ. Sub-family PARINÆ. Genus PARUS.

Cole Tit – Cole Titmouse—Colemouse.

The Coal Tit is found all over the British Isles in suitable localities, but can hardly be considered as common as the Blue Tit, or Great Tit. It is the smallest of our British Tits, being slightly smaller than the Blue Tit, but it is very different in plumage ; for, whereas the prevailing colours of the latter are blue, green and yellow, those of the Coal Tit are black, a greyish colour and yellowish white. Its favourite haunts are the woods and forests, and it is especially partial to pines and firs.

In its habits and actions it very closely resembles the Blue Tit; its antics and peculiar attitudes which

it assumes when searching for food are quite as
amusing, and like it, it consumes a great number of
insects and caterpillars; it also displays a great fond-
ness for small kernels and seeds, particularly the seeds
of the pines and firs. Its note, too, very much resembles the "zit, zit" of the Blue Tit. Like the two
preceding birds it remains with us throughout the
year, but its numbers are increased by migrations.
By some naturalists this bird has been thought to be
the same as the Marsh Tit, but it is now recognised as

COAL TIT.

a distinct class, the plumage showing a decided difference. It may be caged, but it is no songster.

The nest is usually made in a hole in a tree, but
not so far from the ground as the others of its class.
Sometimes it is made in a cavity of a wall near the
base, in a hollow bank, or among the twisted roots
of a tree. Two years ago, when out for a stroll with a
friend one afternoon, I was surprised to see a Coal
Tit rise, as it seemed, out of the ground at my feet.
On examining the spot I found an old rat hole partly

concealed by rotten leaves, and on opening this up for a distance of about eighteen inches, found, at the end, a nest with seven young Tits in it, just hatched. An instance is recorded in the *Zoologist* of a nest built on a window-sill in a box. The nest is composed of moss, with a lining of hair or fur.

The eggs, six to eight, are white spotted with light red; some have a yellowish tinge. If anything they are slightly smaller than the Blue Tit's, but so alike are they that, if they were mixed together, it would be impossible to separate them. It is another case of noting carefully the bird.

MARSH TIT.

PARUS PALUSTRIS.

Family PASSERIDÆ. Sub-family PARINÆ. Genus PARUS.

Smaller Oxeye—Black Cap—Willow Biter.

The Marsh Tit is another bird that lives with us all the year round. It is distributed all over Great Britain, but is very rare in Ireland. It cannot be considered as common a bird as the Coal Tit. Although it frequents the trees and bushes by marshy districts, it does not confine itself to these, but is found in gardens and on trees in the driest soil. Its habits are similar to the other Tits', and its food consists chiefly of insects, though it is also fond of seeds, such as sunflower, lettuce, spinach, etc. The Marsh Tit is a cheerful and happy little creature, and although its song can scarcely be called such, it makes an amusing addition to the aviary.

It is about the same size as the Blue Tit. Its plumage is a dusky grey on the back, the head is

covered with a cap of shining black feathers, the
cheeks are white and the under parts are dull white,
tinged lower down with yellow.

The nest is more carefully made than others of its
kind, and formed of moss, wool, grass, willow catkins,
horsehair and any other soft material, and is placed
in the hollow of a tree. Sometimes this little bird

MARSH TIT.

will bore out a hole for itself, in which case it is always
round, like the Woodpecker's.

The eggs, five to eight, roundish in form, are white,
spotted with light red, generally most so at the thicker
end; in some the spots are large, in some very minute.
Montague remarks that the eggs of the Titmice are so
similar as only to be distinguished by size and weight,
and it is almost impossible to separate them when

once mixed ; we would add that we think size and weight would help you very little, for the same kind vary so much in size.

LONG-TAILED TIT.

ACREDULA ROSEA.

Family PASSERIDÆ.　Sub-family PARINÆ.　Genus ACREDULA.

Bottle Tit—Long Tom—Poke Pudding—Long-tailed Mag—
Huck Muck—Mufflin.

The Long-tailed Tit is common in most counties of England and Wales, in Ireland it is rarer, and in Scotland scarcer still. In Hampshire it is better known to us, perhaps, than any of the other Tits, if we except the Blue. It is not likely to be met with except in well-wooded districts, for it is essentially a bird of the thickets and groves. In colour it is not so gay as the others, being principally black and white. The top of the head, throat and breast are all white. A broad black band runs from the eyes to the back, which is also black. There is also some reddish colouring underneath and on the wings.

These birds remain with us throughout the year. In the winter they are very interesting little objects, when they collect in parties of ten or a dozen and flit about the bushes. Like all the Tits, they never seem to be still, and are very lively in their search for food, which consists almost entirely of insects.

The notes of the Long-tailed Tit are somewhat similar to its relations', but they are very soft and not unmelodious. It is not at all a quarrelsome bird like most of the Tits. Its length is about six inches, of which the tail measures three and a half. On account of its long tail and light body it finds it very difficult to steer its course through a strong wind. I recollect standing on our cricket ground one day when a gale was blowing and watching a pair of these birds trying to beat up against it: in the end they were literally blown away.

The nest is the most beautiful and wonderful of any we know. It takes fully a fortnight for both the little birds working together to complete. It is usually placed in the centre of a bush or shrub three or four feet from the ground ; sometimes however it is placed in an oak ; it has been taken as high as fifty feet from the ground. It is a large nest for the size of the bird; made very much with the same materials as those of the Chaffinch. It is oval in form, composed chiefly of moss, very closely put together, and interwoven with cocoons that cover the chrysalides of insects and eggs of spiders ; externally it is covered with lichens, and inside very thickly lined with feathers. An instance is mentioned in the *Zoologist*, where the outside of the nest was ornamented all over with pieces of paper. The entrance is by a hole at the side, near the top, so that the nest appears domed over ; as snug a little place for the young as they could wish. Morris mentions a case where the feathers forming the inside of the nest were counted, and amounted to the extraordinary number of 2379. What does the bird do with her long tail? According to Seebohm she places it over her back. Some naturalists declare that there are two holes in the nest, the second one opposite the entrance at the back, through which the bird puts her tail; but I have never come across one of this description, though I have seen many of the nests.

The eggs, seven to twelve, and occasionally more, should be looked for towards the end of April ; they are very tiny, almost as small as the Goldcrest's ; often they are quite white, but generally they are spotted with red.

BEARDED TIT.

PANURUS BIARMICUS.

Family PASSERIDÆ. Sub-family PARINÆ. Genus PANURUS.

Pinnock—Least Butcher Bird—Reed Pheasant.

The Bearded Tit must be looked upon as one of our rarer birds, and one which you are not very likely to meet with, as it seems fast becoming extinct, but it still occurs in sufficient numbers to deserve a short account. It is most likely to be met with in the eastern counties, especially about the Broads in Norfolk. In Hampshire we have notes of several nests at Bournemouth and Havant, but all long ago.

It is sometimes called the Least Butcher Bird, as it seems to partake of some of the characteristics of the Shrikes. It has the same lively and restless habits as the other Tits, but may easily be distin-

BEARDED TIT.

guished from them by its long tail, brown back, and beard-like tuft of feathers on its chin. The male bird also has a pair of black moustachios on its cheeks, giving it rather a ferocious look. Its appearance is far more like that of a foreign bird, and one would hardly suppose it was an English resident all the year round.

In its nest and the position it chooses for it, it reminds one of the Reed Warbler. It builds in April, the nest being made of the dead leaves of the reed and sedge, with a few pieces of grass, and always lined with the top of the reed, like the nest of the Reed Warbler, but not so compact; it is placed in the rushes or a tuft of grass, near the ground.

The eggs, four to six, vary a good deal from the different accounts we have, but we may take as a general description that they are white, with purplish red spots and small lines. They are not easily confused with those of the other Tits.

The Bearded Tit may be kept in confinement.

We have now concluded our account of the Tits, and from the description of the eggs, you will no doubt find it impossible to sort out any specimens you may obtain. But we cannot make a distinction where none exists; and once more we would impress upon you that, in order to have a reliable collection, the birds themselves must be carefully observed as well as the position of the nest.

HEDGE SPARROW.

ACCENTOR MODULARIS.

Family PASSERIDÆ. Sub-family PARINÆ. Genus ACCENTOR.

Hedge Accentor—Dunnock—Cuddy—Shufflewing—Hedge Warbler.

We must all be familiar with the Hedge Sparrow and its beautiful blue eggs. It is common all over the British Isles, except in the barest and bleakest parts. It is a sociable bird, preferring the well-cultivated districts and hedgerows. It would be hard to find a garden, too, where the Hedge Sparrow is never seen. All through the year it is with us, and all through the year its song may be heard, for this bird, unlike the House Sparrow, has some lively and merry notes, which are not at all unpleasing, but it is not often heard in the winter time. Its favourite haunts are the bushes and shrubs, and it is rarely seen at any height. They generally fly about in couples, and do not herd together like the House Sparrows. In the winter they will approach close to the houses and pick up the crumbs with the Robins and other birds.

HEDGE SPARROW.

The food of the Hedge Sparrow consists chiefly of seeds; it also consumes a large amount of insects and worms. It is scarcely necessary to describe its appearance, for we must all be able to recognise it; the prevailing colours are reddish brown on the upper parts, dark brown on the wings, and slate grey underneath, shading off to a lighter grey lower down.

It is one of the earliest birds to begin preparations for its nest, and eggs can generally be found by the last week of March and the beginning of April. Meyer mentions one found on the 21st of January. The position chosen is in a thick hedge or bush or in the midst of a growth of closely tangled bramble. An old wall covered with ivy, too, is a common place to find it. When built in a thorn bush, a large thorn may frequently be found protruding right through the bottom of the nest, which must make it very uncomfortable for the sitting bird. It is a pretty nest composed chiefly of moss, and lined thickly with hair, wool, and feathers. It is a very favourite nest with the Cuckoo in which to deposit an egg.

The eggs, four to six, are a beautiful greenish blue in colour, entirely without spots; they are very similar to the eggs of the Redstart, but perhaps a little larger, and the shells are rougher and thicker.

In confinement, Hedge Sparrows are very sociable, and will even make friends with birds of other species. "We possessed one," says Meyer, "which was so much attached to its only companion, a male Redbreast, that on the latter escaping by accident from the cage, the Hedge Sparrow became dull, neglected its food, and sat with ruffled feathers and appeared so drooping and sad, that we thought it necessary to give the poor solitary its liberty, in order to save its life."

It is stated that the Hedge Sparrow will not uncommonly pair with the Tree Sparrow, in which case the male bird is the Tree, whilst the female is the Hedge Sparrow.

WREN.

TROGLODYTES PARVULUS.

Family PASSERIDÆ. Sub-family PARINÆ. Genus TROGLO-
DYTES.

Jenny Wren—Kitty Wren—Common Wren—Cutty—Jimpo.

The Wren is a resident throughout the British
Islands, and common in most parts. An active little
fellow is this tiny bird; he is never still, but spends
all his time hopping around, peeping into this corner
and that, exploring every hidden nook of his retreat.
He is very hardy too, and braves the bleak wilds and
desolate tracts of the north, where he may be found
quite as frequently as in our gardens and copses of
the south.

With the exception of a few weeks in the moulting
season, the Wren's song may be heard all the year
round. It is very lively and animated, and remarkably
loud for the small size of the bird. As an illustration
of the tiny body it possesses, Meyer mentions having
caged one, where twice successively it squeezed

through the bars, which were only just over a third of an inch apart, and escaped. The food of the Wren is chiefly insects ; it is also fond of fruit.

The nest is very large for the size of the bird, but very compactly and firmly put together. It is domed and oval in shape, with the entrance in the upper half. It is difficult to describe the materials of which it is composed, as they vary so much. Perhaps the commonest form is composed externally of moss and withered leaves ; the inside is lined with moss, hair, and generally a quantity of feathers. But the Wren has a wonderful knack of adapting itself to circumstances, and will frequently build its nest of the nearest available materials ; these very often match the surroundings of the nest. This serves a double purpose, for the materials are ready to hand, and the nest is much more difficult to detect. Thus, for instance, one taken in a straw stack was composed outside entirely of straw ; another built near a carpenter's shop had the outside all of shavings ; a third, placed in a wall over a bed of nettles, was composed externally of pieces and leaves of nettles.

The nest is frequently found in low bushes or thick brushwood, in the ivy on trees, or in a low wall where some bricks have been displaced. Sometimes also it is placed on the ground. Occasionally it has been found as much as twenty feet from the ground, but is usually only three or four feet from it.

Instances of peculiar situations which Jenny Wren has chosen for bringing up her family are numerous. Thus, in Leicester Museum there is a nest built in an old hat in a garden in 1884. Another curious place was between the wings of an old crow, which had been shot by a keeper and nailed to a tree. It has also been found in a Martin's nest, in a Swallow's nest, and even amongst the leaves of a Savoy cabbage!

The eggs, four to eight, are white—a beautiful pinky white before they are blown—with a few red spots, generally round the larger end. I have frequently found them with no markings on them at all. The nest is not often found before April is well advanced. In 1881, at the village of Broughton, a mile from Queenwood, a nest containing seven fresh eggs was found and brought to one of our collectors on the 13th January!

The Wren needs hardly any description, as we are all so well acquainted with him. The general colour of the upper parts is dark brown, darkest on the head and neck; the under parts are greyish brown, becoming rather redder lower down.

COMMON CREEPER.

CERTHIA FAMILIARIS.

Family PASSERIDÆ.   Sub-family PARINÆ.   Genus CERTHIA.

Free Creeper—Creeper—Tree Climber.

The Creeper is a very tiny bird, and in colour it so much resembles the trunks of the trees over which it creeps, that even where plentiful we often fail to find it. The difficulty of finding it is increased from the habit it has of running round to the opposite side of the tree immediately it is approached. It is a resident bird, distributed all over Great Britain and Ireland in the wooded parts. It is found most plentifully in the old woods and forests, where the trees have reached a great age, and are large and decayed. There we are

nearly sure to come upon it, running up the trunk of
some old forest tree in search of insects, more like a
mouse than a bird.

The Creeper never descends a tree head downwards,
but always starts near the bottom and works his way
up, holding on with his sharp-pointed claws and keep-

COMMON CREEPER.

ing his tail, the feathers of which are strong and
pointed, pressed against the bark so that it may act
as a kind of prop to support his weight. When he
has arrived near the top he will drop down at the foot
of an adjacent tree and commence a fresh ascent.

The note of the Creeper is not pleasant to hear; it

is very shrill and rapid like the word "tree, tree" often
repeated. Its plumage is dusky brown on the upper
parts, the tail feathers being reddish brown; the
under parts are reddish brown.

The nest is built about the end of April. The most
common site for it is in some old decayed forest tree
where the bark has peeled away from the trunk.
Here, wedged in between the trunk and the bark, we
may often come upon a nest, and very difficult it is
sometimes to get at. Occasionally it will build in a
crevice in a wood stack or in a shed. In 1893 we had
a nest at Queenwood, wedged in between two beams
over the door of a play-shed. It could only be got
at with great difficulty by raising a slate. It was built
of twigs, grass and roots, and lined with feathers.
The Creeper rears two broods in a year, laying more
eggs the first time than the second. The first clutch
consists of six to nine, the second of three to five.
They are white, spotted with brownish red, chiefly at
the larger end. They closely resemble the eggs of the
Tits and the Willow Wren, and it would puzzle one to
have to separate them if once mixed. If you take
them yourselves, however, the nest is quite sufficient
to set any doubts at rest.

The Creeper, we believe, refuses to live in a cage.

NUTHATCH.

SITTA CÆSIA.

Family PASSERIDÆ. Sub-family PARINÆ. Genus SITTA.

Wood Cracker—Nut Jobber—Mud Dabber—Jar Bird.

The Nuthatch is a resident bird found in the central
and southern counties of England. In the northern

counties it is very scarce, and in Scotland and Ireland almost unknown. The Nuthatch is so called from its partiality for nuts; these it will fix in the crevice of a tree, and hammer away at them with its sharp-pointed bill, until it is able to get at the kernel. Very often it has a favourite crevice, to which it will return again and again, until quite a heap of nutshells accumulates beneath. Although nuts are, perhaps, its favourite food, it also enjoys acorns, insects and caterpillars.

NUTHATCH.

Its usual resorts are woods of large oak and beech trees, about the trunks of which, from its peculiar formation of feet and claws, it climbs with astonishing ease and rapidity. The peculiarity of the Nuthatch is that, whether it is ascending or descending a trunk, it moves with equal ease, being quite independent of any support from its tail, which it does not use in climbing like the Creeper or Woodpecker.

It is very plentiful in the New Forest. The country-

men call it the Jar Bird, from the clatter it makes
with its bill against a dead bough or old pole, so loud
that it may be heard two hundred yards away. The
main colour of its plumage is bluish grey above and
white beneath, shading into a red rust colour on the
lower part of the breast and belly.

The nest is made in the hollow of a tree. It frequently uses a hole which has been bored by one of
the Woodpeckers; the reason of this being that the
Woodpecker bores through the living wood into the
rotten heart, which the Nuthatch has not strength to
do—it can only work on the decayed substance. In
Norfolk, Norgate tells us in the *Zoologist*, 1880, p. 41,
it is not a very uncommon thing to see a dead Scotch
pine or alder with as many as a dozen small holes in
it, which only penetrate an inch—these are the
attempts of the Nuthatch to bore for a nest. If the
entrance is too large, the Nuthatch invariably lessens
the size by plastering it up with hard clay. I have
removed a lump of clay entire from the entrance
which weighed nearly nine pounds. In addition to
this the Nuthatch will fill up the hole, if it is deep,
with pieces of bark, so that when sitting it may be
near the opening. As much as two feet of a hollow
tree has been filled up in this way. The Starling
often usurps the Woodpecker's hole as well to rear
its brood in; and on several occasions its dead
body or skeleton has been found in Nuthatches'
nests. This looks as though, after the Starling had
taken possession of the Woodpecker's home, the Nuthatch had fixed upon the same dwelling and partially
clayed up the entrance, when the Starling being im-
prisoned within and unable to get out, perished.
There is very little of a nest built—small flakes of

bark scraped together, perhaps a little grass and leaves, or moss.

The eggs are white, spotted and blotched with reddish brown, similar to the Great Tit's, but generally larger. Some small varieties, however, are indistinguishable from large eggs of the Great Tit.

The Nuthatch is easily tamed, and makes an amusing pet, even going so far as to climb one's legs as it would a tree trunk. He is a mischievous little fellow in a cage, however, if there is any wood in it, for he will soon find out a weak spot, and commence enlargements.

RAVEN.

CORVUS CORAX.

Family PASSERIDÆ. Sub-family CORVINÆ. Genus CORVUS.

Corbie—Corbie Crow—Great Corbie Crow.

The Raven, once so common a resident, is now so no longer in England; indeed it is fast becoming very scarce. In Scotland and Ireland it is still, however, fairly common in certain districts, especially in the Hebrides and Western Islands of Scotland.

In our county, Hampshire, it has been persecuted almost to extinction; the last which we had at Queenwood in a wild state was in 1872, when (probably tempted by the fowls) one paid several visits to " Mr. John's " lawn, but there is no note of any nest being found near. It is a very fine bird, with plumage of a beautiful glossy black all over. It is nearly two feet in length; indeed it has been said that it bears about the same proportion to the Jackdaw in size that the Rook does to the Starling.

It will eat almost any kind of food, for whilst it attacks fowls, ducks, young geese, partridges, hares and pheasants, it will eat fruit, corn and insects; and its partiality for lamb causes the farmer and the shepherd to be among its bitterest enemies.

The nest is placed at the top of the tallest trees, the most inaccessible being chosen; or on some rock or

RAVEN.

sea cliff skirting the ocean. It is extremely difficult to obtain the eggs. The nest is very large and bulky, being made of sticks and twigs and lined with roots and tufts of grass and a quantity of wool. When the birds choose a tree, they generally return to it year after year, piling one nest after another upon the same bough, so that the tree often comes to be called the " Raven Tree ".

The eggs, four to seven in number, very much resemble those of the Rook and Crow; but they are of course much larger. Like the eggs of these birds they vary very much in markings; the ground colour is of a light green shade, the markings vary from pale grey and light green to dark dull olive, and dark yellowish green.

It is hardly necessary to add that the Raven, when taken young, can be easily trained and made very tame. He will also learn to talk with almost as much fluency as a Parrot. The last we had amongst our tame birds at Queenwood was, I think, in 1881.* He was a powerful bird and on one occasion took possession of a staircase leading to an upstairs class-room, and refused to allow his owner or any one to pass, attacking viciously the legs of those who approached him. Needless to say, a peck from his beak was not eagerly courted by the boys.

The note of the Raven is a harsh croak, somewhat like "craugh" in sound. Amongst other things he possesses wonderfully keen sight and smell, and many extraordinary incidents are related of his capacity in these respects.

---

* Summer, 1881, Qd. Notes. " For the greater part of the day it strutted about near the schools in a solemn, ungainly manner, and, if allowed, it would roost for the night on the stairs near the first class-room. It vigorously resisted any one who attempted to dislodge it from its quarters, and sometimes would, even when unprovoked, make an attack on any small boy who attempted to pass.

CARRION CROW.

CORVUS CORONE.

Family PASSERIDÆ. Sub-family CORVINÆ. Genus CORVUS.

Crow—Corbie Crow—Black Crow—Gore Crow—Flesh Crow—
Black Neb—Jim Crow.

The Crow, owing to the strenuous persecution which
it has undergone at the hands of farmers and gamekeepers, is not nearly so common now as it used to
be, yet it is still fairly numerous in most districts of
the British Isles, though scarce in the extreme north.
It is a resident bird, though its numbers are increased in the autumn by others which migrate.
Crows are commonly seen in pairs throughout the
year, and it is believed that they pair for life.

The note of the Crow is a harsh croak, somewhere

in strength between that of the Raven and Rook. In appearance he is similar to the Raven, but smaller, being black all over, with glossy steel-blue feathers on his head and breast; his legs, feet, and beak are all black.

For his food he will eat almost anything, though, as his name implies, carrion seems to be his favourite meal; young hares, rabbits, partridges, and fowls, or even a sickly lamb, all falling victims to him. He will also eat insects, grubs, and seeds, or sometimes he will scavenge along the sea-shore for dead fish or mussels, which latter he flies with to some height and then drops, to break the shell.

Carrion Crows can be kept in confinement, but their bodies have such a disagreeable odour, that it is impossible to keep them in a dwelling-room. They can be made very tame, however, and make almost as amusing pets as Ravens.*

* From the Qd. Report, Summer, 1879. " Three Carrion Crows. These birds were taken from their nest on 19th May, being about a fortnight old. As they had to be fed on raw flesh, the keeping of them came rather expensive, the butcher's bill amounting to a shilling a week. The meat diet was continued for about six weeks, and then the birds were put on barley meal mixed with water. Being constantly cared for by their owners, they got to know them perfectly both by sight and by voice. No restraint whatever was put upon them; from the time of their being able to move about they were allowed to go just where they liked, and they were left out all night to roost. As their powers increased, they would take considerable flights, but they appeared to have no inclination to go far away from the grounds. The boys were their companions, and the birds did not seem happy if none of them were about for them to associate with. They would come to welcome their friends first thing in the morning as they came up the asphalt path from the house to the schools; when the

Unlike the Rook, the Crow is a somewhat late breeder, not often commencing to build before the end of April or the beginning of May. The nest is built in high trees, of sticks, cemented together with clay and lined with roots and a quantity of wool and fur. Hewitson mentions a curious instance of a pair of crows in 1832, which repaired to one of the Fern Islands to breed; there being no trees on the island, the nest was built on the ground, and twigs being unobtainable, it was made of pieces of turf laid upon each other; the wool lining was all brought over from the mainland, a distance of five miles. A curious freak on the part of Jim Crow.

bell for studies had rung, they would perch on the window-sills and watch what was going on in the class-rooms, occasionally cawing to attract attention; sometimes one or other would come into the room and perch himself on the master's desk in front of a class. It was amusing to see how, when the boys were drawn up in line for drill, one or other of these birds would swoop down from a tree, and, flying close over the heads of the rank, firmly light on his master's head or on his outstretched arm. In the latter case he would try to pick a pocket, and if successful, fly off with the spoil. He evidently appreciated the joke of this, as, if pursued, when the order to dismiss had been given, he would withdraw just far enough to be in safety for the moment, and repeat the move when he was again approached. In fact the Carrion Crow seems to be like the Magpie in its propensity for carrying away and hiding objects; anything bright has a special attraction for them in this way. On Sunday last the birds followed us in our afternoon walk, occasionally taking wide excursions over the fields, and then making a straight line again for us in rapid flight. It was quite delightful to observe the thorough confidence they had in the boys.

" It appears to us so delightful that birds can be kept in this way—absolutely free denizens of the air, and yet coming to call as readily as the best trained dog. How different the captive life of the caged songster ! "

The eggs, three to six, usually five in number, are very similar to those of the Rook. Like them they vary greatly. They are usually of a green or bluish green colour, spotted or mottled with grey and brown ; one variety is almost white and without any markings.

HOODED CROW.

CORVUS CORNIX.

Family PASSERIDÆ. Sub-family CORVINÆ. Genus CORVUS.

Royston Crow—Grey Crow—Scare Crow—Dun Crow—Bunting Crow—Hoody.

A winter visitor to England, consequently a rare breeder here. In Scotland, however, it is resident

6

and more common, particularly in the Orkneys and Shetlands. In Ireland also it is fairly common.

It has been thought by some that the Hooded and Carrion Crows are simply varieties of the same species, for no difference can be found on dissection, but there is a great difference in the plumage of these birds, for the Hooded Crow has its head, tail, and wings black and the rest of its body grey; this colouring however varies a great deal with different birds, which is possibly due to the fact that the Carrion and Hooded Crows will frequently pair together.

Like the former species, carrion is the favourite food of the Hooded Crow, but he is somewhat more of a coast bird, and will rob the nests of sea birds of their eggs or young. Small chicks or even leverets fall a ready prey to him, in consequence of which he is terribly persecuted by the gamekeeper and shepherd. He will also feed on worms and insects, and is very fond of mussels. His note, too, is like that of the Carrion Crow, a hoarse croak or "craa" repeated at intervals.

He is also a somewhat late breeder. The nest is placed in the crevices or on the ledges of rocks and cliffs; sometimes in a tree or not infrequently in a bush, eight or nine feet from the ground. It is built of sticks, or, when these cannot be obtained, of seaweed, lined with roots, stalks of plants, wool and hair. He probably pairs for life.

The eggs are usually four or five in number and are quite indistinguishable from those of the Carrion Crow—greenish in ground colour with grey and brown markings. The Hooded Crow will frequently bring down the wrath of other birds upon him by his nest-robbing proclivities. An instance is recorded of a colony of Terns banding together and surrounding a Hooded Crow, which had visited their breeding grounds on a plundering excursion. Driving him out to sea, they gradually beat him lower and lower until he fell exhausted into the sea and was drowned.

He can be easily kept in confinement.

ROOK.

CORVUS FRUGILEGUS.

Family PASSERIDÆ. Sub-family CORVINÆ. Genus CORVUS.

We must all be familiar with the Rook; and we have all, no doubt, watched with interest his move· ments at the rookery. Everywhere in the British Isles, where rich pasture lands and cultivation abound, the Rook may be seen. In Hampshire they abound, and as I am writing this they may be seen in the first shadows of evening "going home" to the Norman Court Woods with that stately measured flap of the wings literally in their thousands. What excitement there is, too, when they reach their destination! What "cawing" and quarrelling and fighting for places, as one after another is pushed off his perch, or shifts for himself to get a better position! By degrees the disturbance grows less loud, the "cawing" grows fainter and more subdued, and at last all is quite still and our black army has settled for the night. But with the first light they are off again, for they are among the earliest birds in their search for food. They will settle in a fresh ploughed field, scouring it in search of grubs and worms, or in the pasture lands, pulling up here and there the roots in which, with their keen sight, they have detected a wire-worm or some harmful insect. On these occasions look-out sentinels are generally posted on the trees around to give warning on the approach of an enemy. Occasionally they do much harm to the fresh sown corn, or young potato shoots; but it is universally acknowledged that the good they do far outweighs the evil, and so they are protected by the farmer, and looked upon as his best friends. There is no doubt that many people often confuse Rooks with Crows. Rooks are generally seen in large companies, whilst Crows are nearly always seen either alone or in pairs. Another distinction between the Crow and the Rook is a sort of yellow skin at the base of the beak in the latter, which is not found in the Crow, the black plumage in it covering the base.

Rooks, you will probably have noticed, are peculiarly quarrelsome in the breeding season; if you have not, it will considerably amuse you to watch the impudent way in which they rob their neighbours of the materials collected for their nests, how they will wait until one has gone off in search of building material and then quietly appropriate what he has gathered, they in their turn receiving the same treatment. So fierce do their quarrels become, that it is no uncommon thing to find a dead Rook beneath a rookery. I once saw one at the top of a high chestnut hanging head downwards, dead, within three feet of a nest. How had he got there? Had he been fixed there by his conqueror as a warning to all the rest so busily employed in repairing the nests all around? I don't know, I'm sure.

As you know, the same rookery is used year after year, the old nests being repaired each season, and occasionally a new one added. They are sociable birds and seem to prefer the tall trees near old mansions and dwellings, and certainly most people like to have them there; there is something in the " cawing " of the Rooks that gives an air of comfort and homeliness to the whole place.

Operations begin as early as the end of February.* The nest is built of sticks and twigs, cemented with mud and clay, and lined with turf, roots, moss, leaves, and a few feathers. It is rather deep inside, and compactly put together. The eggs, three to five, differ considerably. The general type is greenish blue

* Since writing this I have received the following communication from West Dean,'five miles from Queenwood: "A curious date for Rooks to attempt to rear young, 27th October, 1894. There is at the present time a Rook sitting in a nest which has recently been built by a pair of birds on one of the large elm trees which form an avenue adjoining the rookery, and leading from the road to Mr. Wooley's farm, called Church Farm."

in ground colour, marked with blotches of greenish and blackish brown.

The Rook makes a most confiding and amusing pet. We have one at Queenwood now* (the only survivor of five) which was brought up from the nest. "Barkee" is his name, and on being called by it, he will strut gravely up to you, and, hopping on your finger, acknowledge his head being scratched with an approving "Ba-ar, ba-ar". During school hours he will sometimes wander round and make a tour of inspection, peeping in at a half-open door and putting his head on one side in the most critical way, as though he were going to be asked to give his opinion of it all. He is quite a school institution.†

JACKDAW.

CORVUS MONEDULA.

Family PASSERIDÆ. Sub-family CORVINÆ. Genus CORVUS.

Daw—Jack—Kae.

This lively bird breeds in most districts of the British Isles. We are probably all familiar with him, and at once recognise his impudent cry of "Jac, jac," as he flies overhead in company with his relations the Rooks, or with others of his own kind. They are very similar to the Rook in their habits, always being seen in companies, going or returning from their feed-

* July, 1894.

† In a letter dated 23rd June, 1896, his owner writes: "Barkee, the rook, is dead. One day, when we were out with the hounds, he must have gone strolling about the field, and some boys found him and took him home and killed him. We found out who had stolen him a fortnight afterwards."

ing grounds. In size they are much smaller, and as they grow older they assume a grey band of feathers round the neck, which brightens their otherwise sombre appearance. The motion of their wings is much quicker than that of the Rooks, and their flight altogether less sedate. They feed on insects, grain or fruit. They are also very fond of meat or eggs when they can get them.

As a pet, I always consider the Jackdaw *facile princeps*. We have three with us now. Reared from

JACKDAW.

the nest, they will come at their owner's call and perch on his shoulder, or hop on his hand and look in his face with their heads on one side and a look of unutterable mischief in their eyes. They are quickly attracted by anything bright, such as a ring or a watch-chain, and if one is given them they will probably hide it away, like the fabled Jackdaw of Rheims in the *Ingoldsby Legends*. Three years ago we had some exceptionally tame ones. It was the gardener's custom to put a few strawberries in his waistcoat pocket when he came up to the house. The Jackdaws soon got to know their friend, and would swoop down from the trees when they saw him coming, and dive into his pockets with their beaks and draw out the fruit, chattering away all the time in the highest glee.*

"Jacks" always build in colonies: in the crevices of cliffs, in ruined buildings or church towers, or in the holes of trees. Near Queenwood we have a big "Jackery," all the nests of which are built in rabbit warrens. This is all the more curious, as a great number of the young every year are destroyed by rats. The nests are built of sticks and wool. In some cases the birds will drop whole barrow loads of sticks into a hole to bring it up to the height they wish. Instances are recorded of this bird trying to fill up chimneys in this way.

The eggs, three to six, are very handsome. They vary a good deal in colour and markings; they are pale bluish white, spotted and blotched with a rich greenish brown, light brown and greyish white.

* Another tame one from Qd. Notes, Summer, 1885. Account by owner. "Ever since it could fly it has come to me for food, but latterly it has come to me whenever I called it, knowing my voice from any one else's. It can catch a piece of food when thrown four or five feet in the air, flying up and seizing it before it reaches the ground. In going to Broughton it followed me down there, but not liking the village children, it flew on to a house, and did not return till the following morning. Another time I was going to Horsebridge with three other boys, when at the commencement of the beeches we were surprised to see 'Jack' fly to me and settle on my head. We do not know where he came from. He stopped with me on my hand and arm till we came almost to Horsebridge."

MAGPIE.

PICA CAUDATA.

Family PASSERIDÆ. Sub-family CORVINÆ. Genus PICA.

Mag—Madge—Pianet—Pyet.

The Magpie is resident in most wooded districts of England, Scotland and Ireland. It is gradually becoming far less common than formerly on account of its persecution at the hands of gamekeepers, for it destroys many young pheasants and chicks in the spring. When seen in its wild state with its plumage undamaged, it is one of the handsomest birds we have. Its head, throat, breast and back are black, the lower part of the breast is white, the wings are black, richly glossed with green and with a patch of pure white. The long tail is a beautiful metallic green and purple. It makes a capital pet; and by "pet" I do not necessarily mean caged pet, for if fed up from the nest, the Magpie, like the Jackdaw, will remain close at hand, roosting in the trees near by, and ready to fly down to his master the moment he appears. We have one with us now which is very friendly with the Jackdaws. He has been taught to speak, and in addition to saying several words, will cough so much like a human being that, with one's eyes shut, it would be impossible to distinguish it from such.

The Magpie will feed on almost anything; snails, worms, fruit, acorns, young birds, and pheasants' eggs, or, like the Starling, the vermin from sheep and cattle. His note is a harsh chatter.

Though very shy and wary, in consequence of the persecution to which he is subjected, the Magpie is fond of the neighbourhood of houses. In several country villages he is looked upon with awe and super-stition, and the number which are seen together at one time is supposed to foretell coming events. As the old rhyme has it : —

> One for sorrow,
> And two for mirth ;
> Three for a wedding,
> And four for a birth.

The Magpie is an early breeder, its nest being com-menced at the end of March or the beginning of April. This is generally placed in the topmost branches of trees ; but sometimes it is built in hedges, or even in a gooseberry bush. The outside is formed of sticks ; these are cemented together with mud and clay and lined with rootlets ; the whole is covered with a domed roof of sticks. Most of these sticks are sharp thorny ones, and tightly woven together. The whole is a wonderful piece of architecture, and so well protected that it is often difficult to extract the eggs without serious damage to the hand. The birds will frequently return to the same place to nest year after year. Often the old nest is repaired.

The eggs, from six to eight, are small for the size of the birds. There are many varieties; they are bluish or yellowish green, with greenish brown markings distributed all over the surface.

COMMON JAY.

GARRULUS GLANDARIUS.

Family PASSERIDÆ. Sub-family CORVINÆ. Genus GARRULUS.

Jaypie.

The Jay is among the most beautiful of our resident birds, and is found in all the wooded districts of England. In Scotland it is rare, and in Ireland it occurs in the southern parts locally. We are most of us probably more familiar with Jays dead than alive, from seeing them either hung to a tree or nailed outside a keeper's cottage. Here again, as with the Magpies and Crows, the game is the cause. Gardeners, too, lose no opportunity of destroying them, as they are particularly fond of cherries and also of peas; and we fear that not even the beauty of their plumage will prevent their ultimate extermination. A cinnamon brown is the prevailing colour of the Jay; the thighs, belly and upper coverts of the tail are white, the rest of the tail black. But the wings are its chief beauty; they are black on the inner part, but barred on the outer part with black, white and blue. There is a crest on the top of the head of bluish-white feathers, the smaller ones being tipped with black.

Its cry is a harsh scream sounding like a hoarse "rae". It is very shy and wary and keeps to the thickest part of the woods (except when in the summer it approaches gardens to steal the fruit), and will fly off chattering and screaming on the slightest sound of any one approaching.

COMMON JAY.

We had a nest of five last spring which we attempted to rear and tame, but only one now survives. The Jay makes a most amusing pet, for it has a wonderful imitative faculty which it displays to great advantage on occasions. It has been heard to imitate "the bleating of a lamb, the mewing of a cat, the hooting of an owl, the neighing of a horse, the shriek of the Buzzard, the song of the Greenfinch, the human voice, the note of the Kite, the warbling of birds, the crowing of a cock, the bark of a dog and the calling of fowls to their food ".

The Jay indulges in a great variety of food—acorns, fruit, beech nuts, grain, seeds, worms, snails, insects, frogs, mice, or even young pheasants, partridges and eggs.

The nest is built towards the middle of April. It is not generally placed at any great height from the ground. The usual situation is in the lower branches of a holly or yew tree. In appearance it reminds one of a very large Bullfinch's nest, being built of sticks and twigs and lined with small roots.

The Jay lays from five to seven eggs of a dusky green colour, thickly freckled over the whole surface with light olive-brown markings.

CHOUGH.

PYRRHOCORAX GRACULUS.

Family PASSERIDÆ. Sub-family CORVINÆ. Genus PYRRHO-
CORAX.

Cornish Chough—Red-legged Crow—Cornish Daw—Cliff
Daw—Red Shanks.

The Chough is fast becoming a very rare bird in our islands, and from the inaccessible positions in which its nest is placed, young collectors will be very unlikely to secure its eggs themselves. The only places in England where it is now likely to be met with are a few spots on the coast of Wales, or of Cornwall and

North Devon. It is also found in a few select places on the Irish coast, and in some of the islands on the West of Scotland. It was formerly resident in the Isle of Wight, but now is only an accidental visitor. Its plumage is a glossy black, with dark steel-blue feathers on its upper parts. The beak and legs are vermilion red.

The Chough's favourite haunts are the high per-

CHOUGH.

pendicular cliffs, which are perfectly inaccessible to climbers, such as Beachy Head and the Newhaven Cliffs in Sussex, which, however, like many others of its old haunts, it now no longer frequents. In such places as these it builds its nest, placing it in a crevice or fissure, often some way back from the entrance, where it is impossible to get at it. It is stated also that it will sometimes make its nest in buildings. It is built of sticks and heather stems, and lined with roots, grass, and sometimes a bunch of wool or cowhair.

The eggs are from two to five, greenish white in ground colour, spotted with brown. They are somewhat like the eggs of the Magpie, but larger, and the markings are yellower.

The Chough feeds on beetles, grubs, caterpillars, grain and raw meat. Meyer says they are " easily tamed, and are very amusing and clever, and may be taught to pronounce many words ; but they are very inquisitive and troublesome, carrying off and hiding anything they take a fancy to. If confined in a cage, they peck and beat about its boundaries continually, in search of insects." In the *Zoologist* (p. 431, 1882) there is an account of two pairs which were tamed, but allowed to fly where they liked. One of these pairs built a nest in a tower attached to the house and laid three eggs. This seems to be the only recorded instance of tame Choughs breeding.

RED-BACKED SHRIKE.

LANIUS COLLURIO.

Family PASSERIDÆ. Sub-family LANIINÆ. Genus LANIUS.

Lesser Butcher Bird—Cheeter—Flusher—Murdering Pie— Jack Baker—Nine Killer.

A summer migrant reaching our shores at the end of April or beginning of May, and leaving again in September. It is commonest in the southern counties of England. North of Yorkshire it is very scarce, and in Ireland it seems to have been only once recorded. In Hampshire we find it fairly common, and a season seldom passes without some eggs being taken.

Its favourite haunts are in the open and on the tall hedgerows. It feeds upon frogs, beetles, caterpillars and small birds; and when it has killed them, apparently the more readily to tear them in pieces, it transfixes them on the thorns of the hedgerows, thus making the hedge serve as a larder, at a good distance from the nest, using a considerable length of hedge for this purpose. Some suppose (from the fact that

RED-BACKED SHRIKE.

insects are often found in this way, without having received the slightest injury) that they are placed there as baits for other birds; for it is quite certain that it does feed on others of the feathered tribe.

The head, neck and upper part of the tail of this bird are slate grey, the back is a rich red brown, shading off on the sides to chestnut red, the tail is black, edged with white, the wings black, edged with chestnut, the under parts are red, shading into white on the chin and breast. Its song consists of a few notes very quickly uttered; it is also said to imitate the notes of other birds.

The nest is begun about the second week in May. It is generally placed in a thorn bush, at no great distance from the ground; it is large, thick, and made of straw, hay, or moss, and lined with wool and horsehair.

The eggs are from four to six in number, salmon colour, yellowish white, or deep cream colour, with a zone of grey and pale reddish-brown spots near the larger end, and sometimes a few hair lines of deep brown. Occasionally the zone of spots is found round the smaller end.

The Butcher Bird will live for years in captivity, when it is said to frequently display its imitative powers, and even to reproduce the barking of a dog; but it must be borne in mind that it is a *Butcher*, and therefore should be kept separate from any other pets.

STARLING.

STURNUS VULGARIS.

Family PASSERIDÆ. Sub-family STURNINÆ. Genus STURNUS.

Stare—Sheep Stare—Brown Starling—Solitary Thrush.

One of our resident birds, though its numbers are largely increased by annual migrations from the north of Europe. It is also one of our commonest birds in England, though in Scotland it is less numerously distributed, and in Ireland it must be considered

7

more of a winter visitor. It is an exceedingly hand
some bird, nearly all its feathers being black, beautifully glossed with rich metallic green and purple, and
tipped with white or cream-coloured spots; the beak
is a rich yellow.

When the breeding season is over the Starlings
collect in flocks, often many thousands in number, and
wander about in search of food. Sometimes they band

STARLING.

together with flocks of Rooks or Jackdaws. Their
food consists chiefly of worms, slugs, and beetles;
but they are also terrible robbers of the cherry
orchards. Most pertinacious are they in this, and
I have frequently watched them, in open defiance of
the gardener and his gun, wantonly stripping off
cherries and dropping them on the ground, as though
in sheer mischief. No wonder the gardener, whose
pride is in his trees, vows vengeance! And yet pos-

sibly the Starling may sometimes be a useful bird, for I have read of an instance of a nest of young Starlings being fed on wire-worms, and wire-worms only—at any rate, that was the only food found in the vicinity of the nest.

The Starling generally commences to build early in April. Its nest is a loosely put together structure, built of straw, dead grass and rootlets, and lined sometimes with feathers or wool, and bits of string. Sometimes there is scarcely anything of a nest at all. It is placed in the hole of a tree, in the gable of a roof, under the eaves, or in a stack-pipe, sometimes also in a pigeon-cot. In almost any suitable hole it can find the Starling will build.

The eggs, four to seven, are of a beautiful greenish blue, or bluish white colour, rather rough but highly polished, and perfectly free from any markings whatever. Frequently eggs of this bird are dropped on the grass in the breeding season, generally unbroken. Some have been picked up almost hatched. It has been suggested that this is the outcome of quarrels.*

The notes of the Starling are very strange and not easily mistaken for those of any other bird. Some of them are harsh, but others are pleasant and full, and altogether the song is cheering and lively. It also has the power of imitating the notes of other birds.

In confinement it may be made very tame and taught to whistle tunes and say several words. In 1880 one of our Queenwood boys had a Starling

* If the eggs are taken from the nest, the Starling will contrive to replace them with fresh clutches, as many as forty eggs having been taken from one nest in this way. The Starling also will return to its old nesting site year after year.

which he tamed most successfully. This bird was taken from the nest, built in a hole in an ash tree growing in a chalk pit near Queenwood. After being in confinement a short time, it was allowed its liberty, and became very tame and fearless. It would come in at the open window during class hours and hop along the desk to its master. It used to fly about with the tame Crows, and come and perch on its owner's shoulders when called. Perhaps its most interesting accomplishment and favourite amusement was hawking for moths and butterflies. It would come to its owner's whistle, and perched on his wrist as he walked about the playground, would wait until a passing insect attracted its attention, and would then swoop off and return with the captured prey to its post of observation.

Starlings, being very fond of bathing, when in confinement should be given plenty of water, as without it they will not long survive.

COMMON CROSSBILL.

LOXIA CURVIROSTRA.

Family PASSERIDÆ.   Sub-family FRINGILLINÆ.   Genus LOXIA.

European Crossbill—Shell Apple.

We must regard this bird as a late summer and winter visitor, in some years much more plentiful than in others, and sometimes remaining to nest. In Scotland it is a resident in parts, and in Ireland it is an occasional winter visitor. It has been observed nearly every year lately with us at Queenwood.

There is no doubt that many more birds are bred in

England than, from the number of instances recorded, one would be led to suppose; for the nest, from the very early time of year at which it is built, and from the high position in which it is generally placed, is frequently overlooked.

The bird's favourite haunts are the spruce firs and larches, upon which it obtains its food by extracting the seeds from the cones, the formation of its bill being especially adapted for this. It is also extremely fond of the pips of apples, which it obtains by inserting

COMMON CROSSBILL.

its beak and then expanding it, splitting the apple in halves. It is almost impossible to describe the appearance of these birds, for their plumage varies so much as they grow older. The general colour of the male bird is something between scarlet and crimson, and the female greenish yellow. Before the first moult young birds are plain brown.

The nest is usually placed right at the top of tall firs and larches, and is built very early in the year, sometimes even in January. It is built on the outside of small sticks and twigs and on the inside of softer materials, such as dry grass, and a little moss, wool or feathers.

The eggs, four or five in number, are pale greenish blue in ground colour, others are almost white. They are spotted, chiefly at the larger end, with small dark-brown spots, and with underlying spots of reddish brown. Some varieties slightly resemble eggs of the Greenfinch, but they are usually larger. The curious feature of this bird is the bill, the upper and lower parts of which cross. The Cross-bill can be easily reconciled to a caged life, but it is very likely to die when moulting comes on. Meyer had one which "was very fond of climbing about its cage like a parrot, by means of its hooked beak".

BULLFINCH.

PYRRHULA VULGARIS.

Family PASSERIDÆ. Sub-family FRINGILLINÆ. Genus PYRR-
HULA.

Nope—Pope—Alp—Olph—Hoop—Red Hoop.

Most of us, from the frequency with which we see this bird caged, must be familiar with the Bullfinch. It is a common resident bird throughout all the wooded parts of Great Britain, but in Ireland it is not met with so commonly. On account of its shy and retiring habits, and its love for the densely wooded parts, it is commonly looked upon as a much rarer bird than it really is. It may also be sometimes seen in gardens and orchards. Its food consists of berries and fruits and various kinds of seeds; but when in the garden it has a great liking for the young fruit-buds of the trees and bushes, which it devours in great numbers, and in consequence draws down the wrath of the gardener upon it.*

The song of the Bullfinch is very soft and sweet. He can also be taught to pipe very beautifully, and whistle a tune, and for this reason, as well as from his striking and beautiful appearance, he has become one of our favourite cage birds.† The plumage of the head and the greater part of the wings and tail is bluish black, the back is bluish grey, the breast and

BULLFINCH.

* Curiously, too, it only picks off the fruit buds, and passes by the leaf-producing buds. Are birds influenced by colour in their choice of food ? It would almost appear so, for though white currants are much sweeter than red, yet they seldom touch them till they have pretty well stripped the red currant trees. I have said these birds are vegetarians, but Dixon mentions an instance in which he saw one catching insects just like a Flycatcher; it was a female bird, and had a nest close at hand.

† Most, if not all, of these Piping Bullfinches come from Germany, and a well-trained bird will fetch a considerable amount of money.

under parts are brick red, shading into pure white towards the rump.

When the breeding season arrives,* the Bullfinch seeks the dense plantations and shrubberies for a site for his nest, and by his silence and retiring habits, does his best to conceal its whereabouts. It is usually commenced about the middle of April. A very favourite position for it is in a low blackthorn, holly, or young fir, while in Hampshire I have more frequently found it in the boughs of a thick yew bush.

Although by young collectors the eggs may possibly be confused with those of other species, yet there is no difficulty in recognising the nest of the Bullfinch. It is a very beautiful, though loosely woven structure. The foundation is made of small twigs, and the nest being rather flat, it reminds one somewhat on the outside of a very small Dove's nest. The inside of the nest is formed chiefly of rootlets, and sometimes a little lining of wool, hair, or moss is added.

The eggs, four to six in number, are pale greenish blue in ground colour, spotted and streaked with dark purple red, and with some larger and paler blotches. These markings are variously distributed, but in most cases they form a zone round the larger end.

As we said above, the Bullfinch is very easily reconciled to confinement, but care should be taken not to give it too much hemp seed. Gilbert White mentions an instance of a cock bird which he saw in a cage ; it had been caught in the fields after it had attained its full colours. In about a year it began to look dingy, and blackening each succeeding year, it became coal black at the end of four. Its chief food was hemp seed.

* It seems most probable that the Bullfinch pairs for life, as at all seasons of the year they are found in pairs.

HAWFINCH.

COCCOTHRAUSTES VULGARIS.

Family PASSERIDÆ. Sub-family FRINGILLINÆ. Genus COC-
COTHRAUSTES.

Grosbeak--Common Grosbeak—Haw Grosbeak.

I think we may fairly class this amongst our rarer
resident birds, though, on account of its very shy
habits, it is no doubt thought less common than it
really is. It breeds in most counties south of Yorkshire, and occasionally in Ireland, but in Scotland it
seems to be only an accidental visitor. During the
last year or two there must have been several reared
near us at Queenwood, for I have observed many
young ones, two of which were caught in traps and
one old one was shot by the gardener. It had built

a nest containing eggs in one of the apple trees in the orchard.

The Hawfinch can be readily recognised by anybody from the large size of its head and bill, which are quite out of proportion to the rest of its body. It is a handsomely coloured bird, its predominating colours being chestnut, black and yellowish brown, the latter being the colour of the under parts.

Being an exceedingly shy bird, its favourite haunts are the woods and dense shrubberies, or the thickly planted orchards. In these latter it commits great depredations during the fruit season, stripping the cherry trees to get at the stones of the fruit, which it easily cracks with its powerful beak. It also robs the pea sticks sadly; but its chief food is seeds of various kinds, such as those of the hawthorn and beech, also the berries of the yew tree.

The Hawfinch is a poor songster, only uttering very few notes; but in confinement it is said to have imitative powers. In the *Zoologist* (1882, p. 189) there is an account of one reared from the nest which would utter the piercing whistle of a Grey Parrot which was kept near him. He would also repeat the "sweeting" and "clucking" sounds with which his owner addressed him, and was very fond of his own name "Jock," though the "J" sadly troubled him.

The nest is built towards the latter end of April or the beginning of May, and is found in various situations, in oak, fir and apple trees, in thorn and holly bushes, and at heights varying from five to forty feet. It is made of twigs intermingled with lichen; the inside is formed of dry grass, rootlets and sometimes a little hair. It is very similar to the nest of the Bullfinch on a larger scale.

The eggs, four to six, are a pale olive green, spotted with brownish black and irregularly streaked with dusky olive brown. They cannot be easily confused with the eggs of any other British bird.

HOUSE SPARROW.

PASSER DOMESTICUS.

Family PASSERIDÆ. Sub-family FRINGILLINÆ. Genus PASSER.

House Sparrow—Common Sparrow—Sprug.

This, we may fairly consider, is our commonest resident bird. In all parts, whether on the roofs and eaves of our crowded cities, or in the fields and country lanes, this impudent chirper is so abundant that I think he may be looked upon as a real pest, in spite of all the strong arguments which naturalists have advanced in his favour, such as, for instance, the statement of Jesse that a pair, whilst feeding their young, destroy on an average 3300 caterpillars in a week, besides other insects. Dixon says of its destructive habits : " Although it feeds on the seed of the charlock and the dock and other seeds, it is also, unfortunately, very fond of grain. Kept in proper bounds it is undoubtedly a useful bird, but its increase is rapid and its enemies so few, that unless its numbers are kept down by artificial means it soon becomes a perfect pest. I have known farmers in the north of England cease from growing corn at all—or only in the smallest quantities—entirely owing to the inroads of the Sparrow, and I have seen fields of corn so stripped by them that the straw was the only re- compense the farmer got ; of course this is in the neighbourhood of large towns. It is not what the birds absolutely eat, although one Sparrow will take its bulk of corn in a day, but what they waste by shaking it to the ground, or breaking the straws. The Sparrow must be kept under. It has been introduced into the United States, and its increase is so rapid that the day will come when our American cousins will repent of having introduced such a destructive souvenir of home."

In addition to grain and seed, the Sparrow will also feed upon insects, and may be often seen hawk- ing a large fly or butterfly. It is very fond of washing itself in puddles, and also of dusting itself in the road much in the same manner that chickens will.

Instances of affection displayed by these birds for their young, and when caged, for their owners, are very numerous. A large number of these are related by Morris in his *British Birds*. It is said that when caged young with a song bird, such as the Canary, the Sparrow will learn to imitate its notes. The House Sparrow is very quarrelsome and pugnacious. It is a common sight to see two of them after an exciting chase alight on a tree, when their angry chattering attracts one by one all the other Sparrows near, which come to look on and add to the din with their harsh chirping till the fight is over.

Its nest is built in a great variety of situations. Under the tiles, or in the gutterings and stack-pipes of buildings, in holes of walls, or the thatched roofs of barns and outhouses, in trees, in an ivy-wall, or in the deserted nests of other birds; even in the nest of a Sparrowhawk the nest has been found. In the spring of 1894 a nest was built under a carriage of the district railway, supported by one of the cylinders in which the gas is stored, and the young were reared while touring round the city.*

The Sparrow commences to build very early, for two or three broods are reared in the year. It is a life-paired bird. When placed in a hole of a wall or building, the nest is a very slovenly piece of work,

---

* Perhaps the most remarkable situation on record was one chosen by two Sparrows, which in 1885 built their nest on one of the axle-tree boxes of a nine-pounder bronze gun at Woolwich Arsenal *which was fired twice daily ;* and in due time five young Sparrows were hatched in spite of the noise caused by the firing, which one would have supposed would have caused the birds to desert for ever, and the recoil and vibration, which one would think would have disturbed the eggs so much as to render them unproductive.

but when in a tree it is well woven together and completely domed. Straw, grass, and any rubbish the
birds can collect, such as string, worsted, rags, and
paper, are used, and it is lined with a quantity of
feathers.

The eggs are from five to seven in number, white in
ground colour, speckled, spotted, and blotched with
greyish brown, ash colour and dark brown. These
markings vary very considerably. In some the ground
colour is almost completely hidden, while in others
the markings are very fine and faint. I have known
many young collectors deceived into buying Sparrows'
eggs for those of the Water Wagtail, or even the
Cuckoo, so that a word of warning in this respect may
not be out of season.

It is almost needless to describe the House Sparrow;
suffice it to say that the handsome plumage of the
country-bred bird can hardly be recognised as the
same as that of the dirty, dusty, smoke-begrimed
inhabitant of our cities and towns.

TREE SPARROW.

PASSER MONTANUS.

Family PASSERIDÆ. Sub-family FRINGILLINÆ. Genus PASSER.

Mountain Sparrow.

The Tree Sparrow is considered a rare resident
bird. It is commonest in the central and eastern
parts of England; in Scotland it is also found, but
in Ireland it is only of very rare occurrence. Though
on the Continent this bird has become imbued with
much of the impudence of the House Sparrow, and

may be seen with it in the streets of towns, yet in England it has not advanced so far, and while we look upon the House Sparrow as a town bird, we must consider the Tree Sparrow as a bird of the country and wilder districts away from all habitation.

It is a smaller and handsomer bird than the House Sparrow, and may be easily distinguished from it by its chestnut head and neck, a white circle round the black ear covert, and by a double bar on the wing. It is more lively and active than the House Sparrow,

TREE SPARROW.

with which it may often be seen in company, and like it, it is very pugnacious. Its food consists of seeds and insects and sometimes grain, though in this respect it seems to be far less destructive than its namesake. Meyer states that out of twenty individuals examined, there was only one whose crop contained any corn, namely, two or three barley-corns; those of the others contained upwards of fifty seeds of weeds growing in the neighbouring fields.

The Tree Sparrow has a few notes, which are not

unpleasant, but its common note is like the chirp of the House Sparrow, only shriller.

It is a somewhat late breeder, the nest being commenced in April. The favourite position is in a hole of a tree, usually of a pollard-willow, and near the top of the stump. Sometimes, too, it will build in the thatch of barns, and occasionally in the deserted nest of a Crow or Magpie, in which case the nest is domed. It is similar in its construction to the House Sparrow's nest, but perhaps not so large. It is made of hay and straw, and lined with wool and feathers.

The eggs are dull white, speckled all over finely and thickly with light shades of greyish brown. They much resemble those of the House Sparrow, but are smaller, and generally darker and redder. They do not seem to vary much in their markings, and are, as a rule, much more thickly and finely marked than eggs of the House Sparrow.

GREENFINCH.

FRINGILLA CHLORIS.

Family PASSERIDÆ. Sub-family FRINGILLINÆ. Genus FRINGILLA.

Green Grosbeak—Green Linnet—Green Bird.

A well-known bird, whose favourite haunts are the shrubberies of gardens, and the hedges around cultivated fields. In these places it may be found throughout the British Islands. It is a resident bird, but its numbers are largely increased by autumn migrations.

Greenfinches seem very sociable birds, and it is no uncommon thing to find several nests in close proximity to one another. I have found as many as fifteen in the hedge surrounding our kitchen garden. In the winter they collect in flocks, sometimes in large numbers, and visit the fresh sown fields in search of seeds and grain.

The song of the Greenfinch is not remarkable. Seebohm says it bears some resemblance to that of

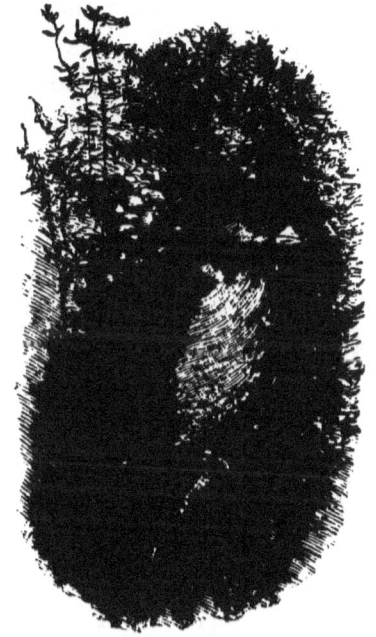

GREENFINCH.

an inferior Canary. It can be kept in confinement, and in that state will pair with the Canary. In its wild state it has been known to pair with the Linnet and Goldfinch. Its food consists of grain, seeds of various kinds, such as charlock, groundsel, dandelion and chickweed; it also consumes insects.

The Greenfinch is a handsome bird, though some-

8

what clumsy in appearance. The general colour of the plumage is bright yellowish green, shading in parts to slate grey. Two broods are generally reared in the season, and the first nest is begun in April. It is very prettily though somewhat untidily constructed. Some nests, however, are much neater than others. The outside is composed of dry grass, moss, and wool, with a few twigs interwoven, and is lined with rootlets, hair, feathers, and wool. I have found the nest lined almost entirely with rootlets. It is usually placed in a shrub or evergreen or in a thorn hedge, and is easily discovered, as very little pains are taken to conceal it. The Greenfinch usually commences to sit after the first egg has been laid.

The eggs are four to six in number, white, or white slightly tinged with blue, spotted and blotched with purple-brown spots and underlying pinky-brown spots, mostly at the larger end. They vary much in shape, one clutch of five in my possession being of a very elongated form, almost as though they had all contained double yolks. Small eggs of the Greenfinch are very similar to those of the Linnet and Goldfinch, so that care must be taken in naming doubtful specimens.

GOLDFINCH.

FRINGILLA CARDUELIS.

Family PASSERIDÆ. Sub-family FRINGILLINÆ. Genus FRINGILLA.

Thistle Finch—Gold Spink—Proud Tailor—Red Cap—King Harry.

The Goldfinch is distributed locally throughout England, less numerously throughout Scotland and

Ireland. It was once much more common with us than it is now; this decrease no doubt is due to the large numbers which have been netted of late years by bird fanciers. A considerable number of these birds remain with us throughout the winter, though many are migrant. The Goldfinch is one of the most beautifully plumaged of our British birds, and is a

GOLDFINCH.

general favourite everywhere on account of its sweet and pleasing song. It must be familiar to all of us as a cage bird. It is very easily reconciled to captivity, and may in this state be taught many interesting tricks. Meyer relates : " We ourselves possessed a bird which had been taught to lay itself down in its master's hand at command, as if dead, which it performed admirably; and such was the retentiveness of its memory, that after it had been nearly two years in our possession without practising this feat, it repeated it again the instant it was called upon to do so ".

In its wild state the Goldfinch frequents our orchards and more especially the neglected wastes on which the thistles and docks abound. It is the " attendant upon the slovenly farmer who does not make use of his odd corners, and is not very careful about his hedgerows; but on those farms where scarcely a weed is left to grow the bird is rarely seen ". It is pretty to see it in the winter time perched upon the thistle heads assuming many dainty attitudes while busied in extracting the seeds, and strewing the ground with their husks. At this time of the year they are mostly seen in small flocks. In the summer time insects form their principal food. The most striking features in the plumage of this bird are the beautiful black and gold wings, and the crimson forehead and chin. The crest is black, the back a reddish brown, the tail black, the breast a light wood brown and the rest of the under parts white; some of the wing and tail feathers are tipped with white.

The nest is commenced rather late, and is not ready for eggs before the middle of May. Like the other Finches', it is a very beautiful structure, somewhat resembling the nest of the Chaffinch, but smaller and less compact, and with more moss in its construction. An apple or pear tree in the orchard is usually chosen for the site, but the bird will occasionally build in a chestnut or beech tree or in a thorn hedge. They frequently return to the same breeding ground year after year; for some years past now we have had four or five nests every year in the orchard at Queen-wood, and that in spite of a very disastrous season two years ago, when nearly all the young birds were massacred in their nests by some birds of prey. The chief materials used in the construction of the nest are moss, grass and lichens; the interior is lined with feathers and a few hairs.

The eggs, four or five, are greenish white, spotted with purplish brown and grey, and sometimes streaked with brown. They very much resemble the Linnet's eggs, but are as a rule smaller; however, the nest when seen at once settles any doubt.

CHAFFINCH.

FRINGILLA CÆLEBS.

Family PASSERIDÆ. Sub-family FRINGILLINÆ. Genus FRINGILLA.

Pink—Spink—Chink—Shell Apple—Twink—Beech Finch—Skelly—Horse Finch.

This is one of the commonest of our British birds, and there are few gardens, hedgerows, or shrubberies in the British Isles where its "pink, pink, pink" may not be heard. In addition to this common note it has a song, short and lively and not unpleasing, which is thought very highly of by the French and Germans, but amongst us it has no very great reputation as a songster.

The Chaffinch is a resident bird, but its numbers are largely increased by autumn migrations. A curious fact in connection with these birds is that towards Christmas the males and females collect into separate flocks and live for some time quite independently of one another.   Much has been written upon this remarkable occurrence, which has gained for the bird its specific name " Cælebs ".   The food of the Chaffinch consists principally of insects, grain and the seeds of weeds.   It is a very watchful bird, and on the approach of an enemy is generally the one to give the note of warning to other small birds.   Instances are recorded of the Missel Thrush building its nest in close

CHAFFINCH.

proximity to that of the Chaffinch, apparently that it may profit by the watchful guardianship of the latter.

The male is much sought after as a cage bird, as much for his handsome plumage as for his song powers. The general colour of the upper parts is slate grey, the wings and tail are dark brown, the under parts are pale chestnut shading into pink lower down.   The nest of the Chaffinch is a most beautiful and elaborate little structure ; it is said that it often takes three weeks to build. It is constructed entirely by the female, though the male assists in bringing the materials to hand. Two broods are generally reared and the first nest is commenced in April. It is placed at heights varying from five to twelve feet, sometimes higher, sometimes on the lichen-covered bough of a birch or ash, or in the branches of the holly or yew, very frequently on the limb of an apple or other fruit tree in the orchard, or in a hawthorn bush. It is made of grasses and moss beautifully woven together with cobwebs and lichens, and lined thickly with wool, hair and feathers. It is particularly noticeable with respect to the Chaffinch's nest that the bird attempts to assimilate the nest to the colour of the surrounding bush or tree, generally with reasonable success; if in decayed underwood, you will find little pieces of decayed wood used; if on a lichen-covered branch, lichens will be used, and a hawthorn bush in flower had scraps of paper used to conceal the nest. The Chaffinch generally rests content with this ingenuity for the purposes of concealment, but a most remarkable instance is recorded by Seebohm of the pains which a pair of birds took at Bastow near the river Derwent to conceal their nest. This structure had no less than two feet of moss attached and hanging to it, all put together by the bird, and containing also lichen and wool, the whole being attached to the ivy by horsehair. The amount of this material woven together was several times more than that used for the nest itself.

An amusing incident occurred at Queenwood some years ago, on the occasion of the haircutter paying his periodical visit to the school. A few days after his departure, a Chaffinch's nest was found in the grounds completely lined with the hair of one of the boys.

The eggs, four to six, are bluish green in ground colour, clouded with pale reddish brown, sometimes very thickly spotted and blotched and occasionally streaked with pale purple brown and dark reddish-brown markings. They are not easily confused with the eggs of any other bird, but there is an uncommon variety which bears a remarkable resemblance to the eggs of the Bullfinch.

LINNET.

FRINGILLA CANNABINA.

Family PASSERIDÆ. Sub-family FRINGILLINÆ. Genus FRINGILLA.

Brown Linnet—Red Linnet—Grey Linnet— Rose Linnet—Whin Linnet—Lintie.

The Linnet is commonly distributed throughout the British Isles, more particularly in those parts abounding in gorse, whin and furze bushes, but it frequents in smaller numbers nearly all parts, except perhaps just in the breeding season. It should be noticed that this bird is described by various names—Brown, Grey, White and Rose Linnet, and sometimes Greater Redpole. We have frequently had eggs brought to us thus distinguished by farm boys and country people, whereas these names simply denote the Linnet in different attire, its plumage at various seasons undergoing great changes.

In the autumn and winter the Linnets join in flocks, packed closely together, and frequent the stubbles and weedy, uncultivated ground. From here they chiefly obtain their food, the seeds of thistles, dandelions, charlock, dock, etc. They also feed upon insects in the summer.

The Linnet is much prized as a cage bird, on account of its melodious song, some of the notes of which are very soft and mellow. It also is said to have the power of imitating the notes of other birds. It can be made very tame. In connection with this, " Mr. John " related to us some time ago an in-

LINNET.

teresting account of a hen bird, which was picked up in the garden of a medical practitioner at Falmouth, before it had any feathers. "The cook, who owns the bird, fed it on bread and milk for three months; it is now two years old. It hops on her hand, and when she says 'Sing, pretty Bob,' it will sing to her, and it will also kiss her when she tells it to. It regularly sits on her shoulder when she is reading. It is hurt if the doctor's wife passes the cage without noticing it. If, when the kitchen is left, a kettle or saucepan should boil over, it calls the servant down. When the tradesmen call, it expects them to feed it— from the grocer some tit-bit, and from the milkman a drop of milk; but should it see cream, it won't touch the milk."

In its breeding plumage the Linnet has a crimson forehead, the rest of the head and neck is brownish grey, shading into chestnut brown on the back; the under parts are of a buffish colour, richly mingled with carmine and shading into buffish white lower down. The tail feathers are dark brown, edged with white.

The Linnet builds its nest in the furze, or in short thick hedges, sometimes too in the evergreens and gardens. It is usually placed about four feet from the ground. It is scarcely so neat in appearance as the nests of the other Finches, but the inside is beautifully formed and rounded. It is formed outside of dry grass and moss and a few small twigs, and lined with wool, hair, and vegetable down, and sometimes a few feathers. Both the nest and the eggs of this bird vary considerably.

The eggs, four to six, are greenish or bluish white in ground colour, spotted, blotched, and streaked with reddish brown to reddish purple of different shades. As previously mentioned, care must be taken in iden- tifying the eggs, as large specimens are very similar to small specimens of the Greenfinch; and small speci- mens are almost indistinguishable from the eggs of the Goldfinch.

LESSER REDPOLE.

FRINGILLA RUFESCENS.

Family PASSERIDÆ. Sub-family FRINGILLINÆ. Genus FRIN-
GILLA.

Common Redpole—Lesser Redpole Linnet.

The Lesser Redpole breeds in the northern counties
of England. It is also resident in parts of Scotland
and in Ireland, but in the south of England it can
only be regarded as a winter visitor. However, nests
have occasionally been found in most of the southern
counties; we have one recorded in 1888 with us at
Queenwood in Hampshire, by " Mr. John ".

The Redpole is a lively and fearless little bird,
smaller than the Linnet, and in its search for food it

adopts very similar antics to those which amuse us so in the Tits; it feeds, when it can get them, on the seeds of the alder and birch, at other times on the seeds of the thistle, dandelion, turnip and other plants. It is said also, like the Bullfinch, to destroy many young buds, but this is probably in its search for insects within them.

As a caged bird the Redpole is a great favourite, and may be taught many tricks; his song too is pleasing, clear, and not unmusical. He will soon become exceedingly tame in confinement. The distinctive feature in the breeding plumage of the Lesser Redpole is the crimson patch on the top of the head; for the rest, the general colour of the upper parts is yellowish brown, each feather having a dark centre to it, the under parts are buffish white, mingled with crimson on the breast.

The nest is usually placed in a low bush, sometimes also in a birch or alder at a greater distance from the ground. It is made of dry grass and moss, and lined with willow down, or with feathers. Hewitson speaks of it as "very small, and of the most elegant construction, thickly and most beautifully lined". It is a late breeder for a resident bird, its eggs being seldom found before June; but in the south of England it has been found earlier.

The eggs, four or five, are pale bluish green, spotted and blotched with orange brown and dark reddish brown, mostly at the larger end. They resemble very much some of the eggs of the Linnet.

REED BUNTING.

EMBERIZA SCHÆNICLUS.

Family PASSERIDÆ. Sub-family FRINGILLINÆ. Genus EM-
BERIZA.

Reed Sparrow—Water Sparrow.

The Reed Bunting, often incorrectly called the
Black-headed Bunting (a doubtful British bird), is a
common resident bird in most parts of the British
Isles, and breeds in marshy districts. It is a handsome bird with head and throat a deep black, the
breast is white, and there is a white collar passing
round the neck; the general colour of the other upper
parts is bright chestnut, the wings are dark brown,
edged with red.

In the winter the Reed Bunting feeds upon grain and seeds of various kinds, and in the summer chiefly upon insects. Its song, like that of the other Buntings, is uninteresting and monotonous.

The birds pair rather early, and the nest is commenced about the middle of April. It is nearly always placed close to the water (though a few instances are recorded of the nest being found right away from any), and is generally placed on the ground, well concealed by a tuft of grass, or a clump of rushes. One nest, which I only discovered by nearly walking over the sitting bird, was so completely hidden that, although I knew the exact spot from which the bird rose, I could find no trace of it until I had torn away the thick surrounding rank tuft of grass. Another nest I found built in the rushes themselves, and some distance from the ground; but this position is not a common one, and when adopted, the nest is never suspended like the nest of the Reed Warbler, but always supported. It is composed of dry grass, moss, and the leaves of rushes, and lined with fine grass, a little moss and hair. The materials, however, vary considerably, sometimes reed and grass stems alone being used.

The eggs, four to six in number, are of a reddish-brown or greyish-brown colour, spotted, streaked and blotched with dark brown of a rich purple shade, some of the spots being bold and large, though toned down at the edges. These eggs bear a certain resemblance in their markings to the eggs of the Chaffinch, but they are of a darker and browner tint.

CORN BUNTING.

EMBERIZA MILIARIA.

Family PASSERIDÆ. Sub-family FRINGILLINÆ. Genus EM-
BERIZA.

Common Bunting—Lark Bunting—Ebb.

The Corn Bunting, or as it is sometimes called, the
Common Bunting, but inappropriately, for it is by no
means the best known of the Buntings in this country,
is found in certain districts throughout the British
Islands, common in some, rare in others. It is a
resident bird, but its numbers are largely increased
by autumn migrations. The tracts it prefers are the
large, open, level-lying, cultivated districts, away from
woods and trees, and away from hills. It is the largest
of the Buntings.

In its habits, the Corn Bunting resembles the Lark,
roosting on the ground at night, and in the autumn
and winter when they collect in flocks they may
frequently be seen in company with the Larks, searching the stubble fields for grain. In appearance, too,
it is not unlike the Lark, being of rather dusky

plumage, the general colour of the upper parts being yellowish brown, and of the lower, yellowish grey. The food of this species consists chiefly of seeds and grain, but in the summer it feeds on insects.

The song is harsh and monotonous, and has no music in it. For its breeding site the Corn Bunting usually chooses some open field, in which it builds its nest on the ground, away from hedges and trees, and protected by some overhanging tuft or clump. Frequently it is found amongst the growing corn. It is not generally finished before the middle of May or the beginning of June, and is frequently brought to light by the mowers. Roots and straw, dry grass and leaves are the materials used in its construction, and it is lined with hair.

The eggs, four to six, usually four, are oval in shape; they are of a pale greyish white colour, tinged sometimes with a dirty pink tint, spotted, streaked and blotched with reddish-brown or greyish-purple markings. They cannot well be confused with the eggs of any other of the Buntings, on account of their larger size. I have seen a clutch of the eggs of this bird very much resembling large eggs of the Greenfinch, but rounder and of a duller ground colour.

CIRL BUNTING.

EMBERIZA CIRLUS.

Family PASSERIDÆ.   Sub-family FRINGILLINÆ.   Genus EM-BERIZA.

Black-throated Yellow Hammer.

The Cirl Bunting is a rare bird, and very local in its haunts, being confined to the southern counties of

England. In Hampshire we have many instances recorded of it nesting in all parts of the county. I have myself found the nest, in which the female sat so closely that I was able to examine her minutely without disturbing her, and almost succeeded in taking her in my hand.

In its appearance, it bears a strong resemblance to the Yellow Hammer, and may sometimes therefore be taken for it. The chief points of difference are in the

CIRL BUNTING.

head and chin. The head and nape of the Cirl Bunting are olive green and the chin is black (in the Yellow Hammer they are yellow). The back and wings are chestnut brown (in the Yellow Hammer they are reddish brown), the breast and sides are yellow, lower part yellow; the tail dusky black, the outer feathers patched with white (in the Yellow Hammer the tail feathers are margined with brown and olive), but there

9

is not so much difference between the two birds in general appearance but that casual observers might well mistake them. The female is even more like the Yellow Hammer than the male, but may always be distinguished by the dark head feathers.

The song of the Cirl Bunting is shrill and piercing, " so much resembling the call-notes of the Lesser Whitethroat, that it requires considerable knowledge of their language not to mistake the one for the other ". It feeds on insects, seeds, and berries. It is easily reared if taken from the nest.

The nest is placed in a low bush or shrub, or amongst brambles and briars, very often in a site similar to the Yellow Hammer, whose nest it greatly resembles. It is made of dry stalks of grass and a little moss, rather loosely put together, and lined with hair and fibrous roots.

The eggs, too, bear a strong resemblance to some eggs of the Yellow Bunting; they are usually four in number, dull greenish white in ground colour, streaked and spotted with very dark, almost black brown. They are as a rule much greener than the eggs of the Yellow Hammer, and the markings are much larger, bolder, and more decided; the thin hair streaks are much less numerous, and the colouring of them is blacker. In shape, too, the eggs seem rounder, and perhaps slightly smaller. It should be remembered that the Cirl Bunting is a rare bird, and its eggs are not likely often to be met with, and from the great similarity between the nest and eggs of this bird and the ensuing one mistakes in classi-fication may easily be made; so that great pains should be taken to observe closely the parent birds, before the eggs are removed.

YELLOW HAMMER.

EMBERIZA CITRINELLA.

Family PASSERIDÆ. Sub-family FRINGILLINÆ. Genus EM-
BERIZA.

Yellow Bunting—Gold Spink—Yoldring—Yeldrock—Yellow
Yeldring.

The Yellow Hammer, or more correctly speaking,
the Yellow Ammer (Ammer being the German word
for Bunting), is the commonest of our Buntings and is
found all over Great Britain and Ireland, its favourite
haunts being the hedgerows, country lanes and fields.
It is shy of towns, however, and the thick woods, preferring to keep on their borders. It is a handsome
bird in its brilliant dress, and but for its common
occurrence in all our country rambles would no doubt
have many more enthusiastic admirers.

The head, neck and under parts are a bright yellow,

the back and wings are reddish brown, the tail feathers are dark brown margined with brown and olive.

The Yellow Hammer is a most pertinacious songster, commencing in February and singing on until September, reiterating his peculiar notes again and again, which Atkinson compares to the words " A little bit of bread and no-o che-ee-e-se". He is also a wonderfully good ventriloquist. In the summer these birds feed on insects, but in the autumn and winter they collect in flocks and frequent the new sown fields and stubble, making their meal off the grain and seeds. They may also often be seen clinging to the stacks and ricks and extracting the corn from stray ears.

As a cage bird the Yellow Bunting will become very tame.

The nest is not often completed before the middle of April. It is built upon the ground or in some low bush or bramble, or sometimes in a hedge; it is made of dry grass and moss, and lined with roots and horse-hair, and occasionally a few feathers. Once the eggs are laid, the bird is very tenacious of her property, and will seldom desert her nest. A curious instance in connection with this was related to us. On 1st August, 1884, a man was digging some potatoes on the Maison Dieu Estate at Dover, and was shaking the roots when a nest containing five eggs of the Yellow Hammer dropped out of the haulm. He collected the eggs and removed them to his tool-shed, but about ten minutes afterwards, seeing a bird hovering near the spot, and thinking it was the parent, he replaced the nest close to where he found it. The bird returned to the nest and hatched the eggs.

The eggs are a considerable trouble to young collectors from the immense variety, both in colour and marking, but they cannot well be confused with any others except those of the Cirl Bunting; some are pale purple-white colour, streaked and speckled with dark reddish brown ; some have been known of a red colour, with reddish-brown streaks and lines; others entirely of a stone colour; others quite white, and others again stone colour, marbled in the usual way; and we could add even to this list, but perhaps this is sufficient to show the almost infinite variety in the colour and markings of the eggs of this common bird.

The male bird takes his share in hatching with the female, which is also the case with the Cirl Bunting.

SWALLOW.

HIRUNDO RUSTICA.

Family PASSERIDÆ. Sub-family HIRUNDININÆ. Genus HIRUNDO.

Chimney Swallow—House Swallow—Barn Swallow.

"The Swallows have returned!" Who, on hearing this, will not admit that there is something cheering and inspiriting in the knowledge that these little birds have come back, bringing with them the announcement of another spring begun, and another winter ended? Referring to some old notes, I find, "12th March, 1884 —Swallows said to have been seen near Bossington (Hants)". This date is certainly very early for the arrival of our friends, and is probably incorrect, the ordinary time being the second week in April, though not infrequently they arrive during the first week, and have been known to be as late as the second week in May. They leave us again in September or the commencement of October, previous to which time they may be seen collected together in great numbers on the housetops and copings making preparations for their flight. I was much interested this last autumn when driving from Eastbourne to Polegate in watching these birds, mingled with the House Martins, packed along the telegraph wires literally in tens of thousands. The lines of birds must have extended for quite two miles; and such a chattering and clamouring for places, no doubt all feeling very cheery and

SWALLOW.

elated at the thoughts of distant Africa! It was formerly imagined—how curious the idea sounds to us now!—that Swallows passed the winter in a torpid state, submerging themselves in lakes for this purpose and burying themselves in the mud at the bottom. Of this Dr. Johnson says: "Swallows certainly do sleep all the winter. A number of them conglobulate together by flying round and round, and then all in a heap throw themselves under water and lie in the bed of the river." But space will not permit more on this interesting subject.

It is said that the Swallow has been kept in captivity two or three years, and has become very tame. It feeds entirely upon insects, caught on the wing; indeed this active little bird scarcely ever rests during the daytime. Its flight is very rapid, being as much as ninety miles an hour, or a mile and a half a minute. Swallows may often be observed chasing birds of prey —Hawks or Cuckoos—their quickness on the wing ensuring their perfect safety.*

The Swallow has the forehead and throat rich chestnut, the upper parts are steel blue, wings and tail brown, and the general colour of the under parts nearly white. Its song, which may be heard very early in the morning, as the bird perches on some chimney-pot close at hand, is more correctly an incessant chatter, but soft and not unmelodious.

Swallows pair for life, and often return year after year to the same spot, building a new nest beside the old one. This is usually placed in an old barn or hovel on one of the joists supporting the roof, or in a chimney, or beneath the eaves of a house. It is built of numerous pellets of moist earth, kept together with bits of straw, and lined with feathers. It is saucer-shaped in form, but when placed against a vertical wall, it resembles a quarter of a sphere. Unlike the House Martin's nest, the Swallow never continues its nest right up to the roof, but the top is left completely open. It has been found in many

* It is a common saying that if the Swallows fly high, we shall have fine weather, and if low, it will be wet. This is because in the damp weather, when the atmosphere becomes heavy, the insects and flies keep low.

curious places. Some years ago a pair of Swallows built in the corner of one of the sitting-rooms at Queenwood, continuing their operations through the open window while people were using the room, and eventually laying their eggs. It has been found in the hole of a tree, in a hanging lamp, in an open drawer, in a disused loft, on the handles of a pair of shears, and in the knocker of a hall door.

The eggs are usually four to six in number, white spotted and speckled with light brown and deep coffee colour. Two broods are often hatched in the year.

HOUSE MARTIN.

HIRUNDO URBICA.

Family PASSERIDÆ.   Sub-family HIRUNDININÆ.   Genus HIRUNDO.

Martin—Martlet—Window Martin—Eaves Swallow—Martin Swallow.

The Martins reach our shores about a week later than the Swallows, and soon spread themselves throughout the British Isles; they leave again as a rule a few days earlier. The Martin is often mistaken by casual observers for the Swallow, but it may easily be distinguished by its shorter tail, its perfectly white rump, and glossy black feathers on the upper parts. Its legs, too, are covered with soft downy feathers down to the toes, which is not the case with others of the Swallow kind. The legs are very short and weak and cannot be used for walking. If it should try to move along the ground it always uses its wings.

Like the Swallow, the Martin feeds entirely on in-

sects, which it hawks for on the wing; but its flight is
not so swift as the Swallow's. The chatter of the
Martin cannot be called pleasing, it is not so rich or
varied as that of the Swallow.

The nest of the Martin is too well known to need
much description. It is built of pellets of mud, each
layer of which is allowed to dry before the succeeding
one is added, and the structure is strengthened with

HOUSE MARTIN.

small bits of straw and grass; the inside is smooth
and lined with a few feathers and a little dry grass.
It is usually placed under the eaves of houses, or beneath a window ledge. It is built right up until it is
roofed in by the projecting ledge, and a small gap is
left for the admission of the birds. The birds return
to the same nest yearly, if it has not been destroyed;
in this latter case, they will often repair it. When the

young are hatched both birds sleep in the nest with them, and after the young have flown, the whole of this happy little family with the parents repair nightly to the nest to roost.

Martins are apparently very fond of one another's company; as many as twenty and, it is said, in some instances even a hundred nests are built by them close together, forming quite a little town. These birds when they have finished their nests are not infrequently attacked by the House Sparrow, which wishes to usurp the home, and a fight takes place in which, I am sorry to say, the Sparrow is often victorious. There is an instance of this recorded in the *Zoologist* in which, when the Sparrows had obtained possession, the Martins banded together, and, leaving one of their number to guard the exit, brought material and walled the robber in, and so starved him to death.

As an instance of the fearlessness of these little birds, "Mr. John" writes: "When I was at St. Gilgen, in the Tyrol, with my brothers, in the sitting-room of the inn in which we had our meals were several Martins' nests. The windows were left open, and the little birds flew in and out at pleasure. Perching on the bell-wires, they seemed entirely indifferent to the company, and no one ever disturbed them."

Two broods are generally reared in the year; but it is sometimes the case that the last ones get left behind to starve, if they are not able to fly when the time for departure comes.

The eggs, four to six, are pure glossy white and very smooth; they resemble the eggs of the Sand Martin, but are slightly larger.

SAND MARTIN.

HIRUNDO RIPARIA.

Family PASSERIDÆ. Sub-family HIRUNDININÆ. Genus HIRUNDO.

Bank Martin—Sand Swallow—River Swallow.

From all accounts, the Sand Martin seems to be the last of the species to arrive in most parts and the first to leave our shores. It is the smallest of all the Swallows, and is much more local in its distribution, though found throughout the British Isles. Its haunts are the sandy cuttings and cliffs, particularly in the neighbourhood of water. Its plumage is dull and sombre; the upper parts are mouse colour, the wings and tail being darker; the under parts are snowy white. Like its relations, it feeds upon insects. It seems to have no song.

On its arrival, the Sand Martin repairs at once to its old breeding ground, the sand-banks and chalk-pits, the old nesting holes being used to roost in at night time. These holes are very numerous and close together. The most numerous colony I can call to mind that I am acquainted with is in the sandy cliffs

along the Suffolk coast between Southwold and Lowes-
toft. These low cliffs seem completely riddled in parts.
I recollect a young sailor telling me that, when a lad,
he would take a long stick with a hook at the end, and
carry home hundreds of their eggs of a morning and
boil them for breakfast. It seems almost incredible
that these holes, sometimes as much as four feet in
length, can be bored by such a small, weak little thing
as the Sand Martin. It works entirely with closed
beak, shovelling out the loosened sand with its feet.
The tunnel slopes gently in an upward direction, and
towards the end opens out into a small chamber in
which the nest is placed. Some of the passages are
straight; others, where perhaps a stone or other obstacle
has been encountered, bend off at an angle. The same
hole is used several years in succession.

The nest is very slight, built of a few straws and
grass and lined with some feathers. Eggs will be
found at the end of May or the beginning of June.
They are perfectly white, four to six in number, with
very thin shells, so that when fresh the yolk showing
through gives them a beautiful pink tint.

Unlike the House Martin, this bird is entirely free
from feathers on its feet.

PIED WAGTAIL.

MOTACILLA YARRELLII.

Family PASSERIDÆ. Sub-family MOTACILLINÆ. Genus MOTA-
CILLA.

Water Wagtail—Polly Dishwasher—Nanny Washtail—Black
and White Wagtail.

The Pied Wagtail is the commonest of our Wagtails and is distributed all over the British Isles.

Many birds stay with us through the winter, but the majority migrate to us in the spring and leave us again in the autumn.

The " Dishwasher " is a general favourite on account of its particularly neat and dainty appearance. Watch them as they run along the ground, turning their heads this way and that, and every now and then darting a

PIED WAGTAIL.

few feet from the ground after some passing insect. How quickly they move their little legs, and how daintily they flirt their graceful tails !   They may often be seen running on the slates of some roof, or on fresh-cut lawns, busied in this way in their search for food ; but their favourite haunts are in the neighbourhood of water, by the banks of rivers and lakes, where they may frequently be seen washing themselves on the shallow margin.

The song of the Pied Wagtail has been described as short and loud, " putting you in mind of the twitter of a Swallow ". It is not often heard. It feeds, as above stated, on insects; it is also said to enjoy minnows. It has been kept in confinement.

The plumage of these birds undergoes several changes. In the breeding plumage the forehead, sides of the head and neck are pure white, the general colour of the remaining upper parts is black; the tail is black, edged with white; the chin and breast are black, the rest of the under parts white.

The nest is placed in all sorts of positions, generally near water, but by no means always; sometimes in a hole in a wall or bank, a hollow in a heap of stones, in the roots of trees, or in an ivied wall. For several years past at Queenwood, a pair has built in a loft filled with rubbish, over the Science Laboratory. The birds return each season and the nest is placed between the rafters forming the floor, a new nest being built each time. The birds enter in a gap between the slates and the wall. They generally rear two broods in the year.

The nest is built of dry grass, moss, roots, and leaves, and lined with wool, hair, and sometimes feathers. It is a favourite nest for the Cuckoo to select.

The eggs, four to six, are of a bluish-white or grey colour, thickly spotted and speckled with small greyish-brown markings. They much resemble some varieties of the House Sparrow, and I have known many a youthful collector " done " by some astute country lad with eggs to sell.

GREY WAGTAIL.

MOTACILLA SULPHUREA.

Family PASSERIDÆ. Sub-family MOTACILLINÆ. Genus MOTA-
CILLA.

Winter Wagtail.

The Grey Wagtail is an uncommon bird, but yet is
met with sparingly throughout England and Wales;
in Scotland and Ireland it is slightly more plentiful.
It is a resident bird, but migrates from one part of
the country to another, breeding in the mountainous
and hilly districts, and wintering in the open and low-
lying parts. It is even more confined to the vicinity

of water than the Pied Wagtail, and is seldom met with away from the banks of streams and lakes. In its habits it much resembles the other Wagtails—the same light, dainty step and flirting of the tail up and down, as it runs about snatching at the passing insects. It is a peculiarly graceful and pretty bird. Seebohm says of it: " In spite of its name, the delicate brilliancy of its plumage entitles it to be considered one of our most elegant native birds. All its movements correspond; nothing can be more graceful than the way in which it will run along the margin of a still pool, leaving the impression of its delicate feet on the sand, or daintily flit from stone to stone in the running stream."

Grey tinged with green is the prevailing colour of the upper parts, and by this and its longer tail it may easily be distinguished from the other Wagtails. It has a black chin and throat, edged with white, and a yellow breast, which becomes grey in the winter.

The nest of the Grey Wagtail is most commonly placed upon the ground beneath some projecting rock, and close to the water; but it has also been found in most of the sites chosen by the Pied Wagtail, the nest of which it resembles. It is made of fine roots and grass and lined with hair.

The eggs, which are laid towards the end of April or the beginning of May, are of a creamy or greyish ground colour, mottled with light brown and sometimes with a few streaks of a darker brown.

The Grey Wagtail will live in confinement, and is not difficult to tame, which may be said of all the Wagtails.

YELLOW WAGTAIL.

MOTACILLA RAYII.

Family PASSERIDÆ. Sub-family MOTACILLINÆ. Genus MOTA-
CILLA.

Ray's Wagtail—Cow Bird—Seed Bird—Seed Lady.

The Yellow Wagtail is a summer visitor to our shores from March to October, and consequently breeds here. It is common in most parts of England and the southern counties of Scotland. Its movements and habits are similar to the others of its species, and it has the same graceful and light-running step. It is not, however, such a lover of the water as the Pied and Grey Wagtails, and one may always expect to meet with it in the cultivated pastures and fields where, it is said, it will follow the plough with as much persistency as the Rook.

They are usually seen in pairs, and are great friends to the cattle, delighting (as do also the Pied Wagtails) to flit about over them and relieve them of many of the troublesome insects which infest them. In addition to insects, grubs and beetles, the Yellow Wagtail feeds upon small worms.

This bird is occasionally heard to sing. Its song

somewhat resembles the Pied Wagtail's. As its name implies, the preponderating colour of the plumage is yellow. The general colour of the upper parts is yellowish green, the under parts are bright yellow.

The nest is built upon the ground, on a mossy bank concealed by an overhanging tuft, or in the corn fields and fallows, sometimes in an old tree stump level with the ground. The materials of which it is built vary; moss, roots, dry grass and hair are used. The bird is rather an early breeder, and eggs may generally be found towards the end of April.

The eggs, five or six in number, are grey in ground colour; this, however, is sometimes completely hidden by the thickness of the pale-brown mottlings. They are, in appearance, very like the eggs of the Sedge Warbler, and, if the eggs of both species were mixed up, it would be almost impossible to separate them. The eggs of the Yellow Wagtail are, as a rule, rather larger perhaps.

As previously mentioned, the Yellow Wagtail can be tamed without much difficulty.

TREE PIPIT.

ANTHUS ARBOREUS.

Family PASSERIDÆ. Sub-family MOTACILLINÆ. Genus AN-THUS.

Pipit Lark—Field Lark—Tree Lark—Field Titling—Grasshopper Lark.

The Tree Pipit is a migratory bird, arriving about the middle of April and leaving again in September. It closely resembles the Meadow Pipit, and is often mistaken for it. It is, however, distinguishable by its

superior size and longer tail, and it is more in the
habit of perching on trees than that bird.   It is a
common bird in most parts of England, but in Scotland
and Wales it is rare and in Ireland almost unknown.

The general colour of the upper parts of the Tree
Pipit is brown ; the under parts are buffish white,
with dark round spots on the breast, becoming smaller

TREE PIPIT.

on the flanks.   Whilst the Meadow Pipit prefers the
uncultivated, you will find the Tree Pipit in the highly-
cultivated and wooded districts. He is a most charming
songster; perched upon the topmost sprig of some tree
or bush, he will rise straight up into the air, after the
manner of a lark, warbling out his sweet and pleasing
notes ; but very shortly he seems to tire, and with

wings stretched out and tail expanded he gently floats down, still uttering his melodious song, until he either reaches his perch again or the ground. This performance is repeated off and on the whole day through.

The food of the Tree Pipit consists chiefly of insects, such as flies, beetles, grasshoppers, and the larvæ of insects.

The nest is always built on the grass—on a green bank in a wood, or amongst the long grass at the foot of a tree ; often, too, in an open field; and it is so cunningly concealed that it is difficult to find ; this difficulty is made still greater from the fact that the bird does not rise into the air direct from its nest, but generally runs several yards before mounting, and in descending it will alight twenty or thirty yards from its nest, running along the ground to it. Like so many other birds, the Tree Pipit will often endeavour to draw off an intruder by " shamming ". I recollect almost treading on a sitting Pipit when out in the woods one day, when she fluttered off, apparently with a broken wing, and lay down a few yards away in such seeming distress that I was convinced I had trodden on her: on going up to her to put her out of her misery, however, she flew away " laughing at me ". I afterwards found the nest in which the young ones were just coming out from the shells, which explained her intense anxiety.

The nest is generally placed in a little hollow in the ground, being made of dry grass, root-fibres and moss, and lined with finer grass and horsehair.

The eggs, four to six, differ greatly, and it is impossible to describe all the varieties. The two most distinct perhaps are greyish white, profusely spotted all over with reddish brown and greyish blue, boldly blotched and streaked with olive brown or dark brown. A great number of intermediate varieties to these occur.

The whole family of Pipits will live as cage birds.

MEADOW PIPIT.

ANTHUS PRATENSIS.

Family PASSERIDÆ. Sub-family MOTACILLINÆ. Genus ANTHUS.

Titlark—Meadow Tit—Moor Tit—Moss Cheeper—Heather Lintie.

The Meadow Pipit is much more common than the Tree Pipit. Unlike the latter, it is a resident bird among us, though doubtless many migrate before winter to more southerly parts, returning again in the spring. It is distributed all over the British Isles, its favourite haunts during the breeding season being the moors and heaths, where its nest may be always found.

In its manners, the Titlark bears a strong resemblance to the Wagtails, running quickly along the ground and flirting its tail continually up and down. It rises from the ground into the air, and then, like the Tree Pipit, spreads its wings and tail and floats down, its song being seldom heard before it begins its descent. The bird does not perch on trees so much as the Tree Pipit. Its song is pleasant and soft, but not very varied.

The Titlark resembles in colour the Skylark; but it is smaller and has a long tail edged with white. The upper parts are olive brown, the feathers having dark centres; and the under parts nearly white, streaked with blackish brown. It feeds upon insects and worms. These birds bear confinement well, and behave very like the Larks, roosting on the ground, and singing very prettily, either when standing or running along the ground. The nest, as previously stated, is most commonly found on the moors; but the bird breeds all over the country. The nest is always placed upon the ground, and is generally difficult to find, either in the middle of a grass or corn field, or on a sloping bank, protected by an overhanging tuft, sometimes at the root of a tree, or beneath a stone in a small hollow. It is made almost entirely of dry grass, and lined with hair.

Eggs may be found about the end of April or beginning of May; they are four to six in number, and subject to considerable variation, though hardly so pronounced as the Tree Pipit's. As a general description we may say that they are of a brownish-white colour, thickly mottled over with darker brown, and pale underlying markings. One uncommon variety closely resembles the eggs of the Pied Wagtail. The Titlark resorts to the same tricks as the Tree Pipit to draw off danger from her nest. The Cuckoo is said to patronise the Meadow Pipit's nest more frequently than any other. Out of four nests found last season by our young collectors at Queenwood, three contained a Cuckoo's egg.

ROCK PIPIT.

ANTHUS OBSCURUS.

Family PASSERIDÆ. Sub-family MOTACILLINÆ. Genus ANTHUS.

Shore Pipit—Dusky Lark—Rock Lark—Sea Tit—Sea Lintie.

This Bird for a long time was, it seems, confused with the Meadow and Tree Pipits. It is a common bird on nearly all parts of our coasts, but never comes far inland. It is an active bird, and has all the habits of the other Pipits; its quick run as it moves along the shore, the flight up into the air and descent with the wings expanded all show its Pipit origin. Its song, which the bird hardly ever utters, except on the wing, is musical and sweet, but neither it nor the song of the Titlark can compare with the song of the Tree Pipit.

The food of the Rock Pipit consists chiefly of marine insects, which it picks up along the shore and from the seaweed. It also feeds occasionally on worms and seeds. The general colour of the upper parts of the plumage is olive brown, streaked with dark brown, the chin white, and the rest of the under parts sandy buff, also streaked with dark brown.

The nest is usually commenced towards the end of April, and is built of dry grass; sometimes this is mixed with seaweed and the stalks of plants growing near at hand, or a little moss, and it is often lined with hair. It is placed upon the shore under shelter of a stone or a heap of seaweed, beneath a projecting ledge, or in a crevice of a rock.

The eggs are four or five in number. They are of a greenish white in ground colour, mottled with small reddish-brown and underlying pale-grey markings. These spots are so thickly clustered together that the ground colour is often completely hidden. The eggs of the Rock Pipit do not vary so much as those of the two preceding birds, and they are of slightly larger size; they resemble certain eggs of the Skylark rather closely, but are not so long in proportion to their breadth.

WOODLARK.

ALAUDA ARBOREA.

Family PASSERIDÆ. Sub-family ALAUDINÆ. Genus ALAUDA.

The Woodlark is not a common bird. It is of most frequent occurrence, it would seem, in the southern counties of England. It is distributed over the British Isles, but is rare in Scotland and Ireland. We have several instances of it breeding around us in Hampshire, in which county it is described as a resident bird, but in some parts of England it seems to be to a great extent migratory.

The Woodlark in its appearance bears a strong resemblance to the Skylark, but is rather smaller; its plumage is yellowish brown, shaded with rusty red; the belly and breast are buffish white, streaked with black upon the breast. There is less white in the tail than with the Skylark.

The Woodlark is a ground bird, breeding, roosting and feeding there, but it may frequently be observed in the branches of trees, very unlike its relation the Skylark. From this position it will soar into the air warbling forth its song, but rising rather in large circles than vertically upwards. It descends in the same manner.

Its food in the autumn and winter consists chiefly of grain and seeds, the rest of the year it feeds largely on insects.

These birds are early breeders, eggs being often found by the end of March. The nest is very compact, and is always built upon the ground, in the grass under shelter of some tree, or beneath a large tuft; it has a more finished appearance than the Skylark's nest and is deeper, resembling half a ball; it is composed of coarse grass and a little moss, and lined with finer grass and hair.

The eggs, four or five, are of a pale wood brown, marked with blotches of reddish brown and underlying markings of grey. They are no doubt sometimes confused with the eggs of the Skylark, but may be distinguished by their slightly smaller size, their lighter and more exposed ground colour and the redder colour of the spots.*

The Woodlark is in great request as a cage bird, it being considered a much sweeter and more melodious songster than the Skylark, though its song is not so varied or loud. It becomes very sociable in confinement, " so sociable," says Meyer, " that when spoken to it invariably answers with a few low liquid notes ". Unfortunately this sweet-voiced little bird but seldom lives more than two or three years in captivity.

* A second batch of eggs is laid as soon as the young ones leave the nest.

SKYLARK.

ALAUDA ARVENSIS.

Family PASSERIDÆ.　Sub-family ALAUDINÆ.　Genus ALAUDA.

Lark—Lavrock.

The Skylark must be familiar to all of us, for it is very common in all parts of the British Islands, and a resident bird, except in the extreme north. Its lively and continuous song when first heard in March tells us of sunshine to come, and winter past. The song cannot be compared to the Woodlark's for music, but its cheerfulness and the persistency with which it is uttered render it a favourite with everybody. Rising from the ground, the bird almost at once bursts into song: up and up it goes, never pausing for an instant in its hymn, higher and higher until we often lose sight of it altogether, and yet we can still hear its clear strong notes; presently we may see it returning once more, drawing nearer and nearer to earth again, till suddenly, with wings closed, it drops like a stone to the ground, and its song is heard no more. It is very interesting to watch the different modes in which a Skylark descends from its height in the air. Sometimes, closing its wings, it will come down as though it were shot to within a short distance of the ground, when, opening them, it will skim along for a short distance and alight; at other times it will gradually lower itself, floating gently downwards with outstretched wings till it reaches the ground.

Perhaps there is no more popular cage bird than the Skylark, for it is easily tamed, and will sing while standing upon its bit of turf as cheerfully as though it were soaring away skywards. As a matter of sentiment, however, it seems hard upon the happy little songster to deprive him of his liberty.

The Skylark has already been described under the heading of the Woodlark. The upper parts are brown, with dark-centred feathers, the under parts buffish white, darkly streaked on the breast. Its food consists of grain, seeds and insects. This bird is hardly ever known to perch on a tree; it is always either in the air or on the ground.

The nest is built on the ground. It is a flimsy construction, said to be entirely the work of the female, the male supplying the materials. It is made of grass, and lined with finer grass, rootlets, and sometimes a few hairs. It is generally placed in fields. Often it seems to be placed by the roadside. Twice this year I have found the nest on a grassy bank protected by a tuft, and within three feet of the road.

The eggs, three to five in number, are white or greenish white in ground colour, variously marked with brown, dark - grey, or olive - brown markings ; often these form an irregular zone round the large end. They vary also considerably in size. Two broods are generally reared.

In October and November enormous flocks of Larks pass down our eastern coast on their migration southwards, and many of them land to break the journey. The Skylark is reckoned a delicacy, and in the old coaching days, and perhaps still, Dunstable Larks were much esteemed. It is stated that from September to February as many as four thousand dozen have been sent from that town to the London market. Possibly most of those were recruited from the annual travellers.

Birds of the Family Passeridæ which rarely, or never, breed here :—

WHITE'S GROUND THRUSH.

GEOCICHLA VARIA.

Sub-family TURDINÆ. Genus TURDUS.

A very rare and accidental visitor. Named after the Hampshire naturalist, Gilbert White.

REDWING.

TURDUS ILIACUS.

Sub-family TURDINÆ. Genus TURDUS.

A winter visitor to all parts. Most common in the midland and southern counties of England, but not remaining to breed. An instance of this bird breeding at Cranbrook, Kent, where identity was made certain by killing the bird on the nest, is recorded in the *Zoologist* for 1886, p. 369. The nest resembles those of the Blackbird and Ring Ouzel; and the eggs are somewhat similar but smaller.

FIELDFARE.

TURDUS PILARIS.

Sub-family TURDINÆ. Genus TURDUS.

A commonly distributed winter visitor over the cultivated parts of the British Isles, but the evidence of it nesting here is doubtful. There seems no room to doubt, however, that it nested at Alresford in Essex in 1869. The Fieldfare in appearance and habits is very like the Missel Thrush, with which bird it is often confused by casual observers.

ARCTIC BLUE-THROATED ROBIN.

ERITHACUS SUECICA.

Sub-family TURDINÆ. Genus ERITHACUS.

A very few instances of this bird visiting our shores are recorded.

ROCK THRUSH.

MONTICOLA SAXATILIS.

Sub-family TURDINÆ. Genus MONTICOLA.

Has occurred two or three times.

BLACK REDSTART.

RUTICILLA TITHYS.

Sub-family TURDINÆ. Genus RUTICILLA.

Tithys' Redstart—Black Redtail.

A regular but very scarce winter visitor to the southern counties of England. It may be distinguished from the Common Redstart by the intense black colour of the under parts, where the latter bird is reddish brown. The eggs, five or six, pure glossy white, are very fragile and delicate ; but the evidence of it breeding in England is not very conclusive.

RED-BREASTED FLYCATCHER.

MUSCICAPA PARVA.

Sub-family TURDINÆ. Genus MUSCICAPA.

Has occurred a few times in Britain ; the last occasion being at Scarborough in October, 1889.

SAVI'S WARBLER.

LOCUSTELLA LUSCINIOIDES.

Sub-family SYLVIINÆ. Genus LOCUSTELLA.

A bird which used to inhabit the ·fen-country in Norfolk, Huntingdon and Cambridge. Since the fens have been drained, the bird has in all probability become extinct.

AQUATIC WARBLER.

ACROCEPHALUS AQUATICUS.

Sub-family SYLVIINÆ. Genus ACROCEPHALUS.

Has occurred four or five times in England.

GREAT REED WARBLER.

ACROCEPHALUS TURDOIDES.

Sub-family SYLVIINÆ. Genus ACROCEPHALUS.

There are at least two well-authenticated instances of this bird appearing on our shores. The last specimen was shot in Hampshire at Ringwood, 3rd June, 1884 (*Zoologist*, 1884, p. 343).

MARSH WARBLER.

ACROCEPHALUS PALUSTRIS.

Sub-family SYLVIINÆ. Genus ACROCEPHALUS.

An occasional summer visitor which has bred here. The points of distinction between this and the Common Reed Warbler are disputed by some ornithologists. Seebohm says: "No doubt they are very closely allied; but in their song, habits, eggs and geographical distribution they differ as much as a Blackbird differs from a Thrush".

ICTERINE WARBLER.

HYPOLAIS HYPOLAIS.

Sub-family SYLVIINÆ. Genus HYPOLAIS.

Four specimens seem to have been obtained in Britain, but it has possibly occurred much oftener than this, as it is a common bird across the water in Holland, Belgium, north of France and north of Germany.

BARRED WARBLER.

SYLVIA NISORIA.

Sub-family SYLVIINÆ. Genus SYLVIA.

There are at least three well-authenticated instances of the occurrence of this bird in England—one at Cambridge shot by a porter of my old college—Queens' —in 1879; one in Yorkshire (*Zoologist*, 1884, p. 489), and one in Norfolk (*Zoologist*, 1885, p. 65).

ORPHEAN WARBLER.

SYLVIA ORPHEUS.

Sub-family SYLVIINÆ. Genus SYLVIA.

A very rare and accidental straggler to our islands.

RUFOUS WARBLER.

SYLVIA GALACTODES.

Sub-family SYLVIINÆ. Genus SYLVIA.

Has occurred three or four times in the British Isles.

YELLOW-BROWED WILLOW WREN.

PHYLLOSCOPUS SUPERCILIOSUS.

Sub-family SYLVIINÆ. Genus PHYLLOSCOPUS.

Has been met with and obtained in Britain.

11

FIRECREST.

REGULUS IGNICAPILLUS.

Sub-family PARINÆ.　Genus REGULUS.

A rare winter visitor to our southern counties.　It
is very like the Goldcrest, but rather larger; the tuft
of feathers on the head is larger and the tail is longer.
The nest is also similar to the Goldcrest's, but it is
not known to have bred here.　The eggs, five to ten
in number, are of a pale reddish-yellow tint, speckled
with yellowish grey.

CRESTED TIT.

PARUS CRISTATUS.

Sub-family PARINÆ.　Genus PARUS.

A rare and local resident, breeding in Scotland.　It
is one of our tiniest birds, being only about four inches
long, and the male weighing only about a quarter of
an ounce; it will be known at once by the crest of
shining black feathers, edged with white.　It builds
in holes of trees a nest of the same material as the
other Tits.　The eggs, seven to ten, are white; according to one authority, speckled with light purple, and,
according to another, spotted with red or brown.

ALPINE ACCENTOR.

ACCENTOR ALPINUS.

Sub-family PARINÆ.　Genus ACCENTOR.

Obtained about a dozen times in England, chiefly
in the south.

WALL CREEPER.

TICHODROMA MURARIA.

Sub-family PARINÆ.   Genus TICHODROMA.

Has occurred once or twice.

NUTCRACKER.

NUCIFRAGA CARYOCATACTES.

Sub-family CORVINÆ.   Genus NUCIFRAGA.

A bird which has been met with about a score of times in this country.

GOLDEN ORIOLE.

ORIOLUS GALBULA.

Sub-family CORVINÆ.   Genus ORIOLUS.

An occasional summer visitor.   Kelsall says it "would nest annually in England if not stupidly persecuted". A very shy bird. The general colour is a rich golden yellow with black wings.

PALLAS'S GREY SHRIKE.

LANIUS MAJOR.

Sub-family LANIINÆ.   Genus LANIUS.

Great Great Shrike.

An occasional autumn and winter visitor, differing from the Great Grey Shrike in having only one white wing bar instead of two.

GREAT GREY SHRIKE.

LANIUS EXCUBITOR.

Sub-family LANIINÆ.   Genus LANIUS.

A regular though rare autumn and winter visitor.
In Hampshire it has often occurred in the New Forest
and in other parts.   In many of its habits it resembles
a bird of prey, sometimes hovering over a mouse like
a Kestrel. The nest is made of twigs, dry grass, leaves
and moss, and lined with roots, wool, hair and feathers.
The eggs, five to seven, are greenish white, spotted
and blotched with olive brown.

LESSER GREY SHRIKE.

LANIUS MINOR.

Sub-family LANIINÆ.   Genus LANIUS.

A bird which has occurred less than half a dozen
times in the British Islands.

WOODCHAT SHRIKE.

LANIUS RUFUS.

Sub-family LANIINÆ.   Genus LANIUS.

A bird of which about twenty examples have been
obtained, chiefly in the southern and eastern counties.

WAXWING.

AMPELIS GARRULUS.

Sub-family AMPELINÆ.   Genus AMPELIS.

An occasional winter visitor sometimes in fair
numbers.   It has been observed in nearly every
county, but chiefly in the eastern ones.   A very
beautiful bird.

ROSE-COLOURED STARLING.

PASTOR ROSEUS.

Sub-family AMPELINÆ. Genus PASTOR.

A frequent accidental summer visitor to almost all counties of England. It has also been met with in most parts of Wales, Scotland and Ireland.

PARROT CROSSBILL.

LOXIA PITYOPSITTACUS.

Sub-family FRINGILLINÆ. Genus LOXIA.

A bird only differing from the Common Crossbill in size and in the strength and thickness of its beak. It has been obtained upwards of a score of times in our islands, mostly in England.

WHITE-WINGED CROSSBILL.

LOXIA LEUCOPTERA.

Sub-family FRINGILLINÆ. Genus LOXIA.

A rare straggler to our islands. It differs from the Common Crossbill in having the wings tipped with white.

PINE GROSBEAK.

LOXIA ENUCLEATOR.

Sub-family FRINGILLINÆ. Genus LOXIA.

An accidental winter visitor which has occurred about half a dozen times in England.

SCARLET ROSE FINCH.

CARPODACUS ERITHRINUS.

Sub-family FRINGILLINÆ.   Genus CARPODACUS.

Has been captured twice on our shores.

CANARY.

FRINGILLA CANARIA.

Sub-family FRINGILLINÆ.   Genus FRINGILLA.

The Canary must be regarded as an accidental visitor; no doubt several recorded instances are those of birds escaped from confinement.

SERIN FINCH.

FRINGILLA SERINUS.

Sub-family FRINGILLINÆ.   Genus FRINGILLA.

An occasional visitor.

SISKIN.

FRINGILLA SPINUS.

Sub-family FRINGILLINÆ.   Genus FRINGILLA.

A much commoner visitor than most of the birds enumerated above, coming over in large numbers in the autumn, but it does not very frequently nest here, only occasionally. The Siskin very much resembles the green variety of the Canary, and it fetches a high price from bird fanciers, it being highly esteemed as a pairing bird with the Canary. The nest is placed in a spruce fir, generally about six feet from the ground, and is made of materials similar to those of the Chaffinch's nest. The eggs vary greatly in size, shape and colour, but are generally of a greyish or greenish white, spotted at the larger end with purple or brown.

BRAMBLING.

FRINGILLA MONTIFRINGILLA.

Sub-family FRINGILLINÆ. Genus FRINGILLA.

Frequently called the Mountain Finch. A winter visitor throughout the British Islands, but irregular and erratic, sometimes occurring in great numbers, at other times being very scarce. It is observed annually in the New Forest in our county, and in many other parts. This bird closely resembles the Chaffinch, so much so that it is difficult to distinguish them: the chief point of difference is the black and white, instead of green, rump. Bramblings and Chaffinches are frequently seen in company. This bird does not, as a rule, nest in this country.

TWITE.

FRINGILLA FLAVIROSTRIS.

Sub-family FRINGILLINÆ. Genus FRINGILLA.

The Twite or Mountain Linnet is a rare bird, which has, nevertheless, bred in most parts of the British Isles, wherever moors and heaths are to be found. In the southern counties it is only a winter visitor. In size, it is between the Redpole and Linnet, and resembles them in appearance ; it is, however, longer and more slender, and is without the red colour on the forehead and breast.

MEALY REDPOLE.

FRINGILLA LINARIA.

Sub-family FRINGILLINÆ. Genus FRINGILLA.

An accidental winter visitor to this country, occurring in varying numbers in different years; for a long time it was considered only a large variety of the Lesser Redpole. In some years large quantities have been taken during the winter season.

SNOW BUNTING.

EMBERIZA NIVALIS.

Sub-family FRINGILLINÆ. Genus EMBERIZA.

The Snow Bunting is a comparatively rare visitor to our shores during the winter months, hardly ever nesting here. Though common during the winter months in the north, only a few reach the southern counties. The plumage varies greatly; in some there is a great preponderance of white, others are much tinged with brown. On one occasion, out of forty shot from the same flock, it is stated that hardly any two were alike.

LAPLAND BUNTING.

EMBERIZA LAPPONICA.

Sub-family FRINGILLINÆ. Genus EMBERIZA.

A rare accidental winter visitor, chiefly to the southern counties. About a score of examples have been obtained.

RUSTIC BUNTING.

EMBERIZA RUSTICA.

Sub-family FRINGILLINÆ.   Genus EMBERIZA.

An accidental visitor which has occurred a few times.

ORTOLAN BUNTING.

EMBERIZA HORTULANA.

Sub-family FRINGILLINÆ.   Genus EMBERIZA.

Green-headed Bunting.   An occasional visitor of rare occurrence.   Many of the examples recorded are no doubt birds which have escaped from confinement, the bird being imported alive in great numbers every year for the table.

WHITE WAGTAIL.

MOTACILLA ALBA.

Sub-family MOTACILLINÆ.   Genus MOTACILLA.

In all probability a few of these birds come to this country every year to breed.   It is a summer visitor to us, but is no doubt often overlooked on account of its likeness to the Pied Wagtail.   In its habits, nest, eggs and food the White Wagtail does not differ materially from the Pied Wagtail, and the only difference in plumage is on the back, which in the White is grey, and the sides of the neck, which are white in this species.

BLUE-HEADED WAGTAIL.

MOTACILLA FLAVA.

Sub-family MOTACILLINÆ. Genus MOTACILLA.

An accidental straggler to us, which has occasionally bred here. It is chiefly found in the southern
and eastern counties.

RICHARD'S PIPIT.

ANTHUS RICHARDI.

Sub-family MOTACILLINÆ. Genus ANTHUS.

Several examples have been obtained of this autumn
straggler.

TAWNY PIPIT.

ANTHUS CAMPESTRIS.

Sub-family MOTACILLINÆ. Genus ANTHUS.

Accidental: less than a score have been obtained at
different times, mostly in the south.

ALPINE PIPIT.

ANTHUS SPINOLETTA.

Sub-family MOTACILLINÆ. Genus ANTHUS.

Has been shot three or four times on our islands.

CRESTED LARK.

ALAUDA CRISTATA.

Sub-family ALAUDINÆ. Genus ALAUDA.

This bird has been obtained a few times, but has probably visited us more frequently than is supposed, being liable to be overlooked on account of its resemblance to the Skylark.

SHORT-TOED LARK.

ALAUDA BRACHYDACTYLA.

Sub-family ALAUDINÆ. Genus ALAUDA.

Has occurred about half a dozen times in our islands. It much resembles the Woodlark.

SHORE LARK.

ALAUDA ALPESTRIS.

Sub-family ALAUDINÆ. Genus ALAUDA.

This bird of late years has visited us annually. In the *Zoologist* for 1883 it is stated a large number were obtained on the coasts of Norfolk and Suffolk.

COMMON SWIFT.

CYPSELUS APUS.

Family CYPSELIDÆ. Genus CYPSELUS.

Devil Swallow—Screech Martin—Black Martin—Squealer.

The Swift is only with us about four months in the year, but during those four months it is a very common and well-known bird in most parts of the British Isles. It is one of the latest birds of passage to arrive, and one of the earliest to leave. About the end of April we expect to see it, and it leaves us again about the middle or end of August.

This bird very seldom, if ever, alights on the ground; indeed it was at one time commonly believed that if by any chance it did so, the shortness of its legs and

COMMON SWIFT.

length of its wings prevented it from rising again; this, however, has now been disproved. If the bird is ever seen at rest, it is usually when clinging to some perpendicular cliff or wall, its sharp claws enabling it to hang on for a considerable time, but this is a very rare circumstance. Generally speaking, the birds remain on the wing the whole day, moving through the air with the most perfect command over their movements, and with almost incredible swiftness. From experiments made, it has been ascertained that the Swift will sometimes travel at the rate of 180 miles an hour.

Its food consists entirely of insects caught on the wing. When feeding its young the Swift, like the Swallow, does not return to the nest with each insect, but keeps them in her mouth until she has a good meal; the stickiness of the saliva holding them fast there. The Swift gets its name of Devil Swallow or Deviling from the fact of its hawking for flies often in the roughest of stormy weather.

Its note is a shrill scream which has been compared to the noise made when a saw is sharpened; from this it is often called the Screech Martin.

The general colour of the plumage is a dark sooty brown, tinged with bronze on the upper parts. The throat is a dull white. The expanse of the wings from tip to tip is fifteen inches.

As these birds are unable to perch, and live almost entirely on the wing, it is impossible to confine them in cages.

The nest of the Swift is commenced about the middle of May. It is usually placed as far as possible from the ground in the crevice of a wall, or in an old tower or spire, sometimes in a crevice in a chalk cliff, or under the eaves of buildings. It is a very slight structure, being made of bits of straw and lined with feathers, all of which have been snatched on the wing. The nest is almost flat, and the materials are generally glued together with the sticky saliva of the bird, which hardens and cakes the nest together. The same spot is returned to every year, and at night the old birds roost in the nest.

The eggs are two in number, sometimes three, while even four have been found. They are white and very elongated, being almost completely oval; they are much larger than Martins' eggs and more rounded.

Other birds of the Family Cypselidæ are :—

ALPINE SWIFT.

CYPSELUS MELBA.

Genus CYPSELUS.

White-bellied Swift.

Something like a score of specimens have been obtained in our islands, mostly in England.

NEEDLE-TAILED SWIFT.

CHÆTURA CAUDACUTA.

Genus CHÆTURA.

An Asiatic bird which has only twice been shot in the British Isles. The last was shot in Hampshire, near Ringwood, in 1879.

COMMON NIGHTJAR.

CAPRIMULGUS EUROPÆUS.

Family CAPRIMULGIDÆ. Genus CAPRIMULGUS.

Goat Sucker—Fern Owl—Churn Owl—Night Churr—Wheel-bird—Fern Owl.

The Nightjar or Goat Sucker is a fairly common bird in England, especially in the south. It also occurs in Scotland and Ireland. It is a migratory bird, and arrives about the middle or end of May, leaving again in September.

The Nightjar, as its name implies, seeks its prey in the evening, feeding on moths, beetles, and such other

insects as come out at night; when on the look-out
for these it will sometimes fly round and round a bush
or tree, the noiseless flapping of its wings being
scarcely audible, reminding one more of the flight
of an owl as it silently flits past. When at rest on
the bough of a tree, it perches lengthwise, not cross-
wise, on a branch, usually with its head downwards.
Strolling through the woods in the twilight on a
summer evening you may hear its long-drawn note—a

COMMON NIGHTJAR.

loud chur-r-r-r or jar-r-r-r-r—like the sound made by
causing one's tongue to vibrate rapidly. Gilbert White
says: "I have always found that though sometimes
it may chatter as it flies, as I know it does, yet in
general it utters its jarring note sitting on a bough.
It is most punctual in beginning its song exactly at the
close of day; so exactly that I have known it strike up
more than once or twice just at the report of the
Portsmouth evening gun, which we can hear when the

weather is still.   In Italy it is said to suck the milk
from the goats.   They fly round the goat merely for
insects.   The Nightjar seems to have an attachment
for oaks, no doubt on account of the insects found
near that tree.   I distinctly saw it more than once
put out its short leg while on the wing, and by a bend
of the head deliver something into its mouth."

The Nightjar may be known by its white-tipped tail.
It is impossible to describe its varied and soft plumage ;
the principal colours are yellow, orange, brown and
grey, beautifully pencilled upon rich dark brown.   It
cannot very well be reared in confinement.

The bird is a late breeder and its eggs are not often
met with before June.   It has been found sitting on its
eggs as late as the 17th of August.   No nest whatever
is made, the eggs being deposited on the bare ground,
on an open grass track through a wood, on a bare spot
amongst the bracken, or at the foot of a tree.

They are two in number, rarely three, and are
amongst the most beautiful of all our British eggs.
They are nearly a perfect oval in shape, resembling
most beautifully grained marble, the ground colour
being white, clouded and streaked with bluish grey
and yellowish brown.   The female has been known
when disturbed to take an egg in her mouth and
hurry off to a spot where she could brood uninterrupted.
If surprised when sitting, the bird will often feign
lameness and, fluttering along the ground, endeavour
to draw off attention from her eggs.

Two eggs of the Nightjar were taken by one of our
young collectors on 17th July, 1883, which were nearly
a foot apart ; one of the eggs was hard set, and the
other quite fresh.   Two birds rose as he neared the
spot.   This seems a singular occurrence.   Were the

birds only hatching one egg? We have no evidence whether both eggs were warm when found, or only one.

The eggs of the Nightjar become seriously damaged by exposure to the light; they lose all their beauty, and, in fact, fade so much as to become nearly white. It is therefore very necessary to keep them well covered up.

COMMON BEE-EATER.

MEROPS APIASTER.

Family MEROPIDÆ. Genus MEROPS.

An accidental straggler, but specimens have been obtained in many counties. It frequents the banks of rivers, and feeds on insects. Its plumage is very brilliant, the forehead light greenish blue, fading in front into white; neck, back and wings reddish brown, passing into yellow towards the tail, which is greenish blue; the throat is yellow.

COMMON ROLLER.

CORACIAS GARRULA.

Family MEROPIDÆ. Genus CORACIAS.

Another accidental straggler, of very brilliant and conspicuous plumage, consequently it is an easy mark for specimen hunters, more than a hundred examples having been obtained. Its main colour is a brilliant metallic greenish blue.

HOOPOE.

UPUPA EPOPS.

Family UPUPIDÆ. Genus UPUPA.

A summer visitor to our islands, but very rare, as it has been almost exterminated owing to the stupid persecution of persons eager to obtain a specimen. In spite of this it still visits us, and has bred in most of the southern counties of England. Its note is a loud "hoop" uttered several times in succession. It is a very handsome bird, with a fine buff-coloured crest, tipped with black. The general colour of the body is a dark buff colour. The wings are barred with black and white, and the tail is black with a white crescent-shaped band. The beak is fully two inches long. Its food is chiefly insects and worms. It is easily tamed and kept in confinement.

The nest is placed in holes of trees, and consists of a few straws, roots, and sometimes dried cow-dung. The eggs are unspotted, and vary considerably. Some are pale greenish blue, some grey, and some stone colour.

COMMON KINGFISHER.

ALCEDO ISPIDA.

Family ALCEDINIDÆ. Genus ALCEDO.

Halcyon.

The Kingfisher resides in most parts of the United Kingdom, but can hardly be called a common bird. It is decidedly the most beautiful of our British birds, and on that account has suffered much persecution and a consequent decrease in numbers, notwithstand-

ing the fact that after death the feathers lose much
of their brilliancy, and the stuffed Kingfisher would
scarcely be taken for the same bird as the beautiful
creature whose colours flash and glisten in the golden
sunlight.

The Kingfisher is a shy and retiring bird, and is

COMMON KINGFISHER.

usually seen alone. It haunts the quiet streams and
pools, the trout streams and ponds, in search of its
food. There it may be seen perched on some favourite
twig over the water's surface—for it seems to return
again and again to the same branch—or flashing

rapidly past like a stream of light. It feeds chiefly on small fish, especially on minnows, but it also eats insects. A fish having been secured, it darts off with it, and usually kills it by beating it against a stump or bough; it then swallows it head first. Occasionally it will hover over the water when several small fish are visible, after the manner of a Kestrel. The plumage of the Kingfisher varies considerably. The upper parts vary from a rich metallic cobalt blue to emerald green, the head is barred and the wings spotted, the under parts are a beautiful orange chestnut, shading into white on the throat. Its note is a shrill "pip," usually uttered when flying over the surface of the water. This bird can be kept in confinement, provided it is supplied with a plentiful stock of its customary food.

It is a pity to have to own that such a beautiful creature as the Kingfisher is, in its nesting operations, most foul and disgusting. Towards the end of April the birds begin to prepare a place to receive the eggs. For this purpose a hole, some two or three feet long, is bored, generally in the bank of the stream from which it gets its food. Occasionally an old rat hole is used. The hole is bored in an upward direction, and is usually straight, and the chamber at the end in which the eggs are laid is lined with fish bones, which the bird ejects in pellets. On these bones the eggs are laid. After the young are hatched the nest becomes extremely foul from the droppings of the birds and decaying fish, and the whole passage becomes covered with a filthy, sticky, gluey substance, emitting a sickening smell. Naturally, before the young leave the nest, it frequently swarms with maggots.

But, like the pearl in the shell of the oyster, the eggs laid on this filthy structure are most beautiful. They are five to eight in number, of a round shape, and perfectly white, though before they are blown, they have a beautiful pink tint, from the yolk inside. Occasionally the nest is found without any fish bones, and as the birds usually return to the same site year after year, some ornithologists suggest that the foul conglomeration which we have observed and described above is the accumulation of previous years; the holes without any bones being new ones used for the first time.

BELTED KINGFISHER.

CERYLE ALCYON.

Family ALCEDINIDÆ.   Genus CERYLE.

Has occurred at least twice; both the recorded times in Ireland.

GREAT SPOTTED WOODPECKER.

PICUS MAJOR.

Family PICIDÆ.   Genus PICUS.

Pied Woodpecker—French Pie—Wood Pie—Great Black and White Woodpecker.

The Woodpeckers can scarcely be called common birds amongst us. The Great Spotted Woodpecker occurs in most English counties; but in Scotland and Ireland it is very rare. This bird is a bird of the forests, and must be looked for in our old woods and

thickly studded parks and plantations.　It nests in the
New Forest, but is described as " thinly distributed
and wandering in autumn ".　It is a resident bird,
whose numbers are increased in the autumn by
visitors from the continent.

The Great Spotted Woodpecker spends most of its
life on trees ; searching their branches and trunks for

GREAT SPOTTED WOODPECKER.

food by day, and roosting in holes in them by night.
Its food consists principally of insects, but it also eats
fruit in summer, nuts and berries in autumn.　It is a
curious sight to see this bird working its way up the
trunk of a tree, peering about in every direction and
tapping on the bark as it goes, travelling round and

round that it may miss no crevice which contains a tit-bit. Sometimes it will descend head first, exploring the small branches as well as the trunk, before it passes on to another tree.

It is no easy bird to attempt to rear. It cannot be kept in a wooden cage, added to which it has an objectionable smell. A very interesting account of the taming of this bird is recorded in the *Zoologist* for 1883, p. 473. In this account it is said that its note resembled the cry of "ack," much like the cry of a young Jackdaw. It was very shy of strangers.

In plumage the prevalent colours of the upper parts are black and white. The under parts are buffish white, shading into scarlet beneath the tail. There is a scarlet patch on the nape. The Great Spotted Woodpecker builds no nest. Its eggs are laid about the middle of May, and are deposited in a hole in a tree. This hole is nearly always bored by the bird; though occasionally it has used a ready-made one. It is most frequently made in a decayed part of the trunk, or where a dead branch has been blown off, and is from a foot to a foot and a half deep.

The eggs, five to seven, sometimes eight, are plain creamy white. They are considerably larger than the eggs of the Wryneck and Lesser Spotted Woodpecker, and smaller than those of the Green Woodpecker. The eggs of the Kingfisher may be distinguished from them by their roundness. They most closely resemble the eggs of the Dipper, but are generally duller and less highly polished.

LESSER SPOTTED WOODPECKER.

PICUS MINOR.

Family PICIDÆ. Genus PICUS.

Barred Woodpecker—Little Black and White Woodpecker—
Hickwall.

The Lesser Spotted Woodpecker is thinly distributed
and resident in most counties south of Yorkshire.   In
other parts of the British Isles it is very rare indeed.
Its habits differ little from those of the other Woodpeckers. It seems however to have a greater liking
for the tops of tall trees than the Great Spotted
Woodpecker, and this fact, coupled with its great sly-
ness and anxiety to put the tree trunk between itself
and its observer, leads no doubt to its being frequently
overlooked.   It will work round and round a tree,

running with great nimbleness over the bark, and occasionally pausing to ferret out insects from every crack and crevice. It will also work head downwards with equal ease. It roosts in holes of trees at night.

In addition to its ordinary cry, which is a sort of " keek " uttered several times quickly in succession, a loud whirring sound may often be heard, caused by the bird tapping very rapidly with its beak on the branches. " This peculiar noise," says Seebohm, " appears to be a call or signal between the sexes, and is most often heard during the breeding season."

The food of the Lesser Spotted Woodpecker is the same as that of the preceding bird, but it does not seem to eat fruit or berries.

In appearance this bird is very similar to the Great Spotted Woodpecker, but is of course much smaller. The chief point of difference is the entire absence of scarlet on the under parts.

The eggs are laid in a hole of a tree, usually made by the bird itself, but sometimes a borrowed hole is made use of. When made by the bird, the hole is perfectly round and extends sometimes to a foot in depth, widening out as it proceeds. It makes choice of no particular tree, nor is the hole bored at any fixed height from the ground. No nest is built, but as with the Great Spotted Woodpecker the eggs are laid on the decayed chips and wood-dust that have been left at the bottom of the hole.

The eggs are five to eight in number, white with a beautiful pink tint before they are blown, which is the case with so many of the white eggs, and highly polished. They are extremely difficult to distinguish from eggs of the Wryneck, but are as a rule smaller and more polished.

GREEN WOODPECKER.

GECINUS VIRIDIS.

Family PICIDÆ. Genus GECINUS.

Rain-bird—Yaffle—Rain-fowl—Wood-spite—Awl-bird—Hew-hole—Popinjay—Pick-a-tree.

The Green Woodpecker is the commonest as well as the largest of the Woodpeckers. Its haunts, like those of the rest of the family, are the well-wooded districts, forests, and plantations. In many of its habits, too, it differs very little from its relations. It will work its course up a tree, usually starting near the bottom, and moving in a slanting direction, supporting itself now and then with the stiff-pointed tail feathers bent down against the trunk, and will search the trunk and branches most assiduously, darting its long tongue behind the bark into every nook and corner, probing for insects, which adhere to the tongue owing to the glutinous matter on the end of it. This tongue, according to Meyer, is seven and a half inches long from root to tip, and the bird is able to project it six inches beyond the tip of the beak. When " working " the trunk of a tree, Seebohm compares its manner of progressing to that of a gigantic fly on a window pane.

The cry of the Green Woodpecker is a peculiar "glu, glu, glu," rapidly repeated, bearing a strange resemblance to a laugh. This laugh is said to be frequently and loudly uttered before a coming shower, hence it is known as the Rain-bird.

Its food is composed chiefly of insects; it also feeds upon the larvæ of wasps. It is extremely fond of ants and their eggs, which it devours in great numbers.

The general colour of the upper parts is olive green shading into yellow on the rump, which latter colour enables the bird to be easily distinguished, as it is very conspicuous; the general colour of the under parts is pale green. The cheeks are marked with scarlet and the crown and forehead feathers are grey, broadly fringed with scarlet.

The Green Woodpecker breeds in various trees, either using an old hole or more frequently boring a perfectly round one in the trunk until it reaches the decayed part, when it works downwards for a foot or so. The eggs are deposited on the decayed chips left at the bottom. The hole is usually some distance from the ground. Hewitson relates an instance of a pair of these birds irreverently boring into the wooden spire of a church in Norway. So rapidly does the bird tap away with its beak when at work, that the head can hardly be seen moving. Sometimes the same hole is used year after year.

The eggs, five to eight, are laid at the end of April or beginning of May. As one might expect, they are white; and of course larger than those of either of the preceding species.

It seems to be almost impossible to rear this bird in confinement.

WRYNECK.

IYNX TORQUILLA.

Family PICIDÆ. Genus IYNX.

Cuckoo's Mate—Snake-bird—Long-tongue—Cuckoo's Messenger—Emmet Hunter—Pay-pay.

The Wryneck is a summer visitor, arriving generally in the beginning of April, and leaving again before the end of September. As the date of its arrival is within a day or two of the arrival of the Cuckoo, it is often called "Cuckoo's Mate" or "Cuckoo's Messenger". It receives its name "Wryneck" from the strange manner it has of turning its head from side to side like a snake, so as to give it a twisted appearance. From this fact, too, and from the loud hissing it will make if surprised on its nest, it is sometimes called the Snake-bird.

It is a fairly common bird in the southern and eastern counties of England; in the rest of Great Britain it is very rare indeed, and in Ireland almost unknown.

Woods, orchards, and gardens where there are plenty of trees are its favourite haunts. It feeds on insects, and may sometimes be seen clinging to the trunk of a tree, but it never climbs like the Woodpeckers, and most of its food is obtained on the ground, among the ant-hills. These it turns over with its beak, and devours the inhabitants and their eggs by thousands, collecting them on its sharp-pointed tongue, to which they adhere by the glutinous matter with which it is covered.

The Wryneck has a peculiar note, a sort of "quick, quick" uttered loudly several times successively, which has been compared to the cry of the Kestrel. It has been reared in confinement, but this is a very difficult matter, and the probability is that the bird will die.

The plumage is not showy. The general colour of the upper parts is greyish white, mottled all over with brown, and barred and streaked with dark brown; the under parts are buff, each feather having a small dark-brown spot.

The Wryneck as a rule returns each year to its same breeding site, and in all probability pairs for life.

Unlike the Woodpeckers, this bird never makes its own hole, but takes any one it can find, consequently its eggs are found at all heights, and the hole is of various depths. A favourite tree is an apple tree in an orchard, but other trees are used, and sometimes an old dead stump. The eggs are laid on the mouldered wood scraped together, at the bottom of the hole. They are six to ten in number, and pure white. As previously mentioned they strongly resemble eggs of the Lesser Spotted Woodpecker, but are as a rule larger and less highly polished.

If the eggs of this bird are removed, she will continue laying a great number. An instance is given in the *Magazine of Natural History* where twenty-two eggs were taken from one nest; in the first instance five, then six, four, and lastly seven ; when, judging it hardly worth while to lay any more for the benefit of others, the Wryneck quitted her nest. In another case related in the *Zoologist* forty-two eggs were taken from one nest. In the following year forty-two eggs were again removed, the third year only one egg was laid, and the fourth year the nest was deserted.

CUCKOO.

CUCULUS CANORUS.

Family CUCULIDÆ. Genus CUCULUS.

Gowk.

Did space permit, quite a large volume might be written on this most interesting of our British visitors. In all parts of the British Isles the Cuckoo is a common bird. We probably are familiar with the old rhyme :—

In April come he will,
In May he sings all day,
In June he changes his tune,
In July he begins to fly,
In August go he must.

This is a trite little summary of the Cuckoo's yearly
life among us.　He arrives at the beginning of April
and leaves in July, the young birds following in August.

CUCKOO.

The peculiar note " cuc-koo " in June is changed, to a
stammer, " cuc-cuc-cuc-koo ".　In connection with
this Gilbert White quotes some; curious old lines
written in 1587 :—

In April the Koo-coo can sing her song by rote,
In June of tune she cannot sing a note ;
At first koo-coo, koo-coo, sing still can she do ;
At last kooke, kooke, kooke, six kookes to one koo.

According to Seebohm the males are much more common than the females; and it would further appear that they do not pair at all. There is still much doubt among ornithologists as to whether the note "cuckoo" is uttered by only the male, or by both birds. From all the evidence, one cannot help being inclined to think that both birds do so.

As we all know, the most interesting feature in connection with the Cuckoo is that she builds no nest, but deposits her eggs in that of some other bird. The reason for this is supposed to be that the birds do not stay long enough in our country to rear their young, and so wisely resign them to some one else.

The egg is disproportionately small to the size of the bird, for whilst the Cuckoo is as large as the male Sparrow Hawk (which bird it very closely resembles in appearance), the egg is no larger than that of a Lark, which seems a wise provision; for were the eggs in proportion to the bird, it seems hardly probable they would be hatched by the small birds in whose nests they are laid. The Cuckoo does not seem to choose any particular species with whom to intrust the bringing up of her young; upwards of fifty are mentioned, but the egg seems nearly always to be laid in the nest of a bird that feeds her young on insects or grubs, these being the ordinary food of the Cuckoo. The favourite nests chosen are those of the Meadow Pipit, Pied Wagtail and Hedge Sparrow.

When the young Cuckoo is hatched, as it requires all the food and room for itself, it generally manages to eject the other young birds from the nest. How it does this has long been a disputed point, but from some very conclusive evidence which appears in the *Zoologist*, 1886, pp. 203-205, there can be little doubt that it hoists them out on its shoulders over the side, where they are left to perish, it being now the only occupant; and from its voracious appetite giving the foster parents plenty to do.

Recent evidence tends to prove that the Cuckoo lays four or five eggs in a season, at intervals of several days, in which she has time to select new nests, for it is a very rare circumstance to find more than one Cuckoo's egg in any given nest, and if two should be found, it is very doubtful if both are laid by the same bird. They are not usually found before May. The Cuckoo may actually lay the egg in the nest, but seems more frequently to lift it in with her beak. I have myself found the egg in a Wren's nest, where certainly the Cuckoo could not have got in. In 1883 one of our number of young collectors found the egg in a Thrush's nest, a very unusual occurrence. There is an undoubted resemblance in the majority of cases in the colour of the Cuckoo's eggs to the eggs of the bird in whose nest they are laid, and it seems likely that this is not from any power which the bird has to impart a particular colour to its egg, but from the probability that a Cuckoo which has been reared by a particular foster parent always lays its eggs in the nests of that species, and so, for instance, in Pied Wagtails' nests, we usually may expect to find the Cuckoo's eggs laid in them resemble one another and the Wagtail's eggs.

The plumage of the Cuckoo varies very much. The general colour of the old bird is slate grey on the upper parts, brown on the wings, breast grey, shading to greyish white lower down. It is a difficult bird to rear. We attempted to bring up a young one this year, but it only survived six weeks. They may be fed on raw meat.

GREAT SPOTTED CUCKOO.

CUCULUS GLANDARIUS.

Family Cuculidæ. Genus Cuculus.

Has occurred twice : once in Ireland and once in Northumberland.

YELLOW-BILLED CUCKOO.

COCCYZUS AMERICANUS.

Family Cuculidæ. Genus Coccyzus.

An American bird which appears to have crossed the Atlantic some half-dozen times.

RING DOVE.

COLUMBA PALUMBUS.

Family Columbidæ. Genus Columba.

Wood Pigeon—Cushat—Ring Pigeon—Queest.

The Ring Dove or Wood Pigeon is the largest and commonest of the Dove Tribe. It is resident in the wooded districts all over the British Isles. It derives its name of Ring Dove from the white feathers which partially encircle its throat. In the winter season these birds congregate in large flocks, and may be seen on the ground feeding upon grain, clover, beech nuts, acorns and the like. It is only during the breeding season they are at all inclined to take up their abode near any habitation ; then they not infrequently build in gardens, and do considerable damage to the young cabbage plants, etc. In the summer the birds feed upon vegetable substances—peas, beans, clover and many kinds of fruit. Gilbert White, speaking of the Wood Pigeon, says: "One of my neighbours shot one. When his wife had plucked and drawn it, she found its craw stuffed with the most nice and tender tops of turnips, which she washed and boiled, and so sat down to a choice and delicate plate of greens." Well, every one to his taste!

RING DOVE.

The soft cooing of the Ring Dove is one of the most delightful and soothing sounds we country people love to hear, and when the birds are pairing, the woods all around echo with the gentle murmuring of these happy birds.

The nest is a most rude one, and it seems marvellous that it is not blown away or that the eggs do not roll out. It consists simply of a few sticks placed across each other in some thick tree or bush ; so thin is it that the eggs can often be seen through the nest from underneath. It is placed at various heights from the ground, and usually commenced in March or April. Sometimes it is built on an old squirrel's drey or an old Magpie's or Sparrow Hawk's nest. Both birds take their share of sitting.

The eggs are invariably very oval in shape and purely white. Two or three broods are reared in the season, two eggs being laid each time. Last year two young Pigeons were hatched in a tree by the Queenwood gates on the 7th of November, evidently a third, or perhaps fourth, brood.

The Wood Pigeon becomes very sociable when tamed, but it is almost impossible to rear it in a cage. Slate grey shot with pinkish blue is the prevalent colour of the upper parts of the Ring Dove ; there is a cluster of white feathers on each side of the neck ; the wings are dark brown, each feather being margined with white ; tail dark brown ; breast pink, shading into grey lower down.

Ruskin, in speaking of the plumage of the Dove in one of his Oxford Lectures, says : " When watched carefully in the sunshine, it is the most exquisite, in the modesty of its light, and in the myriad mingling of its hue, of all plumage ".

STOCK DOVE.

COLUMBA ÆNAS.

Family COLUMBIDÆ. Genus COLUMBA.

The Stock Dove is much less common than the preceding, though probably often confounded with it by the casual observer. It resides locally in England and Wales, but is only accidental in Scotland and Ireland. The Stock Dove and the Ring Dove frequent the same roosting places and often feed in the same field, though possibly on different food, for Atkinson relates that on shooting a specimen of each in the same field, he ascertained holly berries to have been the food of the Ring Dove, whilst the Stock Dove had preferred mustard seed; but the latter bird may be readily distinguished from the former by its smaller

STOCK DOVE.

size, dark-brown extremities of the wings, and entire absence of the white ring round the neck.

The Stock Dove frequents the open country for the most part, but retires to the woods and forests to breed. Its "coo" is scarcely so soft and melodious as the note of the Ring Dove, but its food is similar. It can be tamed without much difficulty.

The nest, when one is built, is very slender, consisting of a few twigs, and is usually placed in the hole of a decayed tree, in a cavity on the top of a pollard (hence probably its name, " Stock "), or in a deserted rabbit burrow, but never on the fork of a tree like the Wood Pigeon or Turtle Dove.   Frequently no nest at all is built, but the eggs are simply laid on the decayed wood collected in the bottom of the hole.   Occasionally the deserted nest of a Magpie or Crow is used.

The eggs, two in number, are laid in the beginning of April and are a pale creamy white, by which they may be distinguished from the pure white eggs of the Ring Dove or Rock Dove.   Two or three broods are sometimes reared, and the birds continue to breed very late in the year. When the young are hatched the parents feed them, as in the case of the other Doves, by ejecting half-digested food from their crops into the mouths of their young ones; so that in attempting to rear and tame young birds, they will have to be "crammed" for some time at first.   A curious case of a Stock Dove appropriating a Song Thrush's nest was discovered near Queenwood by two of our number in 1885.   The Thrush's nest was a new one about ten feet from the ground and well lined with mud.   The Stock Dove had filled the nest in with fine roots, so as to form a sort of concave platform.   Two eggs were laid on this, and when found had been sat on some little time.

ROCK DOVE.

COLUMBA LIVIA.

Family COLUMBIDÆ.   Genus COLUMBA.

Rockier—Rock Pigeon.

The Rock Dove is found on all rocky parts of the coasts of Great Britain and Ireland, being most numerous in the north, and particularly in those parts which abound in caves and caverns. It is about the same size as the Stock Dove, and in former times no distinction was made between the two species, but now the two are acknowledged to be unlike both as to habits, plumage and the localities they frequent. The

ROCK DOVE.

Stock Dove is of a deeper blue grey than the Rock Dove, and the latter has a patch of white on the rump and two distinct black bands on the wings, much more defined than the dark marks on the wings of the Stock Dove.

Although the Rock Dove is a dweller on the coasts, yet it often makes long daily inland journeys for its food; this consists chiefly of grain, but it also eats the seeds of many weeds. Its note, which is heard continually in the breeding season, is a soft cooing, not differing much from that of the Wood Pigeon. It can be very easily tamed, and there seems little doubt that this bird is the origin of the Domestic Pigeon, from which all the numerous varieties now in existence have been evolved.

The Rock Dove, in common with all the Doves, has a very graceful walk. He struts with great dignity, with his head held up high, and nods it backwards and forwards with each step he takes.

Rock Doves pair for life and are early breeders, eggs being often found by the middle of March. Their favourite breeding places are the rocky caves by the sea-shore, a great many birds building in the same cave. Less frequently they will nest in the crevices and fissures of the rocks, and Meyer says they have been known to build in a rabbit burrow. The nest is built of plant stems and dry grass or seaweed, with a few twigs. Like all the nests of this family, it is very scanty.

Two eggs are laid, pure white in colour, oval and generally rounder and smaller than the Wood Pigeon's eggs.

In the wild state the Rock Dove rarely, if ever, perches on a tree; in this it differs from all our other Pigeons.

TURTLE DOVE.

TURTUR AURITUS.

Family COLUMBIDÆ.   Genus TURTUR.

Turtle—Ring-necked Turtle—Wrekin Dove.

The Turtle Dove, unlike the rest of this family, only spends the summer months here, arriving about the beginning of May, and leaving in August or September.   It is found in most parts of England south of Yorkshire, but is commonest in the southern and eastern counties.   In Wales and Ireland it is very rare, and in Scotland only accidental.

It is much the smallest of the Doves, and may be easily distinguished by this, and the much browner general colour which it has.   When flying, the broadly white-tipped tail feathers are very noticeable.   Another distinguishing feature is the black streaks, bordered with silvery white, at the sides of the throat.

The Turtle Dove feeds upon grain and seeds, especially the seeds of the fir, which it always seeks for on the ground.   This bird, like all the family, is very fond of water, both drinking a great deal and bathing itself very frequently.

The Turtle Dove seems to prefer the woody parts of the country and in the breeding season it becomes a very shy and cautious bird, retiring to the thickest parts of the covers and copses to build its nest. This is usually placed in a thick bush or fir, or rather low down in a tree. Frequently it can be reached from the ground. I have, however, found its nest at least thirty feet up in a beech tree. The male birds seek fresh partners every season. The nest is a very slight structure, being a mere thin platform of sticks, through which the eggs can often be distinctly seen. On this platform two oval eggs are laid, of a creamy white colour.

The nest referred to above in the beech tree contained only one egg, from which the bird was just emerging, but possibly the other had rolled or was blown out. These eggs are known at once from those of the other Doves by their much smaller size.

The Turtle Dove can be reared in confinement without much difficulty and becomes very tame, looking very beautiful and graceful as it walks proudly about, nodding its pretty head. If placed with other birds in an aviary, it is said to become very quarrelsome and peevish, a trait in its character which seems unnatural, when we consider the many traditional tales of the affectionate and gentle Dove.

PEREGRINE FALCON.

FALCO PEREGRINUS.

Family FALCONIDÆ. Genus FALCO.

In these days, when game is so strictly preserved, and all birds of prey are ruthlessly destroyed by keepers, our hawks and falcons are slowly and steadily decreasing year by year, and the time will undoubtedly come when these interesting and historical birds will be extinct and things of the past. Of the larger birds of prey, the Peregrine Falcon is the commonest, as it breeds for the most part in inaccessible positions. These, as we might expect, it finds in the

PEREGRINE FALCON.

wildest and most secluded parts of Scotland and Ireland, but it still breeds in a few spots in England. Three years ago, a neighbouring farmer, finding a number of his partridges killed, set a trap in his fields and within an hour a beautiful female Falcon was caught, which he still possesses stuffed. This bird, we concluded, had come over from Salisbury Cathedral, fourteen miles distant, in search of food; the spire of which building, 400 feet high, they have frequented certainly for the last thirty years, and occasionally have bred there.   An interesting account of the Salisbury Falcons may be found in the *Zoologist*, 1882, p. 18.   Possibly, however, it came from the Isle of Wight, which in former times was famous for its breed, and where some still reside.*

The favourite food of the Falcons seems to be Pigeons; they live entirely on flesh, and devour, in addition to the first-named, an enormous quantity of Partridges, Water-fowl, Grouse, Rooks, Plovers, and many other birds.   These are all carefully plucked before they are eaten.

The female is considerably larger than the male bird.   The general colour of the upper parts is slate grey, but the head is black; the under parts are buffish white, spotted and streaked with black.   The nest is usually placed in a crevice in some high perpendicular cliff, or on a projecting ledge, sometimes also in the top of a high fir tree ; it is made of sticks or seaweed, but often scarcely any nest at all is built. In Salisbury Spire the eggs have been found laid in the bare guttering.

* A pair regularly build at Alum Bay, and the fishermen tell you that as soon as one is caught or shot, another pair will come and build there.   One of our number was fortunate enough to get a sight of one of these nests.   He reported of it that "it was constructed only of sticks; there were three eggs, which were about twice the size of a Kestrel's, and very much the same in colour.   The two old birds were caught by means of traps set in the nest, to get at which the fisherman had to be let down the cliffs by a rope.   The female measured eighteen inches.   The Sparrow Hawk, which it very much resembles in marking, measures about twelve."

The eggs, two to four in number, are "a pale yellowish white, and the markings vary from brick red and orange brown to rich reddish brown". Some eggs are much smaller and rounder than others. In the middle ages Peregrines were much prized for the sport of falconry, and the birds were strictly preserved and commanded large prices, the loss of the right hand being the punishment inflicted for destroying a nest. The female, being the bigger bird, was flown at larger game, Herons and such like, whilst the male, called the Tiercel, was loosed at such small game, as Partridges and the like.

HOBBY.

FALCO SUBBUTEO.

Family FALCONIDÆ. Genus FALCO.

The Hobby bears a great resemblance to the Peregrine Falcon in his habits and appearance, but is much smaller. Unlike the Peregrine, the Hobby is only a summer visitor to our shores and has now become a rare bird. It is most likely to be met with in the southern and eastern counties of England, where the districts are well wooded.

The prey of the Hobby consists of the smaller birds, such as Larks and Buntings; but it is very bold and courageous and is said to even tackle such big game as Partridges. When giving chase its pace is terrific; it seems to glide through the air with scarcely any motion of the wings, and will strike Martins and Swallows on the wing, hardly ever missing its bird; and even the Swift, it is said, is not safe from its talons. It also feeds on numerous insects and animals, such as cockchafers, beetles and mice. When on the wing, it may easily be distinguished from the Kestrel or Merlin by its more slender appearance and narrow pointed wings.

The Hobby still nests with us, but it is no common thing to find it. It hardly ever builds a nest of its own, the old nest of a Crow or Magpie being used instead, which it generally lines with hair, wool and feathers. Its eggs, three or four in number, will not be found before June. They are pale red in ground colour, thickly spotted and mottled with deeper shades of red. They are almost exactly like the eggs of the Kestrel, but are scarcely so bright a red or so smooth in texture. Seebohm mentions a remarkable fact in connection with a nest of this bird which was used annually by Hobbies, that "although both parent birds were shot for six or eight successive years, and during that period no young birds were reared from this nest, yet each summer found it tenanted by a new pair".

The Hobby will become very tame when kept in confinement, and may be taught to hawk for small birds, but great care will have to be taken with it in the winter, or it will not survive the coldness of the English climate.

MERLIN.

FALCO ÆSALON.

Family FALCONIDÆ. Genus FALCO.

Blue Hawk—Stone Falcon.

With us in the south the Merlin is only a winter visitor, occasionally remaining to breèd, but in the north of England and in Scotland it appears to be a resident bird, frequenting the wild and mountainous districts in the summer and in the winter coming down to the more cultivated districts.

The Merlin has the same habits as the rest of the Falcons and the same bold and fearless courage; it feeds largely upon small birds, but will not be afraid to chase such birds as Plovers, Grouse or Partridges. It is very swift on the wing, though not so fast as the Hobby; still, it invariably hunts its prey down by superior pace, never swooping down from a height on it like the Kestrel or Peregrine. Like the Hobby it has been captured by dashing through the pane of a cottage window in pursuit of some small bird. It also feeds on large insects.

The Merlin has the habit of sitting upon large stones, especially those favourite ones to which it usually resorts with its prey; for just as the Shrikes have a favourite " larder," so many of the Falcon tribe have their pet " kitchens ". This habit has obtained for it the name of " Stone Falcon ".

On account of its swiftness of flight and great daring, the Merlin was once a favourite bird amongst falconers and was frequently used for hawking small game.

Its nesting haunt is in the wild moors of the north. The nest, though it can scarcely be called one, is made on the ground, just a few stalks of the heather being placed round to give it a shape, and in this three or four eggs are laid, very similar to others of the Falcon tribe and like them varying a good deal. Many of the eggs are difficult to distinguish from those of the Hobby and Kestrel, but they seem to be more brown and to have less of the very red tint of those eggs.

The male and female of this bird differ so much in plumage that they were formerly taken for two different species. The upper parts of the male are slate blue; the lower parts are reddish, striped with blackish brown; the tail has a broad black band on the end, and is longer than the tail of the Hobby, but shorter than the Kestrel's. The bird is also more bulky than the Hobby. The Merlin is very hardy and can endure a great amount of cold; it may be easily tamed and trained.

KESTREL.

FALCO TINNUNCULUS.

Family FALCONIDÆ. Genus FALCO.

Windhover—Hoverhawk—Creshawk.

The Kestrel or Windhover—a name which it has from the habit of hovering in the air—is by far the commonest of our hawks and may be found over all the British Isles. Although many Kestrels remain with us during the winter, it is really a migratory bird; and if, as has been stated, the absence of food is the cause of migration, one can understand such a bird as this seeking a country where mice and beetles are commoner than they are with us in the winter. For birds are not the Kestrel's regular food, and there is not the terror among small birds at its approach that one notices on the approach of a Sparrow Hawk. It is very fond of cockchafers, and one would have thought its partiality for mice would have caused it to

be regarded as the farmer's friend. But, no! it is
credited with occasionally helping itself to a young
Partridge when food is scarce, so down it must come
whenever seen.

No doubt many of us have watched this bird; probably, when first noticed, it was poised in the air, with
its wings fully expanded; then, with a flap or two of
its wings, it has darted off; but, suddenly stopping, it
has hovered again in the air; yet only for a moment,
for, closing its wings, it drops almost like a stone, till
within a short distance of the ground, when it stretches
out its wings, hovering for a second or so, and is lost
to our view; but almost immediately it rises again and
flies away. Why this sudden descent? Doubtless
the bird, when hovering in the air, espied a mouse or
some small animal on the ground and took the quickest
mode of reaching it.

As with the preceding members of this family, the
female always exceeds the male in size and strength,
though the male has the advantage in beauty of
plumage. The latter may be easily distinguished by
its slate grey tail. The head and back are of the same
colour, the rest of the upper parts a light chestnut;
the under parts are pale fawn colour, spotted with
dusky marks.

The Kestrel generally nests in a thick wood or copse.
Its eggs may be looked for with the month of May.
Near us it usually adopts the old nest of a Crow or
Magpie, which it lines with mud. Often the nest
is comparatively low down, and I have found eggs
within ten feet of the ground in an old squirrel's drey.
The same place is frequently resorted to year after
year, and it is supposed that the Kestrel pairs for
life.

The eggs are generally six in number. The ground is cream colour, which is almost completely hidden with rich reddish-brown blotches. These markings, however, are often collected round the large end of the egg, or sometimes are not nearly so thickly distributed. The Kestrel was never a favourite for hawking, though it was occasionally used; its flight is so much slower than that of the Merlin or Hobby. According to old books on hawking, the Sparrow Hawk was considered proper for a priest, while the Kestrel fell to the lot of the knave or servant.

The Kestrel has always been a favourite at Queenwood for taming purposes, as it breeds all around in great abundance; but we have never had them so tame as our Crows and Jackdaws. They can however be perfectly tamed and made to come at call. Some years ago an account was given in the *Zoologist* of a Kestrel which was taken young, and when full grown was given its liberty, but it declined to leave the place. In the spring it paired; the nest was in a dovecot near; the eggs were not hatched that year, but they were the succeeding year. This bird used to come every day to the window of the house, and on its being opened would enter and was fed by the children. His mate never ventured so far, but would stop when within a short distance of the window.

OSPREY.

PANDION HALIÆTUS.

Family FALCONIDÆ. Genus PANDION.

Fish Hawk—Mullet Hawk.

The Osprey belongs to the Eagle tribe, and is one of the smallest of them. It is now a very rare bird

indeed in the British Isles.   Up in the Highlands,
far removed from the haunts of man, by the wild
mountain lochs, or amongst the bleak uplands, this
was where once the Osprey dwelt in considerable
numbers; but now these numbers are thinned, and
we are fortunate if we can still say it breeds here.
" There are still one or two eyries in Inverness-shire
and Ross-shire, and also in Galloway," says Seebohm,
" a sufficient number of birds, if strictly preserved, to
retain the Osprey in the rank of a regular emigrant to
our island."

OSPREY.

The Osprey preys upon fish, as its name—the Fish
Hawk—implies.   These it obtains hovering over the
water like a huge Kestrel, pausing with a beat or
two of the wings as it keenly watches the surface
beneath; suddenly with a dip down to the water it
seizes its prey in its talons, and flies off to a neighbouring rock to devour it.

In America, where the Osprey is still plentiful, it is
said to build for the most part in trees; but in this

country its favourite site is some isolated rock in one of the mountain lochs of Scotland. On the top of this a huge nest of sticks is built, from three to four feet in diameter, it is said. The sticks themselves are very big, some of them an inch and a half in diameter, and lined with dry grass. In this structure three eggs are usually laid, the ordinary variety being white in ground colour, boldly blotched with rich reddish brown, thicker towards the larger end.

The upper parts of the Osprey are dark brown, except the head and nape, which are white streaked with brown; the under parts are white, with a light-brown belt of feathers across the breast.

It is an occasional autumn visitor to the south, and has been noticed in the Isle of Wight and on the shores of the New Forest.

COMMON KITE.

MILVUS REGALIS.

Family FALCONIDÆ. Genus MILVUS.

Gleade—Puttock—Fork-tailed Kite.

The Kite, formerly so common, is now another bird which in most parts of our country may not be seen, perhaps, once in a lifetime. The only places in which it now breeds at all regularly are the Highlands of Scotland and the wildest parts of Wales. It is said to be resident.

The Gleade, or Glide, as it is called, receives this name from its motion in the air, sailing up in slow graceful circles, sometimes to a great height, with wings and tail expanded, for hours at a time. Owing to this proficiency in soaring, it was at one time a very favourite quarry for the falconer; Hawk and Kite circling up until they disappeared sometimes entirely from view.

When the breeding season commences the Kite has been frequently known to rob the clothes-line for material for his nest.   Mr. Cordeaux writes to the *Zoologist*, 1891, p. 313, the following reminiscences of an old man, seventy-seven years of age, who began life as assistant to a gamekeeper in Lincolnshire.   " He well

COMMON KITE.

remembers when he was a boy that the Gleade was very common in the big woods near Louth; he had seen scores of them; during a great part of the day they were on the wing, flying and soaring in circles at a great elevation on motionless wings.   His father kept a good many geese, and almost the first job he was put to as a child was to tend goslings.   If the least remiss in his duty, down swooped one of the ever-watchful Kites, and in an instant one of his charges was carried off.   Not only were they skilful foragers in the poultry yard, but equally adept at carrying off linen from the drying grounds and hedges, illustrating the well-known line of Shakespeare :—

> When the Kite builds look to lesser linen.—
> *Winter's Tale*, Act iv., Sc. 2.

Handkerchiefs, socks, and specially children's clothing, disappeared, to be used as building materials for their nests ; and he had many a time to climb trees in the woods to recover these lost articles."

The Kite, however, is a bit of a coward ; he has none of the daring courage of the Hawks, and may easily be driven away except when his nest is menaced.

It is many years since the Kite has nested near us ; we find, however, in our records that in the spring of 1864 a Kite's nest was taken by Dr. J. Hopkinson of Manchester, and Mr. J. Ashby, J.P., of Staines, both then schoolboys at Queenwood. This nest was placed in the top of a tall fir close to a shepherd's cottage, and was made of a platform of sticks, lined with bones and bits of rag. The old bird was sitting, and when Hopkinson got near the top she flew off, circling round him, and occasionally making darts at him. There were three eggs. These were dirty white in colour, with a few spots or blotchings of red.

In addition to birds and fowls, the Kite shows a great partiality for moles, no less than twenty-two having been found in one nest, so that even the Kite is serviceable.

The plumage of the head is whitish grey ; the general colour of the upper parts is reddish brown, each feather being of a lighter colour round the edges ; the under parts are reddish orange streaked with dark brown.

HONEY BUZZARD.

PERNIS APIVORUS.

Family FALCONIDÆ. Genus PERNIS.

The Honey Buzzard, once a regular summer visitor which bred in most counties of England and Wales, now, alas! must be classed with the many other fast diminishing and scarce birds of this family. At one time Hampshire was the regular summer haunt for these birds, and many pairs resorted to it to rear their young, but they have been hunted down, trapped and shot for the naturalist's collection, until we can no longer reckon them among our annual visitors. Who is to blame for this lamentable result? I fear the collectors themselves more than anybody else. Here is an extract from a lecture given by "Mr. John" at Queenwood in 1874: "The Honey Buzzard is still to be found in the neighbourhood of Fritham in the New Forest, and some eggs as well as birds are, we believe, taken most seasons (for when a nest is found, the birds are generally caught by a trap placed in the nest). They prove rather a good find for the poor man, as a gentleman in the neighbourhood offers fifteen shillings a piece for all eggs taken to him." And the following is taken from Kelsall's *List of the Birds of Hampshire*, 1890 : "About 1860 it was known that several pairs resorted to the New Forest; £5 soon became the price of two British eggs, nearly £40 for a pair of birds ; by about 1870 the survivors were driven away, and if any have returned those who know it have exercised a becoming reticence ".

And all this persecution is carried on against a bird which is practically harmless to game ; its principal food consisting of wasp grubs (though it is said to avoid the full-grown insect on account of its sting). It also feeds upon various other insects, in addition to mice, lizards, frogs, and occasionally a small bird.

The general colour of the upper plumage of the Honey Buzzard is dark brown ; the head is grey, and the under parts are brown ; some birds, however, are found with the under parts of a uniform greyish white.

The nest is said to be a broad structure of sticks lined with leaves. In Europe, however, according to Seebohm, it always used the nest of the Kite or Common Buzzard. The number of eggs taken in the New Forest is generally two, but the bird sometimes lays three. They much resemble those of the Kestrel in colour ; but they differ in size and shape, being larger and very round, the small end being little different from the large end.

It is said to be very easily tamed, in which state it displays quite a gentle disposition.

WHITE-TAILED EAGLE.

HALIÆTUS ALBICILLA.

Family FALCONIDÆ. Genus HALIÆTUS.

Erne—Sea Eagle.

Among the towering and inaccessible cliffs in the wildest parts of the Hebrides, the Sea Eagle most commonly rears its young.   No longer is this bird, once abundant in England, now seen soaring away to its eyrie among the beetling cliffs around our coasts, for the Eagle, with us in England and Wales, is now an extinct bird.   Nevertheless, in the autumn and winter the White-tailed Eagle frequently straggles down to our eastern counties, and numerous instances are to hand of birds shot when the cold weather has set in, and food is more plentiful on the warmer side of the borders. Seebohm writes: "Eagles of all kinds are thorough gypsies in their mode of life—here one day, fifty miles away the next, a flight of a hundred miles being nothing but a morning stroll for an Eagle. This circumstance, coupled with the fact that their haunts are so vast and difficult of access, explains why it is that the birds are so rarely seen, and why the impression is so deeply rooted that the birds are well nigh extinct in Great Britain."

The White-tailed Eagle, though most frequently found on the coasts, is by no means confined to them, and often wanders far inland to some quiet loch or piece of water where high rocks or cliffs abound. It feeds near the sea, chiefly upon dead fish cast up on the shore, but it is not averse to rabbits, dead sheep, hares, ducks, fowls and other animals. "The many tales told of this bird," says Seebohm, "as well as of the Golden Eagle, which are represented as carrying off children, are no doubt myths; for as Saxby in his *Birds of Shetland* very justly remarks, every Eagle's eyrie in the islands is pointed out as *the* one made famous for all time by its owners carrying off that world-renowned baby in times so long ago as to be clouded in deep obscurity."

The White-tailed Eagle pairs for life, and the same eyrie is resorted to year by year; the nest is a gigantic structure, five or six feet in diameter, built of sticks and lined with bits of heather and seaweed. It is annually repaired and enlarged. It is usually placed high on some inaccessible ledge of rock, but has also been found in a tree or even on the ground.

The eggs are about three inches long, of a round shape, two in number, and pure white. They resemble unspotted eggs of the Golden Eagle, but are much rougher and coarser in texture.

The Sea Eagle has the upper parts brown, becoming much lighter on the head and neck; the under parts are chocolate.   As with all this family the female is much bigger than the male, being about thirty-nine inches in length to twenty-eight of the latter.

GOLDEN EAGLE.

AQUILA CHRYSÆTUS.

Family FALCONIDÆ. Genus AQUILA.

Black Eagle.

This noble bird, fitly called the " king of birds," is one of the largest and finest of our birds of prey; it is, like the White-tailed Eagle, now chiefly confined to the wildest districts of Scotland, though it is nowhere so common as that bird. It also breeds in a few districts in Ireland.

The Golden Eagle loves the high and rugged mountain peaks of the Highlands, and it is there he makes his home, not on the sea-girt cliffs like his relation, the Erne—though occasionally he is found there, too —but away up on the bare and rugged face of some awful precipice, upon a ledge sheltered by an overhanging rock, with an uninterrupted view of the surrounding country, there he places his nest. The same cliff is resorted to year by year, for the birds apparently pair for life, but they seem to have several nests, which they use in turn; repairing and relining them before use. The nest is made of sticks and branches of heather, and lined with dried ferns and tufts of grass.

The proud flight of the king of birds is indeed a sight which once seen will not easily be forgotten. I once and once only witnessed it some years ago when climbing near the foot of Ben Lawers in Perthshire, and recall now the grand and majestic image of the bird as he first caught my eye, now hovering for a moment and now slowly sailing onwards till he was gradually lost to my view.

The amount of food consumed by these birds and their young is enormous. Tales are told of men who have stocked their larder through the spring and summer months with game carried off from the eyrie. In one season the Golden Eagle has been known to carry off thirty-five lambs from a Highland sheep-farm, and the remains of as many as three hundred ducks and forty hares have been found in the eyrie of one in Germany.

The bird receives its name Golden Eagle from the

red gold feathers that cover the head and neck; by these and the darker and richer brown of its plumage it may be distinguished from the While-tailed Eagle.

The eggs are generally two in number, sometimes three; they vary greatly. We may describe them as dirty white in ground colour, blotched with reddish brown and underlying markings of grey.

The Golden Eagle is easily kept in confinement, but cannot well be tamed. It is reported to live to a great age, even exceeding one hundred years.

COMMON BUZZARD.

BUTEO VULGARIS.

Family FALCONIDÆ.   Genus BUTEO.

Mouse Buzzard—Puttock.

The Buzzard, once distributed throughout the British Isles, now is chiefly confined to Scotland and Wales. It is a resident bird, and unfortunately has been ruthlessly shot down by gamekeepers, owing to its great similarity to the Eagle, although it is practically harmless to the game, its ordinary food being small animals, reptiles and grasshoppers. It is really a sluggish bird and slow on the wing, quite unable to fly down a Partridge or Grouse, and contents itself with perching on a stone or stump, sometimes for hours, on the lookout for a mole or stray mouse on which to pounce. This latter it is extremely partial to, and is sometimes called in consequence the Mouse Buzzard. It has been calculated that a family of five will consume no less than fifty thousand of these little " farmer's pests " in the course of twelve months; and yet this useful bird is destroyed as " vermin ".

The Common Buzzard builds in the New Forest every year. A man, who was for seven years a keeper in the forest, told one of us he had often seen them and taken their eggs. He found the young ones very spiteful, and they defended themselves vigorously. He said that a man who used to bring eggs to him told him that on getting up to a Buzzard's nest, the

COMMON BUZZARD.

biggest adder he ever saw in his life darted from it. The nest contained two young ones, and he thought the old birds must have taken it up to feed them with.

When these birds commence nesting operations, they may frequently be seen circling high in the air, uttering their shrill and mournful scream ; at other times they fly very low over the ground. The same nest is resorted to for several years in succession. It is nearly two feet in diameter, built of twigs, very flat, and lined with leaves. Sometimes it will use the nest of another bird. The eggs are from two to four in number, and are bluish or reddish white in ground colour, blotched and spotted with reddish - brown markings and underlying markings of grey. Some eggs much resemble the Kestrel's eggs in colour, but are of course much larger, being about two or two and a quarter inches in length.

In plumage the Buzzard varies so much that it is impossible to describe it ; it is said that no two birds are alike ; brown, white and grey, variously disposed, seem to be the prevailing colours, and the tail is marked with several pale bars. It is said that this bird in confinement will become quite companionable and very tame.

MARSH HARRIER.

CIRCUS ÆRUGINOSUS.

Family FALCONIDÆ.　Genus CIRCUS.

Moor Buzzard—Marsh Hawk—Harpy—Duck Hawk.

The Marsh Harrier may still be found breeding in a few parts of England, in such places as the Norfolk Broads ; but its great home—the fen districts—is now all drained and cultivated, and the Harriers, in common with several birds of other species, have left their haunts to return no more. In such places as it still remains, however, it is a resident bird ; and it also is found locally in Scotland and Ireland.

The Harriers are said to derive their name from

the habit they have of quartering the ground in their low flight, reminding one of the hounds, when searching for a hare. They feed principally upon young water birds—Moor Hens, Peewits, and such like, which abound in their marshy haunts—and they also consume large numbers of the eggs of these birds. It never hawks its prey, but always seeks it on the ground, though it is considerably faster on the wing than the Buzzard.

MARSH HARRIER.

I am afraid most of our young collectors will not be likely to meet often with this bird, but it seems occasionally to stray after the breeding season is over, for it is described in our *Hampshire Birds* as a winter visitor to the marshy districts around the New Forest, though it no longer nests with us. It nearly always nests on the ground. The following account I borrow from Seebohm of a nest which he took near Bruns-

15

wick. " It was in a large extent of swampy ground, on the margin of one of the numerous lakes and ponds where the reeds had not been mown down. They are too thick on the ground for a flat-bottomed boat to be forced through ; but the water comes above the knees as one wades amongst them. In the middle of this bed of reeds the Marsh Harrier had built. The nest was very large, the outside composed of two thirds reeds and one third small branches of trees, and the extreme diameter was at least four feet ; but the outside was very loose and straggling. It stood two feet above the surface of the water ; and one could see underneath the nest by stooping down. The inside of the nest was neat and compact, measuring less than a foot across, and warmly lined with dry flag leaves and dry gràss. It contained four eggs of the Marsh Harrier and one of the Coot, which had doubtless been taken thither to feed the sitting bird."

The eggs are a greenish white, and have been compared to Domestic Hens' eggs. Frequently they are marked with small blotches of a pale yellowish brown.

The general colours of the Marsh Harrier are dark reddish brown above, and a rich chestnut beneath. The head and neck are white streaked with dark brown.

SPARROW HAWK.

ACCIPITER NISUS.

Family FALCONIDÆ.   Genus ACCIPITER.

Pigeon Hawk.

Though described as the commonest and most extensively distributed of our resident birds of prey, yet

in our part of the world—Hampshire—the Kestrel is
certainly more frequently met with.   Possibly this is
because the Sparrow Hawk, so universally recognised
as a thief and a robber, enjoys the unenviable distinction of being the only bird of prey in the New Forest
to whom protection is not afforded.   Nevertheless we
frequently have observed the Sparrow Hawk and its

SPARROW HAWK.

nest, and in all the woods and forests of Great Britain
and Ireland it is still to be met with in comparative
abundance.

   The female Sparrow Hawk, as with all the raptorial
birds, is much bigger than the male and is exceedingly
courageous ; of its own accord it has been known to
attack a Heron.   But its usual food consists of smaller

birds—Sparrows, Greenfinches, Linnets, etc.—and it is also a terrible marauder amongst the Pheasant coops and the farmer's Hen coops. In this it differs from the Kestrel, which prefers to these such small animals as mice and moles. When in search of its prey, the flight of the Sparrow Hawk is marvellously swift; it skims along close to the ground under shelter of some hedgerow or fence, and little chance has any small bird which it may startle of escaping its clutches, unless it can gain some thick hedge or cover which the Hawk cannot penetrate. It is wonderful to see this beautiful bird dash through a wood or copse in pursuit of his prey, dodging with astonishing dexterity the boughs and twigs which, one would think, must interrupt him in his chase. In such dread is the Sparrow Hawk held by some birds that, on seeing one, they will throw themselves on the ground as dead. But the pursuer is himself sometimes pursued. I remember some twelve months ago stopping in my walk to listen to the rapidly approaching loud cry of a Blackbird. While I was wondering what it meant, in a moment a Sparrow Hawk dashed across the road and into the cover on the other side, with the screaming Blackbird in hot pursuit. Probably the Hawk had robbed the poor creature's nest. Many of us, too, must have noticed one of these birds pursued by Swallows, which delight to annoy and tease him by constantly following him; he never seems to turn upon them, but usually makes off as quickly as he can to some friendly wood.

The Sparrow Hawk builds its own nest, though it is said to occasionally adopt an old one of the Crow or Magpie. The common position is in a tree, generally a fir or an oak, in the midst of some wood or copse. It is a large nest built of sticks and a few roots. Hewitson compares it to the nest of the Ring Dove, but it is always placed near the trunk of the tree and not at the end of the branches.

Eggs may be found in May; they are three to six in number (eight have been found), and very beautiful. The ground colour is a pale blue, blotched with rich reddish brown. Like all the eggs in this class they undergo great variation.

If the eggs are removed, the Sparrow Hawk will continue laying; fifteen eggs are mentioned in the *Zoologist* as having been obtained in this way.

The upper plumage of the Sparrow Hawk is a dark slate blue; the under parts are white tinged with a reddish tint and barred with reddish brown.

On account of its courage and quickness of flight this bird was formerly trained for hawking. It is stated to have become very tame when brought up from the nest and, according to Stanley, to have associated with tame Pigeons, roosting in their cot at night, and never attempting to interfere with their young.

Other rarer birds of the Family Falconidæ :—

EGYPTIAN VULTURE.

VULTUR PERCNOPTERUS.

Genus VULTUR.

Has been twice captured in England.

JER FALCON.

FALCO GYRFALCO.

Genus GYRFALCO.

A bird of very occasional occurrence.

RED-FOOTED FALCON.

FALCO VESPERTINUS.

Genus FALCO.

An accidental visitor from Eastern Europe and Asia.

SWALLOW-TAILED KITE.

ELANOIDES FURCATUS.

Genus ELANOIDES.

Only three or four appearances are recorded.

LESSER SPOTTED EAGLE.

AQUILA NÆVIA.

Genus AQUILA.

Met with once or twice only in Britain.

ROUGH-LEGGED BUZZARD EAGLE.

AQUILA LAGOPUS.

Genus AQUILA.

A rare autumn visitor, sometimes coming in large numbers. Has once or twice remained to breed.

HEN HARRIER.

CIRCUS CYANEUS.

Genus CIRCUS.

The Hen Harrier, so called from its occasional liking for a young chicken, still breeds in the Highlands of Scotland, Wales, and some of the wilder and mountainous districts of England. Of late years it has been so much thinned down that we must now regard it as a visitor to our islands which occasionally breeds with us. In its habits it is similar to the Marsh Harrier, hawking its food flying low over the ground. The eggs are similar to those of the Marsh Harrier, but slightly smaller.

MONTAGU'S HARRIER.

CIRCUS CINERACEUS.

Genus CIRCUS.

An accidental visitor to Great Britain, formerly resident. It has nested for some years running lately in the New Forest, and would do so in other parts of the country if allowed to. Its eggs are greenish white like those of the other Harriers, but of smaller size than either.

GOSHAWK.

ACCIPITER PALUMBARIUS.

Genus ACCIPITER.

Once a resident bird, but never common ; now only an accidental visitor. In appearance it is like a huge Sparrow Hawk, but is not fleet enough of wing to fly down its game, so it perches and falls upon it unawares. It formerly was in much request for hawking, but was flown at slower and lower-flying game than the Falcon. The eggs are a uniform pale blue colour, quite unspotted.

AMERICAN GOSHAWK.

ASTUR ATRICAPILLUS.

A visitor which has crossed the Atlantic some three or four times.

BARN OWL.

ALUCO FLAMMEUS.

Family STRIGIDÆ. Genus ALUCO.

White Owl—Screech Owl—Yellow Owl—Madge Howlet
—Church Owl—Hissing Owl.

The Barn Owl is the most common and the most showy of all our Owls. It is distributed all over the

British Isles, and is usually seen in the dusk of evening, when it leaves its haunt where it has been sleeping
all day to search for its food. This haunt is usually
the place in which its young are reared—some old
ruin, a hole in a tree, an old ivied wall, or perhaps
even a dovecot. It was generally held that the
young Pigeons were looked upon by old Madge Howlet
as among his greatest delicacies, but it has now been
pretty conclusively proved that he does not interfere
with them at all, and that his ejected pellets never
contain any trace of Pigeon, old or young; he feeds
chiefly on mice, rats, and moles, also less frequently
on small birds, beetles and slugs. Charles Waterton
says: " If it were really an enemy to the dovecot we
should see the Pigeons in commotion as soon as it
begins its evening flight! but the Pigeons heed it not:
whereas, if the Sparrow Hawk or the Hobby should
make its appearance, the whole community would be
up at once; proof sufficient that the Barn Owl is not
looked upon as a bad or even suspicious character
by the inhabitants of the dovecot ".

As many as twenty dead rats have been found in a
Barn Owl's nest, all fresh killed, and yet the stupid
farmer will kill so good a friend indiscriminately, under
the impression that it is harmful to his young fowls
and birds.

The flight of the Barn Owl is very weird and silent,
and there is something quite awe-inspiring and " uncanny " in the noiseless motion of one of these birds,
as it flits past you in the dim twilight of evening when
you are wending your way through some quiet wood-
land path or country lane. Its loud screech is familiar
to all of us who have ever lived among rural surroundings, and even to town dwellers as well—for I

have heard its piercing note within five miles of the
Marble Arch, and well recollect being roused in the
middle of the night by a terrified inmate of the house
in which I was, who then heard its unearthly shriek
for the first time.

The plumage of the Barn Owl is most beautiful. It
is an extraordinary-looking bird, with its heart-shaped
face of the purest silky white feathers; the upper
parts are buff, the feathers being most daintily pencilled at the tips with dark purple and black; the
under parts are white, thinly marked here and there
with dark spots.

The Barn Owl builds no nest, but its eggs are
generally surrounded with numerous pellets which it
has ejected. Its eggs, three to seven, are found towards the end of April or the beginning of May. Two
and sometimes three broods are reared. The eggs
of all the Owls are so much alike that unless you see
the bird, or find the nest, you will be unable to classify
them; for although the different kinds vary in size,
this is very insufficient proof, as the eggs of the same
bird often vary very considerably; they are all white,
very slightly oval or very nearly round; the ordinary
size of the Long-eared is stated to be $1\frac{17}{24}$ inches by
$1\frac{1}{24}$ inches, of the Tawny $1\frac{5}{8}$ inches by $1\frac{1}{2}$ inches, and
of the Barn $1\frac{1}{2}$ inches by $1\frac{1}{4}$ inches.

The Barn Owl can be very easily tamed, even if
captured old; the last we possessed was one whose
wing had been damaged through being kicked by a race-
horse in the Danebury Stables, where it had entered to
search for mice. This, through being carefully tended
and nursed, became very tame, and it was comical to see
the bird solemnly moving its head from side to side, seemingly with pleasure, when its food was brought to it.

The young of the Barn Owls snore: this snoring noise is said to be a call to the parent birds for food.

WOOD OWL.

STRIX ALUCO.

Family STRIGIDÆ. Genus STRIX.

Tawny Owl—Brown Owl—Ivy Owl—Jenny Howlet.

The Wood Owl, or as it is more often called the Tawny Owl, is rapidly becoming less numerous year by year.   It is to be found throughout the wooded districts of the British Isles, but even in many of these it is now but thinly distributed.   In the New Forest, for instance, it is by no means as common as the Long-eared Owl.

It is the Tawny Owl which gives utterance to the long, weird, and ghostly "to-who-o-o-o"; this is shortly followed by a second cry resembling the first, but tremulous, sounding like a loud mocking laugh. It is, no doubt, this hoot which has caused the bird to be looked upon as a bird of ill-omen, and its proximity to any house is regarded as foretelling a death about to occur within.

The Wood Owl's haunts are in the depths of the forests.   Here in a rift in some old oak or elm it will find a resting-place, where it may sleep through the day, and from which it may issue at night to search for its food.   This bird is undoubtedly more of a poacher than the Barn Owl, but still by far its commonest food consists of mice, rats, moles and frogs. It does not always breed in its daily home, as sometimes it will roost in an old ivied wall or in the thickest foliage of a pine or fir.*   It generally breeds in a cavity in a tree, but occasionally will breed in an old Crow's or Magpie's nest, in a squirrel's drey, or even in a rabbit burrow.

* I once, when out for a woodland walk with a friend, remarked, on noticing a hole in the trunk of an elm |where a huge bough had been torn off, that it would be a good hole for an owl, and not thinking for a moment that my words would come true, threw a stick at the place. Out flew a magnificent Tawny, and immediately some dozen or two small birds from the neighbouring trees started in pursuit. Round him they flew, screaming and chattering, knowing they were safe while their enemy was blinded in the sunlight, until the whole flock was lost to sight in a neighbouring copse.

The eggs, three or four in number, and white and round, are generally larger than those of any other British Owls.

The Wool Owl is of a darker hue than the Barn Owl, the upper parts being reddish brown, spotted with dark brown; the under parts are buffish white, barred and streaked with dark brown. All the Owls have the peculiar faculty of turning their heads almost completely round, and it is no uncommon thing to see this bird resting its beak upon its back; the eyes appear to be fixed in the sockets, so that to look to one side it is obliged to turn its head.

The Tawny Owl soon becomes tame in captivity. Meyer relates the following anecdote of one which he reared from the nest. " It inhabited an out-building in which various household affairs were transacted by the servants, to one of whom it was evidently attached, and as the building was much covered with ivy, which obscured the light, it would sit in the day-time and watch her operations with all the familiarity of a favourite cat; no restraint was put upon its liberty, yet it seldom strayed beyond the residence to which it had attached itself.

" This bird amused us frequently by an exhibition which at last cost the poor creature its life. It was fond of washing itself in a tub of water which usually stood in the place where the bird was kept, and the dreadful sight baffles description when this wretch sat on the edge of the tub dripping wet, with its feathers all sticking close to its sides; the only thing imaginable that we can compare the object to, for to call it a creature in that state would be a mockery, is the black remains of a burnt paper candle lighter, surmounted by two glaring eyes. This pastime ended tragically, the poor Owl having once by mistake plunged into a tub of food prepared for the pigs, and ended his career in consequence of the vessel being deeper than his usual bath."

LONG-EARED OWL.

STRIX OTUS.

Family STRIGIDÆ.   Genus STRIX.

Long-horned Owl—Horned Howlet.

The Long-eared Owl is resident in most wooded districts of Great Britain and Ireland. It seems especially fond of those tracts which abound in pines and firs, and though generally thinly distributed, in our part of Hampshire it is even more common than the Barn Owl.

A great many of these birds have from time to time been tamed by our young naturalists at Queenwood, and their comical antics by day, and weird notes when they are confined to their cage at night, are very familiar to us.   These notes remind us strangely of the mewing or squealing of a kitten, only very much louder ; they are very shrill and penetrating, and can be heard a great way off.   The birds seem able to bear the daylight with comparatively little discomfort, and will not blink in the midday brightness.   They certainly are by no means blind in the light, as one soon finds to one's cost, if one attempts to tease them. Some few years back a nest of young Long-eared Owls was taken to be reared.   They were pretty little things, little round balls covered with soft greyish fluff.   They were placed in cages in an old play-shed in the grounds.   To procure them sufficient suitable food was not always an easy task for their owners. One morning several dead mice were found lying in a row in front of the cages.   The following day there was a similar mysterious supply.   This led to a look-out being established ; and it was found that the old birds had discovered the whereabouts of their young. There was an opening in the roof of the shed owing to a slate having slipped, and through this opening they swooped with their prey—a mouse, mole, or young rat.   On one occasion as many as twenty-seven small animals were thus supplied for the young birds.

This bird, in all probability, never builds its own nest, but uses an old one of some Magpie or Crow ; we have most frequently discovered its eggs in an old squirrel's drey.   The bird sits so close that it can sometimes nearly be caught on the nest.   It is no uncommon thing to find young birds and fresh eggs in the same nest, for the eggs seem to be laid at long intervals apart. This, it appears, occurs with other birds of the same family.

The eggs, pure white, are generally five or six in number.

This Owl may easily be recognised by its long ears. Its upper plumage is a mixture of dusky brown and. grey and buff: the under parts are buffish brown, becoming lighter lower down, streaked with dark and light brown.

SHORT-EARED OWL.

STRIX BRACHYOTUS.

Family STRIGIDÆ.   Genus STRIX.

Woodcock Owl—Short-horned Howlet—Mouse Hawk—Hawk Owl.

Great interest attaches to this Owl, from the fact that it differs so much from the rest of its kind in its habits. It is a fairly common winter visitor to the moors and marshy districts of the British Isles, arriving in October about the same time as the Woodcock and frequenting the same haunts, from which it gets the name of "Woodcock Owl". A few pairs, however, are still resident in the country and breed in the marshes and fens of the eastern counties.

This bird seems little troubled by the sunlight, and is often seen by day. From its small head and from the manner in which it quarters the ground for its prey it is frequently—though erroneously—called the Hawk Owl; this name properly belonging to another bird mentioned afterwards of the same family. Its favourite food is mice and small rats; it also consumes beetles, small birds and fish that can be caught on the surface.

The Short-eared Owl must not be looked for in the woods and copses, for it rarely, if ever, visits these. Its haunts are the open fields and furze plantations, the barren moors of the north or the fen districts of the east.

The most interesting feature in connection with this bird is that in this open country the bird rears its young; not in any hole of a tree or sheltered by thick foliage, but in an open nest and fully exposed on the ground. There is scarcely any nest; just a few reeds scraped together perhaps in a slight dip in the ground are all that this bird deems necessary to receive the eggs. As we mentioned above, the nest when of late years observed in England has generally been found in the marshes which abound in these reeds.

The eggs are usually six or seven in number, sometimes as few as four; and like all the Owls' eggs, pure white. They are about the same size as those of the

16

Long-eared Owl, and are practically indistinguishable from these. Perhaps they are hardly so round.

The Short-eared Owl varies considerably in plumage. It much resembles in general appearance the Tawny Owl, but of course is without the long ears which form the distinguishing feature of that species.

It is said to be in some degree tameable, though not to such an extent as the preceding species.

Other rarer birds of this species are :—

TENGMALM'S OWL.

STRIX TENGMALMI.

Genus STRIX.

A rare accidental visitor which has been obtained something over a score of times.

LITTLE OWL.

NOCTUA NOCTUA.

Genus NOCTUA.

An accidental visitor. Described as " resident in the New Forest, but doubtless introduced," since it is frequently imported alive to England, and some no doubt escape.

SNOWY OWL.

SURNIA NYCTEA.

Genus SURNIA.

A regular though scarce visitor, principally to Scotland and the north.

HAWK OWL.

SURNIA FUNEREA.

Genus SURNIA.

Has been obtained some half-dozen times. When on the wing it bears a considerable resemblance to a Hawk. Its note also is said to be not unlike the cry of a Hawk.

EAGLE OWL.

BUBO MAXIMUS.

Genus BUBO.

The Great Owl is a bird of rare and uncertain occurrence. Has been met with chiefly in the north. Several of the specimens obtained are no doubt escaped ones.

SCOP'S OWL.

SCOPS SCOPS.

Genus SCOPS.

An accidental visitor, chiefly to England. Some two dozen specimens have been obtained.

COMMON PTARMIGAN.

TETRAO MUTUS.

Family PHASIANIDÆ. Genus TETRAO.

White Grouse—Snow Chick—Rock Grouse.

We now arrive at the Family PHASIANIDÆ, and no doubt with many of us some of the birds we are about to deal with are more familiar to us accompanied by bread sauce, brown gravy, and currant jelly, than they are in their native state.

Very few of us will have met with the Ptarmigan, for it is only found on the bare and bleak tops of some of the highest mountains in Scotland, though in the winter it will descend some little way down the sides

COMMON PTARMIGAN.

for protection. It is said to have formerly occurred in the mountains of Cumberland and Wales, but the evidence on this point is very unsatisfactory. The bird seems to revel in the snow, and will consume it, instead of descending to the burns for water. "During the night," says Meyer, "the Ptarmigan resorts to the shelter afforded by a stone or heath plant, or by the

snow itself, in which it buries itself up to the neck.
In this latter situation these birds are not infrequently
snowed in, and have great difficulty in keeping a small
loop-hole.   The huntsmen of the Alps profess to
know that, when these birds are snowed in and become actually covered over by the snow, they remain
thus at times for a whole week, when hunger prompts
them to the exertion of extricating themselves, and
not infrequently several birds are found dead in such
situations."

The food of the Ptarmigan consists of the buds and
young shoots of heather and other mountain plants ;
it also feeds on certain berries, such as the cranberry
and bilberry.   Its note is said to resemble the low
croaking of a frog.

The Ptarmigan is the smallest of the various species
of Grouse in Britain.   Its summer plumage undergoes
a most complete change as winter sets in.   In both
seasons it so nearly resembles its surroundings that
it is possible, and in fact probable, that one might
walk into the midst of a flock of them without being
aware of their presence.   In winter the plumage is
pure white, with the exception of a black streak from
the beak to the eye, and a few black feathers in the
tail.   There is a patch of bare red skin over the eye.
In the spring and summer, however, the prevailing
colours are buffish brown and grey with dark spots.
In their summer plumage they seem to lose the neat
appearance which their smooth winter feathers give
them.   Cox writes of two which were shot in July,
1882, at Spitzbergen, " They are incomparably the
dirtiest and most ragged wild birds I have ever seen,
and look more as if they had been prisoners among
the stock of some Seven Dials bird-fancier than birds

killed in full possession of their native freedom, in the wilds of Spitzbergen ".

These birds seldom fly unless obliged to. When they do take the wing, their flight is extremely rapid.

The eggs are laid frequently on the bare stones, generally in a little hollow scraped out in the ground and lined with a twig or two and a few feathers.

Seven to ten eggs are laid of a buffish ground colour, blotched with rich chocolate brown.

RED GROUSE.

TETRAO SCOTICUS.

Family PHASIANIDÆ. Genus TETRAO.

Brown Ptarmigan—Muir Fowl—Moor Fowl—Gorcock.

The Red Grouse is the only bird which is found in no place outside the British Islands. It breeds on the moors of Scotland and Ireland, and also in the north and north-west of England and in Wales, and in spite of the large numbers which are shot every autumn it seems to remain as plentiful as ever from year to year. The Grouse never perches on trees and indeed does not often fly unless compelled to, but when it does take to the wing it flies low over the heather, moving very swiftly with a whirring noise.

Grouse feed chiefly upon the young shoots and buds of the heather, also upon berries. They suffer much from disease in the spring, in which state they become very thin and are often picked up dead; probably this disease is caused by improper food.

When Grouse shooting first begins—the 12th of August—the birds are very tame, and large bags are often made, but they soon become very wild and shy and beating and driving tactics are then resorted to.

The birds pair early, and eggs are laid about the end of March. The nest consists of a slight hollow scratched in the ground and scantily lined with a few scraps of heather and moss. It is usually placed in the heather. Seebohm says: "The edge of a patch of moor where the heath has been burnt off a year or two previously is a favourite place, and an oasis of heather which has escaped the general conflagration is a still more likely locality to find the nest of a Grouse".

The eggs are usually about eight or nine in number, but are often more or less than this, and are some of the handsomest British eggs we can have. The ground colour is buffish or light olive, blotched and mottled all over with rich amber brown.

The plumage of the Red Grouse is very handsome. Its general colour is chestnut brown, the feathers

being beautifully marked with fine black pencillings.
The legs and feet are covered with greyish white
feathers, and as with the Ptarmigan there is a similar
patch of bare red skin over the eye.

The Red Grouse can be kept in confinement and
has been known to breed under these circumstances.

BLACK GROUSE.

TETRAO TETRIX.

Family PHASIANIDÆ. Genus TETRAO.

Black Cock—Heath Cock—Black Game—Birch Hen (female)—
Grey Hen.

The Black Cock, formerly resident in all suitable
districts of Great Britain, is now chiefly confined to
the North. However, it is resident in some districts
of the South, such as the New Forest, and in various
other parts has been re-introduced, though in many
of these it is decreasing.

The Black Grouse differs considerably in its habits
and locality from its namesake the Red Grouse. It
is not a bird of the open heath, but prefers the lower
parts of the hill sides which abound in plantations of
birches and firs. The tracts of country covered with
bushes and uncultivated vegetation are its home, and
if it is seen on the open moors it is always near the
edge where it can quickly retire to the cover near at
hand if surprised. Unlike the Red Grouse this bird
frequently perches in trees, and also roosts in them.
Its food is varied—the young shoots of the heather
when they can be obtained, at other times berries of
various kinds, ants and their eggs, grain and seeds.

. The Black Cock does not pair in the strict sense
of the word. The cocks are very pugnacious in the
breeding season and fight for the hens, just as is the
case with domestic fowls, the victorious ones gaining
possession of many wives. The eggs are laid in a
hollow scratched in the ground and lined thinly with
such scraps as are near at hand, a few sticks of heather
or leaves and a little moss. The nest is generally
well hidden beneath a bramble or under a thick clump
of bracken or heather. The eggs are laid later than
those of the preceding species. They may be found
about the beginning of May, and are six to ten in
number, buff in ground colour, spotted and blotched
with rich brown. They are much larger than eggs of
the Red Grouse, and are not so thickly marked as a
rule. Morris says that the female does not breed
until she is three years old. These birds have often
been known to interbreed with the Capercaillie, Red
Grouse, Pheasant and even with domestic fowls.

The male Black Cock is a handsome bird. The
general colour is a shining black, toning into brown-

ish black on the wings, which are also mingled with white.   Over the eye there is a bare piece of scarlet-coloured skin.

PHEASANT.

PHASIANUS COLCHICUS.

Family PHASIANIDÆ. Genus PHASIANUS.

The Pheasant is not a native bird in the British Isles, but was introduced from the East at some early period in our history before the Norman Conquest. It is distributed throughout the British Isles. It has never really become acclimatised, and consequently

a great deal of trouble is taken by the keepers to rear
the birds and preserve them through the winter,
otherwise a large number would perish annually
through the severity of the climate and the insuf-
ficiency of proper food. If left to themselves to breed,
many of the young birds perish through the dampness
of the ground at nights and other causes, so that in
April and May we find keepers scouring the copses
and undergrowth in all directions for Pheasants' eggs.
Around us, in Hampshire, farm hands and others are
paid a shilling a nest for every one they give information
about to a keeper, provided the nest is found on their
farm land, and not in a place where they have been
trespassing to search for it. The eggs are taken by the
keeper and placed under domestic hens, and the young
are reared in coops with the foster-mother, exactly like
ordinary chicks. Many thousands are reared around
us in this way, and the result is that the young
Pheasants become quite tame, coming to the keeper's
call for their food; and when the shooting season
commences the birds are shot down in great numbers,
until the sound of the gun and the sight of the dogs
teach them to become wary and shy. The keeper's
" pheasantry "—if I may coin a word—is an interesting place with its numbers of coops and hundreds of
little birds running about in front of them, and the
old foster-mothers within clucking and displaying all
the anxiety that they do with a brood of their own
species. Numbers, however, are of course never
found by the keepers and take their chance in the
open.

The haunts of the Pheasant are the covers and
copses in the well-wooded parts of our islands. They
are shy birds by nature, and do not care for the open.

They are essentially ground birds, seldom flying unless
compelled, preferring to travel with their legs rather
than with their wings. They run with great swiftness,
and when they take to the wing their flight is low and
noisy, though fairly rapid. The food of these birds
is varied: young shoots, grain, worms, insects and
berries. Their note is a harsh croak, which is often
heard in the evening when the birds are retiring to
roost in the trees, and is a sure guide to the wily
poacher with his air gun or slipnoose.

The bird makes a very scanty nest, nearly always
on the ground beneath the shelter of some bramble
or fern. Just a few leaves or bits of dead bracken and
grass are scraped together, and on these from eight
to twelve eggs are laid, sometimes more. They are
unspotted, but vary much in colour; some are light
brown, others light green, others again nearly white.

In the last year I came upon no less than three
nests in each of which there was a mixture of Partridges' and Pheasants' eggs. In all three cases a
Partridge was sitting. I ascertained from the keeper
that eggs had not been placed there. Do the
Pheasants around us, by some process of evolution,
begin to recognise that a foster-mother is necessary?
But I notice that other writers have come across
similar instances. Eggs of the Pheasant have also
been found in Wild Ducks' nests; and the Pheasant
will sometimes mate with other species of game birds
and with the domestic fowl.*

The Cock Pheasant rejoices in the most beautiful

---

* The birds do not pair, and in the breeding season some
half-dozen females belong to one male; as soon as the eggs
are laid the cock bird thinks no more about his wives or his
future offspring.

and brilliant plumage : the metallic green, blue and violet colours mingling with the gold and copper and forming a splendid combination, while the long tail adds grace to what would otherwise appear a rather clumsy bird.

COMMON PARTRIDGE.

PERDIX CINEREA.

Genus PERDIX.

A resident bird in all the game districts of the British Isles. It is a much hardier bird than the Pheasant, and consequently is not nursed to the

same extent.   In our county the Partridges are left
entirely to themselves to rear their broods, care being
taken by the keepers to guard their nests and themselves from poachers.

The Partridge is found in well-cultivated districts,
and although it is not a bird of the woods and covers,
but rather of the open fields and meadows, yet it is
not abundant where there are not plenty of hedges to
afford it protection in the breeding season.

In their daily habits Partridges form a very happy
family.   The old birds and their young are constantly
together, frequenting the same feeding-ground, running
together and flying away together if disturbed, while
at night they roost together on the ground, nestling up
in a clump with their heads turned outwards.   The
birds always prefer to run rather than fly, and if
alarmed by the approach of the sportsman will crouch
flat upon the ground, their dusky colour rendering
them so indistinguishable from the soil that they often
escape their destroyer.   They scarcely ever perch upon
trees.

Their flight is rapid, the birds shooting away with
a loud whir-r-ring of the wings, which has more than
once alarmed a passing horse, so startling is the noise
when unexpected.

Partridges pair in April, and remain paired for life,
which is generally too short for one or both of these
sociable and devoted birds.   Eggs are laid in May, ten
to twenty in number, though sometimes many more
are found in a nest; this is probably, however, the
result of two birds laying in the same place.   The eggs
are unspotted and are pale brown in colour, though
they go through the same variations of colour as the
Pheasant's.   The nest is on the ground, generally

beneath the shelter of a hedge or low bush, but sometimes in the open fields amongst the long grass or by
the roadside. It consists of a mere hollow in the
ground, lined with a few leaves and bits of grass.

Partridges are very regular in their feeding habits.
The middle of the day is their principal feeding-time,
when they resort to the turnip fields and roots for
maggots or for the green tops. They also feed upon
grain, insects, ants and their eggs, and berries.

They are very fond of dusting themselves, probably
to get rid of the numerous parasitical insects which
often infest them.

These birds seem very fearless in the breeding
season, sitting so close as to frequently allow themselves to be touched before they will leave the nest;
possibly they rely on the protective colour of their
plumage to escape detection. Montague relates that
one allowed itself, and eggs, to be deposited in a hat,
and thus carried off unresistingly in captivity, where
it continued to sit until the young ones were hatched.

We had a nest, two years ago, placed against the
wall of the science laboratory at Queenwood, where
boys were constantly passing and repassing at all
hours of the day. By opening a window one could
put one's hand on the eggs. The bird, knowing her
movements were watched, carefully covered her eggs
every morning with leaves, while she was laying, until
there were nine in the nest, when nervousness got the
better of her, and to every one's regret she deserted.

The young will run about almost as soon as hatched,
and may often be seen with the old mother in the
midst like a hen with a flock of chicks looking about
for food.

The general colour of the upper parts of the Partridge is chestnut ; the head and neck are brown ; the under parts are pale grey, growing lighter lower down. The feathers are beautifully marked with fine bars and streaks. On the belly are two large chocolate marks.

They have been made very tame in confinement.

RED-LEGGED PARTRIDGE.

PERDIX RUFA.

Family PHASIANIDÆ. Genus PERDIX.

French Partridge—Guernsey Partridge.

The Red-legged Partridge is supposed to have been introduced into England (from France probably) in the reign of Charles II. At a later date large numbers of eggs were imported by several noblemen, and the young birds when hatched were cast loose, principally in Norfolk and Suffolk, in which counties they are now abundant. The bird, however, notwithstanding the number of eggs it lays (ten to eighteen), can scarcely be said to have increased rapidly, for in many parts it is still very rare, though in the eastern and southern districts it is fairly abundant. It does not seem to have taken with our sportsmen, partly because the birds are wilder and quicker on the wing, and spread when flushed, partly because they are very loth to rise, and will run with great swiftness on the ground, often not flying until they are out of shot. Their flavour, too, when cooked is considered greatly inferior to that of the Common Partridge. In its habits it somewhat resembles the latter, frequenting the same districts, though more often seen on commons and waste lands than its namesake. It sometimes perches in trees and on hedgerows, which the Common Partridge never does, unless perchance driven to it by dogs. Its food consists largely of insects; it also feeds upon grain and seeds. The nest is placed upon the ground, and consists of a hollow scratched in the ground and rather more thickly lined than the nest of the preceding with dry grass and leaves. It has also been found several feet from the ground, as for instance on the top of a stack.

The eggs are much larger than those of the Common Partridge. They are of a dull buff ground colour, highly polished, and spotted and speckled with reddish or cinnamon brown.

It is said this bird wherever it is very abundant has almost driven out the Common Partridge, and is consequently treated like the Hawks and Crows as vermin. We, however, cannot yet corroborate this

17

so far as Hampshire is concerned, for although the French Partridge is fairly numerous, the Common Partridge is still very abundant. The French Partridge may be easily recognised by its large size and dark colour. The general colour of the upper parts is brown, head grey, throat white, upper parts of the breast brown, spotted with black, lower part slate grey, shading underneath to chestnut, beak and legs scarlet.

They have been kept in confinement, and have been known to breed in that state.

COMMON QUAIL.

COTURNIX COMMUNIS.

Family PHASIANIDÆ. Genus COTURNIX.

These birds, though such common migrants between Europe and Africa—"the numbers which cross the

Mediterranean on their way to their winter quarters in Africa being counted by millions instead of by thousands "—do not come over here in very great numbers. They arrive in May, and though scattered throughout the British Isles are most common in the South, where they occasionally remain through the winter.

Once arrived they betake themselves to the fields and meadows, where they remain, never rising to the trees, and unwilling to take to the wing unless flushed by dogs. But their whereabouts can be easily ascertained by the note of the male, which is a clear but not very loud whistle, three times repeated, and continued with little interruption during the breeding season. When flying, its movement is rapid and near the ground. Its food consists of various seeds; it also feeds upon grain and insects. The flesh is considered a great delicacy. These birds, like Partridges, are very fond of dusting themselves. Quails are extremely pugnacious birds, especially in the breeding season, and in times gone by they were kept for fighting purposes—fighting Quails affording similar sport (?) to the exhibitions of fighting cocks in later years.

The Quail is easily tamed, and Meyer relates that a person who kept some live birds had among others a Quail which had the liberty of running about his study, and in the same room a favourite setter was allowed entrance; by degrees the two animals became acquainted, and the Quail might frequently be seen to lie on the rug near the dog enjoying with him the warmth of the fire.

The nest of these birds is placed on the ground in the centre of corn fields among the growing corn, or in the middle of a meadow in the long grass. In this latter situation I found a nest last year on the 16th June, containing nine eggs which were slightly incubated. The nest resembled a Partridge's: a slight hollow in the ground lined with a few bits of grass and leaves. The eggs were a warm yellow in ground colour, with spots and small blotches of rich dark olive green. A week later a second clutch of ten found in a corn field, quite fresh, was brought me by a keeper. These were quite unlike the first clutch, the ground colour being creamy yellow, boldly blotched with large and rich dark-brown markings, and with a few spots of the same colour.

The Quail in appearance is not unlike a small Partridge. The general colour is buffish brown, barred with dark and light brown on the upper parts, and marked with pale streaks. The throat is very dark, and the under parts become almost white towards the rump.

Rarer birds of the Family Phasianidæ :—

PALLAS'S SAND GROUSE.

SYRRHAPTES PARADOXUS.

Genus SYRRHAPTES.

An accidental visitor of rare occurrence. It belongs to Central Asia. In 1863 an extraordinary immigration took place, the new comers numbering some thousands, and landing in the eastern counties, they soon spread all over the island. They were however soon exterminated. Another immigration occurred in 1883.

CAPERCAILLIE.

TETRAO UROGALLUS.

Genus TETRAO.

A bird which appears to have inhabited Britain in early times, and been exterminated. Being re-introduced in the present century, it still exists in and around Perthshire and Forfarshire, but in other parts the attempt has been unsuccessful. In the New Forest, for instance, the attempt was made but has not succeeded. It is much larger than any other of our game birds. The eggs are pale reddish buff, spotted finely with orange and reddish brown.

COMMON HERON.

ARDEA CINEREA.

Family PELARGIDÆ. Genus ARDEA.

Hern—Hernshaw—Heronseugh—Crested Heron.

A bird which is now locally distributed throughout the British Islands, and which owing to incessant persecution is greatly thinned in numbers. Formerly, when falconry was the ruling sport, these birds were very strictly preserved, being considered the peculiar game of royalty and nobility, and very stringent penalties were passed upon any one interfering with them. In those days they were common birds. As the greater part of the Heron's food consists of fish, the bird is usually found in the vicinity of water. It may frequently be seen standing in the shallows of a lake or river, some distance from the shore, waiting still and motionless until some passing fish gives it

the opportunity it has been expecting.   Darting its
sharp-pointed bill into the water with unerring aim,
it seizes its prey, and swallows it head first ; the indi-
gestible parts being afterwards cast up in pellets as
with the Owls.   The Heron also feeds upon reptiles,
frogs, mice, young water fowl and small birds.   Most
of its food is obtained at night.   Its flight is laboured

COMMON HERON.

but fast, and when on the wing the bird may be heard
uttering its harsh cry.   In flying it trails its long legs
behind it in the air, and no doubt they assist it to
steer its course.   Though not strictly speaking gregarious birds, Herons build in communities, like Rooks.
The nests are built in the tops of high trees, Scotch
firs most commonly perhaps, and are large flat struc-

tures made of sticks, and lined with twigs and sometimes moss. The nests are repaired every year.

Herons are very early breeders and eggs may be
found by the first week in March, but frequently in
February; they are three in number, but sometimes
four or five, of a uniform pale bluish green colour.
We are said to have a larger number of Heronries in
Hampshire than in any other English county except
Norfolk. Single nests of these birds are occasionally
found, and its nest has also been met with on the
ground.*

The predominating colours of the Heron are slate
grey and white; to these black is added in a lesser
degree in various parts.

Rarer birds of the Family Pelargidæ :—

PURPLE HERON.

ARDEA PURPUREA.

Genus ARDEA.

An accidental straggler to our shores, chiefly to the
southern and eastern counties of England, though it
has been obtained in Scotland and Ireland.

---

* There is a popular belief amongst country folk that these
birds when sitting hang their long legs over the side of the
nests. Mr. Young in the *Zoologist*, 1884, p. 192, states that
a man who had every opportunity of seeing for himself, gravely
assured him that the birds made holes in the bottoms of the
nests through which they put their legs !

GREAT WHITE EGRET.

ARDEA ALBA.

Genus ARDEA.

White Heron.　An accidental straggler of rarer occurrence than the bird last named.　Has been obtained about a score of times, chiefly in the eastern counties of England and Scotland.

LITTLE EGRET.

ARDEA GARZETTA.

Genus ARDEA.

A very rare accidental visitor, which has occurred probably less than a dozen times in the present century.

SQUACCO HERON.

ARDEA COMATA.

Genus ARDEA.

A rare straggler.　It has been obtained in several of the southern and eastern counties, also two or three times in Ireland.

BUFF-BACKED HERON.

ARDEA BUBULCUS.

Genus ARDEA.

Has been obtained three times in England.

NIGHT HERON.

NYCTICORAX NYCTICORAX.

Genus NYCTICORAX.

It has been obtained some fifty or sixty times, and visits chiefly the southern and eastern counties of England. According to Hart it has nested in Hampshire.

BITTERN.

BOTAURUS STELLARIS.

Genus BOTAURUS.

Mire Drum—Bog Jumper.

An accidental winter visitor. Formerly it was resident in our islands, and some century or two ago was a common bird, but the draining of the marshes has driven it from us, and the guns of specimen hunters and others have cleared off the rest. Possibly a few may still breed in the fen district. From its skulking propensities, its habits have not been so completely studied as most birds'. It hardly ever takes to the wing, remaining hidden in the rushes throughout its stay here. In these it builds its nest of dead reeds. It is very difficult to reach the nest. The eggs resemble very large Pheasant's eggs. It feeds chiefly upon fish, frogs, and water insects.

AMERICAN BITTERN.

BOTAURUS LENTIGINOSUS.

Genus BOTAURUS.

A rare accidental visitor, generally in the autumn. Driven over by the westerly gales when migrating.

LITTLE BITTERN.

BOTAURUS MINUTUS.

Genus BOTAURUS.

An occasional rare summer visitor, though probably it has never bred here.

SPOONBILL.

PLATALEA LEUCORODIA.

Genus PLATALEA.

A bird which was formerly a regular summer visitor to us and bred in the fen districts; now it is only an accidental visitor on its migration.

GLOSSY IBIS.

IBIS FALCINELLUS.

Genus IBIS.

An accidental visitor, chiefly to the South and East. Numerous instances of this and the last-mentioned species are recorded from the New Forest.

WHITE STORK.

CICONIA ALBA.

Genus CICONIA.

An occasional visitor, which does not easily escape notice when it pays us a visit. It has been most frequently observed in southern and eastern counties. Several, of late years, have been observed in Hampshire: one at Christchurch in 1884, one near Farnham, 1882, one at Bedhampton, 1887, and two at Hayling, 1887. "Some of these may have escaped from the Isle of Wight, where they are kept in captivity." ·

BLACK STORK.

CICONIA NIGRA.

Genus CICONIA.

A much less frequent visitor than the last-mentioned species.

CORN CRAKE.

CREX PRATENSIS.

Family RALLIDÆ. Genus CREX.

Land Rail—Daker Hen—Meadow Crake.

The Corn Crake is a summer visitor to all parts of the United Kingdom, arriving about the end of April or beginning of May, and leaving in the end of August and beginning of September.

It migrates at night, and once arrived here is more frequently heard than seen, for it betakes itself to the meadows and clover fields and seldom leaves the long grass. It is made to fly with the greatest difficulty, and were it not for its peculiar harsh cry of "crake, crake; crake, crake," we should scarcely know that we had the bird amongst us. Yarrell says this note or call may be exactly imitated by passing the edge of the thumb nail, or a piece of wood, briskly along the line of the points of a small comb; in fact, so well does this imitate it, that the bird itself may be decoyed by it. Meyer relates that he has enticed the bird by winding and unwinding the reel on his fishing rod. It seems to be the male bird which utters the call.

Its food consists of worms, slugs and snails, beetles, insects, various seeds and young grass shoots. The Corn Crake threads its way with wonderful

CORN CRAKE.

quickness and dexterity through the long grass and in and out of the bottoms of tangled hedgerows; if you attempt to track it down by following its cry as it hurries away or doubles back to escape you, you will but find yourself engaged in a fruitless chase. It is a very cunning bird, and if captured will frequently resort to some trick or other to effect its escape. It has even been known on one or two occasions to feign death. In corroboration of this Jesse relates the following anecdote: "A gentleman had a Corn Crake brought him by his dog, to all appearance lifeless. As it lay on the ground he turned it over with his foot, and felt convinced that it was dead. Standing by, however, in silence, he suddenly saw it open an eye; he then took it up, its head fell, its legs hung loose, and it again appeared quite dead. He then put it in his pocket, but, before long, he felt it all alive, and struggling to escape. He then took it out; it was as lifeless as before. Having laid it again on the ground, and retired to some distance, the bird, in about five minutes, warily raised its head, looked around, and decamped at full speed." The body of this bird is very high on its legs; it has a long neck and large head. The plumage is very handsome, the upper parts being yellowish grey, each feather having a blackish brown centre, the wings are brownish red, spotted with yellowish white, under parts slate grey, shading into buffish white.

The nest is placed in the meadows or sometimes in a corn field; several nests are often found in the same field. It is built of dry herbage, stalks and grass, placed in a slight hollow in the ground, and lined with finer grass.

The eggs, seven to ten, are buffish or creamy white in ground colour, spotted and blotched with reddish brown and purplish grey marks. They are very similar to eggs of the Water Rail, but are generally more thickly marked.

The Land Rail is considered a very delicate and savoury article of food. It can be kept in confinement.

SPOTTED CRAKE.

CREX PORZANA.

Family RALLIDÆ. Genus CREX.

Jacky-mo.

The Spotted Crake is a summer visitor to the
marshy and swampy districts of the British Isles,
though in some instances it may remain through the
winter. It is not however a common bird, and from
its skulking habits, which, in common with the other
Crakes, it adopts on arriving upon our shores, it is
possibly considered even more rare than it really is.

In its habits it closely resembles the succeeding
species, the Water Rail, both birds frequenting the
same marshes and swampy districts ; they both nest
in the reeds, and the nests are very similar in their
construction. When compelled to take wing, they
both adopt the same heavy, uncertain, laboured flight,
with their long legs trailing beneath them ; indeed to
any one who has witnessed the apparent difficulty
with which these birds fly, it is a mystery how they
ever manage to cross the sea.

The Spotted Crake feeds upon water insects, worms,
slugs and seeds. Its flesh is said to be considered a
great delicacy. It can be kept in confinement, and
has been made fairly tame.

The general colour of the upper plumage of the
Spotted Crake is olive brown, the feathers having dark
centres and being spotted at the edge with white :
the under parts are slate grey shading into white and
buff, the flanks being barred with black.

Though there is no doubt that these birds breed in
some of our marshes, yet it is no common thing to

find their nest, and any instances should be made a note of. The nest is built in a clump of reeds near the surface of the water, and is made of leaves of the reeds and sedges.

The eggs, eight to twelve, are buff or greenish white in ground colour, boldly blotched and spotted with dark and reddish brown, and underlying markings of pale violet. They may be found at the end of May or beginning of June. The markings on these eggs are much bolder and larger than those on any other of our Crakes'.

WATER RAIL.

RALLUS AQUATICUS.

Family RALLIDÆ. Genus RALLUS.

Bilcock—Skiddycock—Brook Runner—Velvet Runner.

The Water Rail, though a commoner bird than the last species, is not very abundant anywhere. It is a resident bird, though a large number migrate every year as well. It is commonest perhaps in the fen districts, but is found in all parts where there are large marshes. It is so extremely shy and retiring that it appears to be more rare than it really is. Its retreat is among the reeds and sedges, or tangled dank grass through which it threads its way more like a rat than a bird. It feeds upon worms, young frogs, and such insects as are found about the marshes. As previously mentioned, its habits resemble those of the Spotted Crake very closely, and its flight is that of a bird anxious to alight at the first opportunity. It is about the same size as the Land Rail, but differs in its plumage. On the back it is a golden yellow, the

feathers having a black centre; the head and breast
are bluish grey, changing lower down to white, barred
with black. It seems almost impossible to tame the
Water Rail, but it can be kept in confinement. Meyer
gives an interesting account of one which he had for
several years; this had been found in a nest in a hen-
house where it had doubtless gone for shelter from
the stormy weather; it became perfectly reconciled

WATER RAIL.

to captivity, but never became tame enough to feed
when watched, unless perchance tempted by some
special dainty, such as a small frog.

The nest is placed among reeds and rushes, and is
usually made of the same materials; it is carefully
concealed and very difficult to find. We were fortunate enough to come upon one in the Test when
swimming one day, and floundering about in the mud

of a large reed bed searching for Water Hens' nests. It was built of reeds, but also contained a large amount of coarse dry grass. The bird slipped off her nest, and we only just caught a glimpse of it, as it hurried away through the reeds more like a water rat than anything else.

The eggs, five to seven, sometimes more, resemble to some extent the eggs of the Land Rail; but are not so thickly spotted, and are generally slightly smaller. They are buffish or greenish white in ground colour, spotted with reddish brown and violet grey.

WATER HEN.

GALLINULA CHLOROPUS.

Family RALLIDÆ. Genus GALLINULA.

Moor Hen—Gallinule—Marsh Hen.

The Water Hen is a common resident throughout the British Isles. Hardly a river, lake, or large pond but has its pair of birds; and in many cases so domesticated have they become that they will feed with the poultry, and trouble little at any one's approach. Water Hens and Coots differ much in their habits from the other members of this family, for although in their wild state shy birds, they are frequently seen in the open, either in the meadows or on the river banks, or more often still on the water itself. The Water Hen is an expert and graceful swimmer though not web-footed, bobbing its head backwards and forwards with each stroke of its legs. It can dive and swim beneath the surface for a long distance.

Their food is very varied; water insects, worms,

slugs, seeds, young buds and shoots all form part of their fare. They fly heavily, with their legs trailing below their bodies.

The Moor Hen is a dark-plumaged bird. Its general colour is dark olive brown ; head and neck slate grey ; under parts also slate grey, shading into brown ; the

WATER HEN.

forehead is scarlet, as also is the bill, shading into yellow at the tip.

The Moor Hen is an early breeder, and eggs may be looked for in the beginning of April. Two and often three broods are reared in the year. The nest is placed amidst the reeds and sedges, and is usually well concealed. It is frequently built floating on the water,

but often on a bank or supported by the low branch
of a tree. It is a very abundant bird around us on
the various streams and tributaries of the Test, and
scarcely a year passes without some of our young
naturalists finding the nest of this bird at some distance from the ground in a tree; it is not, it would
seem, an uncommon position for it, but it does seem
strange that a water bird should choose such an one.
The nest is constructed of reeds and flags and coarse
grass, and is a large structure.

The Water Hen, when it is breeding, displays great
cunning. I have often, when searching the reeds,
heard a splash where some bird has dived, and on
searching around the spot have at length discovered
the nest several yards away from where the bird
entered the water; seeming as though the bird ran
some way along the bank before she made the splash.
When alarmed like this they will sometimes remain a
long time beneath the surface with only the beak
above water to enable them to breathe. Hewitson
writes : " I once came very suddenly upon a Water Hen,
which dived on my approach ; and whilst I was leaning
over a hedge close upon the margin of the brook,
wondering that it did not again make its appearance
from below, I found that it had approached the surface
of the water, and protruding its bill alone to breathe,
remained entirely submerged ; it was then very near
me, and as long as I remained perfectly still, and that
was for some minutes, it did the same ; but the
moment I moved and broke the spell, the fascination
seemed to paralyse its movements—for it watched me
intently the whole time—it made another rapid somerset, and rose again some distance down the stream ".

The eggs of the Water Hen resemble very large

Corn Crake's eggs. They are buffish or creamy white in ground colour, generally with a slight reddish tinge, spotted and blotched with reddish brown and violet grey. On some eggs the markings are much larger and bolder than on others.

COMMON COOT.

FULICA ATRA.

Family RALLIDÆ. Genus FULICA.

Bald Coot.

The Coot is distributed throughout the British Islands, but is not so common as the Water Hen. It is a resident bird, but its numbers are increased in the winter by large migrations. About two miles from our home in Hampshire is a large piece of water, one half open, the other half covered by a big bed of reeds. On this piece of water quite a large number of Coots have made their homes, and the water always goes by the name of the "Coot Pond". It is in such places as this that the Coot is most likely to be met with, or in the neighbourhood of lakes, broads, and slow-running rivers.

Though more often seen on the water than on land, the Coot is quite at home when on shore, and can run and walk with ease, but its legs being placed so far back, it has rather an ungainly appearance. In many of its habits it resembles the Water Hen; it dives with great celerity, can swim for a long distance under water, and clinging to a reed with its feet will remain there for some time with its beak above the surface to get air. If alarmed the bird will sometimes run along the surface of the water, flapping its wings with a great noise and a deal of splashing.

Its food consists of small fish, water insects, worms, slugs, grain, seeds, young buds, and a great quantity of grass.

The general colour of the Coot is dark slate grey, almost black; there is a white bar across the wings, and a white patch on the forehead. It is a much larger bird than the Water Hen.

The Coot's nest is a very massive structure; it is generally built floating on the water and extends some distance below the surface; it is placed amongst the reeds, to which it is cleverly fastened in such a way as to allow for a rise or fall in the water. It is composed of flags and coarse reeds and lined with finer leaves of the same. Sometimes, however, it is built upon the land, close to the edge of the water.

The eggs, six to twelve, are of a yellowish or greyish stone colour, spotted and speckled with dark brown. When breeding, Coots are very jealous of their own ·

privacy, resenting the intrusion of other birds, and have been known to kill indiscriminately young Ducks and other small water birds that dare to venture near their haunts. The young of both this species and the Water Hen leave the nest and take to the water very shortly after they are hatched.

The Coot can be kept in confinement, providing that a sufficiency of water is obtainable.

Rarer birds of the Family Rallidæ :—

BAILLON'S CRAKE.

CREX BAILLONI.

Genus CREX.

A resident bird, but very rare indeed. It probably breeds every year in the fen districts of Cambridge and Norfolk, but its nests are so inaccessible that they are not often discovered.

LITTLE CRAKE.

CREX PARRA.

Genus CREX.

A rare accidental visitor to the British Isles. It has chiefly been observed in England.

Birds of the Family Gruidæ :—

COMMON CRANE.

GRUS CINEREA.

Genus GRUS.

Until within the last three hundred years, Cranes seem to have migrated to this country annually and bred in the fen districts. It is now only an accidental straggler, chiefly to the southern and eastern counties.

DEMOISELLE CRANE.

GRUS VIRGO.

Genus GRUS.

A straggler which had been observed two or three times.

STONE CURLEW.

ŒDICNEMUS CREPITANS.

Family OTIDIDÆ. Genus ŒDICNEMUS.

Thick-knee—Norfolk Plover—Great Plover—Stone Plover.

The Stone Curlew derives its name of Thick-knee from the knee-joints being very thick, and of Norfolk

Plover from its being found most abundantly on the sandy plains of Norfolk and Suffolk, particularly near the sea coast. It is a summer visitor to us from May to September, and strictly a local one; breeding in some of the southern and midland counties, in addition to the eastern ones. It frequents downs, commons and sheep-walks; the bare uncultivated districts are its haunts, and it is never found in wooded parts.

Unfortunately, this bird is undoubtedly, year by year, becoming scarcer in this country, and its days seem numbered. Mr. Ogilvie writes in the *Zoologist*, 1891, p. 441 : "A few years ago the district of which I write had twenty pairs where now scarcely one can be found, and this notwithstanding the fact that, except in a few instances, they have not been persecuted or molested. This, I believe, is partially owing to the larger number of cattle kept on the heathy commons or moorlands to which they resort, and which, no doubt, with their attendant herdsmen, disturb and frighten them, and also to the destruction of their eggs by Rooks. The amount of damage a Rook does during the 'egging time' is simply incalculable. Nothing in the shape of eggs comes curious to him— fresh, rotten, or just on the point of hatching; all are devoured. I have watched Rooks early in April hunting the meadows for the unfortunate Peewit's eggs, quartering the ground with the regularity of well-trained setters; and again in May, in the early mornings, searching the commons and hedgerows for Partridges' nests. When once a nest is found, woe to the owner thereof, for the robber does his work thoroughly, and leaves behind him but a few egg-shells. The eggs are generally carried away to a distance, but I have seen Peewits' eggs sucked *in situ*, while the wretched parents were screaming overhead."

It is a very shy bird, and when disturbed endeavours to hide itself by crouching on the ground, and if followed will try to escape by running, only attempting to fly if closely pressed. "And jist can't he run!" was the remark of a country lad who brought one of our number some eggs of this bird one season. The Thick-knee flies about at night in search of food or water, and we have frequently heard its cry of " Cur-lui" on our downs in the dusk of evening, said by the poor people to be a sign of rain.

It eats worms, frogs, lizards, mice, insects, and sometimes small eggs.

The upper plumage of the Stone Curlew is reddish grey, the feathers having darker centres of blackish brown; the brow, neck and patch over the eyes, white; the under parts are yellowish white, spotted with dark brown on the breast; quills black, the tail feathers bordered with black and white at their side. There is a yellowish white bar on the upper wing.

The Thick-knee when confined can be easily tamed, and it is said to live to a great age. Eggs may be looked for in May. There is absolutely no attempt at building a nest; a small cavity scratched in the ground serves the purpose, and in this, right out in the open where the bird can have an easy view of an enemy's approach while sitting, two eggs are laid. These are more oval in form than the majority of Plovers' eggs: they are about the size of a hen's egg, and of a light brown or warm stone colour, streaked and blotched with dark brown and other greyer tints. They are very difficult to find among the flints lying loose on the sandy soil, their protective colour rendering them almost invisible to one looking straight at them. The young are able to leave the nest about twelve hours after being hatched. They somewhat resemble eggs of the Oyster Catcher, but are smaller and not so darkly or boldly marked.

Other rarer birds of the Family Otididæ :—

GREAT BUSTARD.

OTIS TARDA.

Genus OTIS.

A bird which formerly was resident in England, and probably frequented the open stretches of the eastern counties and the downs of the South, as in other countries it is never found near woods. It is now an accidental winter straggler. In the winter of 1879-80 some eight or nine of these large birds visited us; no other occurrences are noted till the winter of 1890-91, when seven specimens were obtained. The Great Bustard is said to stand from three to four feet high and to weigh from 15 lbs. to 30 lbs.

LITTLE BUSTARD.

OTIS TETRAX.

Genus OTIS.

An accidental visitor of occasional occurrence.

OYSTER CATCHER.

HŒMATOPUS OSTRALEGUS.

Family CHARADRIIDÆ. Genus HŒMATOPUS.

Sea-pie—Olive—Shelder—Pied Oyster Catcher.

The Oyster Catcher is a resident bird with us, but numbers also arrive for the winter from Europe. When migrating they fly in the shape of a huge V, one bird leading the way. It is essentially a coast bird, yet it is often found on the shores of large rivers and lakes and occasionally in other inland localities. It prefers the rocky and unfrequented coasts, and in other parts is rare. On the coast of Norfolk it is a common bird, and the higher North we go the more abundant does it become.

The Oyster Catcher is a sociable bird, and they are often seen in small parties on the beach. They breed too in numbers close together, and also in the neighbourhood of gulls and other sea-birds, though not in the same situation.

The Oyster Catcher has been provided by nature with a wonderfully suitable bill for procuring its food.

Flattened sideways and particularly hard and strong, it is singularly adapted to scooping out the flesh of the various shell-fish on which it feeds.   Whelks, mussels, limpets and such like are its favourite food, together with sand-worms and small fish.   Its flight is very powerful, and it is also capable of swimming, and when wounded by a shot will often take to the water; but it is not so much at home here as when flying or running, which it does with great quickness.

The plumage of the Oyster Catcher is very handsome. The upper parts are black except the rump, which is white; the under parts are white, and there is a white bar across the wings. The eggs are laid in a hollow in the shingly beach, just above high-water mark; less frequently in the sands. This hollow is lined with scraps of shells and pebbles, which the bird seems to have great difficulty in arranging to its taste. It seems frequently to construct several nests before it arranges one to its liking. In this nest some time in May three or rarely four eggs are laid, cream or buff coloured, blotched, spotted and streaked with dark brown, and underlying markings of grey. They resemble occasionally eggs of the Stone Curlew, but are generally larger and darker; and the structure of the nest of course, if observed, would always settle the difficulty.

The Oyster Catcher can be made very tame if taken young, and will live and roost quite happily with the ducks and fowls of the farm-yard.

RINGED PLOVER.

CHARADRIUS HIATICULA.

Family CHARADRIIDÆ. Genus CHARADRIUS.

Ringed Dotterel—Shell Turner—Wideawake—Stone-
runner—Stonehatch.

The Ringed Plover is one of the commonest of our
coast birds, and perhaps, if we except the Dunlin, with
which species it is frequently found in company, is the
most numerous of all.   It is a resident bird in the
British Isles, its numbers being increased in the autumn
by migrations.   It is most commonly found on the
sandy coast, but is also found less numerously some
distance inland on the sand banks and flats of our
large rivers and lakes.

The Ringed Plover is a handsome little bird.   Grey
is the colour of the upper parts and white of the under
parts ; there is a white ring round the neck, bordered
with two narrow black rings above and below which
broaden out around the eyes and on the breast.

It is shy and wary, and when its nest is approached
will run some little distance along the ground before

it gets up. It will also occasionally feign lameness to draw off the intruder's attention.

Its food consists principally of shrimps, sea-worms, beetles and a large number of insects that frequent the seashore. It runs with great ease and swiftness, and is a pretty sight as it darts over the sands, pausing frequently to catch some insect and then hurrying on a few steps farther, reminding one somewhat of the Wagtails in its movements.

The Ringed Plover makes no nest, but lays its eggs in a small hollow which it scratches in the sand, or occasionally in the shingle. In Norfolk it is known as the Stonehatch from a habit it has of sometimes lining the hollow with small pebbles. This, however, is by no means a common practice. The breeding season commences in April, and numbers of the birds usually breed close together.

The eggs, four in number, are very large in proportion to the size of the bird. They possess the peculiar pointed shape at the small end common to birds of this family, and are usually laid with these pointed ends placed inwards. The colour of the eggs much resembles the surroundings among which they are placed; buffish or stone colour forms the ground colour of the egg, spotted and streaked with black and dark grey.

It can be easily kept in confinement, being of a very hardy nature.

DOTTEREL.

CHARADRIUS MORINELLUS.

Family CHARADRIIDÆ. Genus CHARADRIUS.

Dotterel—Dotterel Plover—Foolish Dotterel.

The Dotterel is a summer visitor to our country, and not a common one. It arrives at the end of April or beginning of May. Its haunts are the barren uncultivated wastes; and on the tops of the highest mountains it builds its nest. It is doubtful whether it breeds often in England now; though formerly it did so on the loftiest mountains of the Lake district and probably occasionally does so still. Its favourite breeding places now are in the wildest and most mountainous districts of Scotland.

It is not at all a shy bird, and frequently allows one to approach within a few yards of it; hence it has obtained the name of "foolish Dotterel". It has suffered much persecution from specimen hunters and sportsmen, for its flesh is capital eating. Its feathers are also said to be eagerly sought after to make artificial flies for fishing purposes.

It feeds upon beetles and other insects ; also worms and grubs. It is a very handsome bird; the upper parts are greyish brown, head dark brown, throat white ; breast greyish brown, bordered beneath with a broad white belt; below this the colour is a rich chestnut, shading into black and again into buffish white beneath the tail.

The nest is said to be a mere hollow in the ground on the highest mountain tops, with a few scraps of moss or lichen placed in it.

The eggs are of a buff ground colour slightly tinged with olive, thickly spotted and blotched with blackish brown and dark grey.

The bird can be tamed but will not live long in confinement.

GOLDEN PLOVER.

CHARADRIUS PLUVIALIS.

Family CHARADRIIDÆ.   Genus CHARADRIUS.

Yellow Plover—Whistling Plover.

The Golden Plover is distributed throughout the British Isles during the winter, when its numbers are increased by very large migrations from Northern Europe.   In the breeding season it retires to the open heaths and moors of the North, where it is fairly abundant.   It is partial to swampy ground, and, as it constantly washes its feathers, water seems a necessity to it.   In the winter these birds collect into large flocks, many thousands in number, and resort to the coast, particularly the eastern counties of England, and marshes, where they obtain their food on the mud flats and sand banks. This consists of small marine animals, and of insects, worms, slugs, etc. They feed principally at night time. The flesh of the Golden Plover is considered very good eating, being in perfection in September and October; consequently large numbers are shot for the table.

These birds may be easily recognised by their slender beaks and feet, pointed wings and golden plumage. In

GOLDEN PLOVER.

the breeding season the feathers on the upper part of the body are black, thickly covered with small green or golden yellow spots ; the entire under side is black.

Few birds vary so much in their spring and autumn plumage. In the autumn the throat and breast become spotted with yellowish grey, belly white ; the black tail feathers are streaked with white, and the black throat has a white stripe.

The Golden Plover is very wary if her nest is ap-

19

proached, and will slip off the nest and run some distance before rising from the ground. It is a very active bird on the ground, tripping about with great ease. The protective colour of the eggs of all this family renders them very difficult to be found.

The nest is on the ground. A few fibres and bits of dry grass are arranged in a small hollow, and in this four eggs are laid, with the smaller ends turned inwards. They have a yellowish stone-coloured shell, blotched and spotted with brownish black and purple brown. They may be distinguished from eggs of the Lapwing by their slightly larger size, broader shape and brighter colour.

"The young ones," says Atkinson, "awkward-looking mottled yellow and brown puff-balls on stilts, run fast and well soon after they are hatched, and do not speedily acquire the use of those wings which, after a time, are to be so strong and swift. Very jealous too are the parents as long as their young are only runners, and very plaintive is their incessant piping if you or your dog approach too near their place of conceal-ment."

LAPWING.

VANELLUS CRISTATUS.

Genus VANELLUS.

Peewit—Crested Lapwing—Green Plover—Te-wit—
Teu-fit.

The Lapwing is far and away the best known of our Plovers. It is universally distributed throughout the British Isles, and many birds arrive in the autumn to increase its numbers. The Lapwing perhaps is better known as the Peewit, a name which it has obtained from its singular wailing and mournful note, which it utters on the wing and which, when heard at night, suggests something weird and uncanny.

The birds collect in large flocks in the autumn and winter and are sometimes seen in company with Rooks and Starlings; they seem sociable birds and in the

LAPWING.

breeding season several of them often breed in close proximity. At this season they become very wary and shy. If their breeding-place is approached the old bird will slip off, and running some distance will then rise into the air and commence circling overhead, ducking and tumbling, rising a few yards upwards and turning over sharply almost with a complete somerset, then darting down within a few yards of one, and all the time uttering her peculiar wailing "pee weety-weet" in her endeavours to draw away the intruder from her nest. So clever are these birds at leaving their nests unseen, that I have walked into a meadow where I knew numbers were breeding and not a bird was visible; no sooner had I got into the field, however, than first one was seen overhead, then another and a third until the air was soon full of their sad notes, yet never a single one did I see leave the ground. I almost believed that they watched when my back was turned. Indeed only twice have I ever been able to walk straight to the spot where I have seen a bird run and come upon the eggs. Yet it is said that so expert do men become at finding them, that they can even tell from the flight of the bird in the air the exact position of the nest. For Peewits' eggs are sent in many thousands to the London markets yearly, being considered a great delicacy, and fetch from fourpence to sixpence each; the very first eggs obtained this last season (1894) were purchased at the price of ten shillings each for the royal table at Windsor.

Peewits frequent the open and uncultivated districts; marshy and low-lying lands are favourite haunts with them. They are very active at nights and obtain most of their food in the evening. This consists of worms and snails, insects and grubs, also seed in the winter. The nest is a small hollow scratched in the ground, and scantily lined with a few bits of dry grass and bents. In this four eggs are laid, all turned towards the centre, and they vary in their colouring to quite an extraordinary degree, and also in their size. The ground colour is variously described from different specimens as yellowish olive, pale green, dull cream-coloured, pale yellowish grey, dull dark yellow, dull yellow with a tinge of red, and buffish brown. They are smeared, blotched and spotted with dark brown, grey, brownish black, and dull green. Most of the eggs are very pointed. They may be obtained through April and May.

The Peewit may be easily recognised by the black crest on his head. The general colour of the upper parts is black, shading to bronze green on the back and wings; the lower part of the head and neck are white, breast black, upper and under tail coverts pale chestnut, the rest of the under parts white.

The young leave the nest almost at once. When bathing in the Test last spring, a young Peewit some few days old, which we had captured, accidentally got in the river; we were interested to find it a most perfect little swimmer, quite seeming to enjoy it and paddling about like a young Duck.

These birds can be made very tame, and will live in a semi-domesticated state.

COMMON CURLEW.

NUMENIUS ARQUATUS.

Family CHARADRIIDÆ. Genus NUMENIUS.

Whaap—Whaup.

This fine bird is a common one on nearly all parts of our coasts in autumn and winter, retiring into the heaths and moorlands of the North at the end of March or beginning of April to breed. It also breeds in Wales and sparingly in Cornwall and Devonshire.

The Curlew frequents the marshes and mud flats which appear about the mouths of some of our rivers at low water. It is a difficult bird to observe at all times on account of its excessive shyness and wariness. It feeds chiefly upon worms, slugs and insects, and also upon small crabs and sand-worms. It has a very long curved beak—some seven or eight inches in length —with which it prods about in the soft soil to find its

COMMON CURLEW.

food. "They are more regular in repairing to their haunts than any other birds; to the minute they will desert the moors and meadows to leave for the coast. How Curlews can tell from inland fields, far from and out of sight of the tide, the exact moment to make for the shore (as if they carried watches in their pockets) is more than I can even guess at. They will arrive just as the ooze is sufficiently uncovered for them to get their food whilst wading. I have watched them whilst several miles from the tide cease feeding, call to one another, collect, and then point for the sea ; and this, too, at the very moment I knew the shallows must be nearly exposed. Spring-tides they will hit off exactly, never late, always on the spot just as the banks begin to show." Seebohm's explanation of this curious circumstance is that scouts are probably placed within sight of the shore to give the main flock notice when the tide has receded sufficiently for them to feed. They move very fast through the air and when in companies fly in two long lines, V shaped.

The feathers on the upper portion of the body are brown, edged with pale yellowish brown ; those of the lower back white, spotted with brown ; the under side, yellowish brown, streaked and spotted with dark brown. The quills are black, spotted and bordered with white, and the tail feathers are white, striped with brown.

The birds retire to the moors in the beginning of April to breed. Eggs may be found in May. The nest is simply a depression in the ground, or rather in the moss or grass, more rarely on the rough soil, and is slightly lined with a few stalks of grass or heather.

The eggs are four, very large and in colour dirty olive brown, shaded with brown and green, and variously marked with blackish brown and purplish grey.

It is not an easily tamed bird.

COMMON SANDPIPER.

TOTANUS HYPOLEUCUS.

Family CHARADRIIDÆ. Genus TOTANUS.

Summer Snipe—Sand Lark—Willy Wicket.

A summer visitor to the British Islands from April to October, but not a very numerous species. It is most common in the moorland districts of the North, where it breeds, but a few birds nest in Cornwall and Devonshire.

The Summer Snipe frequents the banks of rivers and the margins of lakes and streams. It is particularly partial to tidal rivers, where some yards of muddy banks are left as the water runs out; over this it may be seen lightly and quickly running, flirting its tail like a Wagtail, and stopping every now and then to catch a passing insect or pick up some dainty morsel left by the receding tide. Its food is almost entirely composed of worms and insects, and their larvæ. It is rarely seen on the coasts, for it seems to prefer the inland streams in their wildest parts. Its flight is rapid, and it is said to swim and dive well, but probably only when hard pressed. The Summer Snipe is a pretty little bird. Its plumage on the upper parts is sandy and greenish brown, the feathers having dark centres; the under parts are white, mingled with brown on the breast and streaked with dark brown.

These birds probably pair for life, for the same place is frequently resorted to year after year for rearing their brood. The nest is built in May, usually near the water's edge, but being very effectually concealed, it is difficult to find. It consists of a very slight hollow in the sand, for it is generally placed on the banks of the stream, lined thinly with stalks of grass and heather and a few leaves. An overhanging tuft or a small bush hides it from view.

The eggs are very large for the size of the bird, and are four in number; they are placed in the way which birds of this family adopt with their pointed ends inwards, so as to get them into the smallest space possible; "and it will be seen how necessary this arrangement is," says Hewitson, "when we take into consideration the magnitude of the egg and the small size of the bird, which is not a great deal larger than the Skylark". The eggs are yellowish or creamy white, with blotches and spots of deep brown and light brown. They closely resemble eggs of the Green Sandpiper, but as the eggs of this latter bird are not found in this country, we need not be troubled with any fear of confusion.

The bird is said to be kept in confinement without difficulty.

COMMON REDSHANK.

TOTANUS CALIDRIS.

Family CHARADRIIDÆ. Genus TOTANUS.

Redshank Sandpiper—Red-legged Sandpiper—Sandcock—
Tenke—Pool Snipe.

One of the best known birds of this family, the
Common Redshank is found on all parts of our coasts
in the autumn and winter, but in the spring and
summer it retires a little inland to breed. It is a
handsome and striking bird with its bright orange-red
legs and feet. The upper parts are dark brown,
streaked and spotted with yellowish grey ; the under
parts are white, streaked with dark brown.

The Redshank is a resident bird in the British Isles,

but like many other birds that breed in swampy places, it has become less numerous than in former years, since so much marsh land has been reclaimed. Its numbers, however, are largely increased by autumn migrations. It feeds upon worms, insects, and small marine animals.

The breeding-places of the Redshank are the open swamps and salt marshes not far from the sea; many birds often retire farther inland. The nest is placed upon the ground and is usually carefully concealed beneath some tuft of herbage or bunch of heather. It consists of simply a few bits of grass and moss or heather placed in a slight hollow in the ground.

The eggs are four in number, cream colour or rich buff in ground colour, spotted and blotched with rich dark brown and with underlying markings of grey. Several of the nests of this bird may be found in close proximity.

The Redshank is at all times a shy and wary bird, and when its young are hatched it becomes excessively anxious. Atkinson says: "When the young are newly hatched the parent birds betray excessive jealousy and anxiety at the approach of either man or dog to their resort. They have sometimes come and settled on the ground within two or three paces of me, and, at others, flown so directly towards me, piping most plaintively and incessantly the while. This conduct is designated by the term 'mobbing' on the Essex marshes."

The bird is said to be easily kept in confinement.

GREENSHANK.

TOTANUS GLOTTIS.

Family CHARADRIIDÆ. Genus TOTANUS.

Cinereous Godwit—Green-legged Horseman.

Although possibly some of our young readers may meet with this bird, yet they are scarcely likely to meet with its nest and eggs, for it only breeds locally in a very few spots, principally in the Highlands of Scotland and the Hebrides; consequently a short notice is all that is necessary.

To our English coasts the Greenshank is a summer visitor, though not at all abundant, and on its arrival it begins to work its way inland immediately for the high moorlands and heaths, especially in the vicinity of water. It is most partial to the low-lying and flat coasts of the eastern counties.

It is an extremely shy and wary bird; so much so that it is said it will rise in the air and begin calling loudly before the observer is within half a mile of it. Meyer says that the only way to get it within range of a gun is by placing a stuffed bird of the same species on the ground and hiding oneself, when a live Greenshank will probably be attracted, as they are of a very sociable nature among one another.

They feed chiefly upon insects and worms; also, it is said, on small fish and tadpoles. The bird may be easily recognised by its long olive-green legs and feet. The general colour of the upper parts in breeding plumage is dusky black, margined with grey; the under parts are white, streaked with dark brown. The plumage undergoes very great changes.

The nest is on the ground, well hidden amongst the

heather, placed in a slight hollow and lined with a few blades of dry grass or leaves.

The eggs are four in number, placed points inwards, and are described as varying from creamy white to buff in ground colour, blotched and spotted with rich dark brown, and with underlying markings of pinkish brown and grey.

The Greenshank will become tame in confinement, and is a hardy bird.

DUNLIN.

TRINGA ALPINA.

Family CHARADRIIDÆ. Genus TRINGA.

Purre—Dunlin Sandpiper—Stint Churr—Sea Lark—Least Snipe.

This is a bird whose appearance undergoes such complete change in summer and winter that it was formerly supposed to be two distinct species, and was known as the Dunlin in summer and the Purre in winter. It is the commonest of all our visitors on spring and autumn migration, and is seen in flocks of many thousands throughout the winter on our coasts, while a fair number retire to the north of Scotland and the Hebrides to breed; a few also breed in the wilder parts of England, but the great majority depart to the far north of Europe, Iceland, Lapland and Greenland. These birds are strictly gregarious, being seldom seen alone, and their favourite haunts in the winter are the muddy banks at the mouths of our rivers, where they obtain their food—small worms and marine insects.

In breeding plumage the Dunlin has the general colour of the upper parts bright chestnut, each feather having a black centre, wings greyish brown, throat and breast grey with black centres, belly black, the rest of the lower parts white. In winter the general appearance of the upper parts is grey, and the under parts are entirely white. The beak is an inch and a quarter long.

The nest is usually in the midst of the heather, sheltered by an overhanging tuft, and is difficult to find. It is always on the ground, and consists of a slight hollow, lined with a few twigs and dry grass.

Four eggs are laid, which, according to Hewitson, are among the most beautiful of all British eggs. They vary from bluish green to light brown in ground colour, richly spotted and blotched with reddish brown and blackish spots. On some eggs the spots are oblique. The hen bird sits very close, and will sometimes even allow herself to be removed from the nest with the hand. Hewitson mentions an in-

stance where the bird, after the nest had been discovered, undoubtedly removed the eggs to prevent
them from being interfered with. The Dunlin can
be easily kept caged, for it is not a shy bird, but it
is difficult to obtain suitable food for it. Worms
chopped up in bread and milk are recommended for
it, and always a plentiful supply of clean water.

WOODCOCK.

SCOLOPAX RUSTICOLA.

Family CHARADRIIDÆ. Genus SCOLOPAX.

The Woodcock is principally known to us as a
winter visitor, but it also breeds sparingly throughout
the British Isles. We are probably more familiar
with it on the table—for its flesh is a delicacy—than
we are with it on the wing, for it is essentially a
night bird, seeking its food after sunset, and lying hid
throughout the day in the long grass on the outskirts

of our woods and forests. It seems rather to prefer the plantations of small trees than the old forests.

It seeks its food, which consists chiefly of earthworms, in swampy and marshy districts. It is a most voracious feeder. Mr. Coates in the *Zoologist*, 1884, p. 150, speaking of one which he had taken up, it having apparently flown against a telegraph post and being not much the worse, and which he determined to keep in confinement, says: " I fed it twice every day on worms, which I put in a box of mud. I should think it devoured its own weight of worms in twenty-four hours. It did not feed by sight, but if it touched a worm with its beak it devoured it immediately. It became very tame, and I allowed it to run and fly about the room; it always ran to the darkest place that could be found."

The Woodcock is an extraordinary-looking bird, its eyes being placed far back and high up in its head. It has a long sloping forehead and long beak. When flying it moves with its beak pointed downwards, probably to enable it the better to see where it is going. Its flight is very fast, but not so fast as that of the Common Snipe; it has also a habit of curiously turning and twisting about in the air.

It is a handsome bird, of very varied plumage. Generally speaking, the upper parts have a speckled appearance of black, chestnut, and grey; the under parts are buff barred with brown.

The Woodcock is an early breeder, eggs being sometimes found in March, but April is the usual month. The nest is on the ground, usually amongst the ferns and undergrowth on the edge of some wood or copse, and consists of a hollow scratched in the ground and lined with a little dry grass and leaves.

The eggs are four in number, and are not pointed sharply like the eggs of nearly all the other birds of this family. They are greyish or yellowish white in ground colour, with large spots of reddish brown and purplish grey. The young leave the nest as soon as they are hatched.

The old bird has been frequently known to fly with its young from one place to another, carrying them between its legs and pressing them to its breast with its beak; probably, it is said, to assist them to their feeding grounds.

COMMON SNIPE.

SCOLOPAX GALLINAGO.

Family CHARADRIIDÆ. Genus SCOLOPAX.

Whole Snipe—Snite—Heather Bleater.

The Common Snipe breeds throughout the British Islands, wherever swampy ground exists. It is consequently found most numerously in Ireland. Its numbers are largly increased by autumnal migrations. The greater number of birds, like the Woodcock, retire to the far North to breed.

The Snipe frequents the swamps and marshes, however limited in extent, provided there is a long enough growth to keep it concealed during the day, for it is a nocturnal bird, and will not rise in the daytime unless put up by some sportsman or flushed by a dog. Its flight, when startled, is exceedingly rapid, and it moves at first in zig-zag fashion, making it impossible to aim with any certainty; afterwards it adopts a straight course and drops into cover again. It should therefore be fired at immediately on rising from the ground.

In the breeding season, however, Snipes may be seen on the wing in the daytime; they will then rise to a great height, circling round and round as they ascend: on descending they emit a most curious noise, known as "drumming" or "humming". This has been variously compared to the loud buzzing of a bee which has become entangled and cannot escape, to the bleating of a goat, and to the suppressed gobble

COMMON SNIPE.

of a turkey. It has long been, and is still, disputed amongst ornithologists, whether this noise is made by the vibration of the wings, by the throat, or by the rapid rush of air through the feathers of the tail, which are spread out in the descent. The following remarks in the *Zoologist*, 1885, p. 306, go some way to supporting this latter theory: "When walking up the meadows on the 17th June last I heard a Snipe 'humming'. The sound was so peculiar that I stopped to discover, if possible, the cause. As the bird came round 'humming' within twenty yards of me, I saw through my glasses that two or three feathers of one wing were wanting, and one or two also out of the other. The sound produced was quite a treble compared with the usual sound, which I fancy varies very little. In the afternoon I again heard the same bird, and as there was another with full wings 'humming' at the same time, the difference was very marked. Several times both birds came within twenty yards, and I noticed that when the noise was made the tail was spread, the wings quivered, and the beak was closed. The very great difference between the sound produced by the bird with the whole wings and that of the one with several feathers wanting fully satisfied me that the humming sound is produced by the wings. The tail being spread steadies the bird in its downward flight, and may in some degree add to the sound."

The Snipe will occasionally, though not often, perch on trees. It feeds chiefly upon earth-worms, which it bores for in the mud with its long slender beak, also on insects, slugs, water-beetles, etc.

The nest is placed on the swampy ground in a clump of rushes or beneath the stump of a willow. It is a hollow on the ground lined with a little dry grass. Eggs are laid in April and May: they are four in number and exceptionally large for the size of the bird. They vary considerably in colour. A clutch we obtained last year from the water meadows near Queenwood was olive green in ground colour, marked obliquely with rich spots and blotches of dark brown and light brown. Others are greyish or brownish buff in ground colour. The young leave the nest as soon as hatched.

The colour of the upper portion of the body of this bird is brownish black, whilst the under side is white; the breast and sides are spotted with brown.

Rarer birds of the Family Charadriidæ :—

TURNSTONE.

CHARADRIUS INTERPRES.

Genus CHARADRIUS.

Hebridal Sandpiper.

A visitor to our coasts on migration in spring and autumn. Some remain with us through the winter. Possibly it may breed occasionally in Scotland; but its true breeding range is the far North in the Arctic Seas.

LITTLE RINGED PLOVER.

CHARADRIUS MINOR.

Genus CHARADRIUS.

A rare straggler of some half-dozen occurrences in England.

KENTISH PLOVER.

CHARADRIUS CANTIANUS.

Genus CHARADRIUS.

A summer visitor which is occasionally found in the southern and eastern coasts of England. It breeds sparingly in Kent and Sussex. Its habits closely resemble those of the Ringed Plover. The nest is a mere hollow scratched in the sand or shingle and is not lined. The eggs are buff in ground colour, spotted and blotched with blackish brown and dark grey.

GREY PLOVER.

CHARADRIUS HELVETICUS.

Genus CHARADRIUS.

A bird of fairly common occurrence on our coasts, more particularly on the eastern ones. Most numerous in the autumn and spring on migration, but also found in the winter.

CREAM-COLOURED COURSER.

CURSORIUS GALLICUS.

Genus CORSORIUS.

An accidental visitor.

COMMON PRATINCOLE.

GLAREOLA PRATINCOLA.

Genus GLAREOLA.

Collared Pratincole—Austrian Pratincole. .

An accidental visitor, chiefly to the south and east of England : about thirty examples have been obtained. Its flight is like a Swallow's, and its eggs are not pointed like the Plover's ; but its habits leave little doubt about which family it should be grouped under.

AVOCET.

HIMANTOPUS AVOCETTA.

Genus HIMANTOPUS.

Scooper—Yelper—Butterflip—Crooked-bill.

A hundred years ago this was a common visitor to the eastern counties of England and bred regularly in the marshes of Norfolk, Suffolk, and the fen districts. Now it can only be regarded as an accidental straggler, no longer breeding with us.

The plumage is deep black and white, and the feet are webbed. The beak is long, thin and pointed, and turned up slightly at the end.

COMMON STILT.

HIMANTOPUS MELANOPTERUS.

Genus HIMANTOPUS.

Black-winged Stilt.

An accidental visitor chiefly to the south and east of England. Its favourite haunts are the salt marshes near the coast.

GREY PHALAROPE.

PHALAROPUS FULICARIUS.

Genus PHALAROPUS.

An accidental visitor, rare, but occasionally appearing in large numbers. Chiefly observed in the southern counties.

RED-NECKED PHALAROPE.

PHALAROPUS HYPERBOREUS.

Genus PHALAROPUS.

Red Phalarope.

A rare accidental visitor to England, but breeds in the Shetlands and Outer Hebrides. Formerly it bred also in various parts of the Highlands of Scotland. Does not occur in Ireland.

WHIMBREL.

NUMENIUS PHŒOPUS.

Genus NUMENIUS.

Whimbrel Curlew—Half Curlew—Curlew Knot.

A spring and autumn visitor to our coasts on migration. Breeds in the Orkneys and Shetlands and the north of Sutherlandshire. This bird strongly resembles the Common Curlew in its habits and in appearance, though much smaller. It breeds on the heaths near the sea. The nest resembles others of this family, and the eggs are very similar to those of the Curlew, but smaller.

ESQUIMAUX CURLEW.

NUMENIUS BOREALIS.

Genus NUMENIUS.

Has occurred some half-dozen times in the British Isles.

BARTRAM'S SANDPIPER.

TOTANUS BARTRAMI.

Genus TOTANUS.

Has been obtained some six or seven times in Ireland.

RUFF.

TOTANUS PUGNAX.

Genus TOTANUS.

A spring and autumn visitor. Formerly it bred in large numbers in the marshy districts of England. The females are far more numerous than the males; they are called "Reeves". The peculiar feature of the male bird in breeding plumage is the curious feathery ruff which it assumes round its neck. The birds do not pair, one male having many wives; and there are spots, known as "hills," to which they repair systematically to fight for the possession of the females. From this habit of constantly repairing to the same "hill" many birds are netted.

The nest is on the swampy ground, and the eggs, four in number, are greenish grey or stone colour, spotted and blotched with reddish brown and light brown.

SPOTTED SANDPIPER.

TOTANUS MACULARIUS.

Genus TOTANUS.

A bird of very rare occurrence.

GREEN SANDPIPER.

TOTANUS OCHROPUS.

Genus TOTANUS.

A spring and autumn visitor to our coasts. There seems a probability that it has bred in the country, but its eggs are not known to have been taken. Seebohm says: "So far as is known, it is the only Sandpiper which does not lay its eggs on the ground, in a hollow, more or less slightly lined with dead grass or lichen. The Green Sandpiper lays its eggs in a tree, but it is not known that it ever builds a nest. Sometimes its eggs are placed in the fork of a tree-trunk, on the leaves, or lichens and moss, which may have accumulated there; more often the old nest of a Song Thrush or Missel Thrush is chosen."

WOOD SANDPIPER.

TOTANUS GLAREOLA.

Genus TOTANUS.

An occasional visitor, not of common occurrence. It has been known to breed in England. The nest is the ordinary hollow in the ground lined with a few stalks. The eggs are creamy white, buff, or olive in ground colour, spotted and blotched with rich reddish brown.

YELLOW-LEGGED SANDPIPER.

TOTANUS FLAVIPES.

Genus TOTANUS.

Yellowshank—Yellow-legs.

Has occurred some two or three times in the British Isles.

DUSKY REDSHANK.

TOTANUS FUSCUS.

Genus TOTANUS.

Spotted Redshank.

Spring and autumn visitor, principally to the eastern coasts of England, but not common. Only an occasional straggler to Scotland and Ireland. It varies much in summer and winter plumage.

BAR-TAILED GODWIT.

TOTANUS RUFUS.

Genus TOTANUS.

Common Godwit—Grey Godwit.

A spring and autumn visitor, more common on the eastern coasts than the western, and preferring the low-lying shores. Not known to breed anywhere in Britain.

BLACK-TAILED GODWIT.

TOTANUS MELANURUS.

Genus TOTANUS.

Red Godwit.

An occasional spring and autumn visitor, much rarer than the last. It formerly bred in the fen districts, but now does so no longer.

RED-BREASTED SNIPE.

EREUNETES GRISEUS.

Genus EREUNETES.

A bird of very rare occurrence.

KNOT.

TRINGA CANUTUS.

Genus TRINGA.

A winter visitor, principally to the southern and eastern coasts of England. Nests in the polar regions, but very little is known of its breeding places.

CURLEW SANDPIPER.

TRINGA SUBARQUATA.

Genus TRINGA.

Spring and autumn visitor, most numerous on the eastern coasts. In habits it closely resembles the Dunlin, frequently being seen in company with it. Neither the eggs of this bird nor the preceding are yet in any collection.

BONAPARTE'S SANDPIPER.

TRINGA BONAPARTI.

Genus TRINGA.

An occasional wanderer from America.

PURPLE SANDPIPER.

TRINGA MARITIMA.

Genus TRINGA.

Black Sandpiper—Selninger Sandpiper.

A winter visitor to the more rocky parts of our coasts. More numerous in some winters than in others. It is thought that it may have bred with us in the Hebrides and Shetlands, but nothing certain is known.

BROAD-BILLED SANDPIPER.

TRINGA PLATYRHYNCHA.

Genus TRINGA.

A bird which has very rarely been obtained in the British Isles.

PECTORAL SANDPIPER.

TRINGA PECTORALIS.

Genus TRINGA.

A rare straggler across the Atlantic from America.

LITTLE STINT.

TRINGA MINUTA.

Genus TRINGA.

A spring and autumn visitor, chiefly to our eastern coasts, closely resembling the Dunlin in its habits.

AMERICAN STINT.

TRINGA MINUTILLA.

Genus TRINGA.

A bird which has only occurred very rarely indeed.

TEMMINCK'S STINT.

TRINGA TEMMINCKI.

Genus TRINGA.

An occasional visitor on migration in spring and
autumn to the southern and eastern coasts.   Much
less common than the Little Stint, and smaller.

SANDERLING.

CALIDRIS ARENARIA.

Genus CALIDRIS.

Common Sanderling—Sanderling Plover.

A regular spring and autumn coast visitor, often
seen with the Dunlins: breeds in the polar regions.

BUFF-BREASTED SANDPIPER.

TRYNGITES RUFESCENS.

Genus TRYNGITES.

A very rare straggler.

GREAT SNIPE.

SCOLOPAX MAJOR,

Genus SCOLOPAX.

Double Snipe—Woodcock Snipe.

An occasional visitor to our more swampy districts, by no means common, and does not breed here. It flies straighter and slower than the Common Snipe, and is larger; consequently it is a better mark for the sportsman.

JACK SNIPE.

SCOLOPAX GALLINULA.

Genus SCOLOPAX.

Half Snipe.

A winter visitor, thinly distributed throughout marshy tracts. In habits it does not differ much from the Common Snipe. It is much smaller than this bird.

SANDWICH TERN.

STERNA CANTIACA.

Family LARIDÆ. Genus STERNA.

Surf Tern.

The Sandwich Tern receives its name from Sandwich on the coast of Kent, where it was first observed over a hundred years ago. It no longer breeds there, however; its chief breeding haunt on our shores being on the Farne Islands, off the coast of Northumberland. It also breeds in lesser numbers on the coast of Cumberland, Wallney Island, and the Scilly Isles, and in one or two places in Scotland and Ireland.

It is a true sea-bird, never coming inland ; it migrates to us at the end of April and leaves again in September. Its food consists of fish, which it catches by darting down upon them, after hovering above them ; it never dives for them.

In its summer plumage the Sandwich Tern has the top of the head black, the back and wings are pale bluish grey, all the rest of the parts are white.

'; They are sociable birds and breed in large numbers close together. The nest is on the ground, being a slight hollow, either natural or one made by the bird, and sometimes lined slightly with a few bits of grass but often with nothing at all. In a visit which Seebohm paid to the Farne Islands he mentions that so thick were the nests that there must have been on the average one nest per square yard, and it was impossible to walk about without treading on the eggs. Referring to the richness of these islands in treasures for the oologist he mentions that in a *quarter of an hour* he found the nest of an Eider Duck with eggs, several nests of the Lesser Black-backed Gull with eggs, a Ringed Plover's nest with four eggs, two Oyster Catcher's nests both containing eggs, a dozen eggs of the Arctic Tern, and more than two hundred eggs of the Sandwich Tern.

The eggs of this bird are subject to great variations and are among the most handsome of all our sea-birds' eggs. The first week in June is the best week to visit their haunts to obtain fresh eggs. These are two or sometimes three in number, of a buffish or creamy ground colour, spotted and blotched with rich dark brown, and chestnut underlying markings of slate grey.

COMMON TERN.

STERNA HIRUNDO.

Family LARIDÆ. Genus STERNA.

Sea Swallow—Tarney—Gull Teaser.

The Common Tern is not, as its name would imply, the commonest of the Terns. In former years it was confused with the Arctic Tern, but since the two species have been distinguished, the latter one is found to be the more numerous of the two, especially in the North. The Common Tern is found in suitable parts on most of the coasts of the British Isles in the summer months. It frequents the sandy flats and shingles and mouths of rivers, and often follows their course inland. It also is sometimes found on the shores of our inland lakes. It has been observed at Fleet Pond in Hampshire, which is near Basingstoke and many miles from the sea.

It feeds upon small fish, which it catches on the wing; and will often chase and worry small gulls until they drop the small fish they have caught, when the Tern secures them before they reach the water; from this habit it gets the name of Gull Teaser. It is a very graceful bird upon the wing and its occasional swift motions and turns in the air have obtained for it the name of Sea Swallow, but this is not its ordinary mode of flight, as it is usually much more deliberate on the wing than the Swallow.

The Common Tern breeds sparingly in several places on our coasts. In common with other Terns and Gulls, the Farne Islands are one of its favourite breeding haunts. It makes no nest but lays its eggs on the bare shingle or sand, more rarely upon the low rocks, often quite close to the water's edge.

The eggs are two or three in number, and vary considerably. The average type is buffish or stone colour, with rather small blotches and spots of dark reddish brown and underlying greyish ones. They are similar to eggs of the Arctic Tern.

The Common Tern in breeding plumage has the general colour of the upper parts French grey and of the under parts white, tinged with grey. The top of the head and nape are black.

ARCTIC TERN.

STERNA ARCTICA.

Family LARIDÆ.   Genus STERNA.

This is the commonest of all the Terns, especially in the northern part of Great Britain. It breeds chiefly on the western islands of Scotland, and on parts of the west coast of Ireland, as well as on the Farne Islands; it is also found breeding in several other suitable spots frequented also by the common Sand-wich Terns. It is a summer visitor, reaching us in the end of April and leaving again in August and September.   It has occasionally been obtained inland.

It is very similar in habits and appearance to the Common Tern, one of the chief points of difference, amongst others, being the shape of the beak.   In its plumage it resembles those previously mentioned, except that in the breeding season the under parts are pure white.

Its flight is very graceful, even more so than that of the Common Tern.   They are very interesting birds to watch when searching for food: when darting for a fish they drop like a stone with great force to the surface, and the splash they make, says Seebohm, "can be distinctly heard for half a mile across the water".   Most of their day is spent upon the wing, and they are very incapable walkers, seldom attempting to progress more than a yard or so on foot.

They breed in colonies and very closely together. They are often found breeding in the same haunts as the Common Tern; but they always keep separate, each species having its own portion of the island.

They lay their eggs on the bare beach, often close to the water; generally no nest is made, but sometimes the eggs are placed in a slight hollow lined with a few stalks of grass.   The eggs are two or three in number and closely resemble those of the Common Tern, going through all the same varieties of ground colour and markings; they are generally slightly smaller, however, but the birds must be observed to distinguish them with any certainty.

LESSER TERN.

STERNA MINUTA.

Family LARIDÆ. Genus STERNA.

Little Tern.

The Lesser Tern may be classed as a rare bird compared with the other Terns. It is a late arrival, reaching us about the middle of May and departing again at the beginning of September.

It breeds in the Orkneys and on several spots round the Scotch coasts; also on a few spots on the English coasts, principally on the eastern and southern sides, and sparingly in a few spots of Ireland.

In its habits it is similar to those birds of the same family which we have already mentioned. Its food consists of small fish and marine insects, and its appearance is very similar to that of the Arctic Tern, but, as its name implies, it is of course much smaller, being about half the size.

It breeds upon sandy flats and makes no nest but perhaps a slight hollow in the ground. The eggs, generally three in number, vary like those of the Common and Arctic Terns and are very similar in appearance, but are much smaller.

In Hewitson's time (fifty years ago) a colony bred annually on the sandy shore of the mainland of Northumberland nearly opposite Holy Island. He gives the following account of them: "To this locality about thirty or forty pairs annually resort, depositing their eggs upon those small patches of gravel which are most like them, both in size and colour; and so strong in many instances is the resemblance, that an unpractised eye would find great difficulty in detecting the eggs at first sight. Mr. J. Hancock has carefully brought away the eggs, and the gravel upon which they rested; and even thus, without the spreading beach around them to add to the delusion, the resemblance is very close. In a ramble along the coast with the Messrs. Hancock, we had the pleasure of finding at the place I have just mentioned between twenty and thirty nests of this bird, and all within a circuit of a few yards. It was the first week in June."

BLACK-HEADED GULL.

LARUS RIDIBUNDUS.

Family LARIDÆ. Genus LARUS.

Brown-headed Gull—Pewit Gull—Sea Crow—Red-legged Gull.

The Black-headed Gull is a very numerous species, congregating sometimes in enormous colonies. It is a resident bird, frequenting our coasts throughout the greater part of the year, but retiring inland from March to July to breed. It is a far more common bird in the North than in the South, and the majority of its breeding places are in Scotland and Ireland, the nature of the ground being more suitable for its purpose. They breed in swampy districts, and around

BLACK-HEADED GULL.

the inland ponds and marshes. The largest English "Gullery" is at Scoulton Mere in Norfolk. Here some ten or twelve thousand birds build annually. If their eggs are taken, the birds will lay again, and even a third time or fourth time, the eggs becoming smaller in each instance, but only one brood is reared in the year. Large numbers of eggs are collected for eating purposes, where the birds are not protected, as they are without the fishy taste common to the eggs of most sea birds. In the breeding season they feed upon worms and insects, and they may be seen in large colonies, like Rooks, quartering the fields for these. At other times small fish are added to the fare.

The nests are placed upon the ground, and consist of slight hollows, lined with sedges, grass, and reeds.

The eggs are two or three in number, rarely four, and vary very considerably; pale green, grey, or buff being the ground colour, spotted, blotched, and streaked with dark brown and greyish brown. The markings also undergo considerable variation, some eggs being scarcely spotted at all, while others are thickly covered.

The Black-headed Gull in its breeding plumage has a brownish-black hood, the back and wings French grey, the latter margined with black, and the rest of the plumage pure white. After the breeding is over, this bird, in common with several others of the Gulls and Terns, throws off its black hood and its head becomes perfectly white.

COMMON GULL.

LARUS CANUS.

Family LARIDÆ. Genus LARUS.

Sea Gull—Sea Mew—Winter Mew—Sea Cob—Sea Mall—
Storm Gull.

The Common Gull is a resident bird in Scotland and Ireland, but in England is only a winter visitor, having deserted its last breeding colony on the coast of Lanca-shire now more than thirty years ago.

The Common Gull is for the most part gregarious, and generally keeps in flocks. These birds have a great variety of breeding grounds. Either their nests are built on the rocky ledge of some cliff, or on the flat open ground, on the borders of lakes and broads or in marshy places ; sometimes too on high rock. Their food consists chiefly of fish, but they often pick up the insects on the shore, and in the spring may frequently

COMMON GULL.

be seen in flocks in the ploughed fields hunting for worms.

This Gull, in common with others, can easily be tamed, and makes a very handsome and useful gardener, keeping down the worms and slugs most effectually. I had a couple, which for many years led a perfectly happy life in this way, eating almost everything that was given them.   Unfortunately they both picked up some poison from a manure heap and died the same day.   This Gull will often come far inland on the appearance of stormy weather.   Some time ago, when the weather was very rough, one was brought to me by a shepherd which he had found perched in an exhausted state on some sheep hurdles : we were some seventeen miles from the coast then at Queenwood. The stupid man had foolishly knocked it on the head, thinking I would like to have it stuffed.

The nest is made of sea-weeds and dead grass and is a rather large structure.   It usually contains three eggs.   These are found towards the end of May, and are olive or buffish brown in ground colour, spotted and sometimes streaked with dark brown, and underlying markings of grey.

In breeding plumage the Common Gull has the head, neck, tail, and under parts white; the upper parts are French grey ; outer quills black, tipped with white.

LESSER BLACK-BACKED GULL.

LARUS FUSCUS.

Family LARIDÆ.   Genus LARUS.

Yellow-legged Gull.

The Lesser Black-backed Gull is a resident bird in the British Isles.   It breeds locally on the coasts and islands of England and Scotland, and upon the islands of some of the inland lakes, such as at Ulleswater.   The Farne Islands are its great resort, and here it breeds in many thousands.   It is less shy and wild than the other Gulls and can be approached much closer.   It feeds chiefly upon fish and marine insects ; it also may

sometimes be seen ashore in the ploughed fields, feeding upon worms and grain. It is a large bird, being
more than twice the size of the Common Gull, but not
quite so big as the Herring Gull. Its head, neck, tail,
and all the lower parts are white at breeding time, the
back is very dark grey, and quills black tipped with
white.

The nests are placed in the rocky cliffs in any con-

LESSER BLACK-BACKED GULL.

venient little niche, or on the bare grass. They are
large slovenly structures made of dry grass and seaweed. In them three eggs are generally laid, early in
June, varying much in colour and size. The ground
colour is buffish, pale olive green, bluish green, cream
colour or brown, and the spots are rich blackish brown
with underlying markings of grey. It is quite impossible to distinguish some of them from eggs of the
Herring Gull.

When their nests are approached these birds become very bold and aggressive.   Hewitson states that when at the Farne Islands one of these birds, near whose nest he was sitting, " retired to a certain distance to give it full force in its attack, and then making a stoop at his head, came within two or three yards of him ; repeating its attack without ceasing till he left the place ".   Mr. Darling, the lighthouse-keeper, informed him " that the bonnet of an old woman who was in the habit of gathering the eggs of the Sea Gulls was riddled through and through and almost torn to pieces by their bills ".

Lesser Black-backed Gulls can be easily kept tamed ; plenty of water should of course be supplied them.

GREAT BLACK-BACKED GULL.

LARUS MARINUS.

Family LARIDÆ.   Genus LARUS.

Black-back—Great Black and White Gull—Cob Farspach.

This large and handsome Gull is a resident bird amongst us and breeds in a few chosen spots chiefly in

Scotland. Its favourite breeding grounds are either the flat tops of inaccessible rocks or islands in the midst of lakes. It finds the former of these in the Orkneys and Shetlands, consequently it breeds in large numbers in these islands.

The Great Black-backed Gull is by no means so gregarious as the other Gulls, and is never seen in large flocks. Neither do they breed in such close proximity as most of the others of this family. It is very shy and wary, and is therefore very difficult of approach with a gun. It feeds upon fish (dead and alive), all sorts of refuse which is left on the shore by the receding tide, and the eggs of smaller sea birds are taken in large numbers and even the young birds themselves are devoured.

The eggs of this bird are much sought after for eating purposes and are collected as soon as laid, when they can be reached. The birds then lay a second clutch, which is also taken, but the third clutches are left to be hatched out.

The Great Black-backed Gulls are strictly sea birds, and are seldom seen any distance from the coast. Their nests are placed on the ground or in a niche in a rock, and are large loose structures made of grass.

Three is the usual number of eggs. They are brown in ground colour, spotted with dark brown and underlying greyish markings. They can usually be distinguished from the eggs of the other Gulls by their larger size, but very large eggs of the Herring Gull closely resemble small ones of this species.

The breeding plumage of this bird scarcely differs from that of the Lesser Black-backed Gull; but the back is a little darker, and the bird is of course very much larger.

HERRING GULL.

LARUS ARGENTATUS.

Family LARIDÆ. Genus LARUS.

The Herring Gull is a resident bird amongst us and breeds in suitable spots round our coasts. One of its favourite breeding grounds is the Isle of Wight, where it may be found in large numbers. It is very numerous on the south and west coasts of England. Sometimes this Gull will wander inland, following the course of the rivers.

In its habits it is similar to the other Gulls: it obtains its name of Herring Gull from the persistent way in which a flock of them will follow a shoal of these fish, a bird every now and then swooping down and picking up one with its bill or catching one with its feet as it skims just over the surface. Its food, however, is by no means confined to fish, and the Herring Gull will eat almost anything it can get hold of—carrion, the dead carcase of a sheep or horse on the beach, young birds, eggs, worms and grain, the refuse thrown over from the fishing boats, which they follow with great persistency, all kinds of garbage lying on the beach; indeed they are noted for the foul things which their bill of fare contains.

The favourite nesting places of the Herring Gulls are the flat edges of the upper part of a cliff. Other nests are found on the ground in uninhabited islands, such as the Farne Islands, which we might certainly christen "The Sea-birds' Cradle". The nests as a rule are very large and bulky, made of tufts of grass and seaweeds and lined with fine grass. At other times and when on the ground they are much slighter in their construction.

The eggs are usually three in number, greenish or buff colour, spotted and blotched with dark brown and grey. Many of the eggs are quite indistinguishable from those of the Common Gull and the Great Black-backed Gull and even the Lesser Black-backed Gull, so that great care must be taken in making sure of any specimens that one may possess. If the first or second clutch is taken, the bird will continue laying.

The general appearance of the plumage of the Herring Gull is similar to that of the other Gulls, but the grey on the back and wings is lighter in colour.

These birds become very tame in confinement. They require plenty of water.

KITTIWAKE.

LARUS TRIDACTYLUS.

Family LARIDÆ. Genus LARUS.

The Kittiwake, so called from its note, which resembles this word, or "get away," seems to be a resident bird on our coasts, though in the autumn

and winter it often leaves its breeding haunts and
moves southward. In this latter season we find it
generally distributed round our shores, but in the ·
breeding season it is very local on account of the few
suitable sites which can be found for its colonies.
It is one of the commonest of our British Gulls. In
its habits it differs little from others of the same
family, but perhaps it is less shy than most of them.

KITTIWAKE.

Its food consists principally of small fish which it
catches on the wing, striking the surface with a loud
splash as it darts for its prey; it also feeds upon any
garbage or floating refuse which it can pick up. In
confinement it will require to be fed upon fish and
must have a plentiful supply of water to bathe in.

When the breeding season commences the birds
retire in large flocks to the cliffs which rise sheer and

perpendicular from the water. Here all the available ledges are requisitioned for nesting purposes. The nests are large and rather better constructed than most of the Gulls' nests. They are made of grass, which is carried up with the clay and soil sticking to it; this by its weight no doubt helps to keep the nest in its precarious position and to prevent it from slipping off to destruction. The interior is formed of seaweeds.

Two or three eggs are laid, sometimes four, differing much in colour and markings; some are stone colour, some olive brown or buffish brown and some of a greenish-blue type. These are spotted and blotched with reddish brown, light brown, and grey.

The general appearance of the Kittiwake is not unlike that of the Common Gull, but it is rather smaller.

One of the largest colonies of these birds is at Svœrholt, near North Cape, in Norway, which is inhabited by an enormous number of Kittiwakes, of which Seebohm gives the following graphic and descriptive account: "It is the custom to fire off a cannon opposite the colony; peal after peal echoes and re-echoes from the cliffs, every ledge appears to pour forth an endless stream of birds, and long before the last echo has died away it is overpowered by the cries of the birds, whilst the air in every direction exactly resembles a snowstorm, but a snowstorm in a whirlwind. The birds fly in cohorts; those nearest the ship are all flying in one direction, beyond them other cohorts are flying in a different direction, and so on, until the extreme distance is a confused mass of snowflakes. It looks as if the fjord was a huge chaldron of air, in which the birds were floating, and as if the floating mass was being stirred by an invisible rod. The seething mass of birds made an indelible impression on my memory; it photographed itself on my mind's eye, as such scenes often do. I tried to make a sketch of it at the time, but I found it impossible to convey the idea of motion. It reminded me of Gustav Doré's picture to illustrate the passage in Dante's *Inferno* of 'the punishment of sinners, who are tossed about ceaselessly in the air by the most furious winds'. No less an artist than Doré could do justice to such a scene."

RICHARDSON'S SKUA.

STERCORARIUS RICHARDSONI.

Family LARIDÆ. Genus STERCORARIUS.

Black-toed Gull.

Richardson's Skua, which receives its name from Richardson, who accompanied Sir John Franklin's expedition, and brought home specimens from the Arctic regions, is the most common of all the Skuas with us; still, it only breeds within a very limited area, its nest being found in the Orkneys and Shetlands and Outer Hebrides. It is a summer visitor to us.

There are two distinct forms in the plumage of this bird, a dark and a light form. The first form in breeding plumage is of a uniform dark brown all over, tinged with grey on the upper parts. In the lighter form the upper parts are still dark greyish brown, but the general colour of the under parts is white, tinged in parts with brown. A large amount of the food of Richardson's Skua is obtained by chasing and mercilessly persecuting other birds, such as the Kittiwakes and smaller Gulls, until they drop the food which they have perhaps with difficulty obtained. It even devours the eggs of these birds in large numbers and feeds upon any carrion or garbage it can pick up. It will also eat insects and fruit. Its flight has been compared to the flight of a Hawk.

The nest is a slight hollow in the ground, lined with

RICHARDSON'S SKUA.

a few stalks of grass and sometimes a few leaves. It is placed on the open moors and is not easy to find. Eggs are obtained in June.

The number of eggs is generally two, they are olive green or olive brown in ground colour, spotted with dark brown and a few underlying spots of greyish brown. Their shape varies very much. Many of the eggs of the Common Gull and Black-headed Gull closely resemble them. It is said that the bird when sitting will feign lameness or a broken wing, and will adopt other devices to draw off the attention of an intruder from the nest.

22

Other rarer birds of the Family Laridæ :—

BLACK TERN.

STERNA NIGRA.

Genus STERNA.

Fifty years ago the Black Tern bred in many of the fen districts of Lincolnshire, Norfolk, and also at Romney Marsh in Kent; now it is only a spring and autumn visitor, principally to the southern and eastern English counties. It is not a beach bird, but frequents lakes and large ponds, in the reeds of which it builds its nest. The eggs are generally three in number, varying very much in colour and markings. Greyish green to brownish buff are the extreme colours of the ground work, the eggs being spotted and blotched with dark brown and underlying greyish markings.

WHITE-WINGED BLACK TERN.

STERNA LEUCOPTERA.

Genus STERNA.

An accidental visitor.

WHISKERED TERN.

STERNA HYBRIDA.

Genus STERNA.

Another marsh-breeding visitor; of rarer occurrence than the last.

GULL-BILLED TERN.

STERNA ANGLICA.

Genus STERNA.

A rare straggler to our coasts; has been obtained some score of times.

CASPIAN TERN.

STERNA CASPIA.

Genus STERNA.

Also a rare straggler on migration.

ROSEATE TERN.

STERNA DOUGALLI.

Genus STERNA.

A bird which some years ago bred on several of the islands off the coasts of Scotland and Ireland, as well as on the Farne Islands and one or two others; but in all probability it does not now breed anywhere in the British Islands, and must be regarded as an accidental visitor. It lays its eggs on the beach in the sand; they closely resemble the eggs of the Common Tern.

SOOTY TERN.

STERNA FULIGINOSA.

Genus STERNA.

This bird has very slender claims to a place in this work, its occurrence on our shores being only twice recorded.

SABINE'S GULL.

LARUS SABINII.

Genus LARUS.

A rare autumn visitor on migration.

LITTLE GULL.

LARUS MINUTUS.

Genus LARUS.

The smallest of all the Gulls. A rare visitor, but its numbers seem increasing. It generally visits us in small flocks.

BONAPARTE'S GULL.

LARUS PHILADELPHIA.

Genus LARUS.

As its Latin name implies, this is an American bird. It has occasionally crossed the Atlantic, some few examples having been obtained in our islands.

GLAUCOUS GULL.

LARUS GLAUCUS.

Genus LARUS.

Large White-winged Gull.

A scarce winter visitor, most common in Scotland. It is a large bird. A specimen shot by Atkinson measured six feet from tip to tip across the wings.

ICELAND GULL.

LARUS LEUCOPTERUS.

Genus LARUS.

Lesser White-winged Gull.

Another winter visitor, less regular in its visits than the last.

IVORY GULL.

LARUS EBURNEUS.

Genus LARUS.

Snow-bird.

An accidental straggler of rare occurrence.

GREAT SKUA.

STERCORARIUS CATARRHACTES.

Genus STERCORARIUS.

Common Skua—Brown Gull.

An accidental visitor to the British Isles during autumn and winter, but breeds in the Shetlands. This bird is very bold and fierce, and will attack any birds of prey which may visit its breeding haunts. It feeds upon fish and carrion ; most of the former it obtains by chasing and bullying the Gulls and compelling them to disgorge their prey. In spite of its fierceness, however, this bird seems to become perfectly tame in confinement. The nest is composed chiefly of moss, and the eggs, generally two in number, vary from light to dark brown, spotted and blotched with dark brown and greyish brown.

POMARINE SKUA.

STERCORARIUS POMARINUS.

Genus STERCORARIUS.

A winter visitor, occurring in varying numbers. In 1879 they visited us in many thousands on the Yorkshire coast; on the other hand, in some years they are very rare visitors.

BUFFON'S SKUA.

STERCORARIUS BUFFONI.

Genus STERCORARIUS.

A rare visitor, chiefly to the coasts of Scotland and the north-east coast of England. Curiously it is recorded in our district—the New Forest coast—as of more frequent occurrence than the Great Skua.

PUFFIN.

FRATERCULA ARCTICA.

Family ALCIDÆ.   Genus FRATERCULA.

Sea Parrot—Coulterneb—Tommy Noddy.

The Puffin is essentially a sea bird, rarely if ever approaching the land, except in the breeding season; then, however, it may be seen on all suitable parts of our coasts, its favourite haunts being the rocky cliffs and headlands, such as Flamborough, the Orkneys, the Hebrides, the Farne Islands, etc., and many parts of the coast of Ireland. The Puffin may safely be said to have the drollest appearance of all our British birds, its curiously shaped and gaudy coloured beak of various hues as it sits upright upon a rock or cliff giving it a most comical and grotesque appearance; the general colour of its upper parts is black, there is also a black ring round the neck, but the cheeks and forehead are grey; the general colour of the under parts is white.

The Puffin is a restless bird, incessantly moving

PUFFIN.

its body and turning its head when on land; it is also an expert diver, plunging from its perch into the waves head first, and if escaping from an enemy by this means it will swim very fast beneath the surface, spreading its wings and literally flying under water for a long distance. Its flight through the air, though its wings are small, is also very rapid. These birds feed chiefly upon fish, which they obtain by diving; they will also eat marine insects.

Puffins breed in colonies, sometimes many thousands in number, either on small islands or on rocky headlands. They lay but one egg, towards the end of May, which is placed in a hole in the ground usually burrowed by the birds themselves, though at times they will use a rabbit-hole,—often first forcibly ejecting the lawful tenant. The egg is placed right at the end of the hole and is pale greyish white in ground colour, finely spotted and blotched with light brown and ash grey colours. The bird sits very close upon her egg (which is large for the size of the bird) and will often allow herself to be caught when hatching. Hewitson says: "Of this I have often had very feeling experience when seeking for its egg, and after thrusting my arm into various holes to no purpose, have at last had notice of my success by the no means pleasant gripe of its sharp and powerful bill, with which it lays such tenacious hold of the finger that you may draw it out".

RAZORBILL.

ALCA TORDA.

Family ALCIDÆ. Genus ALCA.

Black-billed Auk—Marrot.

This bird is rather smaller than the Guillemot, which it greatly resembles in appearance, and larger than the Puffin. Like these birds it is in all respects a sea bird, keeping throughout the greater part of the year many miles out at sea, though it may be regarded as a resident in British waters.

It breeds in rocky and precipitous places, and in such districts it is a common bird in the spring and early summer.

Razorbills when flying keep mostly in flocks, but fly very far apart, so that the flocks often cover a very large area. They move through the air very rapidly, but are certainly most at home when on the water, swimming about and diving with great ease

RAZORBILL.

and swiftness. Their walk is very ungainly and only practised for very short distances. They feed upon fish, small herrings being a favourite article of food, also upon shell fish, which they will dive to a great depth to obtain. The breeding haunt of the Razorbill is frequently in the vicinity of the Puffins, Guillemots, and Kittiwakes. They lay but one egg, and although it is sometimes placed on a bare ledge of rock, they always prefer to place it in some niche or slight hollow, where it stands less chance of being knocked off by some other bird or crushed by a piece of falling rock or stone. The eggs vary considerably from pure white to buffish brown, spotted and blotched with dark reddish brown and greyish brown. Meyer tells us that when the young bird is hatched it is led to the edge of the cliff by its parents, and then apparently instructed to take the eventful leap into the sea; in this leap it sometimes loses its life by striking against a projecting rock or stone on the way down. Once on the water, however, the young bird soon becomes at home, and begins to dive and splash about, and its birthplace is visited no more.

As mentioned above, the Razorbill much resembles the Guillemot in appearance, but can easily be distinguished by its deep bill and by a white streak between the bill and the eye. In breeding plumage the general colour of the upper parts is black, shading into brownish black on the tail and wings; the throat is also brownish black, and the rest of the under parts white. There is a narrow white band across the wings. Evidence tends to show that these birds pair for life, and the female returns every year to the same spot to lay her solitary egg.

BLACK GUILLEMOT.

ALCA GRYLLE.

Family ALCIDÆ. Genus ALCA.

Tyste—Scraber—Pigeon of the North—Greenland Dove—Sea Turtle.

The Black Guillemot breeds in the Hebrides, the Orkneys and Shetlands. It is also said to breed on the north coast of Ireland, and sparingly in the Isle of Man.

Its habits resemble those of other birds of this family previously mentioned. It is, like them, a sea bird, living upon the water in the winter and coming to the rocks of the above-named haunts in the spring to rear its young. It is a better walker than the Razorbill, but seldom practises it much, and its flight is rapid ; its forte is in its swimming and diving capabilities. Its food consists of the small fry of fish, various marine insects and worms, and crustacea ; and it is said that it will dive as much as sixty feet below the surface to obtain these. Its pace when swimming under water is extraordinary; like the Puffin and Razorbill it uses its wings to assist it as well as its feet, its method of progress being really a flight beneath the surface. Seebohm says that its passage under water is quite as rapid as its progress through the air.

The Black Guillemots breed in colonies, and probably pair for life. They build no nest, but lay their eggs in a crevice in the rock, sometimes high up, at other times right at the base of the cliff, sheltered beneath some fallen blocks of rock, or under some large stones. The eggs are two or three in number, generally the latter, and are very similar to eggs of the Razorbill, but much smaller. Certain varieties also closely resemble the eggs of the Sandwich Tern. They are white or bluish white in ground colour, blotched, spotted, and speckled with rich dark brown and underlying markings of blackish grey.

It is said that these birds are easily tamed, and soon become great pets, but they live a very short time in captivity, chiefly through the difficulty in obtaining sufficient sea water for them.

The Black Guillemot is much smaller than the
Common Guillemot.   The general colour of its plumage
is black, slightly tinged with green; but a large portion
of the wings is white.

COMMON GUILLEMOT.

ALCA TROILE.

Family ALCIDÆ.   Genus ALCA.

Foolish Guillemot—Willock—Tarrock—Murre—Scout—Sea
Hen.

The Common or Foolish Guillemot breeds upon the
headlands and bold precipitous cliffs of our coasts and
islands.   At other times it is an inhabitant of the sea.
Its habits have already been described in the birds
which have gone before.   Like them it is a perfect
diver and swimmer, and its flight is swift and low over
the surface of the waves.   The chief interest in these
birds centres in their breeding.   Towards May they
collect in vast numbers at their haunts, and their eggs
are generally taken about the second week of this
month.   No attempt at a nest is made, but the birds

deposit the eggs (they only lay one) on some narrow ledge of rock overhanging the sea, or on the top of some inaccessible pinnacle, where it might be expected that more would come to grief than is the case. The egg is extraordinarily large for the size of the bird, and as the bird literally sits upon it—not crouching but sitting bolt upright on its tail—it would be impossible for it to cover two.

It has been called the Foolish Guillemot on account of its disregard of danger, the bird remaining upon its egg until it can be approached near enough to be knocked over with a stick or stone. " It will remain," says Hewitson, " so stupidly seated as to allow a noose at the end of a long stick to be passed round its neck, by which means immense numbers of them are annually taken by the inhabitants of St. Kilda, who subsist almost entirely on sea birds." It would appear, how-ever, from some observations by Seebohm that they are not quite so foolish as we might suppose from this. He says that when sitting these birds turn their faces to the rock away from the sea, thus hiding the showy part of their plumage ; in this way a very fair estimate of the number of eggs on a ledge can be formed.

The eggs are laid very close together in some parts. They are reckoned great delicacies as articles of food, and are gathered at regular intervals by men let down from the top of the cliff by a rope passed over a pulley ; after the first lay has been gathered a second and a third are generally laid. At Flamborough Head "from two to three hundred eggs a day" are considered a good take for one man.

It is quite impossible to describe the eggs of the Guillemot. Hardly any two are alike. They go through almost every possible variation of ground colour: bright blue, pea green, brown, reddish buff, cream, white, being amongst them. The blotchings and streaks vary quite as much as the ground colour; some eggs are thickly marked, others hardly at all; the markings are mostly of some dark colour, blackish brown, and pink of various tints being amongst them. It is said that when the young Guillemot is ready to leave its birthplace it is carried to the sea on its mother's back.

The upper plumage of the Guillemot is dark brown, tinted with blackish grey on the back, neck brown, and under parts white; a very narrow white band goes across the wings.

Other rarer birds of the Family Alcidæ :—

GREAT AUK.

ALCA IMPENNIS.

Genus ALCA.

This extraordinary looking and interesting bird is now an extinct species; the last birds having expired some fifty years ago. The Great Auk was an inhabitant of the lands in the North Atlantic, its limits southwards being St. Kilda, where it was formerly a regular summer visitor. Its eggs, of which there are very few in existence, are consequently much sought after by collectors, and fabulous prices are paid when one comes into the market; 160 guineas was paid in 1888 by Mr. Leopold Field for an egg of this species, the highest price ever given up to that time for an egg, and many of us at Queenwood had the privilege of seeing this shell, worth many times more than its weight in gold, and of hearing a most interesting lecture upon it by Mr. Field, himself an old Queen-wood master.   This extraordinary price, however, has now been far eclipsed, and in a recent year, 1894, an egg of this bird was sold at an auction and knocked down for 300 guineas !

LITTLE AUK.

ALCA ALLE.

Genus ALCA.

A winter visitor, chiefly to the Orkneys and Shet-lands and the far North.

BRUNNICH'S GUILLEMOT.

ALCA BRUNNICHI.

Genus ALCA.

Some naturalists regard this bird as a variety of the Common Guillemot, others as a distinct species. They are always found together, and they pair together.   This bird has a ring of white round the eye, which the Common Guillemot has not got.

RED-THROATED DIVER.

COLYMBUS SEPTENTRIONALIS.

Family COLYMBIDÆ.   Genus COLYMBUS.

Sprat-loon—Rain Goose—Cobble--Sprat-borer.

This bird is the commonest of all the Divers amongst us, and may be seen throughout the winter

. on most parts of our coasts.   It only breeds, however,
in the north and west of Scotland, the Hebrides,
Orkneys, and Shetlands.   It is a winter visitor to Ireland.

These birds frequent the sea for the greater part of
the year in the breeding season, and are often seen
round the mouths of rivers ; they are seen too on the
margins of lakes and inland lochs. The eggs are generally laid near the water's edge upon the ground ; sometimes a slight nest is formed of reeds and sedges.   The
eggs, two in number, are of an olive-brown colour,
spotted with dark brown.

These birds feed chiefly upon fish. They are most
remarkable divers, descending to a great depth, being
quite helpless on land and unable to walk, as their
legs are placed very far back under their bodies.   The
Red-throated Diver is the smallest of the family.   It
is brownish black on the upper parts, the feathers
being speckled with grey at the tips ; head and neck
grey, throat chestnut red, and the remaining under
parts white.

Other rarer birds of the Family Colymbidæ :—

GREAT NORTHERN DIVER.

COLYMBUS GLACIALIS.

Genus COLYMBUS.

This large bird is a winter visitor to Great Britain
and Ireland and may possibly breed in some of the
north-western islands of Scotland.

WHITE-BILLED DIVER.

COLYMBUS ADAMSI.

Genus COLYMBUS.

A bird which has occurred only once or twice amongst us.

BLACK-THROATED DIVER.

COLYMBUS ARCTICUS.

Genus COLYMBUS.

This bird is rare, but is known to breed very thinly in the Outer Hebrides and in some of the Highland counties. Its habits resemble those of the other Divers. The eggs are generally two in number, similar to those of the Red-throated Diver, but larger. The bird seems to build a nest when it breeds in swamps, at other times it lays its eggs upon the mossy ground in a slight hollow, occasionally lined with one or two scraps of sedge.

MANX SHEARWATER.

PUFFINUS ANGLORUM.

Family PROCELLARIIDÆ. Genus PUFFINUS.

Manx Petrel—Shearwater Petrel—Manx Puffin—Scrapire.

The Manx Shearwater is the best known of the Shearwaters that frequent the British Isles. It has its name from the way in which it skims with great swiftness over the surface of the water, following the curves of the waves up and down as it darts forward in its flight. From the position of its legs it is unable to walk. It breeds in the Western Islands of Scotland, the Orkneys and Shetlands, and the Scilly Islands, and in a few parts of Ireland. Formerly it bred in the Calf of Man. This bird loves the sea and is seldom seen except in the breeding season. Then it hides in holes in the rocks during the daytime, probably obtaining most of its food at night, consisting of small fish, and any scraps and remains floating on the surface. These birds are much prized by the fishermen of some of the Western Isles as articles of food, from whom in consequence it is difficult to get information as to the whereabouts of the nests, the holes being very difficult to discover unaided on account of the entrance often being overgrown. The holes seem generally to be burrowed by the birds themselves, as in the case of the Puffins, but are better concealed, and are in the wildest part of the district among the cliffs and rocks.

Scarcely any nest is made; just a few dry plants are placed at the bottom of the hole, some little distance from the entrance, and on these the bird lays one egg, perfectly white in colour and very glossy and smooth. It has also a peculiar musky smell. The eggs are laid throughout May and the early part of June.

The general colour of the upper parts of the Manx Shearwater is greyish black; the throat, breast and under parts are white.

Seebohm, relating what Dixon was told by a native of St. Kilda, says: "He told me that the bird is so common there that he had known a boat's crew (of which he was a member), despatched to the island to collect birds and eggs, capture as many as four hundred Shearwaters in a single night, and that their cries were almost deafening; he also said that it is one of the earliest birds to arrive at the islands in spring, coming as early as February, and that it is one of the last to leave in autumn".

STORMY PETREL.

PROCELLARIA PELAGICA.

Family PROCELLARIIDÆ. Genus PROCELLARIA.

Mother Carey's Chicken—Little Peter.

The Stormy Petrel is the smallest web-footed bird in existence, being no bigger than a Sparrow. It never comes to land except for breeding purposes, but wanders to and fro over the deep, where, from the blackness of its plumage and its indifference to the storms and tempests which it weathers, Mother Carey's Chicken is looked upon as a bird of ill-omen by the superstitious sailors, and a forerunner of ship-wreck.

The Stormy Petrel obtains its name from the habit it has of running or walking over the surface of the water. It picks up its food on the surface of the sea—anything oily is no doubt acceptable to it, and the young ones seem to be fed entirely on oil. Their bodies are consequently saturated with oil. "These birds," says Morris, "are made use of by the inhabitants of the Ferroe and other Islands, to serve for lamps, a wick of cotton or other material being drawn through the body, and when lighted it continues to burn till the oil in the bird is consumed. The quantity of oil yielded decreases as the summer advances, and at last fails altogether, probably from their falling off in condition, and the supply given to their young."

The nests of the Stormy Petrel are placed in holes in cliffs and rocks, or under large stones, sometimes in holes beneath the beach, or in an old rabbit burrow. The nests consist of a few scraps of dead grass, in which one white egg is laid; the shell has no gloss and is very rough in texture. The egg is finely spotted with tiny specks of reddish brown, often in a zone round the larger end. Their rough unpolished shells prevent them from being mistaken for the eggs of any other bird. The eggs soon become discoloured from the oily feathers of the bird.

The general colour of the upper parts of the Stormy Petrel is black and of the under parts dark brown; the upper part of the tail and rump are white.

Other rarer birds of the Family Procellariidæ :—

GREAT SHEARWATER.

PUFFINUS MAJOR.

Genus PUFFINUS.

This bird does not breed here but is a frequent visitor, often coming in large numbers to the Scilly Isles and the south-west of England.

DUSKY SHEARWATER.

PUFFINUS OBSCURUS.

Genus PUFFINUS.

A bird which has been twice captured in the British Isles.

SOOTY SHEARWATER.

PUFFINUS GRISEUS.

Genus PUFFINUS.

An occasional visitor.

FULMAR PETREL.

FULMARUS GLACIALIS.

Genus FULMUS.

This bird breeds in and around St. Kilda; to other parts it is a rare straggler. It lays one egg, pure white, which can at once be distinguished by its musky smell.

LEACH'S FORK-TAILED PETREL.

PROCELLARIA LEACHI.

Genus PROCELLARIA.

A bird of rare occurrence, but breeds in St. Kilda. One egg is laid, white, finely marked with reddish-brown specks. It resembles the egg of the Stormy Petrel, but is much larger.

WILSON'S PETREL.

OCEANITES WILSONI.

Genus OCEANITES.

A bird which has several times been obtained in the south-west of England, but is very rare.

GREAT CRESTED GREBE.

PODICEPS CRISTATUS.

Family PODICIPEDIDÆ. Genus PODICEPS.

Loon—Greater Loon—Cargoose—Tippet Grebe.

The Great Crested Grebe is a resident in our islands, but local in its haunts. It frequents large pools, lakes and sheets of water, provided that there are reed beds at hand in which it can place its nest. Such places are found more particularly in the eastern counties, and in Buckinghamshire, Oxfordshire, Hertfordshire and other low-lying counties, where, in consequence, the Loon is more commonly found. When seen on the wing, the flight of the Great Crested Grebe is exactly like that of the Wild Duck, but it seldom

makes use of its wings except on migration; neither
does it walk with any ease, but in the art of diving and
swimming under water it is perfect. It feeds upon
aquatic insects and small fish, which it obtains by
diving.

The nest is built towards the end of April among
the reeds, and is composed of a mass of half-rotten
reeds and water weeds, slightly raised above the
surface. The nest is naturally in a sodden condition,

GREAT CRESTED GREBE.

and one at least of the eggs in a clutch is generally
found addled. The eggs are three or four in number,
and are of a chalky-white colour, but soon however
become stained by the decaying matter which surrounds
them. Should the bird, after she has commenced to
sit, have occasion to leave the nest, she invariably
covers over the eggs with rushes or weeds to keep
them from cold.

If the female is disturbed, according to Hewitson

she "leaves the nest by diving; no bird is seen, but a motion is discerned in the surrounding reeds like a pike making his way through them, but slower and more regular. . . . The female seldom rises within gunshot of the nest, and, if a boat be stationed to intercept her, will tack about and alter her course under water without rising to breathe. . . . No sooner do they build a nest than they become the most skulking, diving, hiding creatures possible; indeed when a pool of water is much overgrown with reeds you can hardly ever catch sight of them, even if several pairs are breeding around you."

The general colour of the upper parts of this bird is greyish brown, the feathers having paler edges, and of the under parts white, shading to brown on the flanks; there is a ruff round the neck which is bright chestnut, edged with black.

LITTLE GREBE.

PODICEPS MINOR.

Family PODICIPEDIDÆ.　Genus PODICEPS.

Dabchick—Dobchick—Didapper—Blackchin Grebe.

The Little Grebe, or Dabchick as it is more commonly called, is a common resident, found in all districts of the British Isles which are suitable to its habits, that is to say, wherever ponds, lakes, and slow-running streams abound.

The Dabchick feeds upon small fish and aquatic insects; most of its food is obtained by diving, at which it is very expert. Frequently large quantities of feathers, apparently its own, are found in the stomach of this bird. This is also the case with the preceding species, the Great Crested Grebe ; possibly they are swallowed to aid digestion.

This bird also is very loth to take wing, always preferring to escape notice by diving. It is extremely shy, and will slip off its eggs and dive directly it is approached, having first taken the precaution to cover

LITTLE GREBE.

them over with damp reeds and weeds, which it takes from the sides of the nest and places over the eggs with great quickness. The nests are generally floating in the water, anchored to the reeds, but not often built amongst them. They are composed of dank reeds and water weeds, often placed quite in the open, and in them, generally in early May, four or five eggs are laid, though occasionally six are found.   The shells are rather rough and their colour is white, but in a short time they naturally become very stained, seemingly from their damp and rotten surroundings. Atkinson says he is quite convinced that in some cases at least this discoloration is intentional on the part of the parent bird, though in others it may be due to the action of the juices of fresh or decaying vegetable substances.   The eggs can easily be recognised from their shape, both ends being equally pointed.

When the young are hatched the parent will often swim with them concealed under her wings, should danger threaten, and will even dive with them hidden from view in this way.

The Dabchick is the smallest of the family of Grebes.   It may be described generally as dark brown on the upper parts, with the cheeks and front part of the neck bright chestnut ; there is a little white on the wings ; the under parts are a greyish brown, being darkest on the breast.

Other rarer birds of the Family Podicipedidæ :—

RED-NECKED GREBE.

PODICEPS RUBRICOLLIS.

Genus PODICEPS.

A winter visitor of regular occurrence, particularly on the east coast of England and Scotland.   It never breeds here.

SCLAVONIAN GREBE.

PODICEPS CORNUTUS.

Genus PODICEPS.

Dusky Grebe—Horned Grebe.

A winter visitor, chiefly to the south coasts.

BLACK-NECKED GREBE.

PODICEPS NIGRICOLLIS.

Genus PODICEPS.

Eared Grebe.

A rare visitor, chiefly in spring and autumn. Much the rarest of any of the Grebes which visit us.

COMMON SHELDRAKE.

TADORNA CORNUTA.

Family ANATIDÆ. Genus TADORNA.

Burrow-duck—Shell-duck—Sheld-duck—Bargander—Bar-goose.

The Sheldrake is the first in the list of Ducks which breed on our shores. It is a resident bird, and is found on the sandy parts of our coasts more or less commonly. It is not of common occurrence in the south of England. The Common Sheldrake is in great request on account of its beautiful and striking plumage, and may be seen on many of our ornamental lakes and waters. Its head and neck are black, tinged with green; beneath this there is a broad ring of white widening out on the breast, followed by a similar ring of bright chestnut; the back, rump, and sides are white, the tail is white tipped with black, and a broad black line runs from the centre of the breast under the belly; the wings are made up of white, black, green and chestnut. It is a large bird, being considerably bigger than the Wild Duck or Mallard. The Sheldrake feeds upon water insects

COMMON SHELDRAKE.

and various water plants, also on marine animals; it does not dive for its food, but fishes for it in shallow water with its head and half its body immersed, its tail being upright in the air. Its flight is slow and laboured, and it walks with ease.

This bird builds its nest in a rabbit burrow; occasionally they will excavate a hole for themselves, but as a rule they have a great objection to doing so, and it is said they will even use a fox or badger's hole to avoid doing this, having even hatched their young while the rightful owner was still in possession. Artificial burrows are sometimes dug in their breeding haunts by those who are anxious to obtain their eggs, when, by a movable piece of turf being placed over the far end, the eggs may be taken out every morning. The nest consists of a little dead grass and moss, and is lined with down. The eggs, seven to fourteen or sixteen, are creamy white in colour.

The bird and the site of the nest should be observed to make certain of identifying these eggs.

COMMON TEAL.

ANAS CRECCA.

Family ANATIDÆ. Genus ANAS.

The Common Teal is a resident in the British Islands, but is local in its haunts, and can only be considered to breed sparingly. Its numbers are largely increased, however, in the winter by migration, so that it is then one of the commonest species of Ducks, next to the Mallard, in our islands.

The Common Teal shows very little shyness in its habits, and will allow itself to be approached quite closely and watched. It is excessively fast on the wing.

Their habits and food are similar to those of the rest of this family; they live upon aquatic insects, young blades and shoots, and various seeds and weeds.

This bird is the smallest of our Ducks and has very pretty plumage. The head and neck are chestnut, chin black, and a broad purplish green stripe with a narrow white edge runs from the eyes down each side of the neck; the tail feathers are brown, edged with white, and the general colour of the body is greyish white covered with close zigzag lines of black; the breast is white spotted with black, and the wings are made up of grey, brown, yellow, and green.

The Common Teal breeds in marshy and swampy moorland districts, either in the open or amongst trees; it seems to prefer haunts removed from cultivation, and here it places its nest amongst the long grass, rushes, or heather, sometimes concealed beneath a willow bush or overhanging rushes. The nest is built of dead grass and sedge and various other vegetable substances; it is very deep, and lined with a plentiful supply of down, with which the bird will cover the eggs when it leaves the nest.

The eggs of the Duck family are so similar that this down found in their nests forms one of the best means of distinguishing between them. The eggs of the Common Teal are eight to ten in number, buffish white or cream coloured; they are, of course, much smaller than eggs of the Common Wild Duck or Mallard, which are the eggs most likely to be met with by young collectors, and they lack the green tint of these latter.

A.Thorburn.

SHOVELLER.

ANAS CLYPEATA.

Genus ANAS.

Blue-winged Shoveller—Broad-bill.

The Shoveller must be regarded as a winter visitor to our shores, but several remain to breed, chiefly in the eastern counties of England and the fen districts. This bird frequents lakes and large pieces of water in open country where there are no trees: it prefers a locality near the sea, though it is a fresh water species. Damp boggy tracts and marshy swamps surrounded with reeds and covered with plenty of water weeds are the places where we may expect to find the Shoveller.

They obtain their food either by taking it from the mud in shallow places, where they may be often seen swimming with only the tail uppermost exposed, or from the water weeds, but they do not dive for it. Their food consists of aquatic insects, tadpoles, the spawn of frogs, small fish, and tender shoots.

The flight of the Shoveller is somewhat slower and

more laboured than that of most of the Ducks.   The
nest is generally placed in the long grass or heath out
in the open, and is made of dead grass and reeds, and
lined with down.

Seven to nine eggs are laid towards the end of May
of a buffish-white colour, faintly tinged with olive.

The Shoveller is a much smaller bird than the
Mallard, and is easily distinguished by its peculiarly
large, broad and spoon-shaped bill.   The head and
neck are black, tinged with purple and green ; the
back is brown, " glossed with purple and green on the
rump and upper tail-cover " ; the breast is white, and the
wings bluish grey with a white bar across, the quill
brown, tail brown edged with white ; the under parts
below the breast are reddish brown, shading into white
and then into black beneath the tail.

This bird can only be kept in confinement where
there is a pond with plenty of duckweed for it.

MALLARD.

ANAS BOSCHAS.

Family ANATIDÆ.   Genus ANAS.

Wild Duck.

This bird is the commonest of all our Ducks.   It is
a resident bird, breeding in suitable localities throughout the British Isles, but its numbers are enormously
increased by migration in winter.   It is said, however,
to be slowly but surely decreasing on account of the
enormous numbers which are shot and decoyed every
year.

The Mallard is the species from which our farmyard

Ducks have sprung, and on that account we have a special interest in it. It is a wonderfully knowing bird and learns to take care of itself with surprising instinct. Seebohm says: "They seem to know perfectly well that they are watched by their enemies, that small ponds are not often visited by sportsmen, and that the sportsman is not likely to be informed of their presence on the larger sheets of water unless they appear in some numbers. They soon learn to distinguish a labourer from a keeper, no doubt from his actions, and

MALLARD.

not from his appearance. If not molested they will breed, year after year, in the same corner; but if the eggs are taken they will not have forgotten the fact a year hence, but will try another hiding-place."

In winter these birds are mostly seen in large flocks flying to and from their feeding grounds. Worms, slugs, water plants, all kinds of water animals, acorns and grain, all form a portion of their food; in fact there are few things they will not eat.

They breed generally in the vicinity of water, but

not often close to it. The nest is a deep one, formed of grasses and lined with down. The eggs, eight to twelve, are buffish green in colour. They may be found as early as the end of March. The nest is generally placed on the ground amongst reeds or in the long grass, but it is often found in most unlikely places, such as in the deserted nest of a Carrion Crow, or in the tops of trees many feet from the ground, in ivy on a ruined wall, and on the top of a straw-stack. A unique instance was recorded by some of our Queenwood collectors in 1884. In this case the eggs were laid in a Rook's nest in an inhabited rookery, on the banks of the Test, over thirty feet from the ground. There were six eggs, and the nest from which they were taken was in a horse-chestnut tree. One paper, the *Nottingham Journal*, attached political significance to the portent: " A Wild Duck has laid eggs in a Rook's nest. Can this have any bearing on Lord Randolph Churchill's reconciliation with the leaders of his party?" while the *Daily News* remarked that " the Romans would have drawn conclusions as to the fate of Kartoum from the prodigy ".

The head and neck of this bird are black, tinged with green and purple; the back is brown, shading to greyish brown on the wings; across these there is a white bar. There is a narrow white ring round the neck, the breast is deep chestnut, belly greyish white finely marked with zigzag lines of dark grey, tail blackish brown.

POCHARD.

FULIGULA FERINA.

Family ANATIDÆ. Genus FULIGULA.

Dunbird—Red-headed Pochard—Duncur.

This bird must be regarded as a rare breeder in our country, and must be considered a winter visitor. It has been found nesting, however, in various parts of the British Isles; amongst others in the New Forest.

The Pochard dives with great skill and quickness, and obtains its food by this means. Diving in shallow parts and pulling up water-weeds from the bottom, it pulls them to pieces when it reaches the surface again and leisurely devours them. It also eats insects and small shell-fish. It is a bad walker, its walk being a literal waddle; its flight also is rapid, the wings being moved with very quick and short strokes. It has a decided preference for fresh water to salt.

The nest of the Pochard is built among the reeds on marshy tracts of water. It is built of dead grass, reeds and sedge, and lined with down. The outside is said to be somewhat similar to the nest of the Coot.

The eggs are eight to ten in number, usually the latter; they are buffish or greenish buff in colour, very like eggs of the Pheasant in their tint.

In the breeding season this bird has its head and neck a rich chestnut, the lower neck and breast are black, and the rump and parts of the tail are dull black; the general colour of the rest of the body is a lavender grey, finely lined with wavy marks of black.

TUFTED DUCK.

FULIGULA CRISTATA.

Family ANATIDÆ. Genus FULIGULA.

Tufted Pochard.

This is another of the Ducks which breed, but very locally, in the British Islands. It is really a winter visitor. Its chief breeding site in these islands seems to be Sherwood Forest.

The Tufted Duck, though seen on the coasts in winter, is to all intents and purposes a fresh-water bird. It is an expert diver, and like the last species obtains much of its food by this means. Consequently it is found on lakes and even quite small ponds provided there is a good growth of waterweed at the bottom. It also feeds upon water insects of all kinds and shell-fish. Its flight is strong and rapid, and performed with quick beatings of the wings. In the winter these birds collect in flocks.

The nest of the Tufted Duck is placed around the margins of ponds and lakes, sometimes under a bush, sometimes in the reeds and rushes, and at other times amongst the tufts of sedge. It is simply a hollow, lined with dead grass and sedge, and coated with down.

The eggs are eight to twelve in number, and resemble in appearance those of the former species—the Pochard. They are laid rather late in the year, towards the end of May. The head, neck, and crest of this bird are black, tinted with green and purple ; the breast is black, the rest of the upper parts are dusky brown, the feathers being margined with black, the belly creamy white.

COMMON EIDER.

SOMATERIA MOLLISSIMA.

Genus SOMATERIA.

Eider Duck—St. Cuthbert's Duck.

The Eider Duck breeds in some parts of the north of Britain, such as the Farne Islands, the Hebrides, Orkneys and Shetlands ; in these parts it is consequently a resident. South of Yorkshire it is only a rare and occasional visitor.

The Eider is essentially a sea bird, and is hardly ever found inland. It dives with ease, and most of its food is obtained by this means. It feeds upon marine insects, shell-fish and crustaceans. These birds are gregarious, more particularly so in winter than in summer; in this country, where the birds do not occur in great numbers, the flocks are small—from ten to twenty birds—but where the birds abound they often collect in very large bands.

Though the male Eider is always a cautious bird and seldom comes within gunshot, the female is remarkably tame in the breeding season. Hewitson, speaking of a visit to one of the islands on the coast of Norway, says: "An old man who had the care of the island, and seemed to derive much pleasure from the charge, accompanied us all over his preserves, pointing out to us the Ducks as they sat around us, apparently heedless of our near approach, and on

A Thorburn.

COMMON EIDER.

quite familiar terms with our companion, who would even stroke them on the back, and was very jealous lest we should fire our guns and thus scare his pets". The nests of the Eider are generally built on the rocks of some small unfrequented island, or amongst the heath on the gentle slopes near the sea. The

nest is composed of seaweed, dry grass, and heather;
and, when all the eggs have been laid, contains a large
quantity of the valuable and much sought after Eider-
down.   " By judiciously removing the eggs and down
from the nests, the birds are made to lay again and
furnish a fresh supply of the precious down.   Each
Duck yields about four ounces of down, which, when
cleaned, is worth about a sovereign a pound."

The eggs are from five to eight in number, of a light-
green or greyish-green colour.   The plumage of this
bird is very handsome.   It might roughly be described
as having the upper parts white, tinged with yellow
in parts, and the under parts black; the forehead and
crown are also black.

This bird can easily be rendered reconciled to
captivity.

RED-BREASTED MERGANSER.

MERGUS SERRATOR.

Family ANATIDÆ.   Genus MERGUS.

Red-breasted Goosander.

This bird is a winter visitor, but in the north of
Scotland and Ireland many birds remain throughout
the year and breed.

The haunts of this bird are the quiet and secluded
rocky coasts, where calm and smooth bays and creeks
abound.   It dives and swims under water, often remaining beneath the surface for as long a space as two
minutes.   Its food is obtained in the water, and consists
chiefly of small fish, crustaceans, mollusks, etc.   Meyer

says: "The small fish which the present species pursues have little chance of escape, as the whole flock of birds present dive simultaneously and pursue them towards the shore under water; the fish have no alternative but to run on the shallows, and then their pursuers make short work of them, and satisfy their greedy appetite".

When alarmed these birds will occasionally take refuge by flight, though more frequently by diving; their flight is strong and rapid.

The nest of this bird is placed in a variety of situations. According to Hewitson the favourite situation is on the woody borders of inland lakes and rivers beneath the shelter of a fir-tree. Seebohm says it always builds on an island, whenever it is possible, and the nest is placed among long grass and heath. It is also said to have been found in a bush, in the hollow of a tree, or in the old nest of a bird of prey. The nest is usually composed of grass, heather, and leaves; when the eggs have been laid the nest is also lined with the down of the bird.

The eggs are six to nine or more in number, of a plain olive-grey colour. They are generally found in June. The head and neck of this bird are black, tinted with green and purple; below this is a white band round the neck; the rest of the neck and breast are buff, streaked with black; the rest of the under parts are white, finely lined with black; the back is black, but the lower part of back and rump is white; tail greyish black, and wings black and white.

Other rarer birds of the Family Anatidæ :—

MUTE SWAN.

CYGNUS OLOR.

Genus CYGNUS.

This is the Swan which is seen in a semi-domesticated state on our lakes and ornamental waters. Whether it has ever migrated to us as a visitor in its wild state is doubtful, but it is probable, since it breeds in Denmark and Germany, that it has occasionally wandered over.

HOOPER SWAN.

CYGNUS MUSICUS.

Genus CYGNUS.

Wild Swan—Whistling Swan—Elk.

A fairly common winter visitor. At Emsworth, in Hants, flocks of a hundred birds are recorded.

BEWICK'S SWAN.

CYGNUS BEWICKI.

Genus CYGNUS.

Also a fairly common winter visitor; most numerous on the west coast of Ireland.

SNOW GOOSE.

ANSER NIVALIS.

Genus ANSER.

An American species, which has been shot occasionally in Ireland.

BEAN GOOSE.

ANSER SEGETUM.

Genus ANSER.

A common winter visitor to all our coasts, but is not known with any certainty to have bred here.

PINK-FOOTED GOOSE.

ANSER BRACHYRHYNCHUS.

Genus ANSER.

Another common winter visitor to the coasts of Great Britain. It is very similar in appearance to the last species, but smaller.

GREY-LAG GOOSE.

ANSER CINEREUS.

Genus ANSER.

Grey-legged Goose—Grey Goose—Wild Goose.

This bird still breeds in some of the Hebrides, and in one or two parts in the northern counties of Scotland.   Before the fen district was drained it bred regularly in the eastern counties of England; now, however, it is only a winter visitor.   The nest of the Grey Goose is very large—often a yard in diameter—built of dead reeds, grass and sedge.   The eggs are six to eight in number, of a dull creamy-white colour. They measure over three inches in length.   This species is kept in a domesticated state by farmers; in this condition, however, it is often quite white.

WHITE-FRONTED GOOSE.

ANSER ALBIFRONS.

Genus ANSER.

Laughing Goose.

A winter visitor of somewhat irregular occurrence. Sometimes it appears in large flocks, but more frequently it is rather sparingly distributed.

BRENT GOOSE.

ANSER BRENTA.

Genus ANSER.

A common winter visitor, and the most numerous of all the species of Geese which visit us; it is also the smallest.

BERNACLE GOOSE.

ANSER LEUCOPSIS.

Genus ANSER.

Barnacle Goose.

Another winter visitor, most numerous on the west coast of Scotland.

RED-BREASTED GOOSE.

ANSER RUFICOLLIS.

Genus ANSER.

An accidental visitor, obtained some half-dozen times.

RUDDY SHELDRAKE.

TADORNA RUTILA.

Genus TADORNA.

A very rare visitor indeed.

GADWALL.

ANAS STREPERA.

Genus ANAS.

Rodge—Grey Duck.

A winter visitor to Great Britain and Ireland. It is said to breed regularly in Norfolk, where it has been introduced. It is exceedingly shy and wary, and so often escapes notice in the thick cover. It lays eight to twelve eggs of a buffish white or cream colour.

PINTAIL.

ANAS ACUTA.

Genus ANAS.

Cracker.

A winter visitor. A few pairs, it seems, breed in Ireland every year.

WIDGEON.

ANAS PENELOPE.

Genus ANAS.

Whewer—Whim.

One of the commonest winter visitors of the Duck tribe, both to the coast and inland. A few remain to breed in the north of Scotland. The eggs can only be distinguished by examining the down in the nest.

AMERICAN WIDGEON.

ANAS AMERICANA.

Genus ANAS.

A bird which has been obtained once or twice in the British Isles, but it may have escaped from confinement.

AMERICAN TEAL.

ANAS CAROLINENSIS.

Genus ANAS.

A bird which has occurred two or three times in Britain.

GARGANEY.

ANAS CIRCIA.

Genus ANAS.

Summer Duck—Summer Teal—Pied Widgeon.

A rare summer visitor, which is said to breed in one or two localities, notably in Norfolk. It formerly bred in the fen district. The eggs are eight to twelve in number, similar in appearance to eggs of the Common Teal, but distinguishable by the down in the nest.

RED-CRESTED POCHARD.

FULIGULA RUFINA.

Genus FULIGULA.

A rare accidental visitor.

WHITE-EYED POCHARD.

FULIGULA NYROCA.

Genus FULIGULA.

Another rare visitor, less common than the last.

SCAUP.

FULIGULA MARILA.

Genus FULIGULA.

Spoon-bill Duck.

A common winter visitor to most of our coasts. Occasionally seen in the summer but not known to breed here. Essentially a sea Duck, and does not venture far inland.

BUFFEL-HEADED DUCK.

FULIGULA ALBEOLA.

Genus FULIGULA.

An American species which is recorded as having occurred here a few times.

GOLDEN-EYE DUCK.

FULIGULA CLANGULA.

Genus FULIGULA.

Brown-headed Duck—Grey-headed Duck—Golden-eyed Widgeon.

A common winter visitor, chiefly to the northern parts of Britain. Seemingly most common in severe winters.

HARLEQUIN DUCK.

FULIGULA HISTRIONICA.

Genus FULIGULA.

A very rare straggler.

LONG-TAILED DUCK.

FULIGULA GLACIALIS.

Genus FULIGULA.

A bird of fairly frequent occurrence, most abundant in the North. It is a bird of very handsome appearance, and its plumage undergoes great variation. It has been seen here in the summer, but is not known to have bred in Britain.

COMMON SCOTER.

FULIGULA NIGRA.

Genus FULIGULA.

Black Scoter—Black Duck—Black Diver.

A common winter visitor to most parts of the coast. It is said to occasionally breed in the north of Scotland.

VELVET SCOTER.

FULIGULA FUSCA.

Genus FULIGULA.

Velvet Duck.

A regular winter visitor, but much less common than the preceding. More common on the east coast of Scotland than in England.

SURF SCOTER.

FULIGULA PERSPICILLATA.

Genus FULIGULA.

A very rare winter visitor of infrequent occurrence.

STELLER'S EIDER.

SOMATERIA STELLERI.

Genus SOMATERIA.

Steller's Western Duck.

Said to have occurred a few times.

KING EIDER.

SOMATERIA SPECTABILIS.

Genus SOMATERIA.

King Duck.

A bird of casual occurrence. It possibly breeds in the Orkneys and Shetlands.

GOOSANDER.

MERGUS MERGANSER.

Genus MERGUS.

Dun Diver—Sparling Fowl—Jacksaw—Saw-bill.

A fairly common winter visitor. "An occasional pair remain and breed in the Highlands." More common in severe winters.

HOODED MERGANSER.

MERGUS CUCULLATUS.

Genus MERGUS.

A very rare occasional visitor.

SMEW.

MERGUS ALBELLUS.

Genus MERGUS.

White Nim—Smee—White-headed Merganser.

A rare winter visitor, most frequent on the east coast.

GANNET.

SULA BASSANA.

Family PELECONIDÆ. Genus SULA.

Solan Goose.

This bird is a resident one, but very local, having some half-dozen colonies where it breeds, among these being the Bass Rock, Ailsa Craig, Sulisker in the Hebrides, and Lundy Island. In the former of these it breeds in immense numbers, every available ledge of rock where a nest can be placed being occupied by a sitting bird.

These birds are mostly on the wing, moving with powerful flight over the water on the look-out for food ; this consists of various kinds of fish, such as herring, whiting, mackerel, etc. When about to seize on of these, the Gannet drops like a stone with a splash

25

into the water and seldom misses its prey. They never dive, unless when winged by a shot, to escape being taken. They are very gluttonous and are often caught through becoming quite helpless with over-eating. In the St. Kilda Group the birds are taken with a horsehair noose slipped over them, in

GANNET.

great numbers, and are used for food while fresh by the native fishermen ; others are dried for winter use. The oil obtained from them is also useful, and the feathers are sold. These birds seem to become perfectly tame when breeding, and will allow themselves to be approached and stroked without leaving the nest. Their nest consists of simply a mass of seaweed, mingled with lumps of turf. On this is laid one egg, white or greenish white in colour, but which soon becomes stained or soiled. If this egg is removed the bird will lay again. It is said that a large number of the eggs of these birds are unfruitful.

The general colour of the Gannet is pure white, but the outer wing feathers are black.

CORMORANT.

PHALACROCORAX CARBO.

Family PELECONIDÆ. Genus PHALACROCORAX.

Crested Comorant—Great Black Comorant—Cole Goose— Skart.

The Comorant is a resident bird in our islands, and may be found wherever rocky coasts abound. This bird is often found some way inland near our lakes and rivers, but its home is really in the vicinity of the sea.

Fish is its food, and for this it will dive, swimming with wonderful ease under water, and using its wings much the same as if it was flying. It is a bird of voracious appetite and will eat fish of great size, having been observed to devour eels two feet in length. When seen on shore it is usually stationary, perched upon a rock near the water digesting its food and possibly on the lookout for further prey. The Japanese and Chinese train this bird to catch fish for them, in which practice it proves very useful.

The Cormorant breeds upon the bare rocks which rise sharp from the sea, but, curiously enough, in some districts it nests inland in the tops of trees, consequently it may be often seen perching on trees. They breed in colonies. When the nests are on the rocks they are built almost entirely of seaweed. They are large structures which are repaired and added to from year to year, so that they sometimes approach three or four feet in depth ; they are lined with the green leaves of sea plants. When the nests are built in trees, however, they are formed principally of sticks and lined with a little fresh green stuff. The colonies of the Cormorants are covered thickly with the droppings of the birds, and, on approaching, the odour from this and the decaying remains of fish becomes very strong and offensive.

The eggs are usually three in number, but often only two are laid. They are chalky white in appearance, but the green ground colour often shows through. Seebohm describes the Cormorant as " intermediate in size between a Duck and a Goose ". The general colour of the bird is black, tinged with purple and green. The head and neck are mingled with narrow white feathers; the cheeks are white; the wings are brown, and there is a white patch on the body above the top joint of the legs.

SHAG.

PHALACROCORAX GRACULUS.

Family PELECONIDÆ.   Genus PHALACROCORAX.

Green Cormorant—Crested Shag.

The Shag is also a common resident in the British Isles, and is found where there are rocky cliffs, especially where caves abound.

The Shag is much more of a sea bird than the Cormorant and is never found inland like that bird, unless, perchance, driven inwards by boisterous weather. Consequently it is never found nesting or perching in trees, but is always observed near the coast when on land.

In its habits it differs little from the Cormorant. It is an expert fisher, and a perfect diver, frequently descending to a great depth —even as much as one hundred and fifty feet in pursuit of its prey.   This it catches with wonderful celerity, fairly swimming its fish down by superior pace, using its wings as though in the air, and, it is said, forcing itself to the surface again by means of its stiffly-formed tail.

The Shag, whenever it can, breeds in caves and hollows in the rocks; in these, on ledges within, many nests are placed, which are resorted to and repaired from year to year; if, however, no caves are to be found, the Shag will place its nest on the ledge of cliffs.   In this case they are generally found singly.

The nests are large and bulky, built of seaweed, turf, and bits of heather, and rendered very disgusting and offensive by the decayed fish and droppings lying thickly in all directions around.   The eggs are usually three or four in number, and resemble the Cormorant's in every particular, excepting that they are somewhat smaller. The plumage is black, mingled with rich metallic green ; the head is surmounted with a tuft of feathers, which it can erect when it pleases ; the wings are tinted with bronze and purple. It is considerably smaller in size than the Cormorant.

INDEX

SUPPLEMENTARY LIST

DIGBY, LONG & Co.'s
NEW NOVELS, STORIES, Etc.

IN ONE VOLUME, Price 6s.

By Florence Marryat.

IN THE NAME OF LIBERTY.

By the Author of "The Beautiful Soul," etc. Crown 8vo, cloth, 6s. —*Second Edition.*

By Mrs Alice M. Diehl.

A LAST THROW.

By the Author of "A Woman's Cross," etc. Crown 8vo, cloth, 6s. —*Second Edition.*

By Robey F. Eldridge.

THE KESTYNS OF CATHER CASTLE.

Crown 8vo, cloth, 6s.—*Second Edition.*

By Capt. Charles Clark.

MY YARNS OF SEA FOAM AND GOLD DUST.

Crown 8vo, cloth, 6s.—*Second Edition.*

By John Ferriss Causton.

A MODERN JUDAS.

Crown 8vo, cloth, 6s.—*Now Ready.*

By John Bridge.

DINNER FOR THIRTEEN.

Crown 8vo, cloth, 6s.—*Now Ready.*

By Jean de la Brète.

FATE'S FETTERS. Translated from the French by Mrs F. HOPER-
DIXON. Crown 8vo, cloth, 6s.—*Just out.*

> "The Author's first two books, 'My Uncle and My Curate,' and 'The
> Romance of a Believer,' had neither of them less than thirty editions. The
> newcomer is worthy of its predecessors, and we doubt not that it will meet
> with the same success."—*La Libre Parole.*
>
> "One of the best novels of Jean de la Brète, and it is just as interesting to
> readers of either sex."—*Gaulois.*
>
> "'My Uncle and My Curate' is one of the novels most relished by the
> French public. 'Fate's Fetters' is most chaste, most distinguished, and
> really a strong work in its melancholy grace."—*Revue Helvétique.*

By Clement A. Mendham.

A TROTH OF TEARS.
Crown 8vo, cloth, 6s. With a Frontispiece.—*End of May.*

By Hattil Foll.

MAJOR CARLILE.
Crown 8vo, cloth, 6s.—*Ready.*

By S. E. Hall.

SYBIL FAIRLEIGH.
Crown 8vo, cloth, 6s.—*At Press.*

By Rupert Alexander.

BALLYRONAN.
Crown 8vo, cloth, 6s.—*Now Ready.*

By Reginald St Barbe.

FRANCESCA HALSTEAD. A Tale of San Remo.
Crown 8vo, cloth, 6s.—*Second Edition.*

> "Francesca is a beautifully drawn portrait, tender, graceful, and woman-
> like."—*Glasgow Herald.*
> "The writer exhibits rare skill in devising a plot."—*Sheffield Telegraph.*
> "This clever and interesting novel."—*Aberdeen Free Press.*
> "Does not fail in interest at any stage."—*Scotsman.*

By Alfred Smythe.

A NEW FAUST. Crown 8vo, cloth, 6s.—*Second Edition.*

> "Told vividly and with spirit. Stephanie is charming . . . intensely ex-
> citing."—*Pall Mall Gazette.*

By Mrs Florence Severne.

THE DOWAGER'S DETERMINATION.

By the Author of "The Pillar House," "In the Meshes," etc.
Crown 8vo, cloth, 6s.—*Second Edition.*

> "A powerful story. The authoress manages her incidents with skill and grace."—*Pall Mall Gazette.*

By Mrs Alice M. Diehl.

A WOMAN'S CROSS.

By the Author of "The Garden of Eden," "Passion's Puppets," "A Modern Helen." Crown 8vo, cloth, 6s.—*Second Edition.*

> "Far above the average of modern novels, and should undoubtedly be inquired for and read."—*St James's Budget.*

By J. E. Muddock.

WITHOUT FAITH OR FEAR.

The Story of a Soul. By the Author of "Stripped of the Tinsel," etc.
Crown 8vo, cloth, 6s.—*Second Edition.*

> "An absorbing narrative. Will be read with interest. It possesses great charm of narrative and grace of literary style."—*The Daily Telegraph.*

By May St Claire (Mrs Gannaway Atkins).

A STORMY PAST.

Crown 8vo, cloth, 6s.—*Second Edition.*

> "A wholesome story of a romantic order, and will be read with pleasure and profit."—*Western Daily Mercury.*

By David Worthington.

EQUAL SHARES.

Crown 8vo, cloth, 6s.

> "Told with spirit and ingenuity . . . very cleverly sketched."—*Pall Mall Gazette.*

By the Princess de Bourg.

THE AMERICAN HEIRESS.

Crown 8vo, cloth, 6s.—*Second Edition.*

> *** Published simultaneously in London and New York.*

> "One of the most delightful female characters in recent fiction ; Kitty Fauntleroy is, indeed, a creation. The story is a refreshingly healthy one."
> —*Aberdeen Press.*

By Bertha M. M. Miniken.

AN ENGLISH WIFE.

Crown 8vo, cloth, 6s.—*Second Edition.*

"A pleasant story, animated by a pure and healthy spirit. The tale is told with great feeling."—*Observer.*

By Albert Hardy.

A CROWN OF GOLD.

Crown 8vo, cloth, 6s. With a frontispiece by the Author.

"The plot is distinctly good, and various types of character are cleverly drawn. The book is one that will be read and appreciated by many."— *Court Circular.*

By Kathleen Behenna.

SIDARTHA.

Crown 8vo, cloth, 6s.—*Second Edition.*

"A book that will keep one in breathless excitement from start to finish. The story is one of those in which the reader will not feel inclined to skip a page, lest he lose a link in the chain of interest."—*Glasgow Herald.*

"There is certainly no lack of incident in Miss Behenna's maiden effort, and Edgar Poe himself could not have given us a more weird conception than the bewitchment of poor Doris . . . the power of the hidden terror is described with a quiet force that is very striking."—*Pall Mall Gazette.*

By Mrs John Procter.

AN OAK OF CHIVALRY.

Crown 8vo, cloth, 6s.

Both hero and heroine engross the reader's warm sympathy from the opening chapter. The reader follows with increasing interest the ramifications of the plot through a series of vivid scenes.

By Val Nightingale.

THE DEVIL'S DAUGHTER.

By the Author of "The World on Wheels." Crown 8vo, cloth, 6s.— *In May.*

By G. Beresford Fitz Gerald.

A FLEETING SHOW.

By the Author of "An Odd Career," etc. Crown 8vo, cloth, 6s.—*In May.*

By Belton Otterburn.

A NEW NOVEL.

By the Author of "He would be an Officer," and "Jilted." Crown 8vo, cloth, 6s.—*In June.*

IN ONE VOLUME, Price 3s. 6d.

By Tivoli.

A SHORT INNINGS.

A Public School Episode. By the Author of "Une Culotte," etc.
Crown 8vo, cloth, 3s. 6d. With a Frontispiece.—*Second Edition.*

By Theresa Molyneux.

A LADY'S CONFESSIONS.

Crown 8vo, cloth, 3s. 6d.—*Ready.*

By J. H. Swingler.

CIRCUMSTANTIAL EVIDENCE.

Crown 8vo, cloth, 3s. 6d.—*Ready.*

By Mrs E. Lynn Linton.

'TWIXT CUP AND LIP.

By the Author of "Patricia Kemball," etc. Crown 8vo, cloth, 3s. 6d.
—*Second Edition.*

Grant Allen's Successful Book.

THE DESIRE OF THE EYES.

By the Author of "The Woman Who Did," etc. Crown 8vo, cloth,
3s. 6d.—*Eighth Edition.*

ACROSS THE ZODIAC.

A Story of Adventure. In pictorial cloth, with a Frontispiece, crown
8vo, 3s. 6d.—*Second Edition.*

"One of the best books of the year. The idea has been well worked out,
and the Author goes far beyond any of Jules Verne's imitators in the
audacity he displays."—*The Morning Post.*
"Marvellous incidents in a narrative abounding in sensation."—*The Daily
Telegraph.*

By Fergus Hume.

A MARRIAGE MYSTERY.

By the Author of "The Masquerade Mystery," etc. Crown 8vo,
pictorial cloth, 3s. 6d.—*Third Edition.*

"The book is a tortuous and mazy tale of mystery, very ingenious in throw-
ing the reader off the scent while luring him on through a cleverly woven web
of mystery, which is only unravelled in the very last chapter."—*St James's
Budget.*

By Dr Gordon Stables, M.D., R.N.

THE ROSE OF ALLANDALE.

By the Author of "289 R: the Story of a Double Life," "The Mystery of a Millionaire's Grave," etc., etc.   Crown 8vo, cloth, 3s. 6d.

By the Hon. Ernest Pomeroy.

SKETCHES FOR SCAMPS.

Crown 8vo, pictorial cloth, 3s. 6d.

"Several of the 'sketches' are full of raciness and humour, and a keen appreciation of character."—*St James's Gazette.*
"One cannot help laughing heartily over it."—*Literary World.*

By A. E. Aldington.

THE QUEEN'S PREFERMENT.

A Historical Romance.   With original Drawings by H. A. PAYNE. Crown 8vo, cloth, 3s. 6d.

"An historical story, short and brisk. The picture is worked up with vivacity and vigour, and not without some command of language and picturesque effects. The story is quick and stirring. The illustrations are purposely quaint."—*Athenæum.*

By Norman R. Byers.

A DOUBTFUL LOSS.

Crown 8vo, cloth, 3s. 6d.

"A nicely written story."—*Pall Mall Gazette.*

By Edgar D. C. Bolland.

DOROTHY LUCAS.

Crown 8vo, cloth, 3s. 6d.

"So fascinating and delightful a story.   It is a most readable story."—*Western Daily Mercury.*

By Fred Holmes, M.A.

A MAN AMONGST MEN.

Dedicated to Human Society.   Crown 8vo, cloth, 3s. 6d.

"A work of genuine ability and considerable interest."—*Dundee Advertiser.*

By Quinton Simmel.

THE WILL THAT WINS.

Crown 8vo, 3s. 6d.   Dedicated to the Earl of Hopetoun.

All readers will warm to the bright picture of the good Bishop and his two soldier boys. Cerena, the charming heroine, is in her way a creation, and the story of her daring flight from a detested suitor is holding from the beginning to the end.

By an Exponent.

CHRYSTAL, THE NEWEST OF WOMEN.

Crown 8vo, cloth, 3s. 6d.—*Third Edition.*

Chrystal, with her many questionings, her high courage, her candour, her truthfulness, and her quaint originality, is charming. Rarely, if ever, has such a close analysis of a child's character, and that child a girl, been given.

By Henry Grimshawe.

Dr FORENTI.

Crown 8vo, cloth, 3s. 6d.

"The interest is evenly maintained throughout. It is not wanting in exciting incident, concisely and well described."—*Birmingham Daily Gazette.*

By H. J. Chaytor.

THE LIGHT OF THE EYE.

Crown 8vo, cloth, 3s. 6d.—*End of May.*

By Mina Sandeman.

THE WORSHIP OF LUCIFER.

By the Author of "The Rosy Cross and Other Psychical Tales." Crown 8vo, cloth, 3s. 6d.—*End of May.*

By Richard Penny.

SCENES FROM MILITARY LIFE.

Crown 8vo, cloth, 3s. 6d.—*End of May.*

By Clos.

LIFE IN AFRIKANDERLAND AS VIEWED BY AN AFRIKANDER.

A Story of Life in South Africa, based on Truth. Crown 8vo, cloth, 3s. 6d.—*In rapid preparation.*

By Frank Hart.

A NEW NOVEL.

Crown 8vo, cloth, 3s. 6d.—*In June.*

IN ONE VOLUME, Price 2s. 6d.

By Jean Delaire.

PRO PATRIA.

A small sketch on a vast subject. Illustrated throughout with Drawings by ALFRED TOUCHEMOLIN. Crown 8vo, cloth, 2s. 6d.—*In May.*

By W. Carter Platts.

THE TUTTLEBURY TALES.

By the Angling Editor of the "Yorkshire Weekly Post." Crown 8vo, pictorial cloth, 2s. 6d.—*Third Edition.*

> "The rollicking good humour is irresistible."—*Pall Mall Gazette.*
> "These lively episodes will be the source of hearty laughter."—*Globe.*
> "Mr Platts reminds us of the American humorist, Max Adeler. He is not an imitator but his fun is of the same kind, farcical of course, but unstrained and laughter compelling."—*The Spectator.*
> "Very amusing. Irresistibly comic. There is not a dull line from start to finish."—*St James's Budget.*
> "Mr Carter Platts is the Max Adeler of the present generation. If one looks about for another writer of the same hilarious kind, he is not to be found."—*Yorkshire Post.*

By Joseph Ashton.

INMATES OF THE MANSION.

Crown 8vo, pictorial cloth, 2s. 6d. Beautifully illustrated.

> "An allegorical subject, and will be found most readable for youths, who will learn a lesson in glancing through its pages."—*The Daily Telegraph.*

By Chleton Chalmers.

THE INSEPARABLES.

A Book for Boys. Crown 8vo, pictorial cloth, fully illustrated, 2s. 6d.

> "High above the average of school stories. There is a strong dramatic interest in the narrative of the disgracing of Lionel Middleton on a charge of which he was innocent that will appeal to every school boy's heart. It is really a first-rate story."—*Pall Mall Gazette.*

By Nemo.

A MERE PUG. The Romance of a Dog. Crown 8vo, pictorial cloth, 2s. 6d.

> "This pretty story of the adventures of a pug dog . . . there are few books of the season that could have been more heartily recommended for children. —*The Standard.*

Digby's Popular Novel Series

In Crown 8vo, price 2s. 6d. per Vol. Each book contains about 320 pp., printed on superior paper, from new type, and bound in uniform handsome cloth, gilt lettered. These novels have met with marked success in the more expensive form.

Those marked with an * may be had in picture boards at 2s.

NEW ADDITIONS TO THE SERIES.

By Dora Russell.
A MAN'S PRIVILEGE.

By Fergus Hume.
THE MASQUERADE MYSTERY.

By Arabella Kenealy.
THE HONOURABLE MRS SPOOR.

By J. E. Muddock.
STRIPPED OF THE TINSEL.

By Annie Thomas.
A LOVER OF THE DAY.

By Jean Middlemas.
HUSH MONEY.

By Mrs Robert Jocelyn.
JUANITA CARRINGTON.

OTHER VOLUMES IN THE SERIES.

By Arabella Kenealy.
* Some Men are Such Gentlemen.—*Fifth Edition.*
* Dr Janet of Harley Street.—*Seventh Edition.*

By Florence Marryat.
The Beautiful Soul.—*Second Edition.*

By Dora Russell.
The Other Bond.—*Second Edition.*
* A Hidden Chain.—*Third Edition.*

By L. T. Meade.
A Life for a Love.—*Second Edition.*

By Jean Middlemass.
* The Mystery of Clement Dunraven.—*Second Edition.*

By Hume Nisbet.
* The Jolly Roger. Illustrated by Author.—*Fifth Edition.*
Her Loving Slave.—*Second Edition.*

By Annie Thomas.
False Pretences.—*Second Edition.*

By Hilton Hill.
* His Egyptian Wife. Picture Boards only.—*Seventh Edition.*

** Other Works in the same Series in due course.

IN ONE VOLUME, Price 1s. 6d. and 1s.

By Hillary Deccan.

WHERE BILLOWS BREAK. By the Author of "Light in the Offing." Crown 8vo, cloth, 1s. 6d.

> "This little volume of stories from the west coast of Ireland, is a refreshing change from the scenery and subject-matter of the ordinary novel. The Author evidently knows and loves the sea, and a fresh breeze as of the rolling Atlantic inspires his work. The Author has a knack of description, and we could wish for more of his Irish stories."—*New Saturday.*

By Aldyth Ingram.

SMIRCHED. Crown 8vo, cloth, 1s. 6d.

> "A pretty and original little romance."—*Black and White.*
> "The dialogue throughout the book is unusually good, the Author showing genuine signs of a gift worth cultivating."—*Manchester Guardian.*

By F. H. Hudson.

THE VAGARIES OF LOVE. Crown 8vo, cloth, 1s. 6d.

> "A love story this of more than ordinary merit. The plot presents some degree of freshness—which is commendation enough—and it is worked out pleasantly, fully and deftly."—*Aberdeen Press.*

By Violet Tweedale.

UNSOLVED MYSTERIES. By the Author of "And They Two," etc. Crown 8vo, cloth, 1s. 6d.—*Second Edition.*

By Gratiana Darrell.

THE HAUNTED LOOKING GLASS. Crown 8vo, pictorial cloth, 1s. 6d.—*With a Frontispiece.*

By Frances England.

SMALL CONCERNS. Long 12mo, 1s.—*End May.*

By Bernard Wenthworth.

THE MASTER OF HULLINGHAM MANOR. Crown 8vo, paper cover, 1s.—*End May.*

By Neville Marion.

SWEET SCENTED GRASS. Long 12mo, paper cover, 1s.—*End May.*

By Blake Lamond.

THE SPORTING ADVENTURES OF MONSIEUR LOLOTTE. By the Author of "The Two Dunmores," etc. Crown 8vo, paper cover, 1s.—*End May.*

By Katharine Renell.

SHIBBOLETH. Crown 8vo, paper, 1s.—*In June.*

𝕽oof 𝕽oofer's Sensational 𝕹ovels
Price 1s. each; Post free, 1s. 2d.

LOVE ONLY LENT.

THE TWIN DIANAS.

TWO MOTHERS OF ONE.

PRETTYBAD ROGERS.

"Mr Roofer is undoubtedly clever ... his smart and witty style." — *The Daily Chronicle.*

"He knows life, the feverish set-on-edge existence of the Wall Street money-maker, and the select, silver-lined life of Fashionable New York." —*Dundee Advertiser.*

"Clever when he treats of finance."— *Morning Post.*

➤ 𝕸iscellaneous ➤

THE BIRDS OF OUR COUNTRY. By H. E. Stewart, B.A. With Illustrations by ARCHIBALD THORBURN, J. GIACOMELLI, G. E. LODGE, K. KEYL, R. KRETSCHMER, etc. Crown 8vo. Pictorial cloth, gilt top, 3s. 6d., over 400 pages.—*Now Ready.*

> In bringing this work before the public two things are essential to its success —firstly, the conviction that such a book is needed, and secondly, that the Author is possessed of the information required for its production. With regard to the first of these :—The price of nearly all the standard works on ornithology places them beyond the reach of the young naturalist, and the information contained in the few cheap books, which at present exist, is in many instances scanty. The aim of the Author has been to place in the young collector's hand, at a popular price, a comprehensive account of every bird which is likely to be met with in the British Isles. The work is illustrated throughout.
>
> *Illustrated Prospectus post free.*

A BEAUTIFUL GIFT BOOK.

WIT, WISDOM AND FOLLY. Pen and Pencil Flashes. **By J. Villin Marmery.** Author of "Progress of Science," "Manual of the History of Art," etc. With 100 Original Illustrations by ALFRED TOUCHEMOLIN, Author of "Strasbourg Militaire." Demy 8vo, superior binding, 6s.

> An *Édition de Luxe*, in Royal 8vo, printed on hand-made paper, and limited to 100 copies, bound in red leather, gilt top, is also issued, price 21s. net.
>
> "A pleasant volume of chatty anecdotes. Bright and piquant. Mr Marmery's book ought to be a treasure to the confirmed diner-out."—*The Standard (Leader).*
>
> "One of the most entertaining collections of anecdotes. The illustrations consist in daintily-drawn headpieces to the various chapters. The present collection of anecdotes is better than most."—*Westminster Budget.*

New Work by Caroline Gearey.

TWO FRENCH QUEENS.

Elizabeth of Valois—Marguerite of Valois. By the Author of "In Other Lands," "Three Empresses." With Portraits, crown 8vo, cloth, 6s.—*Second Edition.*

> "We have the very highest opinion of Miss Gearey's powers, and unconditionally recommend her book."—*Glasgow Daily Mail.*
>
> "Miss Gearey has once more given us a charming collection of historical biographies, compiled with care and written with taste and true womanly feeling."—*Birmingham Gazette.*

IS NATURAL SELECTION THE CREATOR OF SPECIES? By Duncan Graham. Crown 8vo, cloth, 6s.

> This work is a library of reference on the most controversial subjects of the day, and in it Darwin and his theories are analytically tested, and the whole of the teleological argument is set forth with much lucidity. The merit of this work is that it is a compendium of the subject of Evolution, and in itself a small theological encyclopædia made popular.

By Robert Woolward ("Old Woolward").

NIGH ON SIXTY YEARS AT SEA.

Crown 8vo, cloth, 6s. With Portrait.—*Second Edition.*

> "Very entertaining reading. Captain Woolward writes sensibly and straightforwardly, and tells his story with the frankness of an old salt. He has a keen sense of humour, and his stories are endless and very entertaining."—*The Times.*

By John Bradshaw.

NORWAY, ITS FJORDS, FJELDS AND FOSSES.

Crown 8vo, pictorial cloth, 3s. 6d.

> "A book which every tourist may well buy."—*Daily Chronicle.*
> "The work is much more than a guide book, and it is certainly that and an excellent one. It is a history as well of the country, and contains a series of admirably arranged tours."—*Leeds Mercury.*

By Josiah Crooklands.

THE ITALIANS OF TO-DAY.

Translated from the French of RENÉ BAZIN. Crown 8vo, cloth, 3s. 6d.

> "By those who would study more closely the political and social aspects of Italian life to-day, Mr Crooklands's translation should be accorded a hearty welcome and an attentive perusal."—*Public Opinion.*
> "M. René Bazin is a writer whose style we have often praised."—*The Athenæum.*

By William F. Regan.

BOER AND UITLANDER.

The True History of Late Events in South Africa. Crown 8vo, cloth, 3s. 6d. With Copyright Portraits, Map, etc.—*Fifth Edition.*

> Mr GLADSTONE writes:—"I thank you very much for your work, and rejoice that by means of it public attention will be called to all the circumstances connected with the origin and history of the Transvaal, which possess so strong a claim upon our equitable consideration."
> "The writer should be able to speak with authority, for he is none other than Mr W. F. Regan, the well-known South African financier, whose name has been a good deal before the public in connection with the events following upon the 'Raid.'"—*Glasgow Herald.*

By Margaret Newton.

GLIMPSES OF LIFE IN BERMUDA AND THE TROPICS.

With 42 Illustrations by the Author. Crown 8vo, cloth, 6s.—*Now Ready.*

New Work by the Author of "Roland Kyan."

THE REIGN OF PERFECTION. Letters on a Liberal Catholic Philosophy. **By Walter Sweetman, B.A.** Crown 8vo, cloth, 3s. 6d. net.—*Now ready.*

> "The book is ingenious and clever, the spirit of it is admirable, and its temper calm and sweet throughout. . . . The book is certainly significant, while, outside the region of contentious subjects, its intellectual and spiritual merits will command wide sympathy and appreciation."—*Bradford Observer.*

By Percy Russell.

THE AUTHOR'S MANUAL.

With Prefatory Remarks by Mr GLADSTONE. Crown 8vo, cloth, 3s. 6d. net. (*Ninth and Cheaper Edition.*) With Portrait.

> ". . . Mr Russell's book is a very complete manual and guide for journalist and author. It is not a merely practical work—it is literary and appreciative of literature in its best sense ; . . . we have little else but praise for the volume."—*Westminster Review.*

BY THE SAME.

A GUIDE TO BRITISH AND AMERICAN NOVELS.

From the Earliest Period to the end of 1894. By the Author of "The Author's Manual," etc. Crown 8vo, cloth, 3s. 6d. net.— *Second Edition carefully revised.*

> "Mr Russell's familiarity with every form of novel is amazing, and his summaries of plots and comments thereon are as brief and lucid as they are various."—*Spectator.*

⚏ Poetry and the Drama ⚏

By Kathleen Behenna.
THE HISTORY OF A SOUL.
Beautifully printed on Hand-made Paper. Demy 8vo, artistic cloth, gilt edges, 5s. net.

By Frederick J. Johnston-Smith.
THE CAPTAIN OF THE DOLPHIN AND OTHER POEMS OF THE SEA.
Crown 8vo, art linen, gilt top, 3s. 6d. net.

By Cecilia Elizabeth Meetkerke.
FRAGMENTS FROM VICTOR HUGO'S LEGENDS AND LYRICS.
Crown 8vo, cloth, 7s. 6d.

By C. Potter.
CANTOS FROM THE DIVINA COMMEDIA OF DANTE.
Translated into English Verse. Crown 8vo, cloth, 5s. net.

By Lily Overington.
RANDOM RHYMES AND CHRISTMAS CHIMES.
Crown 8vo, cloth, 5s. net.

By Henry Osborne, M.A.
THE PALACE OF DELIGHTS AND OTHER POEMS.
Crown 8vo, cloth, 3s. 6d. net.

By the late Ernest G. Henty and E. A. Starkey.
AUSTRALIAN IDYLLS AND BUSH RHYMES.
Crown 8vo, cloth, 3s. 6d. net.

By Leonard Williams.
BALLADS AND SONGS OF SPAIN.
Crown 8vo, cloth, 3s. 6d. net.

By Walter Thead.
THE STORY OF JEPHTHAH AND OTHER POEMS.
Crown 8vo, cloth, 2s. 6d. net.

By E. Derry.
SOPHONISBA; OR, THE PRISONER OF ALBA AND OTHER POEMS.
By the Author of "Lays of the Scottish Highlands." Crown 8vo, cloth, 3s. 6d. net.

By Alexander Buckler.
WORD SKETCHES IN WINDSOR.
Foolscap 8vo, art linen, 2s. 6d.

ⅅoetry anⅾ the ⅅrama—*continued.*

By Isaac Willcocks, M.R.C.S.

THE MAGIC KEY. A Fairy Drama in Four Acts. By the Author of "Pixy." Crown 8vo, cloth, 1s. 6d.

By An Odd Fellow.

ODDS AND ENDS. Foolscap 8vo, art linen, 1s. 6d. net.

By E. M. Beresford.

SONGS AND SHADOWS.
Crown 8vo, cloth, 3s. 6d. net.—*End May.*

By Evan T. Keane.

A MOORLAND BROOK AND OTHER POEMS.
Crown 8vo, cloth, 3s. 6d. net.—*End May.*

By Maria Greer.

A VISION'S VOICE AND OTHER POEMS.
Foolscap 8vo, cloth, 2s. 6d. net.—*End May.*

By Swithin Saint Swithaine.

A DIVAN OF THE DALES AND OTHER POEMS.
Crown 8vo, cloth, 5s. net.—*End May.*

By T. Disney.

CRICKET LYRICS.
Foolscap 8vo, paper cover, 6d.—*End May.*

By Frederic W. Coulter.

ENGLAND'S GLORY.
Foolscap 8vo, art linen, gilt top, 1s. 6d. net.

By Charles Rathbone Low.

THE EPIC OF OLYMPUS.
Crown 8vo, cloth, 5s. net.—*End May.*

By William J. Tate.

RUBY BLYTHE AND OTHER POEMS.
Foolscap 8vo, cloth, 3s. 6d. net.

₊ *A complete Catalogue of Novels, Travels, Biographies, Poems, etc., with a critical or descriptive notice of each, free by post on application.*

LONDON : DIGBY, LONG & CO., Publishers
18 Bouverie Street, Fleet Street, E.C.

www.ingramcontent.com/pod-product-compliance
Lightning Source LLC
Chambersburg PA
CBHW021343110726
47900CB00005B/1583